About the Author

SANDRA RODRIGUEZ BARRON is the author of *The Heiress of Water*, winner of the International Latino Book Award for debut fiction. She was born in Puerto Rico and has lived in Connecticut, Florida, the Dominican Republic, and El Salvador. She holds an MFA from Florida International University's creative writing program and is the recipient of a Bread Loaf Fellowship and grants from the NALAC Fund for the Arts and the Greater Hartford Arts Council. She lives in Connecticut with her husband and son.

D0377592

Stay
with
Me

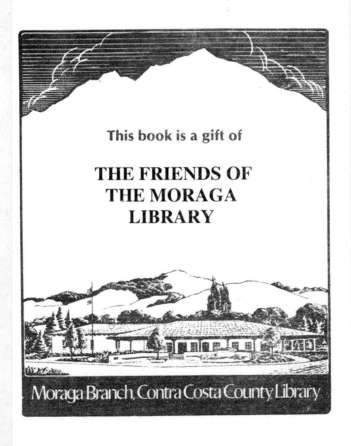

ALSO BY SANDRA RODRIGUEZ BARRON

The Heiress of Water

Stay with Me

A Novel

Sandra Rodriguez Barron

HARPER

NEW YORK · LONDON · TORONTO · SYDNEY

HARPER

STAY WITH ME. Copyright © 2010 by Sandra Rodriguez Barron. All rights reserved. Printed in the United States of America. No part of this book may be used or reproduced in any manner whatsoever without written permission except in the case of brief quotations embodied in critical articles and reviews. For information, address HarperCollins Publishers, 10 East 53rd Street, New York, NY 10022.

HarperCollins books may be purchased for educational, business, or sales promotional use. For information, please write: Special Markets Department, Harper-Collins Publishers, 10 East 53rd Street, New York, NY 10022.

FIRST EDITION

Library of Congress Cataloging-in-Publication Data is available upon request.

ISBN 978-0-06-165062-8

10 11 12 13 14   OV/RRD   10 9 8 7 6 5 4 3 2 1

In loving memory of my father
Juan A. Rodriguez

And for my cherished friend
George H. Wilson

Stay
with
Me

Prologue

1979

Nine days after the hurricane, a boat departed from the southern shore of the Dominican Republic, in the early morning hours of September 8. As its twin diesel engines muscled over treacherous, shark-infested waters, the path was illuminated by a resplendent full moon. By the time the *For Tuna* reached the halfway mark of its journey, the sky had become as blue as the American's eyes, which were fixed, under the shade of a captain's visor, toward U.S. territory.

The boat approached the uninhabited island of Mona, where three-foot iguanas, with their sagging jowls and horned snouts, sauntered out from the caves to sun themselves upon the rocks. A graveyard of crudely made wooden rowboats lay mangled and strewn about on an empty beach, evidence of previous failed attempts of boatpeople to traverse the Mona Passage and make it to Puerto Rico's western shore. The American slowed down and eyed the wrecked boats. She circled Mona Island, searching the beaches, the mouths of the high cliff caves, and the site of the abandoned guano mine. She eyed the rusted, decommissioned lighthouse on the north side and passed around a pair of binoculars. The men surveyed the wild, desolate island from the surrounding waters. Finding no sign of life at all, save a few wild goats roaming a plain, they departed. The *For Tuna* bucked its way across the choppy surface waters of an abyss that drops down to the deepest point in the Atlantic Ocean. The American's eyes stung from the salt in the spray that whipped at her face. It was a violent, gut-twisting ride, and when the men grew seasick and began to vomit, her self-doubt threatened to swell into a full panic attack. But she clung to the wheel and reminded herself over and over that land was just fifty miles away. She was deeply comforted by the sound of children's voices drifting up from inside the cabin, singing Spanish lullabies.

Three hours later, a beautiful sight: Puerto Rico's western shore appeared as a long strip of green along the horizon. Twenty minutes later, the *For Tuna*'s hull cut through a floating carpet of seaweed and hurricane trash—palm fronds, dead fish, empty soda cans, and plastic junk. The American pulled into a docking area a mile south of the city of Mayagüez. She tied the *For Tuna* up to a pier and secured a yellow balloon to the rail of the boat before she left. No one saw her as she hurried down the dock, arms folded over her chest, pressing a tissue to her eyes, sobbing. And no one saw the two dark-skinned men who followed her either. They stepped out of the boat with their heads low, their eyes concealed beneath the brims of their straw hats. One of them wore a black suit; the other was more plainly dressed. The American looked back at the boat several times before she traversed the length of the pier. The men didn't look back at all. Twenty-seven minutes later, two Mayagüez police officers arrived at the site of a waterfront condominium and yacht club complex that was still under construction. It had been abandoned for months, after the developer went bankrupt. An anonymous call had tipped off the police to the dock-ing of a "suspicious-looking" vessel. The identifying balloon was hardly necessary—the *For Tuna* was the only boat in sight. The officers boarded it with weapons drawn. They found the hatch closed, but not locked. Officer Flores pulled it back and peered into the boat's cabin. Without saying a word, he stepped aside, shook his head and let his partner get a look at what was below.

Officer Castillo peered into the dim interior. Curiously, he smelled something that made him think of his infant twins: milky vomit, talcum powder, and soiled diapers. Inside were four toddlers lying across the boat's cushioned surfaces, with their eyes closed. They were dressed in outfits befitting a family who could own such a handsome boat—two of the little boys had button-down shirts and dark dress pants, while another was dressed in a princely sailor suit. The girl was wearing a fancy pink, puffy flowered dress.

"Where the hell are the parents?" Flores said, and the two men scanned the cabin from above. The little boy in the sailor suit lifted his head to look at them. He put his hands over the chests of the two children lying next to him. His eyes lingered on each officer's face. Then he lifted one hand and tried to snap his fingers, or perhaps pinch something, but he didn't say anything. His eyes rolled up to one side. He waited. He did it again. They looked at them expectantly, as if he had asked them a direct question and was waiting for a response. Officer Flores looked at his partner. "Is that sign language?"

Officer Castillo shrugged. He went below, into the spacious cabin and searched the whole boat. He found a fifth child, a little girl hiding under the overhang of an open storage com-partment, this one in a white-and-yellow dress. There were no adults anywhere in the vicinity. There weren't even any witnesses to question. Officer Flores shouted into his radio, "We need medical personnel! I have a boatful of unaccompanied minors! Yes, minors! Children! *Nenes*!" After the ambulance left with the children, the Coast Guard cutter *Borinquen* arrived, and the officials all wrote up their reports, taking photographs and securing the vessel. Everyone was expecting the parents to appear at any minute, shouting and looking relieved and explaining the details of some mishap that had separated them from their children. But none appeared, so they followed protocol and prepared for an investigation that they doubted they or anyone else would have time to pursue anytime soon. The items that made it into the evidence file that day were two empty plastic gallon-sized bottles of water, three plastic baby bottles, cloth diapers, some folded children's play clothes, and a small blanket. One of the little girls clutched an unfinished rag doll without any stitching on the face, which the officers wanted to put in the file, but the little girl threw such a tantrum that they let her keep it. Officer Flores also added that all five of the children had a faded starfish drawn on the tops of their left hands. The drawings, he noted, were sketched with the competence of an adult hand, with a fine-tipped green marker.

There was one item aboard the boat that didn't make it into the evidence file or the notes. Officer Castillo found a can of a Dominican brand of powdered milk on the floor of the boat, stuck behind a cushion. He popped open the lid, and saw that it was still half-full and had a measuring cup inserted into the yellowish-white powder. He sniffed it, took a pinch and rubbed it between his fingers, squinting as he scrutinized the texture of the powder. He turned the can around and around for a moment. Recalling the dark olive skin of at least two of the children, Officer Castillo, whose mother was Dominican born, waited until his partner was not looking, then went up on deck and tossed the can overboard, where it landed among all the other hurricane trash floating around the boat. In the meantime, the American watched him from the roof deck of the defunct condominium building next to the dock, through binoculars.

The discovery of five unaccompanied minors aboard a boat didn't make the news in Puerto Rico that night or in the week that followed. The media coverage was still focused on the death toll and homelessness in the Dominican Republic, and on the virtual obliteration of the Windward Island of Dominica. During the last two days of August, Hurricane David had reached category five strength, with winds that rose to a nightmarish one hundred and seventy-five miles per hour. On August 30, Puerto Rico was spared a direct hit, but it suffered massive property damage and had more than a dozen casualties. President Carter declared it a disaster zone. The next day, David collided with the Dominican Republic's capital city, where it took approximately two thousand lives, both on impact and in the subsequent floods. But it grew weak as it crawled across the high mountain range of Hispaniola's interior, so neighboring Haiti had no deaths and very little property damage. On September 4, the *Washington Post* quoted the Dominican Civil Defense Director as saying, "The situation is catastrophic. Hunger is starting to be felt by thousands of country people isolated by blocked roads." While Dominicans got to work digging out mud-caked cadavers, word spread that yet another storm, Frederic, was thundering its way over from Africa. But mercifully, Frederic didn't live up to its potential—at least not in the Caribbean. Frederic staked out its own territory in Alabama and Mississippi, where it took five lives and went on to become the costliest hurricane in U.S. history up until that date.

After Frederic passed, news media began a slow and gradual softening of its post-hurricane fixation. A week after the children were found on the boat, a hospital spokesperson informed a junior reporter from the San Juan daily newspaper that the children found in Mayagüez were doing well but were still under observation. The next day, Puerto Ricans heard about the incident for the first time, in a small article in the *San Juan Star*, on page twenty-two of section C.

The children of the *For Tuna* were estimated to range from two to four years old, and had limited vocabulary. One of them communicated his needs through some kind of sign language, but one little girl managed to clearly identify herself as Rosita. They didn't know what country, city, or town they were from. Not a single one could name a parent. None of the children resembled each other enough to support the presumption of a genetic relationship, and the forensic methods available at the time were useless in settling the question of family relations between the children. One of the children appeared to have some African ancestry, another had white skin and gray-blue eyes, while yet another had a slightly reddish tint more typical of the Caribbean indigenous people. The other two were dark-eyed and dark-haired but ethnically nondescript. It was clear that Spanish was their primary language and it was noted that they had distinctive Dominican accents, discernible even in the pronunciation of their monosyllabic baby talk. In a televised interview, a hospital spokesperson told a reporter that the children "look Puerto Rican, but sound Dominican." It was this careless, off-the-cuff remark that finally ignited an interest from the public, not for the children's welfare—at least, not initially—but rather, because it reopened old wounds on the subject of immigration and race. "They are members of our Caribbean community," wrote a graduate student at the University at Ponce in a letter to the editor. "Why would anyone bother to wonder if they're 'legal' or 'illegal,' from this island nation or that? They're in Puerto Rico now and it is our duty to protect them."

A week later, U.S. federal authorities had upgraded the case to urgent and assigned personnel with experience in solving crimes involving missing children. Authorities on every Caribbean island were in collaboration with the FBI in a campaign to find anyone who might be able to identify the children and locate their families. It was determined that the anonymous female caller who had alerted the local police probably had something to do with the children's abandonment. The police were still actively searching for her. The call had come through the non-emergency line, so it hadn't been recorded. The dispatcher who took the call said that the woman had spoken in Spanish, "but with a heavy gringa accent."

The *For Tuna* (named simply after its owner's fish of choice), had been lost sometime during Hurricane David. It belonged to retired Army officer Stuart Norwin, who normally kept it at a marina in San Juan. When Norwin heard news of the impending hurricane, he had been fishing off the northwest coast of Puerto Rico. He was forced to tie up in Aguadilla, a city eighteen miles north of Mayagüez. The storm had passed just one hundred miles to the south of Puerto Rico, and the *For Tuna* had been swept away. Norwin was in the process of filing an insurance claim when the police contacted him. He told them that he had never seen the children before and had no idea how they ended up in his boat. Officer Castillo asked him to take meticulous inventory of his boat and its equipment. Norwin concluded that the only items missing were a set of binoculars and his captain's hat. But a month later, he made another discovery. He called Officer Castillo to tell him that he kept a book of nautical maps aboard his boat, and that when he had opened the book he saw that one of the charts had been marked up with a green marker. It charted a short course, beginning on the eastern shore of the Dominican

Republic and ended at Mayagüez. Norwin was sure that neither he nor his wife had marked up the map. An area called the Hourglass Shoals was circled, and a little exclamation point was drawn next to the circle. "Whoever marked up the map knew what they were doing," Norwin concluded, tapping at the exclamation point. "That's the danger zone, where the shoals clash with the currents barreling over from the Puerto Rico Trench." Officer Castillo thanked him and took the map into evidence. The Feds would take it from there, officer Castillo told him. But Norwin never heard anything more in regard to the maps.

The airwaves crackled with speculation: had a group of Dominicans found the deep sea fishing vessel and used it to get into Puerto Rico illegally? But how to explain the children's elegant clothes? The girls, it was noted, were accessorized with headbands and rubber bloomers that matched the pattern on their dresses. What kind of illegal immigrants arrived in one hundred percent cotton linen? It made more sense that they were well-to-do Puerto Rican children, transferred to the *For Tuna* from a boat that had been taking part in some kind of a celebration. But where were the missing parents? And who was the mysterious gringa?

"If they were elegantly dressed, then they are probably of Cuban origin," offered the President of the Cuban–Puerto Rican Society in a televised interview. He was astounded when his comment elicited hostility from the local community. "The arrogance!" shot back the Director of the Dominican Social Club, as he scooped up his baby and held her up for the TV cameras. "To imply that their fine clothes could only make them Cuban!" His small daughter was presented in clouds of pink crinolines, with a matching headband and a huge silk daisy pasted to her bald head. In the meantime, the police decided to release news of the starfish drawings on the kids' hands. This strange detail whipped imaginations into a frenzy. With the world still reeling from the murders and mass suicides in Guyana the year before, everyone wondered: could the children be Jonestown escapees, finally coming out of hiding? Could the starfish drawings indicate membership in a newly formed cult? But the absence of adults didn't make sense in any scenario. As each day passed, the realm of possibilities expanded in the community's imagination. An AM radio talk show suggested a double suicide at sea by the children's parents. Soon, armchair detectives throughout the Caribbean were debating their theories on the marine radio waves and over rumrunners at dockside bars. Mothers gathered outside of schools to debate the circumstances under which they could imagine their own kids ending up on a boat, alone. There were theories involving aliens and phantom cruise ships, the lost city of Atlantis, the Bermuda Triangle, modern-day pirates, drug smugglers, and child traffickers. An international controversy was already brewing in regard to the U.S. Navy test bombings off the coast of the Puerto Rican island-municipality of Vieques. In May of that year, twenty-one activists were arrested for civil disobedience in a restricted bombing area. The Viequenses' theory was that the five children belonged to a group of separatists from the big island who had been secretly murdered by the U.S. Navy. This theory was extremely popular and incendiary, despite the fact that no one was missing. In the end, every theory was easily dismissed. There were no weapons on board. No blood, no signs of a struggle, no note, no clues. And six months later, still no answers.

A black market adoption agency and several known pedophiles plotted to gain custody of the children. Within the year, two people went to jail for their scheming. When the San Juan newspaper tried to run a five-year update, the children's records were closed. All five had been adopted and were living in Arizona, New York, Connecticut, and Florida. One remained in Puerto Rico.

The only peek the public got into the children's new lives was due to a slip on the part of a Child Services spokesperson. She had told a *Newsweek* reporter (a Californian who bore a striking resemblance to Robert Redford), over rum cocktails and lunch, that two of the children had been given names that made reference to their strange story. One little boy had been named David, after the hurricane. The adoptive mother had said that the name paid homage to his astounding resilience, for he had once been either traumatized or speech-delayed but was now "talking up a storm." The New York intellectuals who adopted the precocious Rosita—the tipsy woman confessed—had renamed the girl "Taina," after the indigenous people of the Greater Antilles. The bit about their names made it into an article. Her speculations did not: "They were poor kids. In Spanish we say *jíbaros*, or *campesinos*—hillbillies. Anyway, they were clearly staged to look like affluent children," she said. "You know how I know?" She reached for the reporter's stack of photos and newspaper clippings and rotated one of the photographs so that he was looking at it straight on. "Look at the kids' outfits. What's missing?"

The reporter stared hard into the photo but shook his head.

"Look at their feet."

"They're barefoot," the reporter said. "So what?"

The woman squinted. "Why would anyone put such a gorgeous outfit on a child and then have them run around barefoot?"

"No shoes were found in the boat?"

The woman shook her head. "Isn't that strange? Where are the shoes? And look again," she said, pointing to the photo.

"The soles of that boy's feet are dirty. Wouldn't you give your kid a bath before putting him in a sailor suit?"

"Hmm," the reporter said, squinting. "After the party, the kids were running around in the grass, where their feet got dirty. They got carried into the boat. Dirty feet hardly make them *campesinos*."

The woman couldn't resist the temptation to impress the handsome reporter with her inside knowledge, so she spilled what she knew: "Okay then, here are three more clues," she said, as she leaned forward. She pulled down one finger. "The girls' ears aren't pierced." She used her other hand to give one of her large gold hoop earrings a hard tug. "In Latin America, no self-respecting mother is going to let people mistake her girl for a boy. Newborns have their ears pierced before they ever leave the hospital. It's practically the law." She arched an eyebrow and tapped at the table with her long red nails.

The reporter frowned. "Maybe the parents were just smart; kids can choke on jewelry. Or maybe the parents aren't Latino. I remember my sister wasn't allowed to get her ears pierced until she was twelve . . . You said there are two more reasons?"

The woman leaned in a little more, looked left and right, and whispered, "How about the fact that the boys aren't circumcised? Around here, only kids born at home are uncircumcised. That proves that they're . . . you know . . . *jíbaros*."

The reporter had leaned back in his chair, laced his fingers behind his head, smiled sideways, and said, "I'm not circumcised. Do I look like a *jíbaro* to you?"

The woman choked a little on her cocktail. When she finally stopped coughing, and her eyes stopped watering, she cleared her throat and smiled. But she found it difficult to make eye contact with the reporter, so she held a finger up and ordered another rum cocktail. "Make it *añejo* this time," she told the waiter. For the next ten minutes, she mostly addressed the small potted ficus tree to the left of the reporter's shoulder. "Maybe the children's parents are hippies," she said with a nervous laugh. The reporter, who retained a smirk for the rest of the interview, prompted her for the third clue. At last the woman's capacity for indiscretion dried up. She waved one hand around, shook her head, and said, "I'm drunk. I can't remember. But there's more."

With limited information, a short deadline, and a lengthy word requirement, the reporter was forced to do a little speculating himself. He predicted, in that final update, that if the world was to learn anything new about the children and their background, it would have to be under certain conditions. First, that the children reach legal age in order to speak for themselves—their adoptive parents would understandably try to shield them from the public eye. And second, that they become curious or motivated enough to seriously investigate the question on their own.

Soon after, the reporter was assigned to interview a major-league baseball player who had initiated a reunion with his Puerto Rican birth mother in the months after a near-fatal car accident. He asked the ballplayer to comment about the mystery of the children from Mayagüez. The young man speculated that, since there were five of them, sooner or later, one of them would be compelled to search for their biological families. "I was afraid to know," the athlete confessed from his wheelchair. "And then one day I woke up in a hospital bed, bandaged from head to toe, and decided that I just couldn't leave this world until I knew how I got here in the first place."

As the years passed, the *Newsweek* reporter thought of the five children now and then, but more so when he had children of his own. He thought of them when his wife dressed their daughter in puffy pink dresses for Easter, and when their four-year-old son wore a sailor suit to a wedding. He discovered that the spokeswoman had been absolutely right about the context of the missing shoes. People didn't let toddlers run around barefoot on formal occasions; it probably was a significant clue. And if their story had generated so much print yet still failed to produce answers, how could the question possibly fail to stir the children's own imaginations some day? As a parent, he hoped that their motivator would be simply curiosity, rather than, as the ballplayer had suggested, some soul-shaking misfortune.

Part I

Part I

Chapter

1

August 2007
David

I'm standing on the porch of a Victorian nested high atop a windswept island of pink granite. Griswold Island is the first in an archipelago of three hundred and sixty-five islands known as the Thimble Islands, off the coast of Connecticut. Out on Long Island Sound, colorful sailboats glide across the expanse of water that sparkles in the afternoon sunshine. The air is thick with the fragrances of summer—charcoal and suntan lotion and that fishy smell that never lets you forget you are by the sea. I'm highly entertained by the drama playing out before me. Two seagulls, fierce as gladiators, are battling over a two-pound quahog. The rocks below are a dumping ground for the birds' trash, and they're littered with broken oyster, clam, and mussel shells. I should be helping out inside, but I have to stay and see which bird wins the trophy clam. If Julia's brothers and uncles were here right now, we'd be making bets.

I've been coming here for the last six summers with my girl-friend, Julia Griswold, who is a descendant of the man who built the house in 1886. I intend to marry her. My grandmoth-er's diamond engagement ring is in the right front pocket of my khakis, and I pinch the unbendable platinum between my fingers now and then. I know that the odds are slim that Julia will say yes at this point, but that's another story. I brought the ring with me, just in case, because I can't image a more romantic place than this.

Julia (who refers to herself these days as my "friend") is somewhere inside the house, preparing for the arrival of our guests. The breeze sweeping though the back windows of the house carries the aroma of berries and brown sugar baking in the old stove, along with the clatter of cabinet doors and drawers being opened and shut. I know Julia well enough to know exactly what she is looking for—sterling silver iced tea spoons. Julia knows perfectly well that my brothers and sisters will push away the tea and demand to know where we keep the beer, but she's fussing anyway. Not because of me or because of the rarity of this occasion. No, she's doing it because the ritual of welcoming guests in this meticulous manner has been a family tradition for one hundred and twenty-one years.

There are ten branches of Griswolds who all share the cost and upkeep of this home equally, and since the summer season is so short, the family uses a strict time-share system. Amazingly, each of the ten branches of the Griswold family have cut back their allotment by one day, so that I may host the first-ever reunion of my siblings, which, needless to say, means the world to me. As far as clans go, we are polar opposites. Whereas the five of us are adoptees, the Griswolds have a family history that goes back to the Stone Age. Curiously, they're fascinated by my lack of origins, tantalized by the very *idea* of not knowing anything. Around here, I'm the slightly freakish stray everyone loves. I'm a fixture at the poker games and I've partaken of Scotch withheld from sons. I regularly sneak in nudies for the old guys and beer for their grandsons. The aunts are fond of me too. I'm privy to secrets kept from daughters and I'm the only non–family member to have a house key.

In the butler's pantry, Julia's on her knees, pulling out yellowed boxes of stemware. I reach around her and pull out a tray full of tarnished silver things. "There they are!" She smiles and taps herself on the forehead. I take a handful of spoons, along with a bottle of silver polish and a flannel rag, and I wash the spoons in the long enamel farm sink in the kitchen and lay them out on a checkered kitchen cloth, while she gets to work on the bouquet of flowers from the garden. I squeeze polishing cream onto the chamois and rub up and down until the metal is warm to the touch. I lay them across the counter and they gleam, shiny and fierce as a set of surgeon's tools. When she spots them, her eyes light up. She kisses me on the cheek and gathers them up in the cloth. She heads out to the porch, muttering something about how her great-great-grandmother would be proud of the table setting. Besides the spoons, her dead relatives' contribution to the welcoming ceremony include a hodgepodge of pitchers, glasses, linens, and dessert plates. My favorite is a ceramic sugar bowl and creamer set in the shape of a pair of bikinied lady frogs with huge, drooping boobs. It's a cautionary tale—they belonged to an aunt who left the fold and went to Vegas, and in the end, they're all she had left. But her contribution to the table setting is held in equal esteem as that of the ancestors who passed on the fancy crystal, china, and silver. In this house it's the essence of the family as a whole that counts, and the more kooky or off-beat their personalities, the more vividly they are remembered. The Griswolds are anchored by the meticulous indulgence in each other's idiosyncrasies, tastes, and habits. After a while, you half expect these people to pop up at any time; and this is what is motivating Julia to work so hard in the kitchen, obeying relatives she's never even met. "I imagine my aunts with their hands on their hips, barking out orders," she once told me. "So I do what they say."

Ever since I got sick, I've developed a deep respect for the spirit behind this crazy tradition. It occurred to me one day that people in this family don't really die. Griswolds just sort of become invisible. Their funerals are a blast. There's champagne popping, laughter, dancing. Liquor. Lots of liquor. In fact, I had more fun at Julia's dad's funeral than at either of my sisters' weddings. And yet, seven months ago, I was dismissive of what I thought were silly, wasteful, and time-consuming rituals. In fact, the first time I came, six years ago, I thought the ceremony was for *me*; I presumed that Julia was showing off her future-wife potential. Wanting to dash once and for all any illusions of marriage, I said, "If you're trying to impress me with your domestic skills, don't bother." Back then I sported a goatee, which I tugged as I said with a shrug, "I've got to warn you that I'm not the marrying type."

Her response had been one of visible relief. "That's totally fine. You're not my type anyway," she said. As it turns out, we were both wrong. I intend to right that wrong.

My siblings should be pulling into the small village of Stony Creek by now. I fetch old Uncle Oz's spyglass from a ledge between the eaves of the lower roofline. Oz, who left this world the same year as Woodrow Wilson, kept his instrument on the ledge where he could access it in "emergencies" (defined as the chance to ogle girls in swimsuits). I shut one eye and peer through the tube. It works, but the view is cloudy and there's a crack in the lens. It kind of antiques the world. It's like I'm in one of those films from the roaring twenties. I swear I can almost hear the big band music every time I use it. Through the spyglass, I see that my sibs are boarding the water taxi that will bring them across the mere two hundred yards of water that separate us. Even though we have a motorboat, Julia arranged for this initial taxi pickup because it can handle more cargo and luggage than our small boat can, and this way we can get everyone's belongings over in one trip. I've been Griswold "house-trained," so I diligently replace Uncle Oz's spyglass on the ledge (if you forgot, he'd reputedly smack you silly with a fly-swatter). I look around for something a bit more contemporary, and find a pair of marine binoculars on a coffee table. I raise them to my face. I adjust the focus wheel and the image comes in clear, sharp, and steady. I yell through the screen door to let Julia know that they're getting close.

There is a scale measure to the far left corner of the objective lens of the binoculars. I know I shouldn't do this, but it has become a compulsion to constantly test my brain. I try to figure out the distance, represented by their position on the scale, in meters. I wait for the answer to just come to me. But nothing happens. I simply can't figure it out. An all too familiar anger rises inside me. I grunt a little as I give in to my compulsion to hurl the binoculars over the rail and into the yard. One of the seagulls takes flight as the binoculars sail over the lawn toward a pile of rocks, then land soundlessly in the spongy heart of a hydrangea bush, unharmed and suspended by their strap. I take a deep breath. For a moment, I notice only the smell of the sea, the cawing of birds, and the clusters of sea grass that are hissing and waving in the warm summer breeze.

A screen door slams behind me. I turn around. Julia's got her hands on her hips. She shakes her head as she passes me on her way to retrieve the binoculars. She is elegant and reedlike, with shoulder-length blonde hair. I see that she's been shopping in the attic again: she's wearing a pair of aviator sunglasses that actually belonged to an aviator, a tooled leather belt that went to Woodstock, and a conical bamboo hat that hails from the Vietnam War.

"I aimed for the plant," I say.

"You have to control your impulses, David," she says as she holds up the binoculars, "or you can take your little party back to your mom and dad's house."

"Sorry," I say. "Do I get credit for throwing the binoculars, not the spyglass?" I ask with a sheepish shrug of the shoulders.

She shakes her head, and the frames of her glasses gleam in the sunlight. "Where's your stress ball?"

"Upstairs."

"Doesn't do you any good up there."

"Squeezing a ball when I'm pissed off only makes me more pissed off at how stupid I feel squeezing a ball." I pull my base-ball cap down lower over my eyes. Julia's face softens and she lets out a deep breath. Slowly, she takes off her Vietnam hat and opens her arms, which I dive into like a child. When she finally pries herself out from my clutch she says, "Hey, you haven't shown a hint of aphasia all morning. Did you notice that? Not a skip." She turns and points to the water. "Did everyone make it? Can you see?" she asks, and I know what she's doing—it's one of her teacher tricks. She's leading me down a mental exit ramp, taking the focus off the frustration of my diminishing faculties. That, and the fact that I have the mental acumen of a six-year-old means it works. I find myself looking out over the water and squinting.

"Can I even count anymore?" I harrumph and begin to do the math. "One, two, three, four. Yup, they're all here. One more sibling and I'd need a calculator." I peek out of the corner of my eye . . . yes. I made her smile.

We turn our attention to the approaching water taxi. I've seen both my sister Taina and my brother Adrian in the last few weeks, but we haven't been all together, all five of us, since 1979. Our first full reunion should have happened at both Holly's and Taina's weddings, but someone backed out last minute, both times. And so it turns out that being diagnosed with cancer has a silver lining after all. The zillions of obstacles to a reunion miraculously lift and flutter away, and all of a sudden here they come.

My brothers and sisters disembark along with the smell of diesel fuel and the noise of an idling engine. Ray steps off the boat first. He still has crazy, curly hair down to his shoulders and his wide body blocks the sun for a moment. We slap each other on the arm and he says, "I'm gonna fatten you up, man!"

I pat my belly. "I've gained twenty-eight pounds, man. I'm skinny by reputation only." Over his shoulder, I glimpse boxes of bulky and absurd things: a piñata, a snow-cone machine, a Slip 'n Slide, a karaoke machine. Stuff that should be steak, wine, noodles, paper towels, but that's Ray. And then there's Taina, who has brought more trunks than a Vanderbilt. You never know who she'll be—artiste, hippie chick, urban hip-hop, country-club prep, motorcycle momma, salsa dancer. She's taller than normal today. "Did you grow?"

She twists one platformed foot out to account for her stature. She's wearing a white-and-green palm frond pattern sundress reminiscent of fifties Hollywood, with a neckline that shows off her glassy, golden brown skin, with underlying collarbones that point upward like wings. "Hey! It's the Chiquita Banana girl," I say. Tai squints and then slowly raises a red-tipped middle finger at me.

"Baby boy!" Holly shouts, and she grabs my face and plants kisses on my cheeks and forehead like an overbearing aunt.

"Ew," I say, and wipe them off with the back of my hand. Holly's barely five feet tall and is believed to be the youngest of the five of us, and yet, she is, without a doubt, the big sister. This may have to do with the fact that she's the only one of us that has kids, and is therefore more parentlike, or that she teaches kickboxing, or that she's naturally bossy. And now that she finally broke down and got our clan's signature starfish tattoo, watch out. She holds out her newly inked hand for me to see: a mama starfish with three tiny starfish in tow, representing her three boys. I suddenly understand her long-held reluctance to get it—it's garishly at odds with the Ring-Pop-sized sparkler on her finger. "I finally did it!" she says, beaming and pointing to the tattoo with her other hand.

"Oh man," I say, shaking my head. "You went from high class to no class."

"I know," she gushes. "Isn't it great?"

From behind me, Adrian shouts his sometimes-nickname for me, *"Flaco!"* He slaps me hard on the back, almost knocking me over. His luggage consists of a guitar case and a duffel bag, which he puts down to embrace me. What can I say about my ace? The bastard's as talented with the guitar as he is with the *chicas*. As his brother, it's my job to keep him humble, so I look him up and down and shake my head. "You look like shit."

"Yeah? I stink too," he says and shoves his armpit to my face. I catch a whiff of expensive cologne, but I lean back, coughing and wagging a hand in front of my face. "Don't they have soap in Miami?" I grumble and turn my head. No one enjoys fraternal insults—directed at Adrian, that is—more than our brother Ray. He laughs like a kid on a playground.

"Quick picture!" Julia shouts, holding up a camera.

"Wait! Our hats!" someone shouts. They scramble off in different directions and rummage through bags. Ray slips a Phoenix Suns hat on backward, Holly pulls out a canvas fishing-style bucket hat, and Taina half-disappears under the wide shade of a straw belle hat. Adrian is already wearing a red bandana on his head like a biker, or a pirate. Ray explains by pointing at my head. "It's our way of showing support. You know, for your chemo and all," he says, then looks down. "We're not ready to shave our heads just yet."

I shake my head. "That's so nineties after-school special."

"I told you guys it's passé," Taina scolds as she smoothes the front of her sundress. We crowd together, and Julia snaps the first photo of the trip, with the old house looming in the background. When I peer into the camera's preview screen, I see that Adrian has his hands folded into a gangsta pose, Ray's making horns over my head, and Tai is sticking her tongue out.

I ask Julia to take them up to the house. I point to the water taxi and she nods and takes a couple of bags. I watch them lug their suitcases and boxes of food and liquor up the stone steps. "Need help?" I call out feebly.

"We're fine!" Taina says as she grabs the handle of her leather trunk with both hands and drags it across the crumbling walkway leading up to the house. The boatman from the water taxi runs over to help her. I watch from the bottom of the steps.

Back on the dock, I thank him for his repeated offers to be of service. It's easy to change the subject on a Connecticuter, especially boaters. Just mention the weather and they'll go on about it. When he's done rattling off the forecast for the next month, I ask if my clan tipped him, and he holds up a hand and says, "Plenty."

All the while, I'm trying to remember his name, which starts with an "A" (Albert? Anthony? Andrew? Hell, I've known him for six years). His name is gone. He pulls away and I wave to him while my other fist is curled into a ball. I step off the dock onto the beach and pick up a handful of smooth, heavy rocks and start tossing them hard, one by one. They sail across the water then fall, *falup, falup, falup.* They disappear into the water along with my anxiety. I put a few of the rocks in my pockets for the sake of convenience, figuring that it won't be long before I need to throw something again. Then, remembering Julia's words, I drop them back onto the sand. She's right. I have to control my impulses. The last thing I want is to take my frustration out on anyone—or on the house.

I catch up with the group just as Julia begins to give her famous Griswold House tour. It's both tradition and a measure of security, that everyone be aware of its history. What I'm hoping will happen is that my siblings will begin to get a rare glimpse, as I have over the years, of what it's like to have deep roots; a concept that was totally foreign to me before I met Julia. Their luggage is parked at the foot of the stairs. Julia begins the tour in the foyer. Holly and Ray are sniffing the air, processing the musty, shut-up old home smell that never goes away, the subtle scent of rotting wood and yellowed cotton, of sea salt, old canvas, and citronella. But, if you're to believe Julia, the introductions go both ways. The Griswold spirits are getting to know them too.

Double French doors creak open and we follow Julia into the great room. There are huge, narrow floor-to-ceiling windows that let in bright rectangles of sunshine, but the rich paneling on the walls keep this room feeling gloomy all day long. It's the only formal room in the house, and it stands in stark contrast to the beachy shabbiness of the rest of the house. There are oil paintings and yellowed portraits of Victorian brides and a great gilded mirror over the marble hearth. The heavy, claw-footed furniture has its talons dug deep into the balding scalp of a Persian rug. Sunglasses and hats come off one by one, and we lower our voices, as if we have just stepped into a church. I make a beeline to the wall of shelved books and pull out a heavy, leather-bound tome and hold it up for all to see. "*The Griswolds of New Haven County*," I say, "commissioned by the State of Connecticut Archival Libraries. It has eight volumes." I pause for effect and look them each in the eye. "*Eight* freaking volumes." I plop it in Ray's hands. "That's the last one: 1911 to 1973. Volume nine is being written." I hand out two of the older books. My siblings draw close and start thumbing through them. Holly takes a step back, as if she's in the presence of a Gutenberg Bible. "This is just amazing, Julia," she says. "Amazing."

Taina isn't impressed. When it comes to culture and history, she's seen it all. For starters, she's a New Yorker, and her parents both happen to be art scholars at NYU. So she's hanging back, too cool to swoon over Julia's treasures. Her spine is pressed against the frame of a door. With one hand she's turning an unopened package of cigarettes over and over onto the palm of the other.

Adrian points to an open page. "Julia Abigail Griswold. Born in 1972 at Yale–New Haven Hospital. Daughter to John Crew Griswold and Diane Amelia Sophia Emerson."

"You're four years older than David," Holly says, turning to Julia. "I never knew."

Taina pipes in from the back, "So that whole rush to marriage thing was all about the biological clock, huh?"

Julia drops her head to one side and squints at her. "I think I was more than patient when David and I were dating. You call six years a 'rush to marriage'?"

"In some circles it is," says Adrian without looking up from the book.

Holly hangs an arm briefly on Julia's shoulder. "I can only imagine the pressure on females in your family to fill those books with descendants." She points at the wall behind her.

"Sure. I'll admit it. And it's no joke. We have to produce descendants who will help pay for this place. If the family dwindles, we'll lose Griswold Island. 'Not on my watch' is our motto, as we slave to pay our share of the bills."

I raise a finger and look at Julia. "I keep telling her I'm ready to help. How many babies do you want? Four? Eight? Ten?" Julia gives me a half-smile and shakes her head.

"Wait. The house isn't paid off yet?" asks Holly. "How can that be?"

"Oh, it's been paid off for like, a century," says Julia. "But Connecticut has the highest cost of living in the nation; our local taxes are outrageous. Beachfront? *Ka-ching!* Many of us have had to have two or even three jobs to keep up on the taxes and maintenance bills."

"That part sucks," I agree. "But it's home. And I love that most of the state is forest and wetlands."

". . . But trees don't pay taxes," Julia says. "So we pay over two thousand dollars a month in property taxes, and that's *with* connections at town hall."

"The tax assessor is her uncle," I explain. "Sucks that he's honest."

Holly says, "What would happen if you couldn't keep up the payments, or if the family gets smaller and smaller? Could you actually lose it?"

"Of course." Julia shudders and shakes her head. "It would be like a death in the family." She stops. She can't even stand to think about it. My hand wanders back into my front pocket, and again I pinch the cold, circular hardness of my grandmother's engagement ring. We will have two boys and a girl, I decide.

"Jeeze," says Taina. "Don't you feel trapped?" She points at the books and then opens her arms to include the whole house, and presumably, the whole island. "How do you break away from two hundred years of family history in one city and make your own life? What if you want to move to Paris?"

"I'll never leave because nothing is richer than being a part of a huge, tight-knit clan living in the same region for generations. People leave, but they always come back. They discover that it's lonely out there. So we take menial jobs if we have to, in order to stick with the herd."

Taina straightens and steps away from the doorframe. "I can actually relate to that, but in reverse. It's my *lack* of family history that defines me. It's what makes me fascinating to other people. Without 'the mystery' I'd be just like everyone else. *Bo-ring*," she intones. She looks at Adrian as she speaks; and a conspiratorial look is exchanged between them. Adrian walks over to the baby grand piano and lifts the key cover. *Pink, pink, pink.* He flashes Julia a smile. "Nice," he says. "You finally got it tuned."

Taina twists her head to look at him. "You've been here before?"

Julia ignores the question, and uses her patented method to steer Taina away from the subject. "I want you all to be happy and entertained," she says. "I have an easel and paintbrushes for you, Taina."

"I don't paint," Taina says flatly. "I design textiles. On a computer."

"I was going to ask you," I shift on my feet, "if you would paint my portrait."

"Uh, let me think about it." She looks away, drums fingers on her chin, pretending to mull it over. "No."

"It's either paint my portrait or shave your head. Your choice."

She's about to sass back, when Holly suddenly puts her arms out and chirps, "Did I just die and go to heaven? Ten days of summer in New England?" She clamps her hands together and rests them over her heart, in a gesture that echoes a delighted Minnie Mouse; I can almost see red hearts shooting out of her ears. As Julia walks them toward the dining room, Holly swoons at the glass-front cabinets packed tight with kitchen crap in the butler's pantry. She declares that everything she owns back home is "pure chinz."

Raymond bellows, "As I recall, I paid fifty bucks for *one* fork from your wedding registry. Now it's 'chinz'?"

"I'm talking about character," she laments. "I don't own anything that's more than twenty years old."

Moments later, Ray is standing beneath the cathedral ceiling of the dining room, staring, open-mouthed, at a ship's figurehead that's hung high against the wall. The carving is of a mermaid, all bosoms and scales and sleepy eyes of seduction. Ray pinches the fabric of Julia's sleeve and says, "Whoa. Who's your friend?"

"That's Serena. She came off a Spanish galleon. Someone picked her up at a nautical antiques auction long ago."

Holly jabs an elbow into Julia's rib and mutters, "I'd make sure that puppy's bolted to the wall."

They drift off toward the kitchen. When Julia's out of hearing range, I inform Ray that Serena is the mascot at the uncles' popular poker tournaments. There's even a drink named after her. Guys from all around the Thimbles and Branford come over for the games and the uncles do all kinds of things to Serena, the least of which is put sunglasses, hats, and negligees on her. In the last half-century, Serena's been photographed locking lips with dozens of poker players, including two state governors and one very, very drunk Yale Law School dean.

The next portion of the tour involves a touch of geology. Julia explains that the islands are former hilltops created after the great ice age, as she leads them past the kitchen to the segment of the porch that's at the rear of the house. The entire deck is fitted around the upthrust finger of a large rock. "It couldn't be moved, of course," she explains. "But, with stubbornness being a strong family trait, Ebenezer Griswold, who bought the island for two thousand dollars in 1884, refused to change his blueprints, so they built the porch around the rock. The result is kind of crazy and awkward, but charming," she says with a wink and a quick smile. "Like us."

"Guys," I call out, "check this out! Behold the 'captain's punch bowl,' a trillion-year-old stone beer cooler. Holds up to six cases, plus ice." They step down the dozen steps or so to see a natural depression the size of a bathtub, along a stretch of rock that was mounded high with ice and drinks.

Adrian bends down to fish out a brown glass bottle of Elm City beer. "*Sweeet*."

"Later," I say. "Julia has this whole family tradition she has to do first. It's important. Trust me."

Adrian blinks. "Screw tradition," he says, and twists off the cap.

We lock eyes. "Rule number one. You defer to our hostess." He passes the beer to Taina, who is standing behind me. I hear her take a sip. It pisses me off a little, but I let it go. "Just respect the traditions," I say. "You'll understand later."

We catch up to Julia, who is calling everyone, so she can finish the tour and relax. She takes two steps to the left and points to the ground, where there is a small marble plaque. "My Uncle James is buried here." She stomps her sandaled feet twice, right on the plaque, lifting dust. "Uncle James! You've got company! Meet David's family: Adrian, Ray, Taina, and Holly."

Ray's eyes grow huge. "Are you sure he's okay with you doing that? I do *not* want to be stuck on an island with a pissed off ghost."

They all look down, slightly horrified. Julia tilts her head. "He'd be genuinely hurt if I didn't include him," she says. Ray reads the inscription on the plaque out loud:

If I ever forget who I am,
bring me here and I'll remember
James Alfred Griswold (1847–1930)

"Alzheimer's," Julia sighs. "The family curse. In the end they can only figure out who they are—who any of us are— when they come back here. Maybe it's the sound of the waves, the view, or the smells inside the house that trigger memory. My grandmother used to say that here, on Griswold Island, she could actually hear 'the distant music' that was her life."

"The distant music," Adrian echoes. He pats himself at the chest and hips, presumably in search of a pen.

Suddenly Holly grips my arm and pulls me away from the group. She has a flattering, short, stylish haircut and a cardigan sweater tied around her shoulders, and looks every bit the tidy soccer mom that she is. She's not a natural beauty, like Taina, but she knows what looks good on her and works hard at staying in shape.

"I want to apologize for what I said back in the library," she whispers, pointing up at the house.

I shake my head. "What?"

"I said, 'Did I just die and go to heaven?' I hope I didn't upset you, you know, bringing up, you know . . . death." She cringes, balls her fists up and puts them up to her face. "Oh I'm mortified."

I pull the fists off her eyes and move my head back and forth to force her to look at me. "I don't want you to have to walk on eggshells, Hol. You can say die, kill, croak, kick the bucket, hell you can even say brain cancer, I don't care. It doesn't offend me, it doesn't 'remind' me. Because you know what, I can never forget, not for a moment, of the predicament I'm in. And second," I put my arms around her shoulders, pull her close, and lower my voice to a whisper, *"I'm not going to die."* I put a finger to my lips. *"Shhh. That's a secret."* She looks up at me, eyes brightening, as if expecting me to share some news. When I don't, she looks down and says, "Of course you're not." Her eyes well up with tears and she gets on her tippy-toes and kisses me on the forehead. I turn her and lead her back toward the group.

On the seawall, Taina is lighting up a cigarette. Julia's eyes widen and zoom in on the cigarette. "Don't come anywhere near the house with that. No smoking allowed."

Taina takes a deep drag and blows into the wind. "Don't worry."

"Nasty habit," Ray says, taking it from her fingers. Then he takes a deep, hungry drag, puts it out on the seawall and pockets the butt.

We walk the periphery of the island, which, in some spots involves negotiating piles of rock. Ray shoots photos of the sea, the house, and the distant view looking back to the Village of Stony Creek.

I turn to Adrian and say, "C'mon. I'll show you where we keep the kayaks." He turns and follows me, and it isn't until

we're halfway across the lawn that I remember a comment
Julia made earlier this morning, about how when Adrian and
I get together, we always forget about Ray. I don't turn back,
though, thinking that it will just call attention to our oversight.

We walk out to the boathouse, which is attached to the
dock. Inside there is a Sunfish, a rowboat, a Jet Ski, and eight
multicolored kayaks. I predict that Adrian will spend a lot of
time paddling around in them, at first for the fun of exploring
the islands and to keep up his exercise routine. But in about
three or four days, the charm of our togetherness will begin to
wear off and his claustrophobia will start to set in. He will start
to notice the lack of air-conditioning in the house, the house
rules will cease to be charming, and the constant bickering of
our sisters will grate on his nerves. Maybe the well will go dry
right before his shower, or we'll run out of something essential,
like toothpaste or toilet paper or bottled water. In a week, he'll
be fleeing the arguments about our conflicting memories and
the shadow of our invented fears. He'll want to get away from
me, the one who is forcing it, and then he'll try to escape from
his own brain, from the steady stream of thoughts that will
visit him at night. But that's the whole point of reuniting on a
one-acre island. I can only hope there will be no escape, once
it's started.

I close the door to the boathouse and Adrian starts to tell
me how he might be recording a duet with a famous Colom-
bian singer. I don't know her, but she's one of those so-called
crossover artists. As he's talking, my eye catches something
moving in the water below. It's just our reflection, but for a
split second, I don't recognize the bloated man standing next
to Adrian. All I see is a big head and gut. I'm shocked for
the hundredth time to realize that it's *me*. The steroid-induced
bloating is a reality that I thought I was used to, but I'm blind-

sided in moments like this. I make the mistake of imagining how Julia might compare us, my handsome brother, and bald, fat-headed me. My heart sags at the thought.

When we rejoin the crowd Julia is showing them where to find the cereal, the bowl of hard-boiled eggs, the paper goods, the hard liquor, the ice. She shows Ray the family collection of cookbooks; demonstrates how to open them carefully so the pages don't fall out of the binding. The last room is the boiler room, where they will tend to their laundry, bathing suits, and towels. She points discretely at the mops and cleaning products.

After the tour of the upstairs and the cupola, we clatter and creak our way back down the grand staircase. Along the wall, we pass oversized, melted-glass windows, where we see panoramic vistas of the glittering sea. The stairs groan under us as we head downstairs in a thunderous stampede. Griswolds stare back from daguerreotypes, with their odd details, like topcoats that button on the wrong side. The photographs progress chronologically down the wall, to present-day Sears Studio portraits of the family's most current crop of schoolage children. The elders remind me, with their piercing, yellowed, turn-of-the-century stares, that I can't back down from my decision, regardless of how idyllic the next few days might become.

On the porch, cut hydrangeas sit in hurricane-proof vases that are impossible to tip (one of the many garage inventions that have so endeared me to the family). On the table, ice buckets and pitchers sweat in the sun, perfect stand-ins for the porcelain-skinned gaggle of Victorian aunts who once owned them. The grandfather clock announces the three o'clock hour.

My gang is more polite about the tea and cobbler than I anticipated; they scarf it down, I suppose, because they're tired, hungry, and thirsty. I watch in utter amazement as Adrian

swirls his ice tea with the long-handled spoon under Julia's tu-
telage. "Craps anyone?" Raymond says, as he rolls the sugar
cubes across the table like dice. Adrian puts on a ventriloquist
show starring the sugar-and-creamer frogs, sending Julia and
my sisters into a fit of snorts and giggles. My siblings fill the
porch with a presence as fresh and colorful as sliced watermelon
on a summer day: Holly with her wisecracks and Ray's window-
rattling laughter, Taina with her sarcasm and tinkling bracelets,
and with the reverberation in Adrian's deep, melodic voice. We
sit in a circle of rocking chairs. Our sandals and sneakers lie
abandoned along the wall. We are all barefoot again, like we
were in the picture of us that was taken by the police in 1979.

Bring me here and I'll remember, echoes Uncle Jim from his
grave just a few feet away.

The afternoon sun is really blasting now and Julia claps her
hands and offers our guests the antioxidant pomegranate and
seaweed ice-pops she's been pushing on me all summer. I warn
everyone flat out that they taste like bile. That's what I meant
to say but then the aphasia finally kicks back in and I say "mild"
and so nobody benefits from my warning. I watch my sisters'
worried expressions as they choke them down, lick by torturous lick. I have to admire Adrian's strategy, which is to wave
it around when he speaks and discreetly hold it over a plant
when he's not, until it all melts off. When Julia asks if he liked
it, he raises the empty stick and proclaims that it was "terribly
refreshing." To this I mumble, "Yeah, for the plant," and Ray
tells Julia that Adrian has always been a bit shy about asking
for seconds. Julia rushes to get him another ice-pop despite
Adrian's protests. I high-five Ray and we roar with laughter. So
Adrian dashes off and comes back with his guitar, grips the neck
with one hand and fingers the strings with the other, pretending to concentrate on a few tentative first notes. The unwanted

popsicle is ceremoniously handed to Ray, who hands it to me. What else can I do but eat it? She made them for me, after all; so I dispose of the dripping mess with three airless bites.

Adrian unleashes a warm, sparkling cascade of guitar music that floats down and across the porch. It drifts like foam across the lawn and dissipates when it meets the sea. Adrian's smoky voice is heavier, darker, and much older than the youthful body that produces it. *"Quedate conmigo,"* he sings. Adrian's the only one of us who speaks Spanish, so don't ask me what the song's about. I just know that Adrian's voice is awesome.

Suddenly I smell the sweet scent of tobacco wafting up from the yard. I can easily envision Uncle James, wandering over to check out Taina as he gnaws on his convenience-store cigar. I pat the empty seat next to me, and invite him, in my imagination, to sit. But you can't invite just one Griswold, that would be rude. So I imagine them *all*, hundreds of them, the old and the young, the living and the dead, crowded around the porch. I can see the men in the family lined up against the porch's rail, arms folded over beer guts, watching Adrian play guitar. I can't help but notice that they're all wearing hats: World War II baseball hats and straw boater hats, safari hats, hunting boonies, Navy hats with shiny visors. The women look back and forth at my brothers and sisters, whispering to each other, some in tennis visors, others in gardener's hats. The cougar in the family narrows her green eyes at Adrian from behind a veiled cocktail hat.

I recently started doing this combination of imagining and remembering, in part, out of a compulsion to constantly challenge my brain. It's less frustrating than metric conversions are because I already know so much about these people, both as a collection of colorful individuals, and as a clan. They have such a prodigious genealogical memory that the past is hard-wired into their present. Julia, and the familial spirit embodied in this magnificent old house, is helping me to open up my own past; to unblock the dangerous, clogged artery that is starving off my future. It's not that I think I'm going to die soon, but rather, I've accepted the fact that I now have to live with that probability. I'll always live with the sensation of watching an hourglass drain. But I am incomplete without a beginning. My brothers and sisters, on the other hand, fear that the past will rush in and overwhelm them. The epitaph on Uncle Jim's grave directly challenges the bliss of ignorance with its lament about forgetting. It is indeed profoundly sad to forget who you are, but, I will argue, how much more so never to have known?

Chapter

2

January 2007 (eight months earlier)
David

We were at Taina's favorite New York City café. It was four in the afternoon, and she and Adrian ordered Reuben sandwiches. Without looking at the menu, I said, "Three eggs, scrambled, please. And a pint of that Winterfest ale."

Adrian moaned. "In Puerto Rico they would say, *'por eso es que tu estás tan flaco, nene.'*"

"Translate."

"Dude. You need to eat more fat." Adrian was sitting next to me and he shrugged and folded his hands behind his head. He studied every woman who passed on the sidewalk outside. Taina had her back to the window and looked over her shoulder to see what had attracted his attention. She put her fingertips to her forehead as if she had a headache. "Adrian, you can't go for more than three seconds without scanning for booty." Adrian sat up and looked into her eyes for a couple of seconds, giving her a defiant little squint. A few seconds later, a group of girls with NYU sweatshirts began to cross the street in our direction. Silently, I counted: *one Mississippi, two Mississippi, three*—his willpower crumbled and his eyes betrayed him as they ping-ponged back and forth between Taina and the approaching girls. I laughed and high-fived Taina, who shook her head. Adrian raised an eyebrow and said, "Looking is normal, okay? Every man does it. Even nice, loyal men like your husband."

"Loyal my ass. Doug cheated on me emotionally," she said. "Of course I'm insecure."

Adrian's back curved, as if someone had put a weight upon his shoulders. "What the hell is this 'emotional cheating' anyway? He either banged someone or he didn't. We all know he didn't. So what's the problem? That he *talked* to a female coworker?"

"Basically," Taina said.

Adrian put a hand over his heart. "That dog!"

I have to agree with Rico Suave on this one. Our brother-in-law Doug was having a hell of a time getting over our crazy sister. He must have become addicted to her never-ending drama. Taina had bangles that jingled, leather that creaked, curls that bounced, lips that glistened, and high, meaty cleavage that shook just by her pressing her teeth together. Taina was nothing less than a force of nature.

Our beers arrived and I took a sip. "I agree with Adrian," I said. You're pathologically jealous, Taina. Doug is crazy about you. So what if he poured his heart out to another detective. People do that at work all the time and it doesn't mean anything. In fact, I bet the poor woman is so sick of hearing about you she could puke."

Taina turned her eye on me. "So what's your excuse?"

"Me?"

"Yes you." She said with a tough-girl shake of the head. "You two are the princes of the royal court of romantic dysfunction. At least I *got* to the altar. And you, Adrian? Phew." She drew an invisible upward spiral with her index finger. "Your fear of intimacy is pathological. You go from pick up to breakup in sixty seconds."

"I'm like a Ferrari."

Taina couldn't help a small smile. Yeah, Adrian's a lot more like a Ferrari than any of us care to admit, but we try not to encourage him.

Exasperated with the same old discussion, I dropped my forehead into my hand. "We just go around and around in the same circles. How messed up we all are, blah blah blah."

Adrian got a serious look on his face and lowered his voice. "We're all doing great emotionally. Considering that we were abandoned in such a public way." He sat back, then leaned in again and whispered, "Each one of us has embraced the mission to learn to honor ourselves and each other," he pointed at Taina and me, "even though *someone* thought we were disposable. Do you think it's any coincidence that you turned out to be so talented at art, or that my music career is taking off?" His hands separated and he held an invisible guitar, fingers plucking chords. "David. You love your career. You have a passion for hiking and you have a fantastic girlfriend—"

"Had," I corrected.

"Sorry. Had," he said. "And Holly has her boys . . ." He shot Taina a reproachful look. "Any one of us could be in jail or dead or shooting up drugs. But the very worst that's happened is that we have some trust issues." The waiter brought my $15 plate of scrambled eggs.

Taina held a finger up and pursed her lips. "What about Ray?"

"Isolated case," Adrian said, throwing his cloth napkin across the table. "He was fine until his dad left his mom. Then he started to drink. The point is that despite our weird entrance into the world, so much good has come our way and is still pouring in." He put his hands out, wiggling his fingers as if all those things were raining down, gold coins flowing between his fingers, and he was trying to catch it all.

Just as Tai's and Adrian's fancy sandwiches arrived, someone at the next table said, "Are you Adrian Vega?" Next thing we knew, Adrian was chatting happily with a group of women from Miami. There was the clatter of chairs as the women stood up and crowded in to have their picture taken with him. After ten minutes, Adrian extricated himself from his fans and came back to us. He had turned down pleas from the Miamians to join them for drinks later on. I saw two of the women lean over and size up Taina.

"I love that about you," Taina said, reaching across the table for his hand. "We always come first." Adrian winked at her. His starfish tattoo is a spiny, crawling monstrosity that has wrapped itself around his wrist, ten or more times the original size of the green drawings. Adrian and I both have the first initial of our siblings' names floating over each leg of the starfish. The order of mine is random, *A H R T D*, whereas Adrian's is ordered so it spells *DARTH* (he was into *Star Wars* as a kid).

"Make it move," Taina said, staring intently at his tattoo. Adrian made a fist and squeezed the muscles in his hand and forearm, animating the starfish so it looked like it was moving. Taina laughed and clapped.

Adrian said, "Show us your little dinky tattoo, *Flaco*."

I rolled my eyes and held it out. "I want the record to show that mine is actual size."

Taina rubbed it with the yolk of her fingers, passing large, square blocks of white-tipped fingernails over my skin. She held up her own version, a geometric star that looks more like a crystal.

Adrian says, "It looks like a frozen crab."

Taina pulled her hand away. "It's art."

"It's brilliant," I said. "It's Taina's expression of how our abandonment made her feel."

"Yeah," she said, slapping the table. "Thank you."

Adrian screwed his face up and took a closer look at the tattoo. "You *are* pretty crabby."

"She's frozen," I say. "Emotionally. Not fully alive."

Adrian tapped the table with his knuckles. "*Ah, bueno*, forgive me, then," he said, pointing at my chest. "It's a scar that we each interpret." He raised his beer and offered a toast. "To our biological parents," he said. "May they rot in hell."

He and Taina clinked glasses, but I put mine down. "I won't drink to that. We don't know what happened."

What happened. What happened. What happened. The words echoed inside my head. I felt a vague headache coming on again. I hadn't been taking my breakup with Julia very well, and I'd recently experienced the first nauseating migraines in my life. I had started carrying a bottle of over-the-counter migraine pills in my jacket pocket. I popped it open and downed three of them with the beer. I went to ask the waiter for coffee, hoping the extra caffeine might help, but I couldn't think of the world for "coffee." It was the weirdest thing. After a few seconds, the word "café" popped up.

"Are you okay?" Taina asked. "You look puzzled."

"Mind if we go home soon?" I said. "I'd like to take a little nap before the concert."

That night, Adrian performed with his band in an industrial warehouse that was completely transformed into a swanky lounge as part of a liquor promotion. The venue provided a steady stream of concerts and celebrity events for a month. By the time we got there, the house was packed. Taina happily accepted exotic cocktails from roaming waiters. We were amused, as we always were, to witness the effect Adrian had on his audience. He and his band were mostly a Miami act, so this was an excellent place to perform and expand their fan base in New York.

I took two tiny sips of seltzer water. I still didn't feel well. I couldn't stop my mind from circling something. What, I didn't know. That was the strange part, like trying to remember someone's name, or an important number; something just beyond the reach of memory, something as they say, on the tip of my tongue . . . what?

Beside me, Taina was looking up at Adrian adoringly, mouthing the words to his song, *"Olvídame,"* which I think means "forget me." She doesn't know any more Spanish than I do, but she makes it her business to know Adrian's songs. I saw her lips spread in a slow, Mona Lisa–like smirk, saw her eyelids droop into that dopey-eyed look that Julia used to give me now and then. I had to look away. It's not right for a sister to look at a brother like that. I felt something shadowy spread across my soul; it struggled, batting its wings against my insides, until the music shifted. The lights lowered and went out, then burst back in a shower of white spots that swam over the dancing crowd. The music got louder and a brass section popped up out of nowhere, playing a salsa number that animated every set of hips in the room. I spun Taina around and we swung out the new moves Adrian had taught us earlier at Taina's apartment. We did a slick move called "sombrero" where the girl goes under your arm and both dancers' arms slide across each other in one smooth, elongated, and fluid motion. We danced until I felt the sweat dripping down my face. Taina opened her eyes wide and shouted something into my ear.

"What?"

"I thought he wasn't starting until . . . !"

"What?" I turned my head, hoping the other ear might work better.

"I thought he wasn't starting until eleven!" The tap of a drumstick on a metal disk reminded me of the sound a locker makes when you slam it shut. And that's when it happened. Taina says I just stood there, looking up at the stage with a blank look on my face.

High school. I was facing a little metal plaque with the number "1140." I turned the white-on-black numbers of the combination lock dial. Three clockwise, eleven counterclockwise, turn back and stop at seventeen. *Click.* The lock released. Flesh-colored narrow metal door opening. Book spines were visible on a shelf inside. A blue-and-white wool varsity jacket hung on a metal hook. The vague smell of cold cuts wafted up from the bottom of the locker. On the door, a schedule of soccer meets.

Taina bumped my hip and said, "Wake up!" Adrian hit a high note and threw his head back. The percussion was building and the women in the front were screaming for him. A pair of panties hit the keyboard player on the head and he didn't remove them, just kept playing with them dangling over his eyes. Adrian was glistening with sweat, in that trancelike state he goes into when he's playing; his hands move expertly across the spine of the guitar.

I was both nauseous and dazzled. I wondered, for about a millionth of a second, if I might have fainted or had a kind of mini-stroke, but you don't have either of those things while standing up, do you?

"I need air," I said, grabbing my jacket and turning to look for the nearest exit. I hoped that Adrian didn't see me leave, but I had to escape the noise and confinement. I went outside to an alleyway, taking deep gulps of cold air. I found a dumpster and hung my head over it.

I felt Taina's hand on my back. "Drink too much?"

"Just seltzer," I said weakly.

"Bad food?"

I shook my head, "Something is wrong with me, Tai. I don't know, I think something's wrong. I just had some kind of weird flashback." When the nausea let up, I straightened up and moved away from the dumpster. I sat down on the cement ledge attached to the next building. I folded my arms and looked up at the sky. I was cold suddenly. I desperately wished Julia were with me. Taina hugged me, and the smell of her perfume triggered a violent spasm deep in my stomach, and I threw up. Taina rubbed my back through it. When I was done, she ran back to let Adrian know what happened and that we were leaving.

When I felt better we walked back to her apartment arm-in-arm through the city, not a taxi to be found. Taina's posture was straight and her stride brisk. The high heels of her boots clicked on the pavement and echoed against the buildings. "So what's going on?" she said. "What did you mean, 'I'm having flashbacks'?"

Out of the corner of my eye I saw her turn her head to look at me. I took a deep breath. "I don't think I have an actual illness. I think it's something else." I cleared my throat. "My theory is that I'm having drug-induced flashbacks. I . . . I experimented with some crazy stuff in college."

She laughed. "Drug-induced? YOU?"

"I'm thinking that maybe it's affecting me now. Somehow."

Taina slowed down to a stop. She turned to look at me and raised an eyebrow. "Okay. How crazy? Are we talking a little too much pot or like, acid?"

I scrunched up my face and said, "Neither."

"What then?"

"I don't know." I took a deep breath. "Sophomore year I dated this girl named June Jones. We were lab partners in a botany class. Her family owns a pharmaceutical company. They had a piece of land where her father went on weekends to ride his horses. It was like, the size of Nebraska, but in upstate New York. June kept her own greenhouse and she was a plant connoisseur. Grew hothouse flowers and rare orchids and other things you only hear about if you're hard core into plants."

"Oh boy."

"Yup. Magic mushrooms, opium poppies, cannabis, coca—grew 'em just because she *could*. Anyway, there was a group of rare, illegal tropical plants that I'd only seen in textbooks, the ones nobody knows about. I don't know how she got them, but like I said, she liked experimenting with hybrids and rare varieties. She had succeeded in cultivating this vine that looked like a pumpkin plant, but the fruit was round and had a husk over it, like corn. The strangest part was when you opened the fruit, it had these glistening blue seeds inside. When the first fruit appeared, June made a big ceremony of it. We scraped the kernels, then we dried and crushed them. She said they were sacred to the Mayans and she showed me all these books with hieroglyphics that showed stick figures smoking this stuff."

"How on earth did she convince you to smoke *anything*? That's so unlike you. I couldn't even get you to try NoDoz when you needed to pull an all-nighter during midterms."

"Well, first of all, it's not an opiate. It doesn't affect your nervous system, your heart, or your brain."

"Then what does it do?"

I cleared my throat. "It's an aphrodisiac."

"Really . . ." Her voice trailed off. "Does it work?"

"Oh man. Oh man." I shook my head. "Oh man oh man."

"Really," she said again. "Interesting. So . . . like Viagra?"

"Times a thousand. It's unbelievable. I thought I was going to . . ."

"Enough."

"*Kaboom!*"

Taina put her hands over hear ears. "La la la la la."

We passed a group of women in high heel boots who appeared to be hookers. I didn't want them to think we were looking for some action, so I lowered my voice. "To this day, just the sight of a corn husk gets me . . ." I gave an exaggerated shudder.

Taina made a face. "If you're going to subject me to this torture you can at least tell me what it's called."

"I have a degree in plant biology and to this day I can't figure out what the hell that plant was."

Taina huffed, "You're lucky you're not dead, you moron. You've *always* refused to eat anything complex, foreign, spicy, processed, anything that might have hormones or MSG or pesticides—so you go and smoke up some mystery herb with Patty Hearst?"

"The only reason I agreed to try it is because June knew that I'm a sucker for instruments, especially if they're antique."

"Did she have an antique pipe or something?"

I point a finger at her. "You know me well, my dear. Exactly. She brought out this magnificent Egyptian hookah. It was almost as tall as you are, gorgeous, with a silver framework. The pipe was like, a zillion years old, and it had witnessed just about every important event in Egypt's history. It was going on loan from her father to the Metropolitan Museum the following week. June suggested we take it for a test ride, become a part of Egyptian history, with a Mayan twist. And we did."

"I don't see how it would be affecting you now. That was what, ten years ago?"

"What else could it be?" I practically shouted. "I don't have the flu or an infection anywhere. I haven't hit my head or used any other drugs—if that even counts. But what else could explain flashbacks?"

She shook her head. "I've never heard of an aphrodisiac giving anyone flashbacks, especially a decade later." She paused. "In fact, that's the most retarded thing I've ever heard, David. You could be having a minor stroke," she said, her voice rising a bit. She faced me and put her gloved hands on my shoulders. "Maybe we should go to the ER. Like right now."

I laughed and waved a hand. "It's not a stroke, for God's sake. Look at my face." I pushed my tongue up under my lip, rolled my eyes around, curled my hands up under my armpits and made monkey sounds. A prostitute walking past us did a double take. "I couldn't do this if I'd had a stroke, right?" I said. "Look at my face. No drooping. And look at my eyes," I looked up and down, side to side. "Here, let's step into the light. How do my pupils look?"

A car beeped at us, and when we looked up, it was Adrian in a taxi, and he had the driver pull over. "You okay?" he asked, and Taina and I leaned in.

"It's that same headache I've had all day, bro," I said. "I just need to get some sleep." Adrian said he was off to another party. Did Taina want to come? He had his arms around a woman I didn't recognize. He didn't bother to introduce her to us. "We'll pass," Taina said quietly, stepping back from the car. It pulled away. I watched her profile as she stood, staring into the empty space where the taxi had been. We went home.

Self-revelation must have been in the air that night, because Taina showed me her infamous "bunker." It was a room that was, among other more serious issues, a thorn in the heart of Taina's marriage to Doug. Taina was a severe insomniac who required solitude and militaristic level of discipline in her bed-time routine. Originally a guest room, the "bunker" was an oasis of muted colors and blank walls; equipped only with a bed and a table upon which sat implements in the service of sleep: a silk eye mask, ear plugs, a warming bag, a water carafe and glass. "I'm trying to manage my insomnia without using drugs," she said with emphasis on the last word. "Insomnia is a permanent condition that requires a long-term plan. So I have these strict rituals; I have trained myself."

"But why do you insist on sleeping alone?" I dared. "Does Doug snore?"

"That's the least of it. It's about foster care, David. I shared a room with an older girl who woke up several times a night, screaming. She would run into the closet and curl up on the floor and scream and scream that her eyes were burning. Twenty-five years later, I still hear her screaming every night, in the closet. My body still anticipates the alarm. If there's anyone snoring, moving, or coughing, it's guaranteed to obliterate my chances of getting a good night's rest. But this room is safe. And most nights, I sleep."

Foster care was where our childhood stories diverged: I was adopted almost immediately by the same parents who fostered me, whereas Taina and Raymond spent time with several dif-ferent caregivers before they were adopted. Poor Raymond had been adopted and then returned when he was six—after the family changed their mind. All I could do was kiss my sister on the forehead and wish her sweet dreams. She put one hand on my shoulder. "Davie," she said, "you should see a doctor. That flashback thing is spooky."

"I will," I said. "I have a physical scheduled for next month. And Tai? You should see someone about those nightmares. A little girl with burning eyes? Sheesh. That's creepy."

•   •   •

I was drifting off when Taina's phone, sitting in its charging cradle, vibrated and cast a ray of green light across the table. I looked at the display. It was her husband, Doug. "Miss you so much," he texted. I tapped a reply: "David here. sleeping over. working on her. patience." and hit "send." Now it was me hearing distressed voices in the dark. I lay awake staring up beyond the skylight, at the charcoal New York City sky, which never seemed to darken enough to be called night. I closed my eyes and tried to think about the Yankees and the Giants. Anything but the complexities of Taina and Doug's marriage, which made me think of Julia, of course. Of the parallels between the two situations: one person skittish, one person steady. I finally fell asleep, but a few hours later a noise woke me up. I sat up, trying to shake off a bad dream. I was soaked in sweat and relieved to be awake. This time it was my phone, and I panicked when I remembered Tai's issues with sleeping and noise. I fetched it out of the pocket of my pants, which were on the floor. Doug again. He texted, "let's talk soon." I took a moment to collect myself and I replied, "meet me at grand central at 5 tonight." I tossed the phone back and rolled over. I fell back into a dreamless sleep.

Morning seemed to wash the world clean. We lay around reading the *Times* and talking. Adrian had come in at 4:30 and slept on the couch. We didn't ask any questions. He was the first to get up, even made the coffee. Taina went out and came back with bagels. I didn't tell her that I had made plans to meet Doug, but I told Adrian. Later, we called Holly in Florida but she couldn't really talk because she was watching her kids at a pool party. Ray, who lives in Arizona, works at a restaurant, and you can't reach him until late in the day on Sunday.

At one o'clock, we got out of the house and walked around the park. By four, Adrian had to head to the airport. Taina walked me to Grand Central Station. "Bye, Davie," she said. "Hang in there. You and Julia will figure it out." I wanted to say the same about her and her husband, but couldn't remember his name. My brother-in-law. Her husband. What's-his-name. What *was* his name?

The moment I saw him, twenty minutes later, it came to me. "Doug!" I exclaimed with a flood of relief, already exhausted by my mind's fruitless swirling around the missing name. He was wearing a Yankees jacket and baseball hat. I gave him the thumbs-up on the gear.

"Sorry about last night, man, I didn't mean to invade your privacy. I was sleeping in her room—er, your room, the master bedroom," I said then shook my head, because it was coming out all wrong. "The room that's not her 'bunker,'" I said, making air quotes. He nodded appreciatively. "Man I was having the worst nightmare," I said. "I was sweating and trying to get away, and then the phone rang and I thought, thank you! Your timing was perfect. You saved my ass."

"I'm a detective," he said putting his hands out. "Just doing my job."

"A psychic cop, eh, Dougie? Maybe you should get your own reality show." I meant it too. He looked more like an actor than a cop. Tall with thick, dark hair and the pale blue eyes of a Siberian husky.

He laughed. "I'd never run out of stories."

"Anyway, I didn't mean to intrude. Tai left her phone there in the charger by the nightstand. Adrian was in town for a concert and I wanted to tell you that we had a talk with her, several actually, over the weekend, about you and her and all of us, the relationship failures, and who knows, maybe we got through to her a bit. She's so stubborn, you know."

Doug sat down, exhaled loudly. I sat next to him. He looked at me. "Being in love with your sister is so exhausting," he said weakly. He smelled like cigarette smoke and coffee, which never ceased to amaze me. I'd never quite gotten used to Doug's new cop persona. He used to reek of expensive cologne back in his stockbroker days, back when he insisted on being called *Douglas*. "I would never do anything to hurt her," he began. "You know that, right? She concocted this drama so she'll never have to worry about me leaving *her*. It's ridiculous." He looked up at me. "What I should do?"

"I don't know, man. But if we keep doing the same thing we'll get the same result. She needs more therapy; we ALL need therapy . . . we . . ."

"You need to find out what the fuck happened."

I bristled. "What happened?"

"The storm. The boat."

"Something besides that," I said, with a dry chuckle. "That's Pandora's Box. We don't go there. You know that."

He crossed his arms and sat back. "But the thing is, *someone* has to have the guts to open that stinking box in order to empty it." He knitted his eyebrows. "For God's sake, keeping it locked up only increases its power. It traps hope. It forbids peace."

"Forbids peace?" I echoed. "You're being dramatic."

"Listen. Adrian is convinced that your parents were a bunch of baby killers. But in my professional opinion, he's wrong. And David, believe me, I've read all the clippings and the police reports. I think your families died in the hurricane, that's why no one claimed you. End of story. Sad? Sure. But there's no intention to harm. Just a tragedy."

"Not gonna happen," I said, brushing some lint off my coat. "We can't risk sending Ray back to the bottle."

He slapped his hands on his lap. "Well then, let it drag on. And Jim Beam will always be there. Waiting."

I looked into the crowds of people rushing past to board their trains. Doug nodded, shook my hand. "I have to run. It's always good seeing you, man. I just want to let you know that if you ever want to pursue that big scary thing, let me know, I can help." He smiled and pointed at the back of his hand. "I may not have the starfish on my hand, but I got your back."

"Good to know, bud."

"And by the way, David, my message to Taina—I was just drunk." He gave me a slow slap on the shoulder and said, "See ya." I turned and watched him hurry down the hall, back toward the Lexington Avenue exit. I wanted to say, hey, let's catch a game soon, but I didn't. Of course he wasn't drunk the previous night. He rarely drinks. We both know that he was cold sober and texting Taina at three in the morning out of pure anguish.

"David!" When I turned I saw that Doug was walking back toward me, with a finger up in the air as if he had just remembered something. "I'm just curious, David, what was your nightmare about? The one I woke you up from last night."

I shrugged. "Oh, just stupid stuff," I said, waving a hand, but he stood there, looking at me intently. "Why do you ask?"

"You know why my wife won't share a bed with anyone? Do you really know?"

I turned away, focused on the people boarding the train to the Bronx. "The screaming girl."

Doug nodded. "And you know what happens to Taina when she has this recurring nightmare?"

"She wakes up?"

"She pees the bed. That's why she sleeps alone, David. She's an adult bed wetter. And you know what else?"

I put a hand out. "Ah, man, Doug. This is none of my business. Please."

He ignored me. "There's nothing wrong with her bladder. Whatever is making her pee herself lives in here." He pointed at his temple. Then he slapped me on the shoulder, looked me in the eye, and said, "When you're ready I'll help you open Pandora's Box." Then he disappeared into the crowd.

I hopped the Metro North train to New Haven. Instead of dealing with the thoughts and emotions elicited by my conversation with Doug, I shut them out. At least for a while. I listened to bits of conversation from the passengers around me. A group of women behind me had been prattling on for a while when suddenly one of them said, "If I were ever to become a stalker, Adrian Vega is who I would stalk." The other woman moaned and another disagreed, and the conversation alternated between talk of who was "stalk worthy" and commentary about diapers and preschool. I turned to look at them and was surprised to see that they weren't young like the ones we had met at the restaurant. I texted Adrian, "random MILFs discussing your 'hotness' on train."

From the airport, he texted, "gets old."

"Riiiight," I typed back, since I don't think he's showing any signs of limelight weariness.

The train stopped and picked up passengers in Westport and my thoughts turned to my ex-girlfriend, June Jones, who, last I heard, got a doctorate in botany and was doing research in the Amazon on a big government grant. I thought it might be a good idea to write to her to ask her the name of the plant with the blue seeds. Why not? It was worth looking into. And if they turned out not to be the cause of my episodes, then I might even consider using them for recreational purposes again. I felt my optimism rising, quite literally, at the thought of such an adventure. But with whom? I no longer had a girlfriend.

Across from me, a stunning Asian chick straight out of an anime cartoon was checking me out. She had a nose ring, and she was wrapped in an explosion of pink faux fur. We smiled at each other and played the eye game for a bit and then I grew bored. Ah, women. The past, the present, and the possible. I put my head back. For now, I was happy just knowing I could still catch a girl's eye. But I really didn't want to take action. After all, it wasn't like I didn't love Julia anymore. I did.

I had a good idea of where Julia was right now: in her old bedroom at her mom's house, lying in her girlhood bed. I circled her bed in my mind, around and around, I watched her from every angle, from behind the canopied bed and from behind the white, gold-edged furniture and through slats of the closet doors. I was still floored at how much I had yearned for her when I felt sick. If she was my so-called emotional anchor then why couldn't I commit to her? What was wrong with me, that I couldn't find the courage to show a little faith in love? Could Doug have been right? Were we stunted by the mystery of our origins?

When I got home, Julia's things were gone. Our apartment was almost completely empty. I just walked around for a while as the enormity of it sank in. I felt a wild desperation to reverse the course of this disaster. How could I have done nothing to stop this? Even worse, I hadn't helped her move out. Her brothers moved her while I was in New York partying with Taina and Adrian.

A desperate, pleading declaration of my deepest wish to reconcile and build a future with Julia would have made all the difference at this point. Flowers, notes on her windshield, voice mails, e-mails, and a heartfelt drop to the knees was what I should have done, but didn't. I always thought that I might propose to her in front of her third grade class. How great would it be to embarrass her like that? But instead of *doing*, I kept *thinking*, just like I had been thinking and not doing for years. I felt completely powerless, like in a dream where you can't move. Something was stopping me. I remembered the discussion about Taina's starfish, and yes, *frozen* was a good descriptor. I figured that I just had to make peace with it. Asinine passivity is what it was. Showing a little faith during the good times would have allowed me to hold on to the woman I love in the worst of times. And the worst of times were certainly on their way.

A couple of weeks passed. "This is good," Taina assured me on the phone. "Catching your breath and seeing if you can live without Julia is a kind of test. If you can, then let her go. If you can't, then you have to do something." By the weekend I was so anxious and mentally fried that I had to take the most direct route to happiness. I had to go to the woods.

I studied forestry so that I could be close to nature and ended up stuck in an office all day. I work for the Connecticut Department of Environmental Protection's State Parks & Forests division. I started out as a park project manager and ended up being "promoted" to manage the tech department. It's more money, but I'm cut off from what I love. The only flora I see all day is a sad little Japanese maple outside our office building, the one that they planted last summer next to the employee parking lot. So I went hiking almost every weekend, even if it was just at a local park.

Even though it was late January, the temperature was warm, predicted to peak at fifty degrees Fahrenheit in the afternoon, and there was no snow or moisture on the ground. After a breakfast of three hard-boiled eggs and coffee, I threw together a light backpack and headed out in my Wrangler. I pulled into the range of forested hills and rocky outcrops of Sleeping Giant Park in Hamden and headed toward the picnic areas and the parking lot. My Jeep was dwarfed by a dense pine forest at the foot of the mountain. At 8 a.m. there were already a half-dozen cars in the lot. I dropped my forehead onto the steering wheel. Since the memory of my high school locker combination, I had had two more similar episodes, complete with nausea, headaches, and a sudden flash of a useless, vivid memory. These were also long forgotten and useless brain data, like a conversation I had with a stranger at a bus station, old computer code, and an unspecified moment when I had looked at the face of a clock. I made some notes about it in anticipation of the checkup that I had coming up in a few weeks. I sensed that it could be something serious, but I dared not acknowledge the possibility. In fact, the real purpose of my day in the woods was to remind myself exactly how young, healthy, and athletic I was. I would take the most challenging way up the mountain, the white trail.

I stepped out of my Jeep and took a long, deep breath. I looked up. The sky was ice blue and clear. A few dry pine needles floated down. I put my hand out and they landed in my palm. They were in bundles of five. "White Eastern Pine," I mumbled to myself, remembering the park plans and maintenance I had overseen for several years before my unfortunate promotion. I looked around and surveyed the various types of trees along the path leading up to the mountain. When called a tree-hugger I'd say, "Guilty as charged." I *love* forests, and I also love trees individually. I consider these guys to be my buddies, the black birch, the clusters of hemlocks, the sugar maples and hickory. If any of them is sick, I know how to heal them. Many a tree has been rehabilitated, debugged, defungused, or otherwise protected because of me, which in turn benefits the human and animal community too. I stopped to inspect the blue-gray bark of a beech that had been freshly carved with a pair of initials. I ran my fingers over the inscription and thought, isn't there a better way to say "I love you" than by scarring a tree? Damn kids.

I knew these woods better than I knew my own neighborhood. I had hiked more than half of the seven hundred miles of Connecticut's Blue Blazed trail system. I'd stumbled upon mill ruins, ghost towns, abandoned cellar holes, Indian caves, and crumbling cemeteries. Still, like many life-long hikers, I dreamed of trails yet unseen, of survivalist adventures in the big-league wilds of Alaska. I was thinking about plans I'd made with a group of hiking friends to spend a week camping in Arcadia National Park over the summer, when I heard someone call my name.

I turned, but saw no one. I located a guiding marker, which meant that the path would soon intersect with another trail. I figured I must have heard approaching hikers. Again I heard my name, more distinctly this time. I turned around several times, but there was absolutely no one on the path.

I kept walking, focusing only on my own breathing and the scenery before me. The mountain was already a steep climb at this point, and it rose sharply up seventy feet or so before it leveled off for a stretch. I lifted myself up over the first large boulder in a colossal pile of ice-age trap rock. I noticed the smooth surface of the rock I was climbing. I looked at my hiker's watch: eight twenty-eight and forty-seven seconds. When I was three-quarters of the way up, I heard my name called a third time. I felt that same dizzy feeling I had at the club in

New York. This time, I didn't turn around because I realized that the call wasn't coming from the woods. I was breathing heavy, and sweat dripped off my forehead and into my ear. It tickled, and I shook my head to get it out. Suddenly I smelled urine and boiling milk. I heard the creaking of a hammock as it rocked in its hook. The forest fell away. I landed on my back, inside a crib.

A woman leaned over the edge of the rails and smiled. It was dark, so I couldn't see much more than her dark eyes glistening and her fingers stroking the tops of my hands. She was looking at me but talking to someone else. Later, I would recall, but not immediately understand, her words: *"Javier es el mas fuerte y saludable."* She picked me up and kissed me hard on the forehead. I gripped her finger. She spoke directly to me this time: *"Acuerdate de lo que te digo, mi niño. No tengas miedo. Todo lo que te ha pasado te ayudará. Vas a salir adelante."* She nodded with the sureness of what she had said. Then she lifted me and I smelled her neck, moist with perspiration. Her scent was familiar and safe. She patted me on the back and rocked me from side to side, "Shhhh." I dug my face deeper into her shoulder and I felt the hard edge of her collarbone against my cheekbone. Her "shhh" blended into the hiss of the wind all around me, and the bald branches trembled and the dead leaves stirred on the ground. I opened my eyes and I was on the lip of the seventy-foot pile of rocks. The soles of my boots were three or four inches from the rock's edge. Inside my nylon sports pants, hot urine ran down my legs. I had no memory of climbing up the last quarter of the cliff's face. I had no memory of anything after I looked at my watch. But more than five minutes had passed. I looked back down toward the ground. My stomach lurched.

I scanned the landscape for other hikers but there were none.

I began to shiver in horror and relief: my body had gone on autopilot and finished the climb, like a sleepwalker. I spotted an enormous slab of sandstone hidden among the low branches of a tree and leaned against it, breathing deep. I climbed into the lap of a flat rock, leaning my head in the palms of my hands. I was shaking.

When I calmed down a bit, I turned around and headed back. I got off the white path and onto the safe, flat dirt road of the tower path. At one point, despite being cold and urine-soaked, I had to stop and rest again. The power and clarity of the memory had zapped me. The sun warmed me a bit. I closed my eyes and pressed my fingers into my temples. *Javier.* The woman had called me Javier. The name sounded terribly familiar now, and again I felt a rush of unspecific but powerful emotion, along with that vague sense of dread that had plagued me over the previous week.

I got behind the wheel of my Wrangler. A flag went up—maybe I shouldn't operate a vehicle. But I did. I contemplated going to the emergency room, but I didn't go. At this point I abandoned my convenient blue seeds theory, and realized that Taina was right. This was no small ailment. But within fifteen minutes, I felt *completely* normal. When I got home, I checked my pupils in the mirror, tested my own motor coordination with a few tasks I had been asked to perform in a drunk driving test, and everything appeared to be just fine. Once I felt better, I immediately found reason to question the seriousness of what had actually happened. I downgraded my level of alarm, and comfortably settled back to my earlier suspicions about the mysterious blue seeds.

My first priority was to shower and get into warm, dry clothes. Once dressed, I sat down at the computer. I typed in the Spanish phrases that I remembered from my memory in the woods. But the website couldn't come up with anything because I didn't know how to spell the words. I got out a pad of paper and wrote down the words phonetically, using an online Spanish dictionary until each option matched a real word and then linked them into a string that made sense. When I was sure about each individual word, I checked them off. Then I rewrote them into a single English sentence. I sat back and read the sentence in its entirety. Like the combination from my high school locker, the last word released its meaning all at once.

I didn't read the phrase aloud; there was no need, for in English it was void of context, void of her lovely voice. I had always known these words, I realized. I was only confirming what I instinctively knew. I was the one who had hidden my knowledge of these words, and of the Spanish language itself, somewhere far and deep inside my own head.

"Acuerdate de lo que te digo, mi niño. No tengas miedo. Todo lo que te ha pasado te ayudará. Vas a salir adelante." I stared at the translation on the screen:

"Remember this, my boy. Don't be afraid. Everything that has happened to you will help you. You will succeed."

I rested my chin in the cup of my hand and my elbow on the desk. I stared at the words for a long time. I understood then that there was something really wrong with me. I climbed into bed. Next thing I knew, the alarm went off and it was Monday, time to go to work, which I did, refusing to even think about what had happened the night before.

I worked a half-day. Shortly after lunch, I had a seizure. I was in a meeting with four other people in a conference room when it happened. I woke up in an ambulance, with a mouthful of blood, terrified and thrashing so much that they tied down my wrists. I was admitted into Yale–New Haven Hospital, where I underwent a series of tests. A friend from work stayed with me until my parents arrived. I kept my eyes closed to block out the light. There was a mass inside my head, they told me. Only a biopsy, which they scheduled within twenty-four hours, could determine the exact nature of the mass. They gave me steroids, which reduced the swelling that had provoked the seizure. I immediately felt better. "Steroids. Really?" I said.

"Not *those* kind of steroids, unfortunately," the doctor said, as a nurse took my blood pressure for the millionth time that day. My poor mother looked like she'd aged ten years in the last ten hours. At sixty-five, her hair had already gone completely white, but she also had a playful expression that made people think that she was much younger. But now her big green eyes looked haunted and her voice trembled each time she spoke. I took her hand and said, "Ma, this is a technical problem with a technical solution. We'll find the best brain mechanic to pop open my hood and fix it. I'm gonna be fine."

I told the doctor and my parents about the memory flashes, the sudden and temporary inability to think of common words or names of people I knew well. The doctor explained how it was the tumor pressing against healthy brain tissue. "That contact causes nausea, aphasia, dizziness, and seizures. Hallucinations and personality changes are pretty standard, David," he said, scratching his head. "But eidetic memory? I don't know . . . you could have been hallucinating. We'll know more after the biopsy and some more thorough testing. Was it accompanied by a sense of dread?"

I said yes, and he nodded. "Probably a hallucination." But I didn't believe it. Not for a minute. I knew that what I remembered was real.

That night, when my mom asked me what I needed, I said, "Julia." She looked down and patted my hand. "She's on a cruise to Mexico, Davie. She and her mom can't be reached."

When I woke up after the biopsy the next day, my doctor assured me that I was doing great, and that now we had to wait for the lab results. When I woke up, I answered his five questions perfectly, except the one about my name. I told them my name was "Javier" but I don't remember that. Over the next twenty-four hours, there were a bunch of other kooky moments, especially before the swelling in my brain completely subsided. My night nurse, a cheerful matron who hailed from Cuba, told my mother in the morning that I had warned her, in flawless Spanish, that she should bring the birds' cages inside because there was a hurricane coming.

The doctor came into my room and pulled up a chair. "David," he said, and looked down at his hands. "It is what we were afraid it would be, a high-grade malignant glioblastoma multiforme." He had explained a range of possibilities before. This diagnosis was the worst-case scenario.

I said, "But some people do survive this, right?" He shook his head and leaned forward. "If we treat it with the most aggressive means available—surgery followed by chemotherapy and radiation—you have about a year and a half to live. In your age category, less than fourteen percent of patients with this type of tumor survive the five-year mark. Technically, the ten-year survivorship is 1.7%, but that's just an average. Of course a few do, but it's so rare that it doesn't even bump the statistic up to two percent. That's what we're dealing with here."

I've been asked many times since then what my reaction was after hearing those words. The best way to describe it is to say that I heard the "swoosh" of an axe falling, the splitting of the membrane between normalcy and insanity. Everything that is ordinary, safe, and comforting rips away. I was left in a place of silent, stunned floating. My intestines felt like they had just liquefied, hot acid burning everything in their path. I remember the doctor suggested that one option was not to fight the cancer at all; that the battle would be long and hard and that in the end, this disease always wins. *It always wins.*

My father's stricken blue eyes stared at the doctor from behind gold rim spectacles. "How did he get this?" he asked in a choked voice.

"Cell phones," my mother gasped. "Microwaving with plastic wrap?"

The doctor let out a great sigh and threw his hands up in the air. "My father spent his entire life trying to figure out how brain cancer chooses its victims, but to this day, it remains one of the most intractable forms of cancer. A very small number of people have genetic markers that predispose them, but the vast majority of primary brain tumors are believed to have environmental causes. Exposure to pesticides, plastics, chemicals, radiation, but honestly, it's a big question mark. We just don't know. And nothing in David's history explains the onset at such a young age."

In the meantime, the words "it always wins" echoed across the chambers of my heart. I searched for something to hold on to. A comfort. A beacon. Something to suggest that this was all a big misunderstanding, a nightmare, or a lie. Back in my hospital bed, I closed my eyes and tried to remember the woman who had had so much faith in me. *"Remember this, my boy. Don't be afraid. Everything that has happened to you will help you. You will succeed."*

Had I invented that memory just because I needed some reassurance? Had I known, deep down, that something terrible was on its way? The statistics the doctor had just dropped on me were a kind of tsunami barreling toward me. Before he left, the doctor asked if I needed anything.

"My wife," I said in the impatient tone of someone who's been married twenty years. "I'm waiting for my wife."

"I didn't realize you were married, David," he said. "Where is she?"

"On a cruise ship in Mexico. It's taking her a while to get back."

"That's great that you're married," he said. "I'll tell you, married patients tend to have a better outcome than unmarried ones. To men, a wife is a kind of life raft." He patted me on the shoulder. "You're a lucky guy."

At the foot of my bed, my mother began to sob.

After the biopsy and all the tests and meetings, they let me go home. I was pumped full of steroids and they worked like a dream. I felt perfectly normal, although a bit tired from the biopsy, as would be expected. As the days went on, I waited for the dreaded symptoms to return, but there was absolutely nothing out of the ordinary going on in my head. No memory flashbacks, no headaches, nothing. By the next week I woke up and wondered if the whole thing had been just a bad dream.

Before I checked out of Yale, a series of tests and meetings had been set up with a renowned neuro-oncologist at Memorial Sloan-Kettering in New York in preparation for the next phase: the surgery to remove the tumor, or what they called the "resection." We were aiming for two weeks.

Taina was the only one of my siblings who lived within driving distance, and she had taken two days off from work and had been with me in the days immediately after the seizure. She was in charge of managing the communication with Ray, Holly, and Adrian. My parents handled the extended family, my friends, and the neighbors. Like Julia, Adrian was also missing in action. After the concert in New York, he had gone to perform in a music festival in Spain and wasn't answering his cell phone or replying to text or e-mail messages. No one knew how else to reach him. Taina promised me that Holly was on task, getting word out through whatever channels possible. I really needed to hear his voice. If Julia was my beacon, Adrian was my rock.

Chapter

3

Miami

Adrian Vega was about to unzip the fly of his jeans and dive into bed when he saw, in the blue silky light coming through the floor-to-ceiling windows of his bedroom, the figure of a woman asleep in his bed. His thumb lingered on the tab of his zipper as he leaned forward and squinted, trying as hard as he could to make out her features. She wasn't under the sheets; she was simply lying on top of the down comforter, on her side. She was wearing some kind of dark outfit, and when Adrian took a step back his foot landed on what felt like a high heel shoe. He looked over his shoulder. How had she gotten into his apartment?

The woman stirred, shifted her weight around, but didn't wake up. Adrian stood before the bed, not knowing what to do. He had just gotten home from the airport and was dead tired. He backed up and looked at the digital display next to the bed: 3:15 a.m.

Adrian zipped himself back up and closed the bedroom door. In the living room, he grabbed his cordless phone and stepped out onto the balcony, sliding the glass doors behind him. The moist, salty air blasted him with its fishy seaweed smell. The neon signs on South Beach sparkled on the left, and the sea was dark and invisible. He shook his head, tried for a moment to think straight. *Coño*, he thought. Too fried to think. He dialed building security and asked for the guy on duty downstairs to come up. He wanted the Goldilocks situation to be handled quietly, with the minimum fuss. He also wanted to be safe. Who knew if the woman was armed or crazy? His only desire was to get to sleep sometime before the unforgiving Miami sun came up.

Adrian realized that most people wouldn't handle a home invasion so calmly, even if the perpetrator *was* sound asleep. In fact, the average Miami homeowner would have a gun pointed to her ear by now. Perhaps the woman had been secretly living in his apartment while he was gone. Adrian yawned. Women had been inviting themselves into his bed in the middle of the night since he was sixteen. His father was a social worker and part-time minister who dragged home every glue-addicted loser and prostitute he could find to try to repair their souls with his famous sermon-over-a-hot-breakfast. As a kid growing up in a humble, two-room home in rural Puerto Rico, Adrian had been awakened by the rum-soaked snores and deranged mumblings of strangers with more frequency than he cared to remember. He thought about how his father would handle it: just go inside, shake the woman by the shoulder, and say *¿que te pasa, mujer?* Or maybe he should simply do what most guys would do—bang her *then* kick her out. But he'd outgrown that sort of thing.

Maybe she was a fan. He felt mounting pressure to move into a more secure building, or out to the gated suburbs, which was preposterous. South Beach was the only place for him in the entire state of Florida. And after that, New York and L.A.

After Adrian hung up with building security, the glass slider opened and a voice behind the thin drapes said, "Adrian?" The woman stepped out into the patio; her high heels were back on and they clicked against the clay terrazzo tiles. She pulled her long hair back away from her face. "It's me, Veronica."

Adrian had not seen Veronica Mayorga in over a year. She had lost a significant amount of weight. She looked gaunt and had hair that reached down to her waist, obviously fake because just a year ago, she had been a voluptuous woman with a pixie cut. They had broken up when their relationship reached the three-month mark, which was when Adrian broke up with every woman he dated if she didn't do it first. At three months he always grew bored, and it was time to move on. He blinked for a few moments as he tried to reconcile Veronica with this person. He stepped closer to get a better look, and when he had satisfied his curiosity, he got back to business. "You'd better have a spectacularly good reason for being inside my apartment."

Veronica made a face. "I certainly do. I've been leaving messages for you for twenty-four hours. No one could find you."

"How'd you get in?"

"You never changed your alarm code," she said with a sheepish grin. She held up a key. "And I had a copy. Anyway," she said with a shrug, "I'm still writing for *People en Español* but for the next year I'm also hosting Telemundo's nightly entertainment update *¡Al Dia!* while Lupita Camacho is on maternity leave."

"Congratulations," he said with a yawn. "I guess that explains the new look. I didn't recognize you."

"You like?" she said in a high voice, tossing her thick blanket of hair over one shoulder.

Adrian turned and walked to the other end of the balcony.

He grabbed the rail, squeezing until he saw his veins pop up under his skin. "You still haven't told me why you're here."

"I'm sure that the news about your brother is painful, so I thought you might want to make your statement to someone you know and trust." She blinked both eyes and smiled a tight little smile. "Like me."

Adrian shook his head. "What are you talking about?"

"I'm talking about David."

She held up her notebook, clicked the top of a pen. "Holly could barely talk on the phone, she was hysterical. She had just gotten the call from David's mother in Connecticut." Veronica shook her head, put her arms over her chest and stared at the ground with an almost convincing look of worry. "I'm glad I got to meet David that time he came down to see you."

"What's wrong with David?"

"You don't know?"

"I've been in Spain. I've been trying to get home for three days. Storms, delays, and dead cell phones . . ." He stopped himself and peered in closer, as if seeing her for the first time. "Veronica, what the hell are you talking about?"

She let out a breath. "David has brain cancer. It's fatal."

Adrian sat down, or rather, slid into a chair. He looked down at the floor for a moment, suddenly recalling the weekend in New York, how David had been complaining of headaches and nausea. He took a deep breath and turned to look back at her. "I don't—I can't believe it. I need to talk to him." He rubbed his hand, the place of the tattoo. He found the starfish leg with the letter "D" floating above it and touched it lightly with his index finger. He stood up and turned toward Veronica. "Please leave now."

"Are you sad? Angry?" She tapped her pen against her notepad.

He gave her a one-eyed squint. "Why did you call Holly?"

"Because I check in with her periodically for news about you . . . since I got the new job."

"I have a publicist."

"I *dated* you." She pointed to her chest, and then to his. "That has to count for something. Besides, Holly likes to talk." She placed a hand on his shoulder. "Adrian, please. *Please.*" She moved in closer. "C'mon, it's *me.*" She pressed her chest against his.

There was a knock at the front door. Adrian turned and brushed past her. He walked through the open patio door and let the security guard in. "*Oye*, Frank. This lady needs to be escorted out of the building." The security guard craned to see who she was. In Spanish he replied, "I'm sorry, Adrian. She told me she was dating you and I remembered her." The man bowed. *"Disculpame."*

Veronica clutched his arm. "Adrian, let me sleep on the couch. We can talk in the morning."

"Leave."

She closed her eyes as she spoke. "You don't want to do this."

"This is my house! It's three in the morning. Are you insane, woman?" He looked at the security guard. The guard took a step toward her. Veronica recoiled and said, "You owe me, Adrian."

"Because I dated you? Are you nuts? I've dated half the media in Miami. Get in line."

"I can't believe you just said that," she said, opening her kohl-lined eyes wide.

"I can't believe you broke into my apartment. You're lucky I didn't shoot you."

"You don't have a gun," she said in a mocking voice.

"I'm gonna get one." He made a gun with his fingers and pointed it at her forehead. "Next time, bang!"

"I'll get my story, Adrian. With or without your help."

He wanted to lash out at her, but his dad suddenly popped into his mind, the annoying angel on his shoulder always there to remind him to be a gentleman. The door slammed shut behind Veronica and he stood still until he didn't hear her in the hall anymore. How anyone could deliver that news and behave so selfishly was beyond him. They were all like this, the women he met out here. Smooth and sweet like coconut candy but always out for themselves. He exhaled and rubbed his stinging eyes.

He found his phone charger still attached to the outlet in the kitchen. He plugged in the dead cell phone and listened to his messages. There were almost twenty of them just from Taina, Holly, and Ray. There was one from David's mother, Marcia O'Farrell, spoken in her soft, measured words. "We have some news, sweetie. Please call me as soon as you get this."

Adrian sat for a moment, pressed his hands together. He felt a headache coming on so he reached behind the sofa and found his guitar. He began strumming, aimlessly. Listening. Waiting. At last it came, those first few notes, he played them again to be sure. Those tentative notes were followed by more perfect notes, as if they were living things that were hatching. A simple tune at first, just four chords, but by six in the morning Adrian had composed the first song of his *By Blood and Ink* collection. It contained a veiled confession that he had known that another disaster was coming, a deep and repressed premonition that suddenly seemed inevitable.

As soon as the sun came up, Adrian began returning the phone calls, with apologies to everyone, especially David, who was just home from the hospital. He called to ask Marcia if he was needed right away. Marcia said, "We're fine for now, Adrian. David has us and our relatives and Taina. Julia's on her way back from Mexico, and he has had plenty of friends coming by. We'll know in a day or two what the schedule is for the big surgery. It should be in about two weeks. But like I told the others, not everyone wakes up from brain surgery. You'll want to come before that. Just in case."

Chapter

4

After Holly had exhausted the venues of reaching Adrian in Spain, she remembered the time that he had given her the silent treatment for two whole months. While Holly was known as the family loudmouth, Adrian was the one most likely to hold a grudge. And while he would never purposely go AWOL in an emergency, he did have a record of holing up just because he was in a funk.

The year before Adrian got popular in Miami, he and Holly had gone to a Luis Miguel concert together. Someone had given him the tickets as a gift. Holly had already seen Luis Miguel five times, knew all the songs, had all the CDs. Her husband, Erick, had absolutely no interest in sitting though a concert in Spanish. In fact, Erick only crossed the Broward-Dade county line to get to the airport; he had a deep disdain for anything having to do with Miami.

Holly, who had grown up in Miami, missed the energy and Latino intensity that seemed to evaporate just beyond the North Miami Beach city line. So after Adrian had moved from Puerto Rico to Miami, he had been her ticket to play in the old neighborhood. At first, he had no money, so Holly always paid as long he agreed to go where she wanted. A stroll on Ocean Drive, cocktails and people watching on Lincoln Road, Cuban food in Little Havana. They had gone salsa dancing a few times, but that was harder now that Holly had kids. She always ended up feeling trashed the next day. Eventually, as Adrian got more and more gigs, he had a little more money and less time to hang around with his sister. They hadn't been out in six months when he called to tell her he had the tickets.

Holly was thrilled, but Adrian had criticized the singer throughout the whole concert, and Holly found it distracting and extremely annoying. First it was, "He doesn't play any instruments," and "Only Ricky Martin can turn with his arms spread out like that." Then with a roll of the eyes, "Grown men shouldn't play air guitar."

"Adrian, you play air guitar all the time."

He ignored it and moved on to the next criticism, "The dude's facial expressions are so fake—it totally insults the greatness of that classic song," and, addressing the stage, "What's with the suit, man? Are you moonlighting as a banker?"

Holly could tell that Adrian was wracked with envy. Had they been at a club, Adrian might be getting a lot of attention, but not here. Here he was nobody. Luis Miguel, on the other hand, was an international star, bright and blinding as the sun, which is what they call him in Mexico, *El Sol de Mexico.* The crowd was disproportionately young, female, and crazed. Adrian watched as the young women swooned and waved t-shirts or handkerchiefs for him to wipe his sweat and throw it back at them. During intermission, Holly had asked, "What's the matter with you anyway? Surely you agree the guy's got a voice."

"He's got a voice," Adrian conceded. "But that *suave* act is so fake. He's head over heels in love with himself."

Holly batted her eyelashes and put her hand to her throat. "He's in love with *me*. He was looking at me the whole time."

"See? That's the part I don't understand. Every woman here believes that."

"Well, take notes, baby," Holly said, giving him a fraternal slap on the arm. "That's why it's called performing. You're not on stage to be yourself."

"It is essential to be yourself. It's the rarest thing in the world to find someone who is authentic."

"Alright, are you done? Because you're ruining it for me." She pointed at the stage.

"I'm done." He folded his arms and was silent for five seconds, then started up again. "And then there's the lyrics. People like Juanes and Shakira sing about war and corruption and family and poverty and geography and the environment. Stuff besides love, love, love." When he complained that Luis Miguel sweat too much, Holly flicked her head to the side and replied, "I'd happily lick the sweat off his face and anywhere else it might drip." Adrian looked horrified.

"What?" Holly shouted into his ear, palms out in the air. "I can't say that just because I'm married and have kids?"

"I'm your brother, not your girlfriend," he said. "It's just weird to hear you talk like that."

"Oh, *puh-leeze*," Holly said, slipping into a tough-girl persona. "It's not like we're *really* brother and sister."

Adrian had continued to stare ahead. "I can't believe you just said that."

The music slowed to a ballad and they were able to speak without shouting, so she said, "Look, Adrian, I have three kids, I know what a real brother is." She looked over and saw the expression on his face. She tried to backpedal a little bit: "I'm just saying we didn't grow up together. Even if we are blood relatives, it's not the same. I should be able to say whatever I want and not freak you out. That's what I love about us hanging out. You're better than a brother, better than a friend. You're my 'bro-friend,' a brother without the family baggage. You know?"

Adrian turned stone cold after that. "I want you to apologize for what you said about us not being related. That was mean and if you want to get technical, it's not like you know the truth either."

Holly extended her arm and pressed it to his. The lights were too low to show the subtle differences in their skin tone, and yet they both saw it. "We are different colors. It's impossible." Then she tilted her head, smiled, and wrinkled up her nose. "Unless of course, our mother was a total slut."

Adrian winced, but ignored the last comment. "Is that why you refuse to get the tattoo? Because we have different color skin?"

She made an exaggerated "Augh," and rolled her eyes. "Get a tramp stamp on my hand? No way."

"That's your ultra-conservative husband talking."

"But he's right. It's not like I can hide it on my ankle or my bicep or my butt cheek like everyone else, it has to be right there." She slapped the top of one hand with the other. "Right there for the whole PTA to see."

"Well, that's fine because you don't deserve to be a part of the . . ."

"The what?" asked Holly. "The clan? The brotherhood? The gang?"

"The family," he said.

Holly let out her breath. "I love you guys, don't get me wrong; but I have three boys who love each other and fight every day of their life." She interlaced her fingers and tugged them to demonstrate. "And it's not the same."

"Oh yeah? Well I have a friend whose parents got divorced. His sisters went to live with the mom in another state. He grew up with his dad and almost never saw the girls. So you're telling me they're not siblings, just because they don't see each other?"

"Sure. I'm saying they don't fully exemplify the real definition of a sibling."

"Guess I've been deluding myself," he said, knitting his brow and squinting at her.

"Don't be such a pisser. What's missing in your life, anyway? Why can't you accept that we're just fellow passengers in the boat of life?"

"Siblings," he said, and looked away. "That's what."

"I hear ya, Aidge. But trust me, you'll feel differently when you get married and have kids." She patted him on the back.

"No, I won't," he said. "There's first family and second family, and your siblings are a part of your first family. It's different from parenthood. Siblings are your peers. Everything that predates your husband is the realm of your sibling's memory."

"What memory? We don't share mountains of memory because we don't know anything about ourselves before age two and we didn't grow up together. I return to my original point."

"You know what, Holly? I'll see you later." He spun on his heels and climbed over a row of seats. Holly called his name but he didn't look back. In a few seconds, he had disappeared into the sea of beautiful women, which parted a little bit for him. She could actually see the ripples of his movement through the crowd. The next day, she found out from Taina that he had had backstage passes all along, and that they went unused. She had left him a nasty voice mail, something about him not being very brotherly anyway. She called back again and apologized but she wasn't surprised when several weeks went by, then a month, and then two, and she still hadn't heard from him. "Adrian's so damn sensitive," she complained. Her husband, Erick, had replied, "He has a level of integrity that's out of place in his South Beach nightclub world. I like that about him."

Chapter 5

David

Amazingly, I felt fine after the biopsy. I was restless, bright eyed, and ravenously hungry. My parents' house was filled with flowers and balloons and casseroles. I spent most of the day fielding calls from friends, coworkers, and relatives, but that got exhausting. I stopped taking calls after a while, and only made an exception for Adrian. The day after I came home from the hospital, I asked my mother for the family wedding ring, which had been her grandmother's, a one-and-a-half-carat emerald-cut diamond on a platinum band. She had always told me that it was mine to pass on, since she and dad had skipped it and chose to buy their own rings. When I asked for it, she shook her head and said, "No way. You and Julia just broke up a few weeks ago." She pointed a finger right into my chest. "*You* decided that your relationship didn't have the engine to go the distance. *You* refused to get married when you *didn't* have a brain tumor. You're telling me that now that you have cancer you see the light?"

"Yeah. With brilliant, blinding clarity," I said, opening my eyes wide. "Where my life was once blurry, it now has these sharp, clean edges. I wish it had always been this way."

"It's not fair, David. You can't trap her into a life that lacks stability, peace of mind, a strong future. What about kids? Isn't she thirty-four? She doesn't have a moment to waste."

"You don't believe I can beat this."

"Honey, of course you're going to beat it. And when you reach that place of stability, *then* you ask her. Right now, you can't offer her the 'in health' part of 'in sickness and in health.' You've got to focus on healing, David. Marriage is hard work, and you need to save your energy to fight cancer."

My hand went up to my biopsy cut, which was starting to itch. I couldn't scratch, only wiggle around the bandage. I said, "Being married will help me get through this. You heard the doctor. He practically prescribed it."

"She's a person, not a treatment."

"Julia loves me. She wants to marry me. It took a kick in the teeth to get me to appreciate what I have had all along. The fact remains that she's mine; and I'm not going to let her go."

My mother kept her body rigid as she delicately rubbed my shoulder. "You'd be abusing that love, David."

I got up, stood by the window and looked east, aware that that was the direction of New Haven, where she belonged. Where I belonged. The two of us should be in our apartment, planning our future. And to think that, had it not been for the cancer, I wouldn't have that as a goal. *That's* what gave me hope: that the cancer was visiting me for a reason, a higher purpose, not to kill me but to *fix* me.

I hugged my mother and gave her a kiss on the cheek. She would need time to adjust to the new me, and I understood, but I needed to get on with the business of surviving.

The next disagreement with my parents was about my living arrangements. If they were going to be my chauffeurs, then I had to stay with them. Dad said that it wasn't fair to make them drive to New Haven to pick me up for every little thing. They wanted to keep an eye on me. I argued that New Haven was right on the way to New York. "What about groceries, what about errands? What if you need help in the middle of the night? You can't be alone, David." Excellent point, but still, I refused.

"I can't live with my parents! I don't want you knowing everything I do!" Since that didn't work, I tried, "What if I want to have sex?" My mother flashed me a look and my dad grumbled and shuffled away. But they were right and so I was forced to move into my old bedroom, with the fake log-cabin wood paneling and the bed still covered with a *Star Wars* comforter. That night, I lay my head down on my Luke Skywalker pillowcase. On top of everything else, I was emasculated too.

So I rebelled. One of my hiking buddies came to get me out of the house. He promised my mother that he was taking me on a gentle walk through the woods. We ended up blasting through wooded paths on quads, and I came home covered in mud to her disapproving glare. The next night, a coworker took me to the movies, and we ended up getting plastered on gin and tonics at a townie bar and coming home at two in the morning. My mother was outraged. What she didn't know was that I came *this close* to getting into a fight. I left the bar with three friends, who turned back to talk to someone. I told them I'd wait outside because the smoke was getting to me. This little guido got all pissed off because I was leaning against his El Camino in the parking lot. He had three thugs with him and they circled me. I'm not the fighting type, so I apologized, hands up and all, but when my friends caught up to me, tempers flared, especially since I'd just had surgery. I managed to diffuse the situation and we left. But then the guys in the El Camino appeared again, driving down the street as we headed to the next bar. We ended up side-by-side at a red light. They had golf clubs and one guy got out and threatened us with it. Something in me snapped and I jumped out of the car, beat on the hood of the other car, and shouted, "Let's go. Into the garage where the cops can't see us." I pointed to a dark, empty parking garage. I slammed my fist down again. "And you better bring your golf clubs!"

The guys got back in the car, all of them cussing and flipping us off, but they drove away. I was disappointed, all of my energy draining out of me as I watched their taillights disappear. My friends were also disappointed, but relieved too, because no one wanted to see me take a punch to the head or have to answer to my parents. "We woulda killed them," my friend assured me. "Buncha pussies." By the time I lied down in my twin bed that night, I felt a lot better about myself.

My parents and I had no choice but to endure being trapped together in the same house. Under the dinner table, I texted Adrian, "Dude, I hate the way they chew." I think the friction is what prompted me to dream about finding my "real" parents. I dreamed I was wandering around a strange city, barefoot, unshaven, and unwashed. The city was poor and the buildings were dilapidated, and so I blended in with everyone else, following women around repeating the same question: Are you my mother? Are you my mother? In the dream, no one understood me because they spoke Spanish. There was an increasing wind whipping everything around. There were only women in this village, and they all pointed me to a dark, ruined building, telling me that I could find shelter inside. I went inside to investigate, but the building was nothing but charred wood and broken glass. Rats scurried about. In the center of the building was a half-rotten wood boat.

I woke up to find my mom at my bedside with a damp cloth

and a glass of water. Still half-asleep, I asked, "Are you my mother?"

She cooed, "Of course, David. You're my boy." She stroked my head and stayed by my side until I fell asleep again.

In the morning, over coffee, she asked me if I had had any interesting dreams the night before. "Not that I can remember," I lied. "I slept like a baby."

She raised an eyebrow. "What kind of baby?"

"A happy, safe, loved baby," I conceded. A little smile rose in her lips.

My dad said, "I've been thinking. Those . . . eh, 'visions' you described, the ones you say are flashbacks but the doctor says are hallucinations?"

"Yeah, Pop?"

"You wanna do a little experiment to find out who's right?" His eyes lit up.

I shrugged. "It don't see how it matters."

"I think it does. I think you're going to want to know the difference between the crazy stuff," he said pointing at his head, "and when you've gained unauthorized access to the classified stuff." He raised an eyebrow, like a sleuth in a movie. My dad had worked for the National Archives for a short time when he was in his twenties. He had handled top-secret documents, thus the "classified" reference.

"What'd you have in mind?" I asked.

"Let's test the locker combination," he said.

"What?" I said, making a face. "That's impossible."

My mother put her coffee down and took my hands in hers. "Honey, I know that I've discouraged you to pursue knowledge of your biological roots. I always felt a bit nervous . . . eh, threatened. Perhaps . . ." She looked up at my father and they locked eyes.

My dad took over. "We want you to know that we support you, if you feel that it's time."

I put my hands out. "No, I never . . ."

"Take it from me, son, one day the unanswered question will gnaw at you."

"Okay," I said, "but what does this have to do with the locker? And who cares anyway? Like I don't have more important things to worry about?"

My mother stirred her coffee, shrugged a little. "Those . . . memories about being a baby that you had on the mountain . . ." she said. "I can't stop thinking about them. I think they mean something. It's like the past calling you. And how amazing that a woman spoke to you and said that you'll 'overcome.'"

"Succeed."

"Succeed. Triumph . . . She said that you're the strongest, healthiest one, David, she prophesized that you'd *survive*. It's incredible. You didn't even know you had cancer so it's not like you made it up to make yourself feel better."

I had thought of all this already, of course. But because it was coming from my parents, it suddenly sounded silly.

"Dad," I said, folding my arms. "What makes you think we could test the locker combination, anyway? I'm sure they changed it the very next school year."

Dad was way ahead of me. He had already talked to the principal, and, as he explained in the car, this principal was a pack rat whose policies required the archiving of just about everything, including decades of locker combinations.

A few minutes later, I was sitting in a plastic bucket seat of the main office of my old high school, being stared at by a row of teenagers with lip rings and multicolored hair. Apparently, the fresh-faced, flannel-shirted teens of my day were an endangered species. I remember when leaving your Timberland boots untied meant you were a real badass. These guys (or girls, I couldn't even tell the difference) were pale and looked dressed for Halloween. Would I have kids like this someday? Yuck. And then I felt the weight of my situation pressing down on my shoulders again. I couldn't assume that I would live long enough to raise teenagers, even ones as homely as these.

Acid was building up in my stomach, an empty receptacle slowly filling with fear. I gripped the edges of the chair and let the wave of despair pass over me. Why was I even here? I had a useless recollection about a locker. Who cared? I wanted to go home and wait for Julia. Julia, who was on her way to my parents' house from LaGuardia Airport.

My dad came out and signaled me to follow. The principal's secretary invited us into a long storage hall full of file cabinets and boxed archives. She whipped out a box-cutter and slashed the plastic band on one box, then rummaged through documents for a few minutes. "What year did you say you graduated?"

I cleared my throat. "Nineteen-ninety-five. I believe I was assigned locker number eleven-forty."

She rummaged some more, and then held up a sheet of paper. She blew dust off the edges. "O'Farrell. Here it is."

My father held up a hand to her. "Don't say it." Then he looked at me. "Combination?"

"Three clockwise, eleven counterclockwise, clockwise seventeen."

She nodded. "Yup. That's correct."

My father whooped and punched the air the same way he did when I hit my first home run in Little League. "Steel trap!" he shouted. "You brain is a machine, David. It's *compensating*."

"Oh yeah?" the woman opened her eyes wide. "You some kind of genius?"

"Yeah. I'm a genius. I'm a kind of savant who counts cards in casinos and I can remember top-secret classified data," I said, my voice buckling into laughter as I pointed to the dusty box full of obsolete locker combinations. My dad closed his eyes and pinched the bridge of his nose, and all at once he burst into laughter too. The secretary looked bewildered but gave us a kind smile and said, "If there's anything else we can do for you, honey, you just let us know."

Out in the hallway my father said, "Tell me, David, did you have these numbers written down anywhere? Is there anything that you can think of that could trigger you to remember them, besides your tumor?" I shook my head. He put his arm around me as we walked to the car. "Then you know for sure, son, that what you've been having are certifiable memories. Not hallucinations, not dreams, not imagination, but actual recalled events. That's somethin'."

"I guess," I said. "Maybe next time I'll remember something useful, like where I lost my Spider-Man umbrella in the third grade."

Dad grinned. "Or where you put my cordless drill? Get to work on that, okay? I want it back." He put an arm around my shoulders. "We'll fix it, son," he said. "That steel trap of yours."

Julia. There she was, standing on the front porch of the house, talking to my mother. She had these new light streaks in her hair and she looked so tan and healthy it took my breath away. She held out her arms. We embraced for a long time, so long, that I heard my mother whisper, "C'mon, Paul," followed by the shuffle of my parents' footsteps as they went into the house. I looked straight into her eyes, seeking the permission I needed to kiss her on the lips. But she lowered her eyes and stepped back, a gesture I would see her repeat a hundred times more in the next few months, as my need for physical contact with her increased. She held on to one of my hands. "Turn your head," she said, reaching for my chin. "Let me see your wound."

I took off my baseball cap and turned my head. "It's still bandaged," I said. She gasped anyway.

"God, David. I'm so sorry this is happening."

"Julia, I made a mistake. Breaking up." I shook my head, taking one of her hands and placing it over my heart. "I regret it."

Her eyes filled with tears and she blinked them away. "It is what it is," she said.

"What's that supposed to mean?"

"We broke up. You got cancer. We go forward from here." She tapped a foot on the floor. "We can't go back."

I had backed her into a corner, literally. She dipped under my arm and headed for the front door. "I came to talk to your parents about the logistics of your surgery. I'm taking time off work to help out so I need to know what's going on."

"That's what a girlfriend does," I said, following her into my parents' living room. "So don't pretend that you're not my girlfriend."

Later, I tried to get her to come up to my room, to no avail. I was facing the scariest surgery of my life and to know that she was near was not enough. I needed to *absorb* her, as weird and needy as that sounds. I wanted to know that she was more than my beacon. I needed her to be the very bones that hold me up.

Chapter

6

Julia had begun the process of organizing David's medical paperwork with her usual energetic efficiency. She registered him on websites that linked him to support groups and to stories of survivorship. She had gone to an office supply store and bought a two-drawer steel file cabinet, color-coded file folders, labels, and three-hole punch. She bought printer paper and ink. She was ready to be his medical manager because she could already see that the O'Farrells couldn't handle him. David was extremely stubborn and independent, and he wasn't going to listen to his parents' advice, even for his own good. Now that she had the upper hand in their relationship, she knew that she could use that power to help him help himself. David's first appointment with the renowned neurosurgeon was just three days away and yet none of them had the energy or courage to prepare, probably because the news only got scarier and scarier. When a huge problem loomed before her, normally Julia would begin to break it down by focusing on small tasks in order to move forward. But the enterprise of cancer management was a mountain of intimidating and overwhelming proportions.

There were huge stacks of brochures yet unread. It was vital that David and his parents research and familiarize themselves with glioblastoma multiforme, specifically, which had a very unique set of properties, treatment, and prognosis. But once Julia set up the infrastructure to managing David's care, they found that they could do nothing but ignore the stacks of paper. They all needed, to their very core, to pretend that everything was completely normal, if only for few more days.

Julia had promised to take time off from work around the time of David's surgery and recovery (Dr. Levine estimated that David would be hospitalized anywhere from seven to fourteen days). Julia knew she had to pace herself, so she began a manageable routine: she drove to the O'Farrells' twice a week after work and came by on Sunday afternoons. Marcia O'Farrell scheduled other visitors on the days that Julia wasn't around, so David would have a continuous flow of people around, although he soon began to complain that it was too taxing. "I've always been a loner, why would I want people hanging around jabbering at me now? Listening to small talk hurts my head. I have a brain tumor, not breast cancer." Julia and Marcia had just looked at each other and rolled their eyes. But it was true. The attention was jarring to him.

Julia asked, despite knowing the answer, what she might do to make him feel better. "I guess yoga and green tea are out of the question?" she teased. David answered: "I need a walk in the woods and some hot chocolate."

She shivered at the thought. It was early February, and the temperature outside was just above thirty. But his wish was her command, and so, without another word, she went into the kitchen, melted a chocolate bar in a pan of milk, and poured it into a thermos. She put two foldable plastic recliners and a blanket into the back of her car. They couldn't go tromping up to Sleeping Giant; he was, after all, still recovering from the biopsy. The compromise destination was a popular Christmas tree farm in Shelton, owned by an old friend of his. They set the lawn chairs up at the top of a hill, at the center of a neat grid of blue spruces. They were able to build a campfire in a pit that was set up for shoppers during the Christmas tree season. Even though it was cold, the sun was bright and cheerful. They stared out to the misty, pine-covered hills and into the warm heart of the campfire. They glimpsed a few deer as they sipped their hot chocolate out of robin-egg speckled tin cups. The wind stirred a little bit and David began to talk about the great blight of Christmas pines many years ago. Julia read the newspaper to him aloud. They let themselves be transported by the local politics, the war in Iraq, by the rising fuel prices, the fall in the stock market. They argued with the vigor of people trying to avoid talking about something else. Julia told him about the little girl who imitated her at school, and the boys whose Little League team had made it to the national championships. The fire was mesmerizing and warm and they dozed off a bit. The cancer too, dozed off. There were just the trees and the clear blue sky and the fire and the sweet taste of chocolate in their mouths.

David actually fell asleep. When he woke up, his eyes had a new light behind them. The depression she'd seen in his face earlier was gone. He scooted over in his foldable chair. He opened up his blanket, creating a narrow space next to him. She just stared at the spot.

"I won't try anything," he said. "C'mon. You look cold."

She hopped in, curling up against his warmth. Although she let him lock an arm over her shoulder, she remained guarded and hyper-aware of his every movement. David cleared his throat and said, "Thank you. For bringing me here." He pushed away a strand of hair that was blowing across her face.

"I want to do so many things, see so many places," David said. "Now I have an excuse."

"Focus on your treatment," Julia said. "Now's not the time to go wandering the jungles of Africa, if that's what you mean."

"I mean after. Like once I'm done with surgery, chemo, radiation, and all that business. I have lots of adventures planned."

She smiled. "Adventures? Like?"

He told her what he had experienced on Sleeping Giant Mountain, about the remembered woman, how his dad had set out to prove that they were fragments of recall, not hallucinations. "It's an *invitation*, Julia."

"An invitation to what?" She sat up. "David O'Farrell," her voice trailed off and she opened her eyes wide in an exaggerated look of amazement. "Are you going to start believing in God?"

He gave her a weary look. "Believe me, faith would be a lovely thing right now. But you can't start believing in the tooth fairy just because you lost a tooth. Too convenient. I can't trick myself like that. But I know for sure that cancer isn't intelligent, it's a *thing*, just a kind of flesh rot. So who is controlling the outflow of information from my subconscious, then, if it's not the cancer? It's not my consciousness; I didn't will it. And Julia, nobody has access to such vivid memories of their infancy. *Nobody.* Even people like you who know their full history, who have tons of photos and movie footage and people to tell you stories about yourself. You can't really remember much before what, age three? I'm being summoned by the source of that control."

She shook her head. "And who would that be?"

"I don't know. I've always thought of it as nature with a capital 'N.'" His eyes opened wide and they seemed to sparkle all of a sudden. "It's like catching the glimpse of a creature in the woods. You hear a rustling. The sound of hooves, or maybe antlers being rubbed against a tree. You freeze and wait. It's usually only a few seconds, but it feels like forever. And then suddenly, some low branches tremble and part and there it is! It's magnificent . . . an animal with wild eyes that stare back, and well . . . it's an honor." Julia laughed out loud because his idea of a spiritual encounter involved a beast with horns, sharp claws, and a hide full of ticks; a beast that could rip you to shreds for coming too close.

"I mean it, Julia, it's the closest I've come to believing. I swear it's a glimpse of something holy. And you know what? For some reason, the experience is even more powerful and spiritual if you're alone." His eyes glassed over with the memory of past encounters in the wild.

Julia maintained a more traditional view of God, but she understood what he meant. She had once sailed a boat, alone, cutting across a turquoise sea in the company of a flock of jumping dolphins. She had experienced the quick elation—her heart had swollen with amazement, and then grown solemn and weightless. David was right; you have to be silent in order to hear the footsteps of the mysterious walking across the surface of your soul.

Later that night, she thought about the idea of an invitation—that David's brain had burped out this little hint about his past. How David chose to react to that was a complete surprise. His declaration that he suspected *intention* behind the revelation of his baby name was profoundly out of character.

Chapter

7

David

My resection was delayed by one week. As the date of the surgery approached, I stayed up all night and slept most of the day because it was hard to get continuous sleep. I peed every two hours because of the damn meds. By the early morning, my bladder would wake me up for a measly drop or two; like a dog marking territory. I stood at the toilet, bleary-eyed, holding myself up against the wall with one hand, and said, into the yawning mouth of the toilet, "Now was that worth it?" Then I wondered, who was I talking to anyway? The toilet? My bladder? The medication? Cancer? Who?

I got up at noon, grouchy and annoyed. I had a liver tolerance test in a few hours and it had to be done at Sloan-Kettering. I had just enough time to get dressed, eat, and go. So much for the plans for a morning walk, catching up on the news, and making phone calls. I opened the medicine cabinet and looked for the box of floss. I had never been a flosser, until now. Now that I had decided to live past seventy, I had begun to take long-term bodily maintenance seriously. I dabbed sun block on my face, and rubbed it into the tips of my ears. I poured myself a tall glass of water and drained it, along with my multivitamin and my prescription meds. I took fish oil capsules for my heart, a muscle that would have to go on pumping for decades, despite the daily frights it was suffering. I put on a striped polo shirt and a pair of jeans. They felt unbearably tight. I ended up choosing sweats, feeling disgusted with myself. Julia arrived to take me to my appointment. She put her purse, phone, and a plate of blueberry muffins covered with plastic wrap on the kitchen table. She fed me berries of every variety every chance she could, hoping that maybe the antioxidants could cure me.

Sitting on a side table was the ID card I had been issued at work the week before I was hospitalized. It was likely the best photo I've ever taken in my life. Julia picked it up and stared at it a long time. "You look *hot*," she whispered, oscillating from my steroid-bloated face to the card and back. Then she caught herself and made a lame effort to conceal the obvious by giving me a peck on the forehead and saying, "And you look pretty cute in this ID card *too*." But her reaction to that stark contrast was so plain that it inspired the first vanity crisis in my entire life. I went to the bathroom, locked the door behind me, and looked in the mirror and back at the ID photo and back and forth. I needed a haircut and a shave. My hand went up to the cut on the side of my head where the prickly stitches still poked out. I had managed to convince myself that I resembled a vintage G.I. Joe action figure, but the truth was, I looked like a mental patient. The mirror reflected the image of a guy in distress; someone who was about to get his ass kicked by cancer, a guy who wasn't sleeping, a guy who was facing the scariest surgery of his life with his chin up and his fists clenched. But, I reminded myself, the clean-shaven guy in the photo was in the worst possible place—deep in the bliss of ignorance, with the shock still ahead.

We were both in the kitchen when a postal truck appeared in the window. Julia, who still had her coat on, said, "I'll get the mail," and she ran back out. Our driveway is rather long, so I let the screen close and turned back to whatever I was doing. When she was halfway to the mailbox, the cell phone she had placed on the kitchen table rang. I peeked at the display. The caller ID read "Jonathan Miller." I picked it up, clicked on the green button and said, "Yeah?"

"Hi . . ." a deep but surprised voice said. "May I speak with Julia?"

"Who're you?"

"I'm a . . . friend of hers. Who's this?"

"Her husband," I said. "You wanna leave a message?"

There was silence. "Oh. No message. Thanks." I hung up before he did.

Julia appeared a few seconds later with my parents' mail.

"Thanks," I said. "Who's Jonathan Miller?"

She turned and looked at the phone, still sitting on the table; gave it a hard and disapproving look, as if it had misbehaved, then she picked it up and dropped it in her purse. "Just someone I met on the cruise. He lives in New York," she said lightly, as if that was the end of it.

"Someone you're going to see again?"

"Don't know. Someone I'd like to talk to again. That's all I can say at this point."

And then I did it. I played the cancer card. I said, "Julia, when I go into surgery, I need to know that you're waiting for me on the other side." I put one arm around her waist, the other around her neck and I pressed my mouth into hers. Taken off guard, she allowed herself to be kissed. Then she put her hands on my shoulders and shoved me away.

"Cut it out." She folded her arms in front of her. "Listen to me. Our breakup was a huge blow." She put a hand over her heart. "You, we, everyone who loves you, is in crisis mode until you come out of that surgery. After that, we'll let out a big sigh of relief. And then we have an even bigger hill to climb when you start chemo. I'll be here," she said, pointing at the floor. "I'll be here for you but only if you respect my boundaries. I don't have the emotional energy to keep fighting you every time you want to start your groping, and neither do you. Just stay cool, stay close, and let's keep our eyes on the road. Do we have a deal, yes or no?"

"Will this *Jonathan* character be taking his eyes off the road too?"

She looked away and shook her head. "He's just a friend. I met him on the ship."

"Did you make any other 'friends' on vacation?"

She put a finger to her cheekbone and then pointed at me. "Eyes on the road. Take it or leave it." She offered her hand. I shook it, but reluctantly.

"I'm not kidding about needing *all* of you, Julia. I want you to be the one to make medical decisions if I can't. I want you to have durable power of attorney."

Julia blinked. "What about your parents?"

"It's too much for them. It would kill my mother."

Her forehead wrinkled up with worry. She pulled away from me and looked me in the eye. "Just one question, David."

I stared and waited.

"Do you have siblings?"

I smiled a bit and looked away. "Yes, I have siblings."

"Then they're your next of kin."

"Not if you marry me."

She ignored that last comment. "Which one? Which one would you trust with your life?"

I shrugged. "Adrian."

"Okay, then, we just made an important decision here, David." Her entire face relaxed and she hugged me. She looked utterly relieved and proud that she had shoved responsibility back at me, as in, if Adrian and I are going to talk the talk, we've also got to walk the walk.

"Let's put it in writing," she said. "This will mean the world to him." She smiled and pointed upward to indicate that she had had a great idea. "Let's put a LoJack on him. We can't afford to lose track of him again."

Chapter

8

While David was inside the doctor's office, Julia's phone rang. She felt a thread of electricity zip across her stomach when she saw the name displayed. Jonathan Miller, a name that invoked sweet-oak and citrus-scented cologne, pressed linen shirts, and the festive, twinkling lights of a cruise ship. An invitation back to vacationland. She let it ring and eventually, it stopped. She was in David's world now. She would call Jon later.

She hadn't been entirely truthful with David about Jon. She had given Jon her phone number and agreed to have dinner with him after their ship docked. They had sunbathed and danced for days on end and kissed a little bit on that last night. They had not been romantic so much as they had spent five days flirting with each other. He seemed like a nice guy: good-looking, smart, funny. Like Julia, he sailed, kayaked, and enjoyed fishing, history, politics, music, and dancing. Two things she appreciated in men were gregariousness and style, the exact qualities David lacked. She should have been bowled over by Jon. But her heart wasn't in it. Dating felt foreign, but she accepted it as part of the adjustment period, and had decided to march forward despite her awkwardness.

Two days before their ship returned to Puerto Vallarta, the steward had brought the urgent messages from Julia's brothers. Julia had immediately called the O'Farrells and talked to Marcia. When she heard the words "brain tumor" Julia began to shiver. Not as one who is cold might shiver, but with a bristling inner quake, like someone who has just crawled out of a car wreck. She went to the bathroom, and her stomach yielded its contents quickly and without labor.

Now Jonathan Miller was calling for a date, and it felt a bit like a vacation hangover. But at the same time, she knew that things would never be the same with David either, that his blow to their relationship had been fatal. And even though she returned to the same port after the cruise—then to the same airport, then to the O'Farrells'—she had come back with something less, or perhaps something more, depending how one looked at it. What had changed was that her future was in her own custody again, and she wasn't going to be so careless with it this time.

Across the room, the little frosted-glass doors opened and Julia heard someone call her name. "Me?" she looked around. Then David repeated her name from somewhere inside and the receptionist smiled and waved her in. Her first reaction was to think: *Me? Why? I'm just his chauffeur.* But she nodded at the receptionist and went inside.

In the nurse's station, there were several people standing around holding clear cups filled with yellow fluid. Again Julia felt a sense of disorientation. Then she saw the grocery store chocolate cake on a table, and two black-and-orange bottles of Veuve Cliquot champagne. Dr. Levine himself greeted Julia and handed her a glass, then addressed the group, which included his staff and a middle-aged couple. "To Frank Lorens," he raised his cup to a bearded man next to him and turned to his staff. "Ten years ago we diagnosed Frank with a glioblastoma. And here he is, despite the odds."

"Still a pain-in-the-neck," the wife said, then laughed, and gave her husband a little shove. A portly woman in her late forties, Sue Lorens looked ten years younger than her husband. Everyone clapped and cheered and toasted him. A few minutes later, Dr. Levine introduced Julia to the Lorenses as "David's lovely wife."

"Julia Griswold," she said, shaking their hands. "David and I are just friends." There was an awkward moment when Dr. Levine looked utterly baffled, so Julia turned the subject back to Frank Lorens's victory. "Your success here is encouraging, doc. Congratulations to all of you."

"I'm honored to mark this day with you," David chimed in.

"You'll have to invite us to *your* decade party," Frank said, tipping his plastic cup to David's. David pointed at the champagne bottles. "Put one of those babies in your wine cellar for me now, will ya, doc? Actually make that four bottles for four more decades. I plan to see my seventieth birthday." There was polite laughter after Dr. Levine pretended to balk at the high cost of all that champagne. The staff scattered and the three men drew into a huddle: they folded their arms and drew their heads closer. "You're a biological lottery winner," David said to Frank. "You're the two percent. How the hell did you do it, man?"

The wife, Sue, locked her eyes on Julia. "Are you really just his friend?" She tipped her head toward David, with one eyebrow drawn up. Julia didn't get a chance to answer, just let out a sigh. "I didn't think so," Sue said.

The women turned away and faced the window, speaking

in low, calm voices, as if they were discussing something they had observed in the street below. Julia explained the state of affairs. "Oh, honey," Sue said. "You can't stay with him out of guilt. This is a long, hard road if things go *well*," she paused, turned her head, and looked off to the distance for a moment. "I'm sure you're well aware of the statistics. It's not a matter of *if* it comes back, it's *when*. And after the *when* there will be thirty or forty years of your life still to be lived," she put her hand upon Julia's, "*without him*. It's what I think about every night when I put my head down on my pillow, Julia. It's coming. I just don't know when. So I live my life in a kind of limbo." She squinted, put a hand up to shield her eyes as a large cloud slid past the sun. "David and Frank, on the other hand, need to live in denial. But you shouldn't, not deep down."

Julia lowered her eyes. "Do you have children, Sue?"

"Nope. We were married a year and a half when he found out." She looked at Julia. "Do you want kids?" Julia nodded. "Julia, forgive me, but if you were already married, I wouldn't be saying any of this. I've been to dozens of support groups and I know a lot of people going through this. This is a *different* kind of cancer. It's not like other people's cancers. It's cruel because it steals the body, then the mind, and some say, the soul. Your decision to stay with him has to be very deliberate, because it's going to be one scary ride and you never know when they're gonna let you off."

Julia reached out and squeezed Sue's hand. "I hear you," she said. "And thank you for the talk."

Frank called for Sue. "I have to go," she said. She rummaged through her purse and handed Julia a card. "I hope I wasn't too bold," she said. "I just want to pass on what I know. Call me anytime."

Julia examined the card and tilted her head in surprise. "Cancer Solutions LLC?"

"I'm fighting brain cancer by importing special vitamins and natural medicines. Reishi mushrooms, powdered kelp, and sea cucumbers are *the* thing now. I'll send you some free samples and recipes if you e-mail me." She lifted her chin, forced a smile, and tapped Julia on the shoulder like an old friend. "Girl, you can make the most amazing antioxidant jams, pies, cookies, and ice-pops out of berries and seaweed. Just throw in lots of sugar and a few sprigs of mint to mask the taste."

Julia smiled weakly. "So what are you, the Martha Stewart of cancer?"

"Coming!" she shouted over her shoulder at Frank, who was standing outside the door. She looked at Julia pointedly in the eyes and whispered, "Run. If you can. If you can't, then welcome to the club."

After the Lorenses left, Dr. Levine said that he had one more test for David, and so Julia went back out to the waiting room, alone. She scrolled down the list of calls that she had missed, and listened to the messages: Taina, Holly, Adrian, and Raymond had all called for updates. There were two messages from Jonathan, describing his surprise when David had answered the phone and identified himself as her husband. She experienced a strange mix of emotions at the irony of it. She was both sad and angry that the man she had so patiently waited for was finally showing some competitiveness for her love, now that it was too late. There wasn't a chance for them anymore; she had made this abundantly clear. But apart from withdrawing completely from his life, how could she make him understand that without hurting him? Sue was right. She had to have an exit plan.

The glass window opened and a nurse poked her head out, holding up a bottle. "Bit more champagne?" Julia accepted a half-cup and sat back down. All at once, she remembered the last time she had had tasted Cliquot. It seemed like years had passed since their breakup, but it had been just a little over a month before, on her birthday. She tipped the cup to her lips. It had been the worst birthday of her life.

Julia chose Tre Scalini, the fanciest restaurant on Wooster Street, to celebrate her thirty-fourth birthday. The waiter had just taken away their empty dinner plates when David slid a small black velvet box across the table. *Finally!* Julia thought. She sat up tall, pressed her lips into a tight, prissy smile, and stared down at the box. She reached for it, felt the prickly softness of the velvet on her palm. She heard the soft creak of the spring hinges release as she pulled back the top. Inside, a pair of sparking stones stared back at her like the glowing eyes of a black cat. Her heart sank.

"Studs? We can't afford these."

"*I* can afford them," David said firmly.

She looked back down at the earrings, hoping they had magically morphed into a single stone. But no, there they were. So separate, so lonely. Maybe they weren't real, she thought, her hope half rising again. Because if they were real, then there wasn't going to be an engagement ring anytime soon.

"Like 'em?"

"Depends."

"On *what*?" his voice rose to a falsetto.

She scrunched up her face at the bad taste in her question, but she had to know what she was dealing with here. "David, are these real?"

David threw his head back and laughed. "You think I'm *that* cheap?" He took her hand. "Of course they're real. Put them on."

Julia's eyes filled with tears while David just sat back, pleased at the waterworks he had caused, imagining that he'd made her so happy that she was weeping with joy. That he was so clueless about the real cause was even more depressing.

The waiter arrived with a bottle of Veuve Cliquot and filled the glasses. David wished her a happy birthday and she managed to raise her glass for his toast. She watched him take a long swig, without tasting it herself. She asked point blank, "Why did you buy two diamonds instead of one?"

David blinked and turned his head slightly. "What would you do with only one earring?" She couldn't tell if he was joking or not, but she guessed not.

"Is this a consolation prize? A 'thank you for your patience' gift?"

"It's a birthday gift." He drained his champagne and put it down.

She continued to hold hers up, suspended in midair. She stared at the rising bubbles, still unable to take a sip.

"I know where this is going," he said. "But I'm not even forty yet."

The glass came down, spilling champagne over the rim. "*Forty?*" she gasped.

Chocolate lava cakes appeared on the table. Hers had a lit birthday candle in it. David immediately gutted his cake and began to wash it down with champagne and water.

She slid the box across the table. "I can't accept the earrings, but thank you. I don't want you to think that I'm happy with the way things are."

"I'm not ready for forever," he said bluntly. "Aren't you going to blow out the candle?" The candle was still burning— long, high, smoky flames, burning and whittling down to the little striped wax stump.

"I don't even know what to wish for anymore, David."

"Well I do," he said. Then he took a deep breath and blew her birthday candle out. She stared at the burnt wick until it stopped smoking. She sensed that something big had just happened, that some inner light had gone out along with the birthday candle. For God's sake, what did David wish for, if not a life together?

She stood up, excused herself, and went to the ladies' room. Once safely inside a stall, she masked her sobs by flushing the toilet. Someone asked if she was okay. She took a deep breath, and reminded herself that her life didn't have to implode tonight. Maybe, just maybe, what he needed was a push. The point was that they—no *she*—had to move out of their stagnation.

Back at the table, David had already paid the bill. As they made their way out of the restaurant and down the street back to their car, Julia watched, with an unfamiliar sense of envy, several groups of twentysomethings, some Yalies, some locals, flirting with each other, years of their youth still stretching ahead of them. And for the first time in her life, Julia felt old.

Their apartment had little furniture, mostly cheap, temporary stuff from Ikea, the clutter of a couple shacking up rather than starting a home. Their bedroom floor was littered with piles of clothes, projects, magazines, and sports equipment, and they slept on a queen-sized mattress on the floor. The only real piece of furniture was a scratched wood dresser Julia had bought at a consignment shop in college. Granted, they had only been living together a year, and it had been an unusually busy year, but it was obvious to Julia now that the spirit of nesting had never quite taken up residence.

Julia took her second shower of the evening, just to comfort herself. She put on pajamas and towel-dried her long hair. She stood in front of the mirror. She saw a pair of coppery, half-moon shadows beneath her eyes. Looking at herself critically made her even more sad and tired, and she dropped into bed and fell into a deep sleep.

That night, she dreamed about a new man. She woke up from the dream because there was motion in the bed as David got up to go to the bathroom. She could see the lighted outline of the bathroom door, heard him flush the toilet. She dug her head deeper into the pillow, grasping at the last shreds of the vanishing dream. David turned out the light in the bathroom, then turned it on again. She flipped over to avoid the light, growing angry at losing her grip on the dream. Come back, she pleaded. Who are you and why do you love me so much? Had she ever been loved this way? She felt as if she had known such a man, lived such a life. But she hadn't, she was sure. She could hear the rattle of pills in the bathroom. David shuffled back to bed.

"I can't sleep. Upset stomach again," he said. "I took an antacid."

The dream was gone, but she was drunk with longing. She reached out to David. "C'mere," she whispered. "I know something you can do while you count sheep."

But he kissed her on the forehead, a light dismissive peck. "Not now, it's late."

"Oh, c'mon. I was having a sexy dream."

"Good for you," he said, pulling the blanket tight over his shoulders as he rolled over. "Those are always fun."

A week passed. When they woke up the next Saturday morning, the weather was unseasonably warm, and the sun was out. Julia suggested that they head down to the pier at Long Wharf.

The water had gentle caps sweeping over the surface in the morning breeze. The waves slapped against the edges of the pier. They looked out to the water and the rusty barges and industrial smoke stacks across the bay. David embraced Julia—partly out of affection, and, she suspected, partly to keep warm. The pale winter sun was in her eyes so she closed them.

"David," she said softly, "will you marry me?" He smiled at first, and then his smile faded and he looked into her eyes. "Yeah," she said. "I'm really asking."

He blinked a few times. "But Julia," he said, "you deserve to be asked."

"So ask," she said. "The hard part is done."

There was a moment of limbo, a long embrace. He rubbed her back and whispered for her to hush, even though she was silent. He held her longer than she wanted to be held. She wondered if he could feel her shaking, or hear her molars chattering against one another. She pulled away and looked up at him. He looked stricken, pale. He lowered his lids, so that she could no longer see his eyes. It seemed like an eternity before he spoke. He lifted his head to give her a pained look. "Can we talk about this a little bit more?" he said. She shook her head, no.

"I can't do it," he whispered. "I just can't."

"I knew it." She stared out to the water, trying to hold a focus on the barges, the pier, the few people walking their dogs, the sky, anything to keep from having to look at him.

There was nothing more to say, really. They drove home in silence. He must have been completely shocked, as she was—shocked at the frankness of their exchange after so many years of dancing around the subject, shocked that their time had run out and that now things were unraveling so quickly. Earlier that morning, they had gone for a jog together, they had made coffee, read the newspaper, and folded their laundry. The morning had been so lovely, so routine. For Julia, the wound hadn't even begun to hurt; there was just numbness.

Back at home she began to throw some things into a duffel bag. She'd go to her mother's house for the next day or so and take it from there. She threw an overnight bag over her shoulders and went down to get her purse, phone, car keys, and sunglasses. David was lying on the sofa with one of the cushions on his face.

"I'll be back after work on Monday. We'll need to talk about the lease and, well, everything," Julia said flatly.

"I have the worst headache of my life," he said. "Can you do *one* thing for me before you go?"

"What?"

"Can you bring me the mop bucket?"

She put it next to him.

"Are you okay?"

"Nauseous," he said. "Definitely the flu." He lifted his head and turned toward the bucket and dry heaved. Drama, she thought. Just drama. If he did in fact have the flu, then he absolutely should suffer alone. It would do him some good. She gathered her things, put her shoes on, and headed toward the door.

She had no idea how she made it to her mother's house. A few days later she had no memory of it. She had gone on autopilot, her mind far, far away from the act of driving. Fortunately, the house wasn't far. Her mother was still at work when she let herself in. She was grateful to be alone. She crawled into her childhood bed, a twin four-poster that still had the matching pink bedspread and canopy, walls covered in movie posters. How sad it felt to return to her younger self, she thought. She had gone in a big circle.

But in the meantime, Julia wondered if David had thought to put a cold cloth on his forehead, if he took a pain reliever, if he drank water. She knew deeply, and most humbly this: that she had wanted to marry David because she loved him and wanted to spend every day of her life with him. But now, she was so deeply disappointed in him, and even more so in herself. It had been a desperate and ridiculous gesture to ask him to marry her. She had known, deep down, that he would say no. But she did it because it forced *her* in a new direction, because it had become all too clear that they weren't moving in any direction at all. Something, or *someone*, had to change and it wasn't going to be him. He was, and would always be, devoted to the status quo.

She returned to their apartment at three-thirty on Monday, after work. David would be at the office for another three hours, and that gave her some more time to pack. She knew that she would have to be the one to go. She was the one actively seeking progress, so it seemed natural and even fair that she would bear the burden of motion. Julia's mother had a home nearby with an extra bedroom, whereas David's parents lived an hour away, in rural Connecticut, rather far to commute to work. Julia realized how much of her life was tied to David and to their families, friends, and shared hobbies. She had thought that this meant that they were transitioning from being twentysomethings into the next stage, the married thirties. But David was either emotionally stunted, irreparably damaged, as he himself had suggested, or he just wasn't in love with her. If the latter was true, then, Julia thought, she had been deluding herself all along. And that both frightened and infuriated her.

At five-thirty, she was done with the boxing part of her packing. There was a pile of miscellaneous things she wasn't sure what to do with, divisive things, photo albums and videotapes that archived their lives together; books signed and dedicated to both of them. It was a good thing they hadn't gotten around to finding the right dog yet, she realized. David walked in at six, as she was making the last trip to her car. Her brothers would have to come back for the large boxes and the furniture. David stepped out of his Jeep Wrangler dressed in his daily work uniform: long-sleeve oxford shirt, Gap khakis, polished dress shoes. As they stood chatting, awkwardly, under the light of the front door, she noticed that he had his first strand of gray hair.

"How's your headache?" she asked.

"It's gone," he said. "It got really bad on Sunday night."

She harrumphed, gave him a few suggestions on how to avoid headaches, then got to business. "Taina called," she informed him. "She said something about you going to New York this weekend."

He nodded. "Adrian has a show."

"Sounds like fun."

"Wanna come?"

Julia shook her head no.

David stepped closer, took her hand in his. "Julia, I'm so sorry that I'm hurting you. I do love you."

"Are you seeing someone else?"

He pulled his head back. "Where did that come from?"

"Just making sure I understand all the forces at work," she said.

"*Juuuuulia*," he intoned, slowly, like it contained all the disillusionment of the universe. "C'mon, you know me better than that. I'm the most faithful guy who ever lived. And you're the one leaving, not me."

She let out a sigh. She believed him. Again she forced herself to stay on task. "I was counting on your help to move me out. But you're going to New York, apparently, instead of being present in this colossal thing that's happening to us."

"I can help you next week, if you can wait a little." He shrugged. "You know how it is Julia, family comes first."

Julia gasped a little at that last, thoughtless, and highly ironic statement. "I thought that we *were* a family, you and I." Later, Julia would pinpoint that moment as the coup de grâce. His rejection seared itself into the meat of her heart. Almost immediately, a translucent but impermeable scar grew over the injury.

After her conversation with Sue Lorens, Julia got the idea of a summer gathering at Griswold Island. David needed to be surrounded by an army of emotional cheerleaders. He needed a purpose; something big enough to sustain his tolerance for pain and to embolden his fighting spirit. "Bravery is nourished by purpose," an ancestor had once written in the margins of *The Griswolds of New Haven County*, volume two. In an instant, Julia bridged this old wisdom with the conversation she and David had had at the Christmas tree farm; how he had described the memory flashes as "an invitation." This was the connection that David himself had just begun to figure out, Julia thought, with rising amazement. This was to be her gift, her role, her purpose—to enable David to fulfill his before it was too late. After that, the siblings would take over, and she could get on with her life. And so she decided that she would have to convince her own family of the solemnity of their small sacrifice. The starfish children of Mayagüez needed to gather. And what else characterized the Griswold family, with their one-hundred-and-twenty-one-year-old house, more than genealogical self-knowledge? Yes, it had to happen this summer, and it was vital that all five be reunited at Griswold Island. They would be changed by the experience, she knew. They would grow closer. And then she would quietly slip away and begin to rebuild her life.

Chapter

9

Holly's husband, Erick, was a stoic man who got alarmingly more attractive with age. He was an excellent provider and Holly was very proud to be married to him. She hated the old clichés about pilots, but now and then she worried about the thousand-mile rule. To keep herself in shape, Holly taught aerobics at the local gym. It also gave her the energy she needed to keep up with the kids. They lived in Lighthouse Point, a community of pink houses in various scales just outside Fort Lauderdale.

Holly's parents showered her with rewards for being such a good sister to their natural-born child, Audra, who was five years older than Holly and had cerebral palsy. She had saved the family from an existence that would have been isolated. By being athletic, popular, bold, and willing to take Audra under her wing, Holly enabled Audra to move in circles she would never have otherwise experienced. Everyone knew they were a package deal. If anything, Holly taught everyone in high school to be respectful to the mentally disabled. Being Audra's sister had given her a lifetime of self-assurance, a nurturing spirit, and had awakened her sense of responsibility. She loved watching out for Audra and knew early on that her calling was to be a mom.

Initially, Holly had a little problem with the timing of Julia's proposal for a gathering in August because she wanted another baby. Her husband, on the other hand, was done. Erick had already scheduled a vasectomy in early September. The gate to parenthood was closing, and she had to figure out a way to sneak under it. The truth was that Holly didn't just want a fourth child, she wanted a *daughter*, first and foremost, and secondly, she needed to spawn a child that actually looked like her, with dark eyes and black hair, medium skin—rather than the red-headed, blue-eyed, long-boned, freckled copies of Erick. This meant that if she were to spawn another Erick clone, then she would want a fifth, or a sixth or however many it took to get her brown-eyed, brown-haired, warm-skinned girl. But Erick said they already had one more child than he wanted. Holly was appalled that he would say that, but he said it's just honest. It had crossed her mind to stop the birth control pills and just say oops. But Erick knew his wife was capable of a little trickery to get her way. So when he said he had made the earliest possible appointment with his doctor for a vasectomy, she had a fit; she cried and cried, but he said it was all set. Holly felt horrible about her hesitance to agree to the sibling gathering, but this was an absolute emergency. The next few months would be her last chance to steal sperm from her husband. After all, September was only six menstrual cycles away, and it had taken her an average of eight months of trying, per child, to get pregnant. According to her calculations, she would be ovulating during the trip, and she didn't have enough of a margin. On the other hand, it would be so great to catch a break from her hectic family life, absolutely lovely to get out of South Florida during the most oppressive weeks of summer. The contrast between the two places was so stark. New England, with its cool, rocky coast and forested hills, was the polar opposite of hot, flat, and crazy South Florida.

When Holly was nineteen, she visited David in Connecticut. He took her to Chatfield Hollow State Park. Holly remembered visiting a covered bridge, painted a rich shade of red, in the spring. It was as if she could hear the trees groaning with the surge of energy of the sun and warm air. Holly stood on the bank of this stream and listened to the water tumbling over those dark, smooth rocks. There was a strong smell of water and moss and wet earth. The smell of nature's sex. She got a sense then that she was born to be a mother, that she felt most in-sync with the world when she was a part of this process. She loved being pregnant, loved nursing, loved raising kids. And because she cherished her family so much, she was devastated for David, and felt a deep sense of mourning for the loss of the family he'd never have.

Erick's doctor had a cancellation just a few days after Erick had made his decision. A few hours later, despite her tears and pleas, Erick got a vasectomy, and Holly's hopes to have more children were dashed with a single snip. But when Erick returned home and plopped down on the couch with a bag of ice on his crotch, Holly informed him that he would have to nurse himself back to health, make lunch *and* host the kids' afternoon playdate. She slammed the door behind her for emphasis. On her way to the car, through the wooden fence of the backyard, she heard her middle son report to his two brothers, "Guys! I think she kicked him in the nuts!"

Holly jumped into her minivan and headed to Miami. She walked into the Tarpon Tattoo and asked for Carlos, an old and dear friend from high school. Carlos had been anticipating this appointment for years. Wiping away tears, Holly instructed Carlos to make three tiny starfishes floating over the appendages of the main starfish, symbolizing her three boys. As Carlos's needle pierced her skin, she began to bawl, so he stopped, thinking that she couldn't endure the pain.

"I've had three babies, Carlos," she said. "Two natural, one C-section. Plus I had my tonsils *and* an appendix removed," she said, pointing to the site of those organs. "I've been carved up more than a pumpkin on Halloween. I can handle pain." When she explained why she was crying, her friend asked how many babies it would take to fill the void, and why, exactly, a brown-eyed girl might end her longing. She didn't have an answer.

So Holly got her starfish tattoo, which did double duty as a connection to her siblings *and* symbol of protest against Erick's vasectomy. The first person she called was Raymond. The skin on her hand was still burning when she reached him at work. "I did it," she said. "I look like a soccer mom turned bar fly, but I love it. I can't stop looking at it, Ray. I feel connected, like I'm officially part of a secret family. I wish I had had it done years ago. I know how much the tattoos mean to you, kid. I'm so sorry it took me this long to understand. But I get it . . . I totally get it."

Raymond believed that he was Cuban. At least, that's what he chose to tell people. He had admitted to Holly that he wanted to dissociate himself with the plight of Mexicans in his home state, not wanting to shoulder their particular brand of prejudice. "I got enough crap to deal with without taking on illegal immigration," he once told Taina. "I don't like the theory that we were Dominican, either. That could make us illegal aliens. That's scary. What if they revoked our citizenship and sent us back to a place we don't remember? I could say I'm Puerto Rican and avoid citizenship issues entirely, but then there's always East Coast prejudice. As far as I can tell, Cubans are at the top of the Latino food chain. They're golden the minute they set foot in the U.S., so if no one knows for sure where we're from, why not be Cuban? It's more glamorous anyway. Copacabana and cigars and mambo and all that."

Ray had been adopted by a Germanic-looking couple who had given him an idyllic childhood right up until Ray turned sixteen. His father left his mother for an aspiring ballerina, moved to Mexico City, and never came back. Last Ray heard, his father and the new wife were running a dance school in Puebla. Ray began to drink heavily. At first, he drank tequila just to be ironic—a manly nod to his father's newfound freedom. But as his father's absence grew longer, he lost his sense of humor about it. He grew more and more depressed. He became a chronic overeater and he drank more and more as memories of his first adoptive family returned. That family had kept him for a year, but the older son in the family had not adjusted to life with the new sibling. Ray was sent back into foster care at age seven. The next year, those foster parents decided to adopt him. The new couple was focused entirely on him. It hadn't been an easy transition, but it worked. So when his graduation ceremony came and went with no sign of his father, Ray almost drank himself to death. Ray's mother called Taina from the emergency room to tell her that Ray was getting his stomach pumped. Taina's parents had generously arranged for Taina and Holly to fly to Arizona to be at his side at the hospital. At Ray's bedside, Taina had come up with the idea of a tattoo as a substitute for DNA. "It's a symbol that we belong to each other," she had promised. At the time, Holly's parents had forbidden her to get the tattoo, just as Erick had strongly objected later on. Still, Holly had experimented with the idea by having it sketched in henna several times. It was the kind of thing you have to be sure about, she thought; you ought to really *want* a tattoo to get it in such a visible place. The other four siblings had immediately gone to tattoo parlors that very week, without asking permission, and had each had a starfish tattooed on the tops of their hands, in green ink. The symbolism behind the gesture was powerful. According to Raymond, he regained control of his life the very same day that he got the tattoo. He quit drinking, but started up again at age twenty-one, when he was old enough to get into bars legally, a privilege he couldn't resist exercising. He fell back into a destructive pattern of binge drinking for two more years, until he went cold turkey again. Holly had always felt a little guilty about being the holdout, and since then Adrian had repeatedly challenged her commitment to their sense of family. But she didn't want to appear to be caving to peer pressure, or doing it to appease her pain-in-the-ass brother; she had come to the decision all on her own. Sadly, it had taken David becoming ill to get her to seriously consider it. The final blow was the loss of the opportunity to have a daughter, a closer genetic manifestation of life's spiraling staircase to immortality.

Chapter

10

The five toddlers' outfits were released by the authorities to Taina's parents in 1989. Taina's dress had been white linen, size 2T. It was a curious and unique dress, hand-embroidered with yellow ducks that tumbled from the pockets and then landed on their feet and scattered across the fine yellow piping of the hem. On the seat of the dress, one little duck has its little tail feathers sticking up in the air. Finery with a sense of humor. One-of-a-kind.

The craftsmanship of the dress was what inspired Taina to study textile design. Taina and her mother, Natasha, had examined that dress with the care of forensic scientists. Taina became knowledgeable about fabrics and makers of children's clothing in an effort to discover something about herself through the history of the dress. She consulted experts and a psychic or two about the nature of the fabric, the design, style, and crafting, but she knew very little to this day about where it came from. There was a tag, in English: "Lilly Pad Designs. Cotton linen. Handwash. Warm iron as needed." There had been a small company in Boston specializing in children's clothing called

Lilly Pad Designs, but it had closed in 1985. The owner, Lilly Patterson, was deceased.

The dress takes thirty minutes to iron, Taina timed it herself. The high-maintenance quality of the dress, she decided, was evidence of her early exposure to beauty and good taste despite whatever calamities marked her infancy. She eventually came to feel that she was born in that outfit, that nothing before mattered because her life was a single continuum from then on. The dress had given her a life, a passion, a focus. After attending NYU, Taina found work in the New York garment district, for a prestigious fabric designer. There, she created a unique fabric theme, called "Caribbean Lagoon," a line of rich cottons and linens that evoked a tropical vacation. Even her abstract patterns, such as argyle, implied a life of white wicker on terraces overlooking swaying palms and a turquoise sea, lemons and pineapples and poolside gardens of hibiscus and birds of paradise. The designs had sold to a label that catered to the Palm Beach country-club set. Her parents were her biggest fans, and as soon as the temperature hit seventy in New York, they went to work wearing absurdly bright outfits made out of her "Lagoon" fabrics.

The week before David's surgery, Taina had been on her way to work when she spotted Doug a half-block behind her. She knew that Doug had seen her too. She *felt* detected. This encounter had been prophesied the night before by Holly, a.k.a. Big Mouth. Holly had taken it upon herself to inform Doug about David's illness. "Be ready, Taina" she had warned. "You know how Doug *loves* to be a hero, and he's still very much in love with you."

Taina felt Doug's eyes on her back. She darted into the yawning mouth of a church. In the dim light, she made a sharp left and sunk her knees into the pads of a kneeler, pulling up the hood of her raincoat and bowing her head before a row of candles glowing softly in the shadowy darkness. Doug passed behind her, and when she turned to look at him, she could see him scanning to the left and right. She heard the size-thirteen shoes clicking distinctly across the marble despite the din of tourists' voices, each step carrying him deeper into the gloom of the church. She dashed out the door and exited to the street. Once at a safe distance, she bought coffee and a bottle of water from a cart and headed back to the office.

But Doug was already waiting for Taina in her studio. He was fingering the bolts of fabric that she had left on her work table, a cream-colored, textured raw silk that, based on orders alone, was destined to become all the rage next season for brides, flower girls, first communions, and bat mitzvahs. He looked up at her, then back at the bolt of fabric, which looked like a small, pearly mummy, aglow under the wash of soft track lighting. Doug said, "Lucky you. You work with beauty every day." Taina reached past him and yanked the bolt of fabric away. She placed it on a shelf, feeling his eyes on her backside. She was anxious to get to work. If she had any chance at all of being able to take time off to be with David, she would have to work twelve- and fourteen-hour days in the weeks ahead.

"Doug," she cleared her throat, put her hands on her hips, and said, "let's cut to the chase. David is going to be *fine*."

Doug folded his hands in front of him. "Taina," he said softly, "it's a grade-four primary brain tumor. You know what the doctors call this type of tumor amongst themselves? They call it 'the terminator.' Your brother is dying and he doesn't have much time." Doug sighed. "He called me. He said that he thinks it's time. You know." He reached over and tapped the top of her hand. Taina pulled it away, as if he had touched her with a burning cigarette. "The boss is watching me." She pointed at the clock on the wall.

"I'm going to help you, Taina. I've already started."

"Help *me*?"

"Help David. Help you. He knows what it would mean to know. To give you your life back."

"I don't want my life back," she said. "You can keep it."

"Let this be my final gift to David. And to you. We don't have to tell the others. If they don't want to know, that's their business. But you—you ought to know. It's the only way . . ."

"The only way for what? For us to get back together?"

"Yeah," he said, relieved. "It's my last hope."

Taina shook her head. She made a cutting gesture with her hand. "We're done, Doug." She plopped into her chair, then swiveled her body around on the stool to face her computer.

He left. Her hand was shaking as she turned back around to reach for the water bottle she had been sipping, but it was gone. She looked out the window and saw Doug walking in the opposite direction, three levels down, on the sidewalk. One arm hung beside him as he walked. In the other, he carried something close to his body.

Taina had met Doug while walking her dog near her parents' house on the Upper East Side. Doug had been a stockbroker, the only son of a couple who lived in the same row of brownstones as her parents. He always wore expensive cologne and dark overcoats that in retrospect Taina had thought of as a kind of yuppie super-hero cape. He was tall and bulky, busy, sporty, manly. His voice had the rich, sonorous chime of a grandfather clock. He could figure out a waiter's tip in seconds, pick up the bill, and say, "Let's get out of here," as if she needed to be rescued from a five-star restaurant. At first, he courted her in the

old-fashioned way, by opening car doors and taking her to expensive restaurants. But there wasn't enough chemistry there to
take things up a notch. She certainly wasn't going to sleep with
someone she only liked. Besides, she had this paranoia about
Caucasian men. Did he think she was easy because her skin was
bronze? Five dates and all she gave him were kisses on the cheek
and awkward hugs. She knew he would tire of it eventually, and
he did. He stopped calling and she let it be. She didn't see him
again for a year. Then she walked into a hospital room after a
neighbor had been assaulted and had her car stolen, there was
Doug with his mother. Doug's eyes popped out when he saw
her walk in. Everyone wanted to help the neighbor get her life
back to normal, and so by the end of the visit, the bed-ridden
woman had assigned them all some kind of a task. Doug and
Taina volunteered to make a three-hour drive upstate to fetch
a vehicle borrowed from the victim's elderly aunt. After three
hours in a car together, they relaxed. Doug took her hand and
said, "I want to get to know you for real this time." Then he
said, "I'm gonna have to kiss you, just to take the edge off." So
they kissed good and hard right there in front of the neighbor's
mother's house, and Taina saw the old aunt peel back the curtain to see why they were still in her driveway. They knew that
they couldn't start up their boring formality again. So instead,
they walked the dog, ordered Chinese, and played board games.
He killed her at Monopoly, but she won at Scrabble. Soon they
had found a new, strangely sexy, endearing comfort zone. There
were six more low-budget weekday dates before they moved to
Sunday afternoons. They went bowling, to the museum, on a
long bike ride, to a dog obedience-school graduation ceremony,
and to a Cajun cooking class.

Two months passed before they promoted each other back to
Friday and Saturday nights. He took her sailing on his parents'

boat. They had so much fun that they forgot the time. They ended up having to sleep on Block Island. By then they were all worked up from a whole day's worth of kissing and pressing themselves against each other, drunk with a combination of white wine, lust, and all that sunshine. Taina opened up then, quite literally, and experienced what became one of her all-time favorite life moments: falling in love surrounded by inky, starlit darkness.

They made love three times that night. Then they headed back to the boat before dawn. They jumped into the cold water, and, shivering, wrapped each other in towels and had coffee and watched the sun come up. "This is so much better than those stiff dates we had," Doug said.

"Of course it is. We had sex."

"It's not because of the sex," he said, in a gentle scolding tone. "Hell, I had sex last week and I didn't feel like this." He instantly regretted what he had said. "It was just—" he said helplessly. "Err. I shouldn't have said that. I'm sorry."

She looked away. "I knew it. *I knew it.*"

"What I was trying to say . . ." He fell to his knees and looked up at her. "Is that I'm really enjoying getting to know you. I want to see you again tomorrow and the next day and the day after that. Okay?"

She looked at him sideways. "That depends on whether you plan to continue shagging people while you're 'getting to know me' better."

He laughed. "No. That's the point. I've been 'unhappily shagging.' I will unhappily shag no more."

So they continued to date in a way that felt natural and friendly and fun, and eventually they added some conventional stuff now and then. She took him on a few of her business trips. He was so leading and confident that his reaction to their separations always amazed her: "What? I'm not going to see you for a *whole week*?" Or if he had a big power meeting at work, he'd give her all the credit for getting him though it. "I get to see your face at night, so I can put up with anything during the day." Then he would give her that *look*.

The next phase of their courtship was the meeting of the families. They proceeded with caution, formality having been established as the undisputable enemy of their relationship.

Fast-forward a year. Doug's mother was diagnosed with breast cancer the same day that his dad is named president of a global charitable foundation. It soon became impossible for Doug's father to shoulder his wife's illness, so Taina and Doug stepped in, watching over her and taking her to chemotherapy appointments. His mother had always been polite with Taina, but after that, she adored her. For Taina's birthday, she gave her a white gold and diamond heart locket from Tiffany's. There was an anniversary party for the parents that year, and with secret joy, Taina basked in the admiration and gratitude of the family's friends and extended relatives for being such a great support to the family. She had never been happier; and Doug began to talk about marriage.

A month later, Doug's mother reached the stage of baldness. She was throwing up in the next room, when Doug held up a ring and asked Taina to be his wife. The timing and location of his marriage proposal was perfect, given their aversion to tradition. Taina said, "Of course," and they went into the rancid-smelling bathroom to give his mom the good news. The woman's skin went from green to pink in ten seconds, and she had named her grandchildren and great-grandchildren before she even made it out of the bathroom. Months went by and she went into remission. Life went back to normal, but the family was fatigued so the wedding was put on hold. Then, bad news.

Doug got fired from his high-power job on Wall Street for "underperforming." He had spent too much time caring for his mother. He had a flurry of lunches with other firms, but Taina could see that he was deeply affected. His heart wasn't in it anymore.

Doug and Taina got married in a small ceremony attended by only twenty guests. Holly was the only sibling missing, since she was in her thirty-fifth week of pregnancy and on mandatory bed rest with her second child. Shortly after the wedding, Doug announced that he would never set foot on Wall Street or in corporate America again. For a while, after having talked to Frick, he toyed with the idea of becoming a pilot. Law school was a little closer to the mark but he just couldn't get himself to apply. Several sessions with a career counselor led him back to his childhood dream of being a homicide detective. He had abandoned the dream because his parents had vehemently discouraged it. He knew he had to start at the bottom, as a beat cop; and the idea of it utterly electrified him. Six months later, he began training at the police academy. They had to give up their apartment, and move to more modest quarters.

Technically, Taina was in favor of his "unconventional" new career, but in reality, the change rattled her to the core. She had been toying with the idea of a professional transition herself. She had done well in drawing and painting and college, and felt that she could be a "real" artist as well as a designer. She attended a lecture on the subject of Latinos in the arts, where they discussed the dangers of assimilation into mainstream American culture, using mutually understood terms like "othering" and "post-identity." In these circles, the worst kind of self-betrayal by an artist of color was to produce work that was culturally anonymous. Taina sat through it, looking every bit Latina, with her bronze skin and black hair pulled back shiny and flat like a salsa dancer, but everything they talked about was foreign to her. Inside, Taina felt as white as a Swiss milkmaid; and this, she feared, was a basic failure of integrity. She felt like a fraud culturally, artistically, and perhaps most grievous of all: emotionally.

Taina's own personal anxiety just heightened the tensions at home about Doug's career change. He was a person whose very identity was undergoing transformation too, but rather than make Taina feel closer to him, it felt like she'd hitched up with someone just as confused as she was. One day, they were having lunch in the city on a Saturday, when his mobile phone rang. He was in the restroom so Taina answered. It was a woman. Taina asked the caller how she knew Doug. The caller said that they had met at the police academy, that they were friends and had plans to meet for lunch the following Monday.

When Doug returned to the table, Taina simply looked at him and said, "So I hear you're dating again."

Doug pulled his head back. "Huh?"

She picked up the phone and held it up. "Katie called."

He blinked twice, licked his lips. "Yeah?"

"She filled me in."

"Filled you in on what? We just went to a few happy hours together after training," he said with a strained voice.

"You're cheating on me, aren't you?"

"Taina," he begged. "You're my life, baby. You have absolutely no reason to be jealous. Trust me."

"You slept with her," she said flatly. "I can tell."

"Look at me," he said, pointing at his own eyes. "No. I did not cheat and I never will."

"That's what they all say," she said in a zombie-like voice. And when she got up from her chair, Doug saw that she had wet herself.

Doug made several grandiose attempts to reassure her. He sent huge bunches of roses to her at work, an embarrassment. What else could two dozen roses mean, really?

She "forgave" him eventually, but back came the dreaded formality, a way to punish him or keep him at arm's length. They went back to the peck on the cheek at the end of the night, only this time she expected to be treated like a diva. She even made him buy her silk roses from a street vendor in front of all his work friends, really tacky ones with wax dewdrops on their fake petals, which she tossed in the garbage on the way home.

Taina began to talk about Adrian a lot. Adrian this, Adrian that. She played his music constantly, had his lyrics memorized, even though she didn't speak Spanish. She began to throw Spanish words around and act Latina, as if to make Doug feel the same disorientation he had felt when he switched from a stockbroker to a policeman. Their relationship was out of the corral again, bucking and running off into the hills. In the meantime, Doug had never been happier at work: he was already a star at the NYPD, and his new line of work fulfilled him like never before. In an unfortunate coincidence, and through absolutely no fault of his own, he was assigned to work with an unusual number of women. He was put on a big case that required frequent contact with a renowned criminal profiler, a very attractive blonde who looked like she had stepped out of her own TV show. His partner? A woman. His immediate boss? A woman.

"Do you work at the NYPD or at Victoria's Secret?" David had joked. But Taina didn't think it was so funny. She couldn't adjust to his new life, his new persona, his new vocabulary and street accent, even his new happiness was confusing. Then he made the colossal mistake of revealing an extremely intimate fact about their marriage to a coworker (Taina overheard him on the phone with someone, probably the dreaded Katie, saying that Taina was "a raging insomniac"). Worst of all, he let it slip that she had begun sleeping in the other room. Outraged, Taina changed the locks and kicked him out for good. She went to see a divorce lawyer that same week. Doug's next move was to visit Taina's mother at her office at the university. Natasha Brighton had experienced her daughter's ups and downs and didn't hesitate to help him, although she made him promise to keep her contribution a secret. She had handed Doug two files: one labeled "news clippings" and another labeled "adoption file."

Doug never once considered that Taina didn't love him, nor did he believe that she could possibly love Adrian. Adrian's name came up after every argument they had ever had; he represented some kind of emotional refuge for her, an excuse to focus her energy elsewhere. It was true that Doug had betrayed their marital secrets but only after her insecurities had really gone berserk. Later, he had consulted with a trusted colleague who knew a great deal about the psychology of traumatized children. Taina, he was told, was being manipulated by fears so deep and so old that even she didn't recognize them as imaginary anymore.

When David was diagnosed with brain cancer, Doug had been saddened and shocked like everyone else. But his first concern was for his wife. If David died, Taina might never recover emotionally, she might lose trust in life itself. And the psychologist at work had been spot-on about David's reaction to his own illness. He predicted that David would suddenly want to resolve the mystery of his origins, so Doug wasn't a bit surprised; in fact, he was ready, with research in hand, when David e-mailed him a message two weeks after his diagnosis. The message contained just a few lines confirming his desire to proceed with the search; a message with the words *"Ready to open Pandora's Box"* written in the subject line.

Chapter

11

David was scheduled to have surgery at six in the morning, and the surgery would last six to eight hours. His doctor wanted him to check in the afternoon before, so they could monitor his every breath. David shooed his parents and Julia out in the late afternoon, told them to go home and get some rest. They decided to drive back to Connecticut, have some supper, sleep in real beds, and get up at 3 a.m. to be back at the hospital by 5 a.m., a full hour before he went into surgery. Julia was to spend the night with the O'Farrells, so they could ride in together. After that, the plan was for the O'Farrells to stay in Taina's guest room and on to a hotel if David's hospitalization lasted more than a week.

On the night before the surgery, Marcia and Julia hung out together in their bathrobes. They watched the celebrity gossip channel because suddenly everything else on TV seemed dark and depressing. Everything reminded them that David was all alone in the hospital with "that thing," as Marcia called it, growing in his head. Julia was in the kitchen pouring boiling water for tea when she heard the crackle of what could only be the pages of a photo album being turned in the next room.

"Would you mind grabbing my glasses, hun? I think I left them on the counter."

Julia brought the specs out on a tray with the hot tea, and they curled up on the couch together, looking at photo albums. They laughed at David's pictures when he was a young boy and commented on his evolution through adulthood. "Paul and I have always suspected that he was older than they said," Marcia said. "The growth chart they used was based on Caucasian standards. I think they underestimated the age to the children's advantage, to make them more attractive for adoption. We all know that the younger they are, the better their chances are of being adopted. In fact, this just came up the other day, when we told Dr. Levine about how we had gone about testing the validity of David's memory flashes. We think that David was small for his age, plus he was speech-delayed. He might have been close to four when he was found, which would explain how he could remember so much. It would mean that he crossed into a kind of maturity, where his memories were being linked to language."

In the meantime, Julia was doing the math, remembering David's argument that he was too young for marriage. "That means that he might be up to two years older than he thinks," she said, amazed. "He's probably actually my age, thirty-four or even older . . ."

Marcia smiled a little and shook her head. "That's right. He's not the spring chicken he pretends to be."

She turned the page and there he was on Holly's wedding day, looking like a feral cat that had been dragged out of the woods and bathed, perfumed, and dressed in a tux. "Look at my boy," intoned Marcia. "He's miserable in every picture where he's had to dress up." She held up a photo of David making his first communion. "He's scowling in every picture. I could have killed him. And look, he looks exactly like that at Holly's wedding, only taller." She chuckled softly and shook her head.

Julia sighed. "You can't force him into anything. Even if it's for his own good."

Marcia eyed Julia over the top of the spectacles, but said nothing. She turned the page and they skipped over the ceremony photos, to get to the reception where she knew they would find pictures of a jolly and relaxed David, his tie off, shirt unbuttoned, sleeves rolled up. There was a photo of the siblings lined up: David in the middle, his arms around Taina, Holly, and Adrian. "Ray was the one who couldn't get time off work," Julia recalled.

Marcia said, "Paul and I wish that we had tried harder to gather them when they were kids. All of them—not just Adrian, who was always David's first choice. I don't think any of us parents realized how much they needed each other. Heck, I don't think we imagined that *we* would ever need each other as parents. I've talked to Natasha more in the last month than I have in my whole life." She pressed a hand on Julia's, to demonstrate the next comment was on the side. "I had no idea Taina had had so many emotional issues as a child. I guess we got lucky with David."

"So how do *you* feel about David pursuing his biological roots, Marcia? Has he talked to you about it? He seems to be getting more serious about searching. You know, after he gets better."

Marcia looked back toward the hall, as if David could overhear. She turned back to Julia, who saw her for the first time in her life; really saw Marcia. Her skin was lacking in freckles or any markings but was deeply lined at the forehead and between her nose and mouth. Her eyes were hazel, with flecks of a thousand shades of yellow, brown, and green. Irish eyes.

"I told him it was okay with me," she said.

"No, I mean how does it make you *feel*? I guess I want to know that it's not hurting you."

Marcia's eyes grew large. "Why that's the sweetest thing I . . ." She paused. "When David was small, I definitely would have felt threatened. But that time came and went." She looked down. They were quiet for a moment, each lost in thought. After a few minutes, Marcia pointed to one of the photographs in the album and said, "Oh, this reminds me—a little something I remembered when I was reading a journal I kept after we adopted David."

"Tell me," Julia said, leaning forward.

"Well, it was the week before Palm Sunday and my mother was hosting a gathering of church ladies. They were in charge of making the palm crosses for the weekend masses. They were also supposed to be watching David while I ran out to do some errands. Well, the ladies got to chatting, and when they finally remembered to check on David, he had gotten into a bag of palm leaves. He had twisted all the palms into perfect crosses, you know how there is this certain way they wind the palm into an 'X' pattern around the center to hold it together? David had made forty or so of these, and kept doing it without looking up at them, like someone working an assembly line. We asked ourselves, where the heck would he have learned to do that?"

"In a very Catholic household."

"Yes, but think about it. Even children of extremely devout Catholics are taught to make these what, one once a year, right? He would have had to make an awful lot of them to have that kind of muscle memory."

"So you think maybe they lived in the fold of the church?"

"Something like that. And another thing. In my mother's

journal, a habit I was terrible at keeping up, I did write down that David once called for 'Miguel.'"

"Miguel," Julia whispered.

"He had a high fever when he was around seven or so. I came into his room and he was saying 'Miguel' over and over. I don't remember it, but it's written there in the diary. The adoption agency asked me to keep the journal during the first year that we had adopted David. But like I said, I was terrible at keeping it up. I wish I had more to contribute." She closed the photo album and turned to look at Julia. "I hope you kids do find something, even if it only serves as an interesting distraction from this awful cross that he's bearing." She clasped her hands together. "Ohhh," she sighed. "How I wish you two had married before all this." She shook her head. "You could've been the one to save his soul."

Julia shook her head a little bit. "Me?"

Marcia zipped the gold cross that hung by a chain back and forward across her chest as she spoke. "It says in the Catechism, 'the unbelieving husband is consecrated through his wife.' I looked it up because I'm worried. Even in light of this crisis, he refuses to accept Jesus into his life. And who can help him now? Your relationship ended and he won't lift a finger to save his *own* soul. He won't even admit he has one," she said wearily.

Chapter

12

David

There was video and audio track documenting my surgery. In it, one can see that the anesthesiologist's machines were beeping unperturbed. The EEG display proves that I was in a state of complete electro-cerebral silence. My head had been sawed open by the surgeon who did the prep work. Dr. Levine stepped in only to do the actual tumor removal. He muttered quietly to his assistant without looking up. The motion of his fingers was tiny and delicate, like an artist painting with his finest brush, he went over the same spot again and again. I read a profile about him in a magazine where he describes what goes on in *his* head during those grueling surgeries. He hopes that the scraping doesn't rob the patient of any major abilities, like speaking. The tiniest miscalculation on his part could trigger a hemorrhage or leave the patient mute. In the last day or two, he has undoubtedly spent hours in front of a computer viewing a three-dimensional diagram of my brain, plotting his every move. He can't just yank the thing out because it's wired to my brain, and so he must decide which vessels are feeding healthy brain tissue and which are feeding the tumor. All the while he knows that he won't get it all, that glioblastoma multiforme always leaves behind invisible seedlings, offspring left to fulfill the deadly mission of the parent.

Dr. Levine put chunks of my tumor in a flat dish. The staff around him eyed the moist contents of the dish nervously from behind their surgical masks. Someone made a joke about the cafeteria. Dr. Levine looked at the heart monitor, at the flutter of timid waves. Then he gave it one last scrape.

I would view the recording several months later. I would learn what my brain looks like from the inside. Logic dictates that it is impossible for the brain to contemplate itself, physically. So when I viewed the film, it violated some nameless law of nature that in turn produced strange consequences later on. Once I saw it, I had access to more crib memory. That's my theory anyway, and I never asked Dr. Levine to explain it because I know very well that he would be speculating—they just don't know everything. But it's obvious that the scalpel's intrusion exposed neuro-data which I retrieved months later. As Dr. Levine prodded at my brain tissue, it was as if he altered the status of a neuro-data file from "inaccessible" to "accessible." The memory would sit, albeit inactive, until my brain came back online.

When the anesthesia began to wear off, I would smell the rain coming in through a broken window, feel the agitation of the wind on my skin, and see the thick clusters of coconut palms. The palms were storm-blasted and bowing down before a darkened sky, cowering, reverent, submissive. A woman's long skirt filled with air and flapped around like a bird, and I watched her struggle to close a window. There was broken glass all over the surface of a twin-sized bed. I looked down at the floor and saw a small coconut—just a big seed, really. I picked it up. There was a blonde woman, blue-eyed. She took my hand and spoke to me in Spanish.

While the camera recorded the image of me being wheeled off to the ICU, the blue-eyed woman strummed at a guitar. Now we were in a room that was quiet and safe. She looked at me and said, *"En Inglés . . ."* then she began to sing, "How many roads must a man walk down . . . before you call him a man?" She patted me on the knee. "C'mon, Javier." She continued, "The answer, my friend, is blowin' in the wind, the answer is blowin' in the wind."

My brother always materialized where there was music. Sure enough, a few seconds later, I heard his bones clatter against the tile floor next to me. His eyes were big and round and shiny and he pointed at the guitar and then at himself. She took him onto her lap and began to show him the strings. She continued singing, looking at me, "How many years . . ." She nodded, prompting me. I was shy, so I signed, like she taught me, *I am afraid*. Outside, the wind was bending the branches and the rain was pelting against the window. She put her arm around my shoulder and I was instantly comforted. "When you can't talk," she said, "you can always sing." She looked back down at the guitar. "What's the matter with you guys? You want to sing *en Español*?" She made a face. "Aren't you sick of *'de colores'*?" She was floating, fading, dispersing like smoke. A new screen opened up in my consciousness.

"Can you tell me your name?" someone was asking. I was confused. Was I a boy or a man? I was both, for a moment, and I slid back to singing with Adrian and the woman. Yeah, come to think of it—I *am* sick of *"de colores."* I opened my eyes. "What's your name?" Two voices now, more insistent. What is my *other* name? My adult-name? My mouth was dry, my lips stuck together. All that came out was a croak at first, so I cleared my throat. The blue-eyed woman poked my rib and said, "Sing your name." She prompted me: "Fe fei fo . . . Banana fana fo . . ."

I clear my throat again. "Fana-fo . . . favid." The vibration in my throat felt good. "David. David bo-bavid. Banana-fana-fo favid. Fe-fei-mo-mavid. David."

The clipboard fell out of Dr. Levine's hands onto the bed. "Well aren't *you* the show off!" I didn't need to read any magazine article about him to know that he was experiencing a colossal sense of relief. He had this huge grin on his face as he turned to my father. "Twenty years of neurosurgery and this is a first. I've never had a patient come out of brain surgery singing 'The Name Game,'" he said in an oddly high-pitched voice.

"You're *good*," a nurse said.

"You're the best, Dr. Levine," said another.

"Thank you," said my mother, her hands pressed together.

Dr. Levine's face flushed and he struck a brooding, serious look. "Thank you for your confidence," he said with a little bow and busied himself with a monitor, but it was obvious that he was damn pleased with himself.

My head felt enormously puffed, as if it had recently contained a series of small but hot and spastic explosions, like a bag of popcorn. Julia was standing next to my parents, at the foot of my bed. I felt a sharp empathy for her as I imagined what I must look like all bandaged up. Was it my nausea or hers that clenched at our stomachs as our thoughts merged into one and we both thought, *Dear God, who is this poor bastard?* My eyes found hers and she smiled weakly. "Hey," I said.

"Hey," Julia replied.

"Sorry to give you all such a fright," I said, meaning it figuratively. But then her eyes rolled up and I watched her slowly slump forward. She slammed her chin on the footboard of my hospital bed and hit the ground with a loud thud.

13

For the most part, his answers were perfect: "I'm at Memorial Sloan-Kettering. I just had brain surgery. I live at ten-fifteen Orange Avenue in New Haven, Connecticut. I work for the State Department of Forestry Services." He looked at his parents. "My mother is Marcia, my father is Paul." He even answered the trick question correctly, "I don't currently own a pet but I would like to have a dog."

Julia couldn't get past the foot of the bed. Although David's head was bandaged, she could see some of the black stitching poking through, like barbed wire. A rivulet of blood had dripped down and dried on his forehead and they had failed to wipe it. It reminded her of the crucified Christ. She realized that up until that moment, it had all been theoretical. David had dismissed the surgery as "just a mechanical problem" and she had believed him, apparently, and had been in complete denial, all along, of the physical reality. She had believed, down deep, that Dr. Levine's occupation was similar to that of the cable guy, a technician with a master key who opened a neat little box where he might cut a few fried wires, tie it all up, and leave a bill on the table. No, she had not envisioned the horror of what had actually taken place.

The thought of getting any closer to the bed made her stomach do a quick flip. Her head rushed with dazzling lights and she heard a loud ringing noise. She felt sick and afraid. Then, there was blackness. Pain. Her chin.

She woke up on a vinyl couch. On her right was a nurse jamming smelling salts under her nose and pressing a bag of ice against her chin, which made it hurt even more. Another nurse reached over her to wrap and pump up a black pressure sleeve. The room was full of people in scrubs, but now three nurses were attending to Julia.

"I'm sorry," Julia whispered when Marcia passed a hand over her forehead. "I'm so embarrassed." Marcia squeezed her hand and called her "darling girl." But all Julia saw was the disappointment in Marcia's face. Julia had failed. If she was a coward, so be it. She had no choice in the matter of tolerance. Sue Lorens, the ten-year survivor's wife, had failed to mention the possibility of passing out cold as part of the "challenge." Julia just wanted to go home.

The staff kicked them out of the ICU long before Julia felt better, so Paul and Marcia followed her to a small sitting area nearby. Marcia sat across from Julia, while Julia lay prone on a couch. Paul waited near the door, arms folded, as if standing guard.

"Where's Adrian?" Julia asked suddenly. "And Taina?"

"Taina's on her way," Marcia said. "And Adrian will get here in the morning. He had a contract to play at ten o'clock tonight at a big hotel in Miami Beach. He has a red-eye out of Miami into JFK."

"Marcia, do you trust him?" Julia asked. "With your son's life?"

Marcia raised her chin a little. "I understand that David doesn't want us to ever have to make the decision to take him off life support." Her eyes filled with tears and she looked away. "But," she paused to dab at her eyes with a tissue, "I trust David to make the best decisions for himself at this point. That will change, of course, as the disease progresses. But if he trusts Adrian," she made a fist, "then I'm going to trust Adrian."

Julia nodded. "I've only met him a half-dozen times before, but he seems like a solid person. I can't relax until he gets here, since he's the, you know, the decision-maker."

Marcia put her hands out in a gesture of uncertainty. "David was sent into our keeping, Julia—you, me, Paul. Don't worry that you're no Florence Nightingale, honey, there are other people who can handle the medical stuff. You, you have another role. You and I both know that David was attracted to your family roots, to the presence and stability of your life, but that he really wasn't investing himself into the relationship. He never thought beyond the here and now and he was always trying to wiggle his way out of emotion, commitment, and vulnerability, especially with women. A few days ago he talked to me about how much he loves and admires you." She put her hand over her heart. "I was stunned. He never talks like that, Julia. You have opened him up."

Taina arrived at the hospital about an hour later, but they weren't welcome in the ICU, so they went down to the cafeteria and had dinner. After they ate, the conversation turned to heredity, and Paul told Taina that none of the others had to worry about brain cancer because according to the research, the disease wasn't genetically linked. When Paul got up to get some dessert, Taina leaned in and said, "When we were girls, Holly and I scoured our bodies for genetic similarities. We literally stripped naked and went inch by inch. We compared every last mole, bump, and freckle. We compared our earlobes, our fingernails, and the shapes of our toes, we measured the circumference of our knee caps, the length of our eyelashes, grimaced into mirrors to compare our teeth. We were desperate to find a similarity." Marcia and Julia looked at each other. They didn't bother to ask if she had found any. "Not a thing." Taina bumped the top of the table with one finger, as if she were delivering some startling news. "Which is fine with me," she lowered her head. "Don't tell her I said this, but my sister has the most hideous feet I've seen in my life. The little toes kind of cross over the big toe like this." She demonstrated with her fingers. "I don't know why she insists on wearing sandals," she said, and plumped her shiny lips.

Marcia's haunted-looking eyes brightened for a moment. "Are they that bad? I'll have to notice Holly's feet next time," she said, looking at Julia.

"I tell ya," Taina continued. "She should cover up those suckers. Hide them in orthopedic boots till they decide to behave. You know the kind that lace up to the knee? I'd lock 'em up in those kind of boots and throw away the key." She tossed imaginary keys over her shoulder.

Julia chuckled. "Your children will have ugly feet, you know that, right?"

"If Holly and I are biologically related . . ." Taina shook her head. "I just pray to God that those feet genes don't follow me."

"I'd say you're definitely mean enough to be real sisters," Marcia said.

"I don't know what to think," Taina said. "I know we look nothing alike, but we keep thinking that our children will hold the answer, you know? If my child has ugly feet then, there you have it, we're blood. And if Holly could produce a daughter that wasn't flat-chested, it would only be because I'm their aunt." She looked left, then right, then passed a hand over her ample bosom.

Julia raised an eyebrow. "Holly's boys don't even look like Holly, much less you."

Taina pretended to look shocked. "Really?" she said. "Ha! Is that unfair or what? Here Holly has kids because she wants to clone herself and the three of them look exactly like Erick. Red hair, pale skin. Freckles. All of them look like Ron Howard. Ahhh. God has a sense of humor."

Marcia chuckled this time. "Heavens, that *is* rather unfair."

Julia glanced at Taina and gave her a secret thumbs-up and a subtle nod for succeeding in making Marcia smile. If it registered as such, she didn't know, but Taina kept up her chatter, and her presence that day was a like breath of fresh air.

"Don't tell her I told you this either," Taina continued, tapping her nails on the table. "Holly wants a fourth kid. She's hoping that if it's a girl, maybe the Latino influence will come through." Taina held up her hand and pointed at her starfish. "In the meantime, this is all we've got. I've been trying to convince her to get one, but she held out." She sighed. "But when David got sick she wanted one all of a sudden." Her smile faded a bit and she looked away.

"What's happening to David can rock anyone's foundation," Marcia said, shaking her head, slowly sinking back into her worried state. "I admit that I am just now starting to appreciate the significance of the bond that you kids have with each other." She wrinkled up her nose. "But I still don't approve of tattoos."

"I'm not a fan of tattoos either, Marcia," Julia said. "For the most part, they're faddish and silly, something people do to prove they're cool. But *these* tattoos are different." She took

Taina's hand and held it up to Marcia, as if it were something independent of Taina's body. "Taina said it herself. In biological terms, this tattoo is a stand-in for DNA. She put Taina's hand down. "It's deeply intuitive. Socially, it's the equivalent of a shared last name, which they've never had. Anthropologists would call it a tribal marking. Historians would equate it to a family crest or a coat of arms. As Catholics, Marcia, we know that symbols of belonging are very important and extremely powerful."

Marcia nodded, and pulled out a gold cross on a chain from inside her shirt. She looked at it; then she held it up for them to see. Julia pulled a similar one out from inside her shirt. She leaned forward and tapped it with Marcia's.

"Let's hope there's some magic in that," Taina said softly. "Because we need a miracle."

Chapter

14

The day after the surgery, Julia went to work then drove back to New York when school got out in the early afternoon. By then, Adrian had been watching over David for sixteen hours straight. He seemed like an entirely different person from the last time she had seen him, eight months before. His edgy-coolness was gone. He was wearing baggy Levis and a long-sleeve cotton t-shirt with a pizza house logo on it. His eyes were bloodshot, his hair was sticking up on one side and he had razor stubble. David was asleep. They stepped out into the hall to drink the coffee she had brought for both of them, peeking into the room now and then. Adrian told Julia about the "sad, pathetic" way he learned about David's illness from Veronica, the ex-girlfriend reporter, whom Julia remembered.

Something about Adrian had always rattled Julia a little. He was cosmopolitan, confident, self-possessed, and handsome, especially when he smiled. But his allure was something darker, a mysterious and unsettling quality she found hard to define. Julia always got the feeling that he knew something she didn't, and so she was never entirely comfortable around him. Faced with the prospect of hours of idle time with him, she honed in on the one thing about him that she liked the most: the fact that he adored his dad.

They chatted easily for close to an hour, first about his father, Reinaldo, who still lived in Puerto Rico. Julia had heard the other siblings rave about what a great man he was. "I grew up surrounded by deadbeats, but it has provided me with heaps of material for my songs," Adrian explained. "I think people relate to them because they're gritty and real. But I wish my dad wasn't so . . . generous," Adrian confessed. "He gives away every last shred of time and money he has. Whatever people need, he gives. That always left very little for us, and I think that some of those people don't deserve it. People use him." Next, he talked about his mother, whom even David knew little about, and who had divorced Reinaldo when Adrian was twelve. He told Julia that she lived in Spain now, and that he had seen her briefly during his last trip. Julia inquired about his life in Miami and the progress of his music career, and told him that she loved his music, that she had studied enough Spanish in school to understand and appreciate his lyrics. He smiled, turned his face to one side and asked her to name one song. Without hesitating, she said, *"Tenemos Que Hablar."*

He raised his eyebrows. "So you really do listen to my music."

"You're testing me?"

He shrugged, smiled out of one side of his mouth. "I like to know who's blowing smoke up my ass." When he saw the look on her face he smiled broadly and winked at her. He steered the conversation to her life and she told him about her own father, who had died four years earlier, after a massive stroke. "He was a good man," Julia said, "but he was closer to my two brothers. I apparently ruined my relationship with him by becoming a teenager." Adrian leaned closer. "He was headmaster at a private school for girls," she continued. "We were inseparable until I was about twelve. After that, he always spoke to me with a turned head, hands always engaged in fixing something in the house, watering plants or making a sandwich. I think he lost interest in me, or perhaps became distrustful of who I might become—presumably a woman, like so many of the girls at his school. I think he thought that young women were unpredictable, beastly messes, and he couldn't stand to think that I was one of them."

Adrian blinked. "Women *are* beastly, unpredictable messes."

"I guess."

He reached over and mussed up her hair at the crown. "Aw, I'm kidding. You're the exact opposite of a 'beastly mess,' Julia, and you know it. I'm sure that your dad was very proud of you." He gave her an over-the-imaginary-bifocals look. "I'm sure that beautiful daughters are a huge pain. You probably stressed him out with all your parties and boyfriends."

She nodded. "I tried."

"Kidding aside, Julia, I'm sorry that you lost your father so soon. That sucks."

Julia sighed. "Strangely enough, I feel him all around me, so no, I don't actually miss him. What I do wish is that we had been closer when he was alive, so we could stay that way now that he's gone." She threw her hands up. "I don't know if that makes any sense."

He narrowed his eyes. "Yeah. It does. If you reach this level of closeness," he lifted a hand over his head for a moment, "then it can stay that way forever."

"Exactly. I think you've reached that with your dad." She unfolded her arms and took a deep breath. "Hearing you talk about your dad, in the context of this . . ." She gestured toward David's hospital room. "I don't know why I'm telling you this stuff. I've never even admitted it to myself before. But there it is. I'm disappointed in that relationship. It could have been more. And the opportunity to improve it is gone, and that hurts."

"Believe me, I understand." He tapped at his heart. "David's crisis is making all kinds of crap float up for me too." Julia never got to hear what that "crap" might be because out of the corner of her eye, she saw Dr. Levine marching up the hall with his entourage. They went into David's room, and when they came out they informed Adrian and Julia that David had developed an infection and was running a slight fever. He ticked off the steps he would be taking over the next twenty-four hours, and gave them permission to go back in after the nurse finished up. Julia fished a small notebook and pen out of her purse and asked him to repeat the specifics, then did the same with the nurse, writing down all the details and flipping back to her previous notations. "I have to repeat this clearly and accurately for the O'Farrells," she told Adrian.

They were alone again in the hallway. Adrian said, "Look, Julia, I know that my brother wishes that he had behaved differently." He tilted his head in the direction of David's door again. "He disappointed you too."

She shrugged. "Water under the bridge."

Adrian closed his eyes for a couple of seconds and hung his head. "I have to tell you something, Julia. Up until today, I was afraid to see David. I was literally terrified. But I had to come, of course. And now he's my hero," he said. "And frankly so are you. You've been at his side from the moment you got back from your vacation. Taina says you passed out cold when you first saw him in the ICU. And here you are. He disappointed you, but you don't have the heart to disappoint him."

She chuckled bitterly, covered her eyes, and said, "I'm terrible at this, Adrian. I just figure it sucks less than having a brain tumor." Adrian put his arm over her shoulder briefly, and gave her a reassuring pat. Wanting to change the subject, Julia said, "So if you think I'm such a good old gal, why'd you feel the need to test me about your songs?"

He gave her a bashful look. "I figured I'd catch you in a little white lie," he said. "You look like someone who sticks to gringo rock." He bobbled his head from side to side, as if to dislodge the name of a band. "Dave Matthews?"

"You think I'm a provincial Yankee."

He made a face like he was seriously considering the question. "No . . . just a goody. What I mean is . . ." He squinted, like a fortuneteller struggling to read an aura. "Do you recycle? Pack a lunch everyday? Floss? Check the fire alarm batteries on a schedule? Are you in bed by ten every night?

She burst out laughing. "Yes to all of them. But for your information, I love hip-hop and rap. And reggaeton."

"Seriously?"

"Sure. I don't limit myself. And I'm pretty sure I can whip your butt when it comes to Latin American history."

Adrian grinned widely and shook a finger at her. "Now it's you that's underestimating *me*. Bring it on."

She rubbed the palms of her hands together. "You got it. This summer."

Suddenly his smile faded. He was pensive for a moment before speaking again. "Hey, I know that you were David's first choice as 'decision-maker,' and that you refused the role. I just want you to know that it does mean a lot to me. I'm his brother, after all. So thank you." He opened his arms and she stepped into them. She noticed, fleetingly, that he smelled faintly of cologne, something David never wore. She was thinking about how different the two brothers were, when, from down the hall came a bright flash of light. A man with an enormous zoom lens had just taken a photo of them. He disappeared so quickly that Julia wondered if she'd seen him at all. She figured she'd end up on the cover of a hospital fund-raising brochure or a newsletter or something like that. She turned back to Adrian and saw that he had a worried look on his face. She realized then that he wasn't just cool, he was complex. Suddenenly, she liked him.

Chapter 15

David

According to Dr. Levine, I'm having a "fantastic" recovery. I don't see it that way, but apparently most people have a lot more complications than I've had, especially if they have other medical conditions, which fortunately, I don't. "You have the heart and liver of a bull," Dr. Levine joked. There was a blood clot in my lungs followed by several infections. But in the strange and twisted world of brain cancer, this somehow qualified as "fantastic."

Days dimmed into night and the mornings turned over and over again. People came and went, came and went, while I remained in a kind of netherworld. After eight days I still couldn't read. I looked at a page of text and it was just a series of letters from our alphabet that meant nothing to me. I had some right field-of-vision problems. But there was hope, at least, in the fact that my brain was still swollen. Some or all the cognitive issues *could* go away as the swelling went down. In the meantime, my brain was behaving mischievously. As it turns out, language is encoded by sound for storage. So when the brain can't access a word, it selects another word that sounds similar. Like the time

I was discussing medical issues with Dr. Levine and I referred to my stern-faced, silver-haired cardiologist, Dr. Butterfield, as my "partyologist."

"Tom Butterfield is an excellent heart man, but as a partyologist?" Dr. Levine turned to his physician's assistant. "I just can't picture Tom Butterfield in a Hawaiian shirt passing out tequila shots, can you?"

The PA shook his head. "No. And I hope I don't *ever* have to see Dr. Butterfield do the Macarena."

The next day, my dad was with me when my day nurse came in with a tray full of what looked like hypodermic needles. She was the beautiful one, but that didn't even register, I just didn't want to get poked anymore. I pointed at the metal tray in her hands and asked her if she was planning on giving me an erection. My dad blushed violently and covered his mouth. "*Injection*, my son meant *injection*," he said over and over as his body shook with laughter.

After the surgery, Taina gave me these "Caribbean Lagoon" pajamas and a bathrobe to match. The funny thing is that I absolutely loved them because they were lined with the softest, warmest flannel on the planet. They always keep it so damn cold in hospitals. Everyone who came to visit was highly amused by my "pimp" pajamas. The pretty nurse came to check on me while the guys from work were visiting me. They took one look at her and that was it, they started calling me "the Hef." The PJs turned out to be a bottomless source of jokes and a welcomed icebreaker, especially for some of the guys who didn't know what to say. In fact, three of my hiking buddies rode me so hard about my "fabulous" pajamas that they managed, in an hour's visit, not to make a single reference to the fact that I was sick. And I'm totally cool with that. They came and that's what counts.

Laughter did me good and cleared my head. And when the fog lifted I noticed that Julia was writing down every word the doctors said: what times I got my meds, when I ate, when I peed. She wrote in this pink notebook, with her brow furrowed, biting her lower lip. "What's that little blue pill for?" she asked. "Didn't he get two last time?" and "Aren't they going to hang up another liter of IV fluids before that one runs out?" and "When is he supposed to get his next dose of pain medicine?" Once, she even stopped me from drinking someone's urine sample off a cart when I thought it was apple juice. I thought of all the pills I took without thinking twice, how I just submitted without question. I took Julia's left hand in mine and ran my fingers along the length of her ring finger. I said, "You just wait till I get out of this mess, Julia. I can't wait to show you how much I love you." Her response was always vague or dismissive: *you just worry about getting better* or *I know you would do the same for me.* Then she'd do something nice, like hum a tune or read softly to me, even though for the most part, I only wanted silence. So I'd close my eyes and drift off, and there would be that feeling of a window opening, a pop-up on the computer expanding across my vision, the audio kicking in. Piano music.

The blonde woman took my hands and we sang, *"Ah-beh-cé-ché-dé-eh-efe-gé-hache-eee-jota-kah . . ."* We went through the whole Spanish alphabet that way. When we were done, there was clapping. I turned around. Behind me were more children, maybe a dozen, sitting on the floor. "A-E-I-O-U," I said, and the children all shouted back, *"¡El burro sabe mas que tú!"* We dissolved into giggles. The screen closed and I was back on the homepage of my life. I couldn't have said how many days passed like this before they let me go home, but it was a bunch. Later, I learned that I had been in the hospital for ten days.

•　　•　　•

At home, I was tired and too over stimulated to even watch TV. Turns out watching TV isn't such a passive activity after all. When my relatives came over, I felt like I was at a rock concert. Eating and mundane tasks like brushing my teeth and getting a glass of water required reserves of energy that I didn't have. I keep telling myself to be patient, but recovery was taking way too long and it made me mad. I was seized by rage at the smallest things, and I had tantrums, just like a little kid. The most pathetic one was when I threw a piece of pizza to the floor, enraged because my mother had forgotten that I never, ever, eat pepperoni. Even Julia saw my nasty streak. She was helping me wash my scalp in the sink, so I wouldn't get my wound wet. She was supposed to use the medicinal shampoo they had given me at the hospital. I shouted, "Not *that* kind!" as I slapped the half-empty bottle of Prell out of her hand. It clattered across the tile floor and landed quietly on the bath rug. She just stood there, stunned, while I hunched over the sink with my head full of the wrong kind of suds. In the bathroom mirror, I saw the effort in her face. I'm sure that she wanted to smack me upside the head with the hairbrush, which is exactly what I would have done. But Julia is the very definition of self-control. She put her hands up in the air, took a step back, said see-you-later, and went home.

At first, Julia came by the house every day after dinner. I was terrified to ask if she'd seen Jonathan, so I didn't. She reserved Friday and Saturday nights for herself and I suspected that that was when she stepped out of my world and into someone else's. I lay awake in bed, worrying that she might meet someone else, that she would stop coming to see me.

Chapter

16

In February, March, and April, Julia thought of cancer and work and not much else. She was in constant communication with a vast network of people, from David's close family members to acquaintances of acquaintances who offered hope in the form of e-mails about new treatments and stories of long-term survivors, or just jokes to cheer him up. Then, as the weather grew warmer, the hats began to arrive. Not knowing what else to do for David as he went through chemotherapy, people began to send them as gifts (presumably to conceal his balding head) along with cheerful notes explaining that he would need a good hat for the upcoming season of days spent outdoors. One friend brought him a brimmed, waterproof hiker's hat with an adjustable chin strap; another gave him a "packable" straw hat. He got an Irish tweed cap from his uncle and a baseball cap with a waving Brazilian flag courtesy of his old flame, June Jones, who was in the Amazon.

At David's request, Taina had phoned June, now on the biology faculty at Cal Tech. They had talked one afternoon, and since then, June had been sending cancer-fighting botanicals by the bushel. By March, the FedEx guy was showing up once a week with products from either June Jones or the Lorenses. David figured he had nothing to lose, so Marcia and Julia made "miracle" shakes and sprinkled kelp flakes on his pizza and tacos, especially since Sue taught them that tomato masked the taste very well. One day, David tried to convince Julia to try some lovely lapis-blue seeds that June had sent, seeds that to her looked like something you should wear rather than eat. He assured her that they were perfectly safe and "great for circulation." Unfortunately for David, June had included a note reminding him what they were for and urging him, as always, to check with his doctor before taking any of her botanicals. Julia's first reaction to his offer was surprise. She doubted very much that David had the energy to entertain the effects of an aphrodisiac. Then it hit her. For David, there was only the here and now. There was no time for contemplating the consequences of an impulsive act. So rather than point this out, she just decided to be on guard. She refrained from having any frontal contact with him whatsoever. In the moments that he broke down and talked about how scared he was, she hugged him from behind. She held him tight and let him know, by that gesture, that she stood behind him, not with him, on his journey. David's intense period of recuperation was no time to test their friendship. There was too much at stake.

In the meantime, Julia had made no progress in her quest to move on after their split. Twice she had kissed Jonathan Miller's scratchy face and twice it failed to stir up her libido. It just made her feel sad and empty. There was an early kind of grief unraveling inside her, and it had some of the strains of widowhood, since she and David had once shared a home and presumably, a future. There was also the anger and disappointment one felt in a divorce. She was in a kind of emotional limbo.

When the first of the daffodils began to bud, Julia saw two of her girlfriends for the first time in months. They took her to the movies, to see a comedy. A few weeks later, Julia invited them to her messy apartment for dinner on the condition that the menu wouldn't include anything super-healthy, certainly not fish or berries or green vegetables. Instead, Julia grilled the fattiest steaks she could find, mixed bacon with the mashed potatoes, dipped the corn in melted butter, and salted everything with abandon. They drank coconut rum and pineapple juice instead of red wine. One of her friends, a fellow teacher, presented her with a monstrously large chocolate cake. "Julia, David should eat like this everyday. The 'anti-cancer' diet is a waste. Think about it," she said as she dragged a finger through the brown glaze. "There are only so many cakes, beers, steaks, vacations, and games of strip poker you're allowed to have in a lifetime. He should be skydiving like the country song says. David should be drinking and feasting and screwing like a Roman emperor," she said, as she licked a dollop of chocolate off her finger. "His time is running out."

Julia held her chin up with her fist and looked into her friend's eyes. "That's basically what his doctor said. Although not exactly in those words," she said with a weak smile. "As for David's attitude about it, he goes back and forth," she said. "He buys a bonsai tree one day and calls old friends to say good-bye the next. He talks about having grandchildren and in the same breath he's wondering who will inherit his Wrangler. It's like watching a pendulum go back and forth, back and forth. Where it will stop? Nobody knows."

"Oh, but we do know," Julia's other friend, a nurse, said. "It's the *when* that's the question."

Chapter

17

David

Radiation therapy was a painless but creepy procedure, beginning with the waiver I was asked to sign absolving the practice of all responsibility if I ended up with brain damage. A technician put a soft, netlike contraption over my face and head, hit the gas pedal, and beamed God knows how many units of DNA-zapping photons into my head. One week after I finished radiation, Julia came over with steaks and chocolate cake and champagne to celebrate. I began a one-year high-dose chemotherapy routine, with a cycle of MRIs every two months.

Dr. Levine mentioned that a group of medical students would be viewing the surgery he performed on me. I asked him if I could see it and he said no. A few days later, Julia discovered a web link for medical students with video footage of brain surgery on Dr. Levine's university web page. It didn't require a password to view because the patient is anonymous. I confirmed that it was me by the time and date stamp visible at the bottom of the screen. But even that wasn't necessary because I knew from the quickening of my heart the moment the footage started up, that it was me.

I sat down to view it on the computer. I was completely mesmerized. When it was over, I must have slept for three days straight, waking up briefly to eat and use the bathroom. On the third day I sat up in bed and told Julia and my parents what I remembered. "Her name is Kathy," I said. "And she told Adrian and me that when we can't speak, that we should sing." I looked at my father. "I know I teased you about calling it all 'classified' stuff, but you're right, Dad. I remembered that this woman taught Adrian to play guitar. I think she protected us, but from whom or what I don't know." My dad pointed out that if I could harness the power of that access, that I could move my siblings from the precarious state of mystery into the power of knowing. They could finally control their fears and insecurities and build a new foundation. But I felt impotent, because there I was, in bed most of the time, nauseous and exhausted after each cycle of chemotherapy, barely able to move. I keep reminding myself that some energy would return, eventually.

My parents and I spent Easter Sunday with the Griswolds at Julia's uncle's house in Hamden. After the cheesecake with thimbleberry topping, the patriarch, Uncle Mick, announced that the family had come to an agreement. They would give me my own turn at the house and island in August. They were happy to enable the first reunion of the "starfish children" at the Griswold homestead. After the next chemo treatment, even as I was throwing up, I imagined this distant happy dream. There was so much work to be done in preparation. Go away, cancer, I thought. I don't have time for you.

Chapter

18

One Saturday in mid-May, Julia found David bawling, his head resting on his arm, his shoulders heaving violently. She put her hand on his back and asked him what was wrong. He said, "I need to learn Spaniel. And I can't." Julia looked bewildered, so he pointed to a stack of Berlitz Spanish audio books he had gotten from the library.

Julia said, "David, if you injured your ankle you wouldn't expect to ballroom dance the next day, would you? You'd need therapy; first you'd walk, then run, *then* dance. Learning a second language is like asking your brain to ballroom dance in high heels. It's not fair to ask that of yourself right now."

But David's dark mood was really about the news he had received that day: Dr. Levine had declared that the swelling in his brain was gone. This meant that his recall and reading abilities weren't going to get any better. His expressive aphasia was mild but permanent.

"I'm just so tired," he said. "I'm tired of trying. And nothing's happening."

"But David . . ."

"I'm so tired," he said. "Stop making noise. Please." He got up and heaved himself onto the daybed in the office. He barely made it, and one arm and one leg were hanging off the edge, so she pushed him deeper into the bed. His was a face of transformation, of pain, even labor, if that was possible. He was trying to stand in physical, mental, and spiritual defiance of what was happening inside his body. Each time he did this, he would need to remain without mental or sensory stimulation for at least twenty-four hours. His eyes were shut tight. He needed total silence.

Before she left, though, Julia rubbed his shoulder, like a mother encouraging a child. "Hey," she said excitedly, "you said 'I need to learn *Spaniel*' when you meant to say 'Spanish.' Just aphasia, right? But you know what I just realized, David? You combined the word 'Spanish' with 'Español' and you got '*Spaniol*.' At first I thought you said 'spaniel' as in the breed of dog, but that's only because I'm an English speaker. Your brain is compensating, David. It's smarter than you are. And now you're half-bilingual!" A soft snore interrupted her. His breathing was slow and deep. She touched a hand to his forehead, but his temperature was normal. She noticed, suddenly, that his skin was not its usual sallow gray, but rather, that he was glowing. His face and hands were bright and translucent, as if he was releasing a steady flow of soft, inner light.

Chapter
19

David

A neighbor volunteered to come every day for an hour to read me a copy of Lance Armstrong's memoir about surviving testicular cancer. Lance is my hero, and I studied his method, which was to commit to his future by bombarding himself with statements of faith in his survival. I loved that idea, so I start making long-term plans too. I sent my dad to the antiquarian book dealer to buy vintage, leather-bound copies of the poetry of Robert Frost, of *Walden* and Henry David Thoreau's journals and poems, and of Ralph Waldo Emerson's *Complete Works*, all of which cost big bucks. I'm not a huge reader of classic literature, but I love those guys because they're naturalists. I envisioned these essential works in my library when I'm an old man, so I acquired them as a way to build a bridge to my twilight years. I also bought a chess set. I called my financial planner and asked him to buy annuities. I'm building a tiny forest of bonsai trees. And I convinced my mother to let me have the diamond ring.

Julia had just left for the night. I was alone in my bed, thinking about our old bedroom, the queen-size mattress and box spring on the floor, the plain wood dresser, how she said she had to show me something in the Bassett showroom. We fought non-stop for a week over the decision to invest in "grown-up" furniture. I refused, of course, feeling it was akin to being dragged to the altar. The old adage "you made your bed, now sleep in it" couldn't be truer. There I was, lying in a twin bed, trying to recall what it was like to make love to Julia. What did her breasts look like? What did it feel like to push up inside her? I had no freakin' idea. Hell, I couldn't remember *ever* having sex. I scrolled through my mental little black book. There was Mary Smitty in high school, Lizzy Mancini freshman and sophomore years of college, June Jones junior year, and Elaine Freedman and a handful of others my senior year. A few stray cats after that, and then Julia. But it was like the memory was on lock-down. Classified! Was this a joke? The good stuff was a blur, cannibalized into the compost pile of unremembered things, with no med school video footage to help me through this one. Even watching porn didn't help. It was just gone.

But while my language and memory centers were clearly damaged, apparently my imagination was working just fine. Imagining must happen in the tough-as-nails frontal lobe, then, because I easily envisioned popping the pearly buttons off the black cardigan Julia had been wearing that night. I imagined myself carrying her upstairs and dropping her on the bed. The sheets weren't child-themed, but a dignified white. The bed a king. I lowered my face to hers. But before I got to do what I wanted, I tumbled, head-first, down into sleep.

When I reached the bottom of what could only be described as the rabbit hole of my subconscious, I remembered two large boys climbing into my crib. I saw the outline of their figures in the dim light, felt the mattress sink where they were standing. One climbed on top of me, the other, onto my brother.

A hand pressed over my mouth. Next to me, my brother cried out. I bit down deep into the bone of one of the boy's fingers. He screamed. A light went on. A pair of arms encircled my shoulders and I knew that I was safe—for now. And I understood then that this assault had been the final straw, the moment when someone decided that it was the time to get us out of there.

Chapter

20

In the last week of May, *People en Español* published an article with the headline: *"¡Crisis familiar para Adrián Vega!"* with David's illness as the hook. The by-line credited Veronica Mayorga. There was a photo, dated November of 2005, of Veronica, Adrian, David, and Julia at the Delano in Miami, with the hotel's signature white curtains billowing behind them. Adrian was dressed in jeans and a black jacket, his arms around Veronica and Julia. David looked freshly showered and was wearing jeans and a wrinkled navy blue polo shirt. Adrian recalled how hard he had tried to get David to dress up a bit, told him he looked like a frump, even offered him the pick out of a closet full of linen *guyaberas*. But David refused, arguing that "comfort trumps beauty." Toward the bottom of the article, there was a photo of Adrian embracing Julia in the hallway of a hospital. The caption read, *Adrián Vega comforts Julia Griswold, his brother's fiancée.* Several of Adrian's ex-girlfriends, most of them from the Miami area, were quoted as saying that the brothers seemed to "trust only each other and their immediate families." Adrian's publicist was thrilled. By the middle of the week, Adrian's download volume tripled. Adrian tossed the magazine in the garbage and waited anxiously for the week to pass and for the new issue to replace it on newsstands.

In mid-May, the O'Farrells needed help. They wanted to visit some elderly relatives out of state, and Julia was busy winding down the school year. Taina was traveling to spring fashion shows for work. Adrian had agreed to "David-sit" for a week. Julia was to pick Adrian up at Bradley Airport in Hartford. David was spending the day at home in the company of an old hiking buddy. He had had a dose of chemo the week before, so he was tired but on the way up, energy-wise.

Adrian was accustomed to the hustle of the airports in Miami, San Juan, and New York. Arriving at this quiet airport made for a striking contrast. Julia was waiting for him at the baggage claim. She looked stately even though she was dressed very simply in jeans and a white, long-sleeved blouse and a pair of riding boots. The combination of loose, blonde hair and equestrian boots gave her the air of a prep-school blue blood. But rather than allow himself to be impressed by her, Adrian chose to tease her, as an older brother would, by inquiring where she'd tied up her horse.

After a half-hour of waiting, Adrian discovered that his checked luggage (just an acoustic guitar and case), along with those of several other passengers, was on a flight that wouldn't arrive for another hour. They decided to wait it out at the airport hotel bar.

Julia ordered a glass of red wine and Adrian ordered a gin and tonic. Then Julia called the house and talked to David's friend, who told her that David was napping. She hung up and tucked the phone into a leather case clipped to her belt loop.

She raised her glass to his. "To time," she said, with a great sigh. "The only real commodity we have."

Adrian looked into his drink, full of sparkling bubbles and festive lights reflected from the bar. He held it up. "May we spend it well then." They clinked glasses and each took a sip, their eyes registering faint smiles over the rims of their drinks. Her gaze dreamily trailed the path of a departing jet. "I'm glad you're here," she said. "I'm happy to get a break."

As he drank, Adrian remembered how envious he had been when David appeared with Julia on that trip in Miami. How pretty, how dignified he had found his brother's New England girl. David had confessed, late one night, that while he loved and admired Julia, he wasn't sure if he was *in love* with her. Who could have guessed that she would one day become someone so vitally important to their family, a sixth sister, a partner and hands-on manager in David's care. What he had not known, but learned in the course of draining the gin and tonic, was that she and David weren't together as a couple anymore. That was the most remarkable part of it to Adrian, because when he broke up with someone, that was it. He could no more imagine nursing an ex-girlfriend back to health than he could imagine becoming a priest. That Julia was nothing more than just a friend now to David was baffling, but admirable nonetheless.

"So are you seeing anyone?" he asked casually, two friends arriving at an inevitable topic.

"You're spying for your brother. How sweet," she said.

"I'm not spying," he protested with a laugh. He tilted his head a little. "I'm just curious."

"Why, you got a guy for me?"

"Not a chance. We're keeping you in the family."

Julia confessed that she had tried several times to move on, but that her decision to help David through his illness didn't leave her much room to socialize. "How about you, Adrian," Julia asked. "Who's your latest conquest?"

He was totally stumped by the question, not because there wasn't a name but because there were so many. He had to pick just one?

"No one special," he said, and he wasn't lying, because the women he was dating were, in fact, equally beautiful, smart, successful, interesting. They illuminated the marquee of his life like rows of white lights in the night, all of them dazzling but indistinguishable from one another. And very much like light bulbs, his lovers were bright and then suddenly dull. They were replaceable, unreliable, fragile, and occasionally, cutting.

Chapter
21

It was time to start carting supplies to the house on Griswold Island. Julia's trunk was full of paper towels, cleaning products, bottled water, potting soil, and fertilizer for the garden. She had promised her mother that she would make a run out there, even though it really wasn't prudent to go alone. "What if something happened?" her father used to say. "Who would hear you scream?" On the way home from the airport she asked Adrian if he wanted to "preview" Griswold Island. This way she could unload the supplies without breaking her promise to her father never to go alone. Adrian agreed, and they picked up some fast food and drove to Branford. They parked at the Stony Creek town dock parking lot and Adrian helped her load the water taxi.

Adrian remarked that the chunky rock bases of the Thimble Islands reminded him of Maine, that he had the sensation of being farther up the coast than Connecticut. Julia explained that the Atlas Mountains in Northwest Africa fit neatly into Branford like pieces of a puzzle, and that they have granite exactly like Stony Creek granite, because those two places were believed to have been connected before the continents ripped apart.

Even from the dock, the Griswold house looked desolate and unkempt. The late Victorian had three stories and a cupola. Double-deck, wraparound verandas framed the first two floors of the house. The shutters were closed and the gray wood shingles were weathered. But the house maintained its old-world dignity, with its varied rooflines, gables, double chimney stacks, and cupola tower. It pointed up, cleanly and proudly, toward the sky.

Up in the gnarled old cedars, birds built nests and added their music to the cheerfulness of the timid sunshine, but the air was still chilly. Julia and Adrian wandered down the slate path that wound around the island, through small forests of sea grass and clusters of early-flowering bushes. Adrian peered closely at the unopened flower buds, twisted into tight little knots, and the tender yellow-green shoots in the trees. "Living in the tropics, you don't get a sense of seasons," he said. "I'm always amazed when I come up here."

The empty porches were strewn with sticks and dead leaves. Julia threw open the grand, creaky doors of the house. Adrian was behind her, carrying a wholesale-sized package of paper towels. They went from room to room, and he helped her open shutters and curtains and lift windows to let the air in. They had to push their shoulders against sticky doors to get them to open. In the great room, she pulled back the folds of the curtains and tucked them into a wall hook, like a girl tucking a strand of hair behind an ear. The sun flooded though the tall windows, and a beam of sunshine illuminated the grand piano like a spotlight. Adrian lifted the cover and turned his head sideways to test the sound. "Needs tuning," he said. Then he sat down and began to play "Piano Man" but the notes were off. He looked up at the open book of sheet music. "Someone was having a romantic night," he said. "'This Guy's in Love with You.' Herb Alpert. Nineteen sixty-eight. Harry Connick Jr. did a great cover in *One Fine Day*."

"Oh, will you sing it? I mean this summer, if I promise to get the piano tuned?"

"Deal," he said, then got up and roamed the room, looking at the items on the shelves and studying the artwork on the walls. He ran a finger over the leather spines of the family's history books.

"Just a bunch of dusty books about people who are, themselves, just dust," Julia said. "But among those tedious accounts of births, military careers, illnesses, and deaths there are these little bits of wisdom. So many of our soldiers managed to come back alive from Germany, France, Korea, and Vietnam, against all odds. And then they spent their last days sunning themselves out on the porch." She pointed to a window. "Some of them with pieces of metal still lodged in their bones, mercury in their livers, and the taste of blood in their mouths."

"Would that be one of them?" Adrian pointed to a yellowed human skull that was serving as a bookend on one of the shelves.

Julia laughed. "No. That came from one of the anatomy labs at Yale. One of my aunts worked there in the sixties. When they moved to a new building, the skull was in a pile labeled 'miscellaneous junk,' so she brought it home. It's been a part of the family ever since. Would you care to see our record collection?" The skull was forgotten the second Julia threw the lower cabinet doors open to reveal the family's vast collection of vinyl. Adrian made an exaggerated gasping noise. "A phonograph," he whispered, "I've never seen a real one before." He pointed at the contraption on the bottom shelf.

"The 1910 compact Victrola XI," Julia said. "It still works. I think we have some of the original 78s."

"Can I hear it?" His eyes were as wide as a child's. Julia stepped aside and let him pull the Victrola out of the cabinet, because she knew it was heavy. "Whoa," he said, as he strained to pick it up. He set it down and Julia wound it up with the handle, like her uncle had shown her. It only played about a quarter of a song before it had to be wound up again. Adrian chose romantic-sounding titles like "There's a Girl in Havana" and "Sugar Moon." "Too bad they all sound alike," Adrian said after a few minutes of listening. "That same prewar piano banging away."

"Try something else then." Julia pointed at the rows of records. "They're grouped by decade, and they stop at 1980. Anything after that is considered too modern for this house." She pulled one out and held it up for him. "Do you like the Platters?" Adrian took it from her, wound the machine and dropped the needle onto the disc. As the first crackly notes of "Only You" filled the room, he leaped up and offered his hand. Julia took it and they danced, each singing out loud, with his hand resting firmly on her lower back. He swept her around the room in ballroom high style, then dipped her to "*thrill me like you do.*" The notes got lower and slower and the song wound down completely. They stood in place, awkwardly, for a moment. "Bummer," Adrian said, staring down at the motionless turntable. "How can you dance if you have to wind the thing up every two minutes?"

Julia laughed. "You see? The good old days weren't always so good."

Adrian dropped back down to his knees and read the titles aloud. "'*La Marseillaise,*' 'I Didn't Raise My Boy to Be a Soldier,' 'The Girl Wears a Red Cross on Her Sleeve,' 'When Johnnie Comes Marching Home.'"

"You interested in war stuff?"

"Hell yeah. Especially World War I."

"Oh," said Julia, "then you'll definitely appreciate this." She walked across the room and opened the heavy doors to a large armoire, where she began to hand him American flags folded into triangles, several of them encased in glass boxes. "Vietnam, Gulf War, Korea, World War II, and the rest of them," she ran a finger over eight of them. "World War I. We sure took a hit with that one."

Adrian touched each flag and said, in a low voice, "When they hand the mother the folded flag, they always say something like, 'On behalf of the President of the United States and the people of a grateful nation . . .' Oh, it kills me because I don't think most people nowadays give those guys a second thought."

"You come from a military family?"

"Nah," Adrian replied. "My grandfather was a naval mechanic. Never went offshore, though. We used to love to watch war movies together. *Pearl Harbor* was the last one we saw together . . . What's this?" He reached deeper into the cabinet, sliding out an old ceramic wash bowl. It was full of men's watches.

"That's everyone," Julia said. "Not just the soldiers."

"Holy crap," he whispered. "This place is really something special."

"You won't believe how beautiful it will be here in the summer."

Without taking his eyes off the watches he said, "It's beautiful here right now."

"Yes. It *is* beautiful here right now," she echoed, unsure if there was a hidden meaning in that simple, indisputable truth. Even in the dimness of the pale spring light, it was indeed a stunning and mysterious place to be. She turned and looked up at his profile. He turned his head and looked her straight in the eye. She felt tiny, electric pinpricks, as if a school of fish were nibbling at the tips of her fingers, toes, inside her belly, and around her lips. He looked away, and the magic between them suddenly evaporated. All that was left was a sudden awkwardness. But it was done. Something inside her awoke, opened its eyes, stretched, and found itself cold and hungry.

On the empty porch, they ate the cold chicken they had picked up at a drive-through on the way back from the airport. They straddled the thick railing and looked out at the sea, which was all around them, choppy, gray, and irregular, slapping noisily onto the granite rocks below. As part of her house duties, Julia had brought her family's share of table wine. She plucked one out of the case and opened it. They drank directly from the bottle, which they passed back and forth. "Griswolds have simple taste in wine, thank goodness, especially since we drink so much of it over the course of a summer," Julia said, a little embarrassed by the quality. But Adrian said he wasn't a big wine drinker anyway.

"I couldn't tell the difference between a cab," he held up the bottle and looked at the label. "And a taxi."

She laughed. "That's definitely a taxi."

He ran his hand across the rail of the porch. "Julia, most people don't have this. This is a fantasy. You know that, right? You have this mini-version of the Kennedys in Hyannis."

"*Really* mini," she said, pinching her fingers together and taking the bottle from him with the other. "You won't see any polo trophies on our mantel."

"Well, I love it here," he said. "Even without the polo trophies."

"Maybe you'll come back soon," she dared, pretending to be fascinated by a passing boat but blushing violently. She thought, *whoa. That was bold.*

"I bet you say that to all the boys."

She laughed nervously. "Back in the day I did."

"And what 'boys' have there been in your life, Julia? What was going on before David sucked up six years of your life?"

There had been lots of boys, especially in summer. In the Thimbles, it was easy to fall into an outdoor activity with a stranger. She had dated the full range of personalities, from the son of a Wesleyan University provost to a cute loser who was in jail for holding up a deli. Several of her cousins had big, aching love stories attached to the Thimbles, but not Julia. Julia easily found plenty of guys to like, but rarely love. She had grown to care for a few guys, but not cripplingly so, and as much as she liked the idea of having great loves tucked away in her past, she didn't. She just had a handful of memories of heartache for people who wouldn't have been right for her in the end. And so far, it seemed, no one was ever right for her, not even David.

After lunch, Julia gave Adrian a tour of the upstairs, which was mostly unremarkable, rooms upon rooms partitioned into more rooms, decorated with cheap beach-motif bedspreads and knick-knacks from the dollar store. "As the family got bigger, we had to chop it up," she told him. "Some of the rooms don't even have a window. We're probably in violation of about eleven fire codes." She gave his arm a quick squeeze. "Why don't you help me decide where to put everyone this summer?"

They chose the two prettiest guest rooms for Holly and Taina; rooms with creaky, wide-plank floorboards and exposed beams, wicker furniture, lace curtains and Amish quilts, and double tub fixtures that offered a choice of fresh or saltwater. They chose smaller, less fussy rooms for Ray and Adrian. Last, she took him up to the master bedroom, with its views of the water on three sides. Julia opened a small door with an iron spiral staircase at the center. "The cherry on top is definitely the cupola," she said, but Adrian refused to follow her, citing claustrophobia. He scanned the room that Julia said would be her inner sanctum during the gathering. The bed was a king and he noted that this room had the only air-conditioning unit in the house. There was also the only piece of modern art in the house, a large canvas of watery blues that evoked a morning horizon. His eye was drawn to the small collection of nautical instruments on the mantel above the fireplace, just below the modern painting. He noticed a beautiful old barometer. The tip of the ornate needle was thin as the proboscis of an insect, and it pulsed ever so delicately, over the word "change."

David was standing by the mailbox at his parents' house. To Julia, the bloating around his face and neck seemed to stand out. His friend was just pulling out of the driveway, and she noticed that there was yet another car in the driveway. Once she parked, Adrian practically jumped out of the car. *"Flaco!"* he shouted and stepped forward to embrace David. The mystery car turned out to belong to Doug, Taina's soon-to-be-ex-husband. He stepped out of the shadows and Adrian shook his hand and then slapped his back with the other.

"Honey!" David bellowed at Julia. She pulled her head back and made a face at him. He had never called her "honey," even when they were dating. He made a big show of hugging her. It was obvious to Julia that David was feeling territorial because she had taken Adrian to Griswold Island.

Doug said, "I roused his sorry ass."

Inside, there were Styrofoam cups of coffee that Doug had brought. The guys dove into the couch and David unmuted the baseball game they had been watching. The room filled with the sound of a crowd cheering and Julia said her good-byes.

"Hey, Julia, thanks for the ride," Adrian said, and thumped his heart twice with his fist.

Chapter

22

David

Doug is the one who began to crack Adrian. Doug and I had been talking about my origins long before Adrian arrived. I had told him everything I could remember and Doug brought a letter he had received two weeks before, something he had pursued all on his own, because even professional locators wouldn't take our case. There was nothing to start with. He had a letter addressed to Taina from the post-adoption services unit that had arranged her adoption by the Brightons: "After reviewing your file, it appears that you were abandoned and that there is no other information regarding your birth family. Unfortunately, this means that there isn't enough information for us to begin an assisted search. The record states that you were found without any identifying information."

"No kidding," Adrian said, turning over the letter to see if there was anything on the back.

Doug said, "The guy who owned the *For Tuna* has been dead for ten years, so he's no help. A professional locator suggested I look into the more public venues like mutual consent reunion registries, websites, and DNA banks."

Adrian pressed his hands together and squinted. "What are the chances that our bio relatives are looking for us, eh? Or that they even know what the hell DNA *is*?"

Doug shrugged. "You never know. Traditional venues aren't going to help you, we've established that," he said, looking at Adrian. "All you have are the bits that David is remembering. I would say the next step is to get DNA siblingship tests. Just to figure out what your relationship is to each other."

"Not me," said Adrian. "Whatever you two find out you keep to yourselves. I don't want any part of it."

Doug sat back. "Too bad because there is one very obvious way of blowing the whole thing open."

Adrian blinked, very slowly, and looked up. "My private life is private, if that's what you mean."

"Any one of those Spanish magazines would love to publish your story. They love you already, and they have no idea that you're one of the 'starfish children from Mayagüez.' Your sales would skyrocket."

"I repeat. My life is not for sale. *Punto final*."

Doug looked at me. "You don't need Adrian. It was an international news story."

I sighed. "I won't do it unless we all agree."

"Good. Let's drop it then," Adrian said as he glanced up at the muted TV. "Where's the remote?" he said, as he patted the cushions of the sofa.

I turned to Doug. "Never mind that I have fucking brain cancer. Or that it's my last, dying wish."

Adrian threw his arms up. *"Ave Maria,"* he said, which is what Puerto Ricans say when they think you're being unreasonable.

"It's not like I'm asking for bone marrow, Adrian," I said, "All I'm asking you to do is to scrape the inside of your cheek with a Q-tip for Christ's sake."

Adrian didn't say anything for a moment, but I could see that he was working up to it. He found an empty can of soda on the floor under the sofa and squeezed and released it, so it made that *check, check* sound. Then he put down the can and reached for a framed photograph of the five of us, as kids, that was sitting on an end table. He held it up and said, "You know why it's important that we *not* look into the question of sibling-ship?"

"Ray?" Doug and I said at the same time.

"There's more to it than Ray getting a little 'thirsty' when he's upset," Adrian said, narrowing his eyes. "It's because choosing to be a family is hard work. If we're not related, then each one of us will feel less responsible for each other." He put the photograph down and looked pointedly at me. "David, be-cause of your situation, *you*—more than anyone—need the rest of *us*," he said as he clapped a hand over his heart, "to believe that you're our brother."

Doug cocked his head. "Are you suggesting that every-one will just go their separate ways if the group doesn't have common DNA? Or that no one will be attuned to David's health needs?"

"Not right away, but eventually, yes. It takes time and money and energy to maintain our uncertain family identity. One day Erick's going to say, 'Holly. How come we gotta drag our kids up to Connecticut? You're not even related to these people. For the same money we could go on a cruise.' And one day that's going to make sense to Holly. It's hard enough to split yourself between 'his side' and 'her side.' We all know that 'family time' is a huge imposition and a general pain in the ass. Do you really want to let us off the hook by getting our genes tested? Who needs us to maintain the sibling illusion more than you do, David?" Adrian was leaning forward and his eyes were moist.

He wasn't just being stubborn. I could see that this was a big deal to him.

"But it's our life story, not our DNA, that's our blueprint," I insisted. "And that part is undeniably shared."

Adrian shrugged. "That will erode," he said, "as the years go by."

"This is about your mom, isn't it?" I dared.

He lowered his head. "Adopting me was Dad's idea," he began. "And so when my parents divorced, my mom disappeared out of my life. She found a husband and had children of her own. Her bond with me grew weaker and weaker. When I was thirteen, two years after she left, I came down with pneumonia and was hospitalized. I kept expecting to see her, but she never came. Sure, she called and she talked to me every day but she didn't take the extra step to get on a plane and be at my side. Now, I hear from her once a year, at Christmas. All her time is for her 'real' kids." His voice sounded strangely small. I could see that he was in pain. I had always had a sense that he had contemplated, more than any of us, the reasons and the consequences of our abandonment. He was obviously carrying the burden of a second injury just like Ray, which explained his sympathy and concern for Ray. I could see how just talking about it was affecting him physically—the struggle underneath the shoulders, the muscles accommodating some sharp hurt within. "It's time to show you something," he said suddenly, looking at Doug. He lifted his shirt and pointed to a series of small, round scars on his belly and his back. "I had these scars already, when they found us."

Doug leaned in to get a closer look. Adrian twisted around to show him more of the small circles. When Doug looked up, he looked stunned. "Who knows about this?"

"Only David and my parents. Girlfriends notice them of

course, so I keep a couple of stories in my back pocket. My favorite one involves bow hunting," he said with a wry smile. "But you're a cop, you know what these are."

"They're cigarette burns," Doug said.

"That's right," he said. Then he pulled his shirt down and put his jacket back on. He sat back and folded his arms so the leather of his jacket creaked. He leaned over so one shoulder was touching Doug's, and he spoke while staring straight ahead. "To me, those scars scream *stay the fuck away.*" Then turning to me: "And you know what, guys? I think I'm gonna do just that." He parked his socked feet up on the coffee table, grabbed the TV remote, and ended the conversation by filling the room with the sound of the latest Coke commercial.

Chapter
23

Three weeks before the trip to Connecticut, Doug was waiting for Taina in their living room when she got home from work. "Don't worry, I'm not staying long," he said, holding up a hand. He dropped a manila envelope on the coffee table.

"What's this?" Taina asked. She still couldn't get used to seeing him looking so physically fit. Gone was the slight paunch resulting from too many rich lunches during his stockbroker days. He had lost weight and had a harder, more muscular look, which instantly triggered a flash of jealousy. Who was he trying to impress, anyway?

"Here are the results of a full siblingship test, Taina. Both your maternal and paternal DNA against David and Adrian. I lifted their coffee cups when I was over there. Just to answer the question for *you*."

Taina stared down at the papers, unblinking.

"Since there's no parental DNA to compare it to," he began, "It's not a perfect test. Even full siblings can have few or no genes in common. Anything over ten percent indicates a strong probability of some common genes," he said, "but neither of these scores are even close. It's all in the report." He snapped a finger against the envelope. "Your infatuation with Adrian isn't quite as incestuous as you might think," he said, his voice dripping with bitterness. "And you're not biologically related to David either; less than one percent chance. It's up to you what to do with that bit of information, babe. I've been talking to David about it over the last few months, by the way. He's given me the green light to help him find *his* origins. I'm not telling anyone but you about this test, and I prefer you not tell Adrian or David that I did this covertly. They should resolve the question as a group. A family, I mean."

Taina was mute. She couldn't even summon the word "good-bye" as he pulled the door closed behind him. When he was gone, she took a cab to Central Park. She sat on a bench and watched the dog walkers and the children, the working people and the tourists. She sat like that, until nightfall, then she went to a movie theater that played old movies at all hours. She knew that there was no way she was going to get to sleep for a long time. Days, perhaps. And if she dared sleep, behind her eyelids crouched a girl who screamed and covered her eyes but refused to run from the smoke that was rising up from the floor to engulf her.

Part II

Chapter

24

August

On the very first night at Griswold Island, Raymond grilled skirt steaks rubbed with sea salt. He manned the grill, with everyone else standing around watching, drinking, laughing. He filled the Griswolds' chipped cider pitchers with sangria. A piñata served as the table centerpiece, and after dinner he strung it up to a beam in the ceiling of the porch and handed Adrian a red-and-white bandana, which Adrian tied around Julia's head to cover her eyes. To Julia, the sounds of their voices became louder as Adrian spun her around. She felt her way around the porch, fingers gripping the edges of windows, jumping when her shoulders were tickled by the petals of a hanging petunia. She swung the stick around like a blind woman, and tapped her way across the porch. They laughed when she tripped a little and she could hear them moving around her. Someone said, "Whoa, watch that stick," and someone else shouted for her to turn around, turn left, no, the other way, and suddenly she was inside a pair of arms that were guiding her. She knew by the scent that it was David, even as he led her back to the edge of the porch, where she lifted the bandana and handed him the stick. They each took turns, and Julia thought that Taina drew out the task of blind-folding Adrian for a little longer than what was necessary. Finally, they broke it open and the treats rained down and they all dove on the ground, laughing and shoving each other and arguing over the biggest prizes, which were all sorts of un-usual candies, popcorn balls, and gag gifts that Raymond had brought with him from Arizona.

"I miss my boys!" Holly said, pressing a toy train to her heart.

"You do?" Taina asked, frowning.

"Are you kidding me? This place would blow their little minds."

"They would take us all prisoner," Taina said.

"We should have invited Erick to come too, with the kids," David said distractedly. "We didn't even think of that."

Taina sang, "Oh well, too late now."

Holly pointed at David. "That's a great idea, David. That would be wonderful. They could pretend they are pirates or Harry Potter or—"

"*Lord of the Flies?*" Taina offered.

"Do you mean it, David? Can I Julia? Oh, could we? Erick can jump-seat, so they could get here tomorrow."

David looked at Julia, and she said, "It's *your* week."

David nodded. "They're my nephews. They should be here."

Holly was already halfway up the stairs before David finished the sentence. A few minutes later, they saw her wade over to the big rock, waving her hands and shouting into her cell phone.

"You don't know what you've done," Taina told David, shaking her head.

"Yes, I do," he said, watching Holly from the porch. "But I'm gonna do it anyway."

·   ·   ·

The only espresso drinkers were Ray and Adrian—and David, who couldn't stand being left out of anything his brothers did. After dinner, they drank more sangria (except for Raymond, who had his signature seltzer and cranberry juice cocktail) and played charades for a little while. Julia abruptly ended the game and asked that they all help clean up the kitchen. When David wasn't around, Julia leaned in between Taina and Holly, who were washing wineglasses by hand in the sink. "I didn't mean to be rude by cutting off your game," she said, in a low voice, "but David was getting frustrated. He wants to keep up, but we have to be careful not to over-stimulate him. When he's tired, the aphasia gets worse and he gets pissed off. We have to make sure he rests."

Holly said, "Man, Julia, you're never off duty, even with two sangrias in you. It's like being a mom." She shook her head and looked down into the suds.

Taina held a thin, tulip-shaped glass up to the light, alternately rubbing the edge with a dishcloth and inspecting it again. "If it were me, I'd just keep on playing charades until he melted down in a puddle. He'd just have to tell me outright."

"Well, you're self-absorbed," said Holly matter-of-factly.

"Being unaware is not the same as being 'self-absorbed,' Holly. You're so damn judgmental."

Holly opened her mouth to retort but David wandered into the kitchen, collapsed into a chair, and began rubbing his eyes. Julia sprung up and said, "David. Bedtime." David smiled and put his arms out, as if he expected her to carry him up to bed. She pulled him out of the chair, almost toppling them both, then leaned down and whispered something in his ear that made him nod his head. She went to the refrigerator, handed him a glass of milk, and began dispensing an assortment of pills, which he popped into his mouth one after the other.

"I cooked," Raymond said, carrying in a pile of dirty plates. "Where the hell is Adrian when it's time to clean up?"

"Outside. Trying to get a signal on the rock," Holly called from the pantry, delicately opening the cabinet to replace the wineglasses. When she returned to the kitchen, she put her arms around Raymond. "We're always going to remember this first dinner here together. You did great, Ray." Ray parted his lips as if he was going to say something, but then just nodded. Julia leaned out of a window and shouted, "Adrian? Would you mind helping out with the dishes? I'm gonna tuck David into bed."

From outside they heard, "Coming." He walked through the kitchen door a moment later.

Ray arched an eyebrow and locked eyes with Julia. "How the hell did you do that?" he said under his breath. "He never listens to anyone."

Julia reached for David, but he made a face and pulled his hand back. "I don't need anyone to 'tuck me in,'" he said tersely. Then he turned and climbed up the stairs alone. Julia mouthed *he's exhausted*, and sprinted up the stairs behind him.

Adrian was sitting on the big rock, looking back at the house, listening to the water slapping the rocks. Chirping crickets replaced the daytime cawing of birds. He could hear what he thought might be a flag snapping in the darkness and the faraway sound of ropes and hardware clinking against sailboat masts. He figured it was around eleven, the time he was normally starting his workday in Miami. The earliest he could get to sleep was one o'clock. He had finished his cigar and was drinking a finger of cognac out of a plastic cup, refusing the cut-crystal cocktail glass that Julia had offered him. The house had one lit window hiding among the black leaves of a tree.

There was no moon, and except for the pub, the village had gone dark too.

He heard a screen door open and close. He saw Julia standing out on the porch. Was she looking for him? His heart knocked hard one, two, three times against his chest. He stood. "Julia?"

She turned toward his voice and walked across the lawn, then over the rocky bridge of smooth stones that connected with the big rock. He reached into the darkness and found her hand. He pulled her up to the rock. She wiped her cheek with the back of her hand.

"What's the matter? Is everything okay?" he whispered.

"Oh yeah," she said softly. "David was getting ready for bed when he found my uncle Charles's toupee in the closet and put it on. Oh . . ." Her voice got higher. "In the eighties, my Uncle Charles wanted so badly to look like Sylvester Stallone, but he was skinny and bald, and the hairpiece was too dark for his pale skin, so we hid it from him. Anyway, David just found it in a cubby hole in his room, and tried it on." She sighed and dabbed at her eyes with the sleeve of her blouse. "Lord, I haven't laughed that hard in so long." She took a big gulp of air, and her teeth shone in the moonlight. Then she looked up at the sky. "I love David, you know? The way a very old couple loves each other. Without the . . ." Her hand rotated a few turns. She let the word drop.

"A little early in life for that kind of love, don't you think?"

She snickered. "Sometimes he's just a guy and sometimes it feels like he's about ninety years old." She sighed. "Those medications . . ." She shook her head. "But you're right. It's too early in life for *me*. And after this gathering, I'm going to start to let go. That's why I pushed to get the house and to invite you guys here, Adrian, to hand over the reins. David is blessed with wonderful parents and brothers and sisters and even though I love him *like* an old wife, I'm not his wife, and I'm not old. I have to get on with my life."

"Of course," Adrian said. "Of course."

"Thank you," she said.

"No, *thank you.*"

Adrian saw that someone was watching them through a darkened window on the first floor. He could see Taina's distinctive hourglass silhouette, backlit by a light in the hall. Julia must have seen Taina too, because she immediately rubbed her elbows and said, "It's getting buggy out here. Let's go inside." They turned toward the house and Taina quickly disappeared from view.

Julia was about to jump off the rock, when Adrian held her back. "Wait," he said, "let me help you," and he jumped off first. Once on the ground, he offered both his hands, and Julia slipped her fingers between his as she stepped down off the rock. When they separated, their hands slid away from one another slowly, reluctantly.

Chapter
25

Taina lay in an ancient bed that she swore could speak. Each creak of metal and groan of wood had a human-like tone, as if the bed coils somehow mimicked the sounds of the generations that had slept on it. When she sat, it went *creep!* If she got up quickly it sounded like, *whoa.* She amused herself by sitting up and down, and getting the bed to exclaim, *whoa creep, whoa creep!*

The light from the pub at the Village of Stony Creek came through the window because the curtains were too thin. Inside the house, someone got up to flush the toilet. She could hear a wind chime come to life with a passing breeze outside in the garden, and Raymond's thunderous snoring three rooms away. She fetched a fan from the closet and plugged it in. Four hours had passed since she had laid her head on the pillow, and yet she was still awake. It wouldn't be long before the sun came up. She got up, threw on a bathrobe, and stepped out on the balcony. When she stood in the doorway, the edge of the balcony appeared to extend beyond the shore and created the illusion that she was standing at the bow of a ship that was sailing toward Long Island Sound.

She had to admit to herself that she would have enjoyed having Doug here tonight. For all their trouble at home, they were at their best when they could travel and enjoy the company of others. He complemented her role as the wild child; and he fit right in with the boys. She wondered what he was doing, a world away. The ribbed undershirt she was wearing to bed was Doug's. She crossed her arms around her chest. She wondered how many times, if any, he had tried to call. She opened her cell phone. Zero messages. Then she remembered that she had to go out to the big rock to get any service. She closed the phone. Why did she care if he called? They were divorcing. She pushed against the sticky bedroom door and creaked down the hall, down the stairs, out the door and stepped into the cool night. She walked barefoot through the creaky old house, trying to remember her way through the maze of halls to find her way outside. She passed through the kitchen and stepped out the screen door onto the back porch with the rock finger jutting through the floorboards and the pothole that was always filled with cold beer. Barefoot, she wound her way around the narrow gardens, realizing too late that she had walked over the brass lettering of the uncle's grave. The salty breeze stirred and she smelled seaweed and fish. On the rock, she sat listening to Doug's three messages: *I love you. Enjoy your time with your family. Let me know that you're safe.* She could have sent an e-mail or a text message, something brief to acknowledge or thank him for his concern, but she didn't. She couldn't.

She went back inside to retrieve the pack of cigarettes and the lighter she had left on the windowsill above the kitchen sink, and headed back out to smoke. But she saw that a dim light had been left on in the great room. The light was coming from a floor lamp with a heavy tapestry shade and a thick, dangling silk fringe. Taina went to turn it off, and was looking for the switch when she saw them. Her eyes scanned the room for a quick first impression. Adrian and Julia had fallen asleep. They were seated opposite one another with a coffee table in between them. But when she took in the details of the room, they hinted at a new and secret connection.

Adrian's head was supported by the scalloped edge of a wing chair, below a huge colonial painting depicting a late summer harvest. Two empty low-ball glasses and a bottle of cognac sat on the coffee table. There were books and maps and nautical instruments strewn about; there were piles of photographs and some very old-looking medals and military decorations on the table. There was a huge, footed globe at Adrian's side. There was a map on the floor with colorful pieces of beach glass placed in a pattern that seemed to track a journey across Latin America. But what was most astonishing was that Julia had fallen asleep with one hand curled around a brownish-yellow human skull. What kind of person, Taina wondered, could curl up with a skull and fall asleep? When she looked down, Taina saw that *The Griswolds of New Haven*, volume eight, was open to the page that archived Julia's birth. She remembered how Adrian had read it with admiration in his voice, as if it were a document that certified the quality of a gemstone.

Taina had never glimpsed the depth of her loneliness and insecurity until that moment. She felt herself lacking in the rootedness that Julia had in such absurd, vast quantities. Julia Griswold, she realized, was her complete opposite—blonde, with slim, athletic proportions, a cute sprinkle of freckles across her nose, and placid blue eyes that reflected a calm, nurturing spirit. But she also had a rare and impressive command of historical facts because her family had actually lived it. Who could compete with that? Their differences couldn't be more stark. Julia was formed from cool and transparent minerals, while she,

Taina, was made up of warm, dark, opaque matter. Taina suddenly recognized the perfect chemistry between Adrian and Julia, and it enraged her. She remembered what he had said the first day that they arrived, how he had sat at the piano and said, "So you finally got it tuned?" Julia had changed the subject. And David? She didn't know how her brother fit into that scenario but he was still talking like he was going to marry Julia. Taina was jealous, but also angry for David. Was Adrian capable of messing around with the girl their brother was so clearly in love with?

The lamp bathed the sleepers in a light that suddenly reminded her of the color of urine. She ran a finger over the top edge of the Griswold family history, lifting the page and pinching it between her fingers at the point where it was sewn into the binding. She pressed the book flat with her other hand. She began to pull the page, slowly, watching Julia's eyelids and Adrian's peaceful sleep. *Kkkk* the linen paper ripped away. When she held her breath, she could feel her heart bashing itself like a bat inside its cavity. She ripped some more. Julia stirred, and let go of the skull. It rolled over and turned its huge, empty sockets away, as if it were too upset to watch. *Kkkk*. Taina ripped the page out, stitch by stitch, as quietly and slowly as possible. Finally, the page came detached. She closed the book quietly, slipped the page into her bathrobe, took a step back and retreated from the room. She went back out to the big rock again, sat down, and lit a cigarette with her lighter. She clamped the cigarette between her teeth and squinted against the smoke. She looked over her shoulder once. Then she lit the edge of the page on fire. She tossed the burning paper toward the water below. A breeze caught it and it floated, yellow and bright, like a butterfly with wings of fire, gliding across the darkness. It crashed into the water and faded into the dark.

When she finished the cigarette, she felt calm again. Some great imbalance in the universe had been offset, if only by the weight of a sheet of paper. She went upstairs and slept deeply and hungrily, until she woke up two hours later, gasping for air and soaked in sweat and urine.

Chapter
26

Almost immediately, the guests separated into night owls and morning people. By seven-thirty, Ray had the coffee maker puffing steam into the air and egg sandwiches waiting to be eaten. Ever-present on the table were bowls of blueberries, cherries, pomegranates and the dreaded shaker of kelp flakes.

Ray decided that morning was when the house was most beautiful and spirited. Outside, pink and white hydrangea blossoms framed the edges of the windows. A lush green lawn surrounded the house and met the rocky edge of the island. Beyond the grass was the sea, where egg-yolk-colored sunlight rolled around the surface of the water like gobs of paint.

Morning was also when the ghosts stirred. Their presence was subtle but unmistakable to Ray, especially when he was alone. They were a warm and welcoming bunch. More than once Ray had seen a lace curtain part for him when there was no wind, just in time for him to see a boat full of girls motor by. When he bathed, he heard big band music from deep inside the plumbing, and there was the zingy scent of lemonade in the shower's mist. When he riffled through a particular lady's cookbooks, he got a whiff of roses in bloom even though there weren't any roses blooming in the garden.

The bedroom he was staying in had porch access with a spiral staircase leading to the yard on the side of the house where the dock was. This meant that he could get out of bed, and, in a series of quick steps reminiscent of a firehouse drill, he could be outside, with the sun bright and big in front of him. The dock, which seemed to extend into infinity, beckoned him. On the second morning at the house, the tide was high and the water was deep enough that he could dive in without a problem. At the end of the dock he raised his hands and plunged into the oblivion of silence and cold. There was the brief shock of salt to his eyes, then nothing. Above his head was the light and below was the brown murkiness and an occasional gray fish. He came up for air and got to work on his swimming. He circled the entire island, and when he got tired he did a leisurely floating-and-paddling combination, watching the Victorian from every angle. He pulled himself up on the dock and lay across the wood planks, soaking in the sun.

This was the first vacation of his adult life. Ray was a cook, not a chef, as his boss was quick to remind him. He worked one job to support himself, and held a second job to pay for the extras. He had little leisure time. Taking leave for ten days represented a huge financial sacrifice to Ray. And now that he had gotten away, he didn't want to return to life as he knew it. But what exactly, he wondered, was wrong with his life anyway? Sure he was over-worked, but he loved cooking. He was over-weight and lonely, but none of that changed here. He was still himself, only happy. It could have something to do with the fact that he felt valued for once. Julia had not counted on having so much help from him, and he could tell that she really appreciated him taking over the cooking. She was beginning to hand over more and more tasks; letting him drive, allowing him to pretend that it was *his* house and that *he* was the host. He loved the compliments and the easy camaraderie.

After recharging in the sun, Ray used the outdoor shower and dried off. He hung his bathing trunks behind the lattice-work fence, and put on the shorts he hung out to dry the previous day. The line was full of their clothes. There were two racy thongs, one lime and white and one black, undoubtedly Taina's. There was a pair of so-called "boyfriend" underwear and a sports bra. Holly's, he guessed. And then there was a plain white stretch cotton camisole and matching bikinis that had a crisp, orderly appearance that echoed Julia's persona. He liked the plain white cotton best, and took it in his hand and caressed the fabric with his thumb.

"Is it dry yet?"

Ray jumped. He turned. Julia.

"It's still damp," he stammered, putting his hands in his pockets. He blushed violently.

"Well, sleeping beauty won't need these until after one or so. They should be dry by then."

"The sensible cotton belongs to Taina?"

Julia leaned in and whispered, "She brought a suitcase full of them—all white—not beige or pink or black or anything. Just white."

"She's militant."

"I'm not so sure it's militant," Julia said, squinting with one eye to find the right word. "Hmm. I'd say it suggests a secret longing for innocence and order." She turned her head slightly, as if she were going to share something, then thought better of it. She put her hand underneath the dancing camisole, bunching it in her hands and held it out. "Smell it," she said. "When was the last time you smelled clean cotton that air-dried in the sun?"

Ray stuck his face into the cloth and inhaled. "It makes me think of being a baby."

"That's what everyone says," Julia said. "It reminds them of a way of life that we've lost since the advent of modern conveniences."

"I'm not sure I ever lived without conveniences, but it reminds me of that anyway," Ray said. "I think they chemically insert the memory at the Tide factory."

"Maybe," Julia said, then pointed to the other clothes on the line, behind Ray. "I need to get to my undies there if you don't mind."

"Oh, sure," Ray stepped aside.

She grabbed the thongs hanging by a single clip.

"*Those* are yours?"

Julia laughed, and Ray noticed that one of her front teeth was just a tiny bit crooked. The underwear easily disappeared into her fist, which she held up.

"I'm sensible on the outside, but I'm wild at heart," she said with a wink, and disappeared down the path of tall seagrass that led back up to the house.

Oh, no, he thought. If Julia was conservative on the outside but wild at heart, her perfect opposite was someone bold on the outside but tender on the inside, and that person wasn't exactly David. He had noticed, on the previous night at dinner, the way that Adrian followed her constantly with his eyes or completely avoided her. If Adrian was gunning for Julia, the vacation would undoubtedly end in disaster. David had shown them the diamond ring he had brought with him, "just in case." But it was obvious to everyone that the ring would never be on Julia's finger. Ray suspected that David's chance to seal the deal had come and gone. He remembered when the pair had started dating. Upon meeting her for the first time, Adrian had described her to Ray as "elegant and serene" and that he thought she was a mismatch to their stubborn, nonconformist, feral brother. Although Julia wasn't Ray's type (all his lust was reserved for unattainable centerfold-types), he understood what other men might see in her, and certainly how other women might admire or envy her. And this made him extremely proud that she liked him. For the first time in his life, he felt like one of the popular kids, and he wanted it to stay that way. So after breakfast, he got to work mopping the wood floors. Julia gave him the thumbs-up and said, "You're definitely invited back." He grabbed paper towels, sponges, and several bottles of cleaning agents and headed to the dining room. He tried to open the windows, but the wood frames were so swollen that they stuck. When he managed to lift them all, the breeze cascaded into the house, and dust and papers took to the air. Curtains fluttered. A half-hour later he went back for more paper towels, sweating with exertion of cleaning. Adrian was just standing around talking to Holly and Julia, who were both cleaning too. Adrian wore long bathing trunks and a t-shirt with the sleeves cut off. "Perfect timing, man," Ray said, putting his hands on his hips. "We could use some help."

"I'm going kayaking," Adrian replied. He stood in front of Julia, giving Ray his back, and leaned in and said something Ray didn't hear. Next thing she was handing him the sunglasses that she had propped up on top her head, and Adrian put them on.

"Oh, I *love* aviator glasses," Holly said.

Ray balked. "Aren't those antiques?"

"World War II," Julia said. "But I trust Adrian. He won't lose them."

"They make you look like a prick," Ray said.

"Then I'll guard them with my life," Adrian replied, and headed out the door.

When Adrian had left, Ray said, "Why does he always get away with it?"

Holly said, "He doesn't get away with anything, Ray. I know you won't believe this, but Adrian works his ass off. He's extremely disciplined in everything he does, from his music to exercising." She shrugged. "But I know what you mean. He answers to no one."

Julia turned and began to rub the wood cabinets with a cloth. "I think he does answer to someone," she said. "He answers to *all* of you," she said. "As a group. He's a family man down to his core. And you know what else? He's paranoid about being 'too nice.' He tries so hard not to be just like his dad."

Chapter
27

David

It's taken me three full days to bring *it* up. We're on the porch, close to lunchtime. When I turn to Adrian and Ray, I try to sound casual. "So. Ray thinks we're Cuban," I pitch. "I'm starting to think that maybe he's right." A total lie. But I'm banking on the fact that none of them can resist the temptation to shoot down each other's ideas, and sure enough, it gets the ball rolling.

Julia is sitting across from me, eating ripe, juicy cherries from a bowl. I know she's about to stain her white sundress any minute, and the tension of waiting for that to happen has me on edge. Or maybe it's because I can't imagine anyone not noticing how sexy she looks sitting there, with a strap of her dress fallen off one shoulder, lowering cherries into her mouth by the stem. "Cuba?" she echoes on cue.

Holly is using the porch rail to do some hamstring stretches. She waves a hand around. "Impossible. The island of Hispaniola is a huge barrier between Cuba and Puerto Rico. There's no way."

Ray pulls his shoulders back, speaks slowly, trying hard to restrain himself from rushing at her with too much conviction.

"Families who want to give their kids a chance to live in freedom might keep their mouths shut if they themselves are not free. Who's not free? Cubans."

"Sure, your theory has political logic but it ignores the laws of physics. Ray, we know for a fact that Cuba isn't an option," Taina says, joining us at the table and pulling the shell off a shrimp. "*Newsweek* tested that theory and rejected it, along with other departure points, because of the weather and the currents." She pointed at David. "I showed you the paperwork my mom collected, right? I have a map of the currents, which were moving in a northeast-to-southwest direction. For Cubans to have found the empty boat, it would have had to drift in a direction opposite the current. Impossible."

Ray points at her with an empty bamboo skewer. "We also know that objects move in every direction around the swirl of a hurricane."

"Give it up, Ray," Adrian chimes in.

Ray shakes his head. "No way. I'm as Cuban as . . ." he looks around for a prop. His face lights up and he reaches into Adrian's breast pocket and pulls out a cigar. He holds it up, his eyes sparkling with amusement at his luck.

Adrian snatches the cigar from him and points at the band circling it. "It's a Dominican, *pendejo*." He throws his head back and laughs.

"Well I'm Cuban," Raymond insists. "Seriously though, given the fact that we don't know jack, why wouldn't you just pick being Cuban? It's so much more . . ." he searches for the right words, mashing his fingers together.

"Tidy?" Adrian offers. "You can take it out and look at it and think how heroic our families were, and then you can fold it up and put it back in its little box, labeled 'My Elián Gonzalez Story' and then you put it up on a shelf. Your 'Pandora's Box' has the shape of a cigar box." He sticks out his lower lip and points at Ray. "Very convenient."

Ray bites the sharp tip of the skewer and spits it out. "It's not half as dumbass as your theory." He leans in. "Tell them what you told me in Phoenix."

Adrian shakes his head. "Give me that," he says, pulling the skewer from between Ray's fingers. "You're making me nervous."

"What is it?" Taina says. "C'mon, fess up, Adrian."

Ray smirks and half-closes his eyes, pointing with one pudgy finger at Adrian. "This one over here believes that he sprang from the sea, *parentless*. And you tell me that my Cuban exile story is delusional?"

Holly makes a face. "Parentless?"

Adrian folds his arms in front of him. "It's artsy but it works for me."

Taina said, "You teased me about my geometric starfish. But I, on the other hand, will respect your 'interpretation.'"

Adrian nods. "Thank you. I appreciate that."

"If stupid and artsy are the same thing, then it's certainly artsy," Ray says rolling his eyes up. "A lame story not even a kindergartner could believe."

"I have my own delusions," Holly says, tucking a strand of hair behind her ear. "When I was a kid I told everyone that my parents were drunk and irresponsible millionaires who dropped me off the edge of the family yacht by mistake."

"Hmm. That's lame too," says Ray, with a dismissive wave that mimics the one she gave him earlier.

I segue to the next item on my agenda: "The only thing left to do is publish our story in a major Spanish-language magazine, especially one available in the Caribbean. Someone will step forward if we approach it without being ornamental."

"Ornamental?" Holy echoes, her head cocked to the side.

"Aphasia," I say, then prompt them to help me. "It's a word that means that you think you're better than others."

"Judgmental!" shouts Ray, jumping out of his seat. When he sits back down, the table shakes and the ice cubes clink and sway in their glasses.

I point at him. "That's it. Thanks."

Ray looks pleased with himself, then repeats the sentence. "Someone will step forward if we approach it without being judgmental."

I look at Adrian and ask one more time. "Call a reporter. Any reporter. We'll get more press from the ones you've slept with."

Adrian doesn't say anything. Instead, he stands up, grabs the corners of his polo shirt, and pulls it up. He's pulling out the big guns again, I think to myself. None of them know about the scars but Doug and me. So I watch as Adrian stands before us, bare chested. Holly frowns, "Whatcha doin', Aidge?"

He points to the scars on his flank. They are, without a doubt, disturbing, so I look away. Julia openly admires his six-pack. Then her eyes go lower, just a little, as she follows the narrow line of hair that descends from his navel into his low-rise jeans.

"What the . . ." whispers Taina. She reaches over and touches one of the scars, running her finger over the small bump. Adrian pulls away, as if her finger has burned him. Taina's eyes harden and she sits back.

"Dude," Ray begins, "they look like . . ." But he can't finish the sentence.

"Cigarette burns? Yup," Adrian pulls his shirt back down. Holly lets out a little shudder. Adrian looks around. "So as long as we're playing show and tell, does anyone else have anything they'd like to share?"

No one speaks.

"I didn't think so," he says, and tosses a napkin across the table.

Julia always acts all chipper when she's uncomfortable, so I'm not surprised that she leaps up, goes over to the buffet table and busies herself handing out individual plates of freshly shucked clams, raw and presented on the half-shell. "Local," she says over-enthusiastically, like she's selling them.

"But the women I remember were so loving," I insist, happily partaking of the clams. I pop a trembling clam into my mouth. "They wouldn't hurt anyone, Adrian. Trust me. And none of the rest of us have scars, so obviously we were kept safe."

"David," Adrian says tersely. "I'm not going to rely on your hallucinations to guide my decision. You believe what you want to believe."

I grab the clams and oysters off of Adrian's plate and begin to chuck them, one by one, at Adrian. His arms fly up in defense, and he pushes his chair backward, increasing the distance between us. Almost immediately, seagulls appear out of nowhere to eat. Their cawing is loud and frantic.

"What the hell?"

Julia grabs my wrist. "David. Stop it!"

"Are you nuts?" says Adrian. He stands up, then leans over the table and tries to pry the plate, which still has a few oysters, out of my hand. I pull away even harder. We struggle for a moment until the plate flies out of my hand and clatters to the floor. The oyster meat sticks to the wood siding of the house for a moment. It rolls down, wet and obscene-looking, followed by a slow-moving trail of cocktail sauce, like clotted blood. Almost immediately, Julia reaches into a canvas beach sack and presents me with a stress ball. I want to throw it too, but I squeeze it first. I squeeze it again, and something inside me slithers away and disappears.

I remember Julia's father suddenly, John Crew Griswold, with his Columbo mustache. I remember him in a white panama hat with a black band. He gives me an encouraging nod from a rocking chair on the opposite end of the porch. So I muster all the courage I have and say, in a calm and controlled voice, "I'm sorry, Adrian. I lost my cool."

Adrian is wiping his shirt off with a napkin, and stops to give me a sideways look. "Alright. Sorry I said 'hallucinations.'"

I nod to him and we allow a moment of silence. Then I raise a finger like Jesus. "There are four DNA kits in the refrigerator." I look each one of my siblings in the eye. "Comparative siblingship tests for all of you," I point to each one of them, "against me."

"I'm not doin' it," Adrian says, "I told you." He's still patting himself with napkins.

Holly, who has always been the most resistant (or perhaps competitive) to Adrian's leadership in the family, says, "Oh please. What's the big deal?"

Taina clears her throat to speak. She dabs at the corners of her mouth with her napkin and takes a deep breath before saying, "Doug lifted some DNA from your coffee cups." She looks at Adrian. "Yours, David's, and mine. And if you're wondering what happened to your toothbrushes that time you came to visit, he took those too." She closes her eyes and rests the tips of her fingers on her forehead, hiding her eyes. "And now I know."

"Don't say it. I forbid you," Adrian says.

"*You* forbid *me*?" Taina says with a dry laugh. "Are you kidding me?"

"Yes, as the leader of this family, I forbid you."

"Who made you boss?" says Ray. "I don't remember voting."

Taina glares at Adrian "You're not my brother. Ninety-nine point eight percent says you're not. So screw you."

Adrian pivots, grabs his guitar with one hand, puts the other palm down on the railing of the veranda, and catapults his body sideways over the rail. There's a thud as his feet hit the ground and then the sound of the gravel crunching underneath him. In a moment we hear a door slam at the boathouse and we see him motoring across the water to Stony Creek. Ray laces his hands behind his head, turns to Holly, and says, "I'd kill for a little bourbon right now." I suspect that he wants to remind us that he, not Adrian, is the one that has always been at the center of our controversy, and that he wants the attention back. He puts his hands out and says, "Just kidding."

No one laughs. No one even blinks.

"Lighten up." He lifts his glass of cranberry and soda. "I'm over it." He turns and puts a hand on my shoulder. "I can handle not being related to you. Really. I'll take the test. It's cool."

"I . . . app—" but I can't finish the word. I look to Julia for help. "When you're happy?"

"Appreciate?"

"Yes. I *appreciate* your support." I want to say more, but sometimes it's too much work.

Ray holds up his tattoo and says, "We're brothers and sisters no matter what. Isn't that the whole point?" He looks at Taina and Holly. "No matter what?"

I nod. We bump our starfish tattoos.

After we've eaten, we wrap up Adrian's lunch and put it in the icebox. I bring down the DNA kits. I explain how simple it is: Open mouth. Use buccal swab to scrape inside of cheek. Drop swab in bag. Seal. Send to lab. I detail the cost too, because it's not cheap and I'm only footing the bill for comparisons to *me*—several hundred dollars for each, since we're testing maternal and paternal genes. Matters are further complicated by the fact that there's no parental DNA to compare it to. "They'll make us pay dearly for that," I tell them. "But I figure that we could save some money by using 'if-then' logic to draw certain assumptions, then we can avoid testing every possible relationship." I explain that they can choose comparative tests to each other if they wish.

I ask Julia to summarize the letter that comes with the kit, explaining that the siblingship testing can often be frustrating and inconclusive. "Unlike paternity testing," she paraphrases, "there are no genes that siblings must share. So any combination is possible. Therefore, a DNA sibling test cannot provide absolute answers. Theoretically, if two people are full siblings, then half of the tested genes should be identical. If they are half siblings, only a quarter should be identical. In practice, genes from the two parents combine randomly. So these are *averages* rather than exact numbers." She turns the paper over and scans the back. "Rush orders cost extra. Tests with no parental DNA cost extra. A lot extra."

Ray holds his chin in his knuckles and says, "Tell me again how this will this help us find our birth parents?"

"It won't, Ray," I say. "I see it as piece of the bigger puzzle."

He shakes his head, "Well, Taina just blew a hole in the sibling ideology, whether we like it or not. Is it still worth doing?"

"I was going to keep it a secret," Taina says, first looking apologetically at Holly then accusatorially at me. "It just kind of popped out."

"It's still worth doing," I insist. Doug tested Taina against Adrian and me. I want to repeat that test to confirm, then test against the rest of you."

Holly leaned forward and said, "Is it what you really want, David?"

I make my final sales pitch: "Yes. Absolutely." I turn to Ray. "Being open to the truth about our history doesn't dishonor the people we love. In fact, it does the opposite; it demonstrates a certain level of emotional—" I struggle with the word until they help me arrive at *stability*. "To do this," I continue, "we have to have a confidence in who we are and what we believe. And I believe in us, and in our commitment to each other as a family."

Holly exhales with force, which makes her bangs flutter. "Hell. Doesn't marriage contain the same kind of magic? If the 'two become one' by pact of law or religion, then why would siblingship be so farfetched? Our tattoos don't symbolize DNA; they're more like symbols of commitment. Like wedding rings."

"I'm in," Ray says, touching his tattoo and looking up at our sisters, then at me. "Maybe we can get the results before we leave."

"Are you sure about this?" Taina asks, putting her hand over Ray's.

"No," he says, eyes wide. "But hiding from the truth doesn't seem right either. We're getting too old to stick our heads in the sand."

As I wait to fall asleep before my afternoon nap, I think about what had happened that afternoon. The knowledge that Taina isn't my blood sister doesn't bother me at all. The bonds formed from love and shared experiences are so much more powerful than shared genes. After all, we all know the world is full of blood relatives who can't stand each other. I firmly believe that we are bound first and foremost by a deep understanding of each other. It's all going to melt into one great alloy, then fuse into a whole that's stronger than its divisive parts. I have seven more days to gather consensus and then smooth out Adrian's ruffled feathers. I'm thinking like a salesman: I have one week to close the deal.

I took a seven-hour nap so there's no way I can go to bed when the first crew goes to bed that night. I heat up a glass of milk and figure that I'll just have to join the vampires. I hear them talking through a window out on the porch and smell the smoke of Taina's cigarettes wafting into the hall. I look through the window. Taina is straddling the porch rail, holding up a cigarette, which glows orange against the dark backdrop of the water. Adrian is standing, leaning against the same rail, arms crossed over his chest. They look tense but not combative. He glances at her sideways now and then as he kicks at something with a bare foot. Adrian and I have never talked about Taina's crush, so I don't know if he knows. She and I have never discussed it either, but Holly-big-mouth confirmed it when I asked. The whole idea of it makes me feel dirty, and I know that Adrian would be appalled.

Adrian is talking about Ray, and I catch bits of the conversation. He squeezes the tips of his fingers together when he says, ". . . If it turns out that he has no genetic relatives."

Taina replies, "Ray was seventeen when 'it' happened."

Adrian half-whispers, "Once you're capable of drinking yourself to death, you're always capable."

Taina points her cigarette at him. "You told me once that you had friends in gangs." She blows a huge cloud of smoke into the breeze. "Did you do something bad, Adrian? Is that why you're afraid to give your DNA? Because not even Ray believes that your resistance to this is about Ray."

Adrian stiffens. "Sure I hung around bad people, but I don't trust the law, either. I have too many friends who've ended up in jail for being in the wrong place at the wrong time. Cops think they have X-ray vision into our dirty little Latino souls. I don't want anyone to have my DNA, and I'm pissed at your husband, by the way. I want him to get rid of it. I'm the watch dog in the family, Taina. I'm the one with proof of past abuse. I'm the only one who grew up poor. I've seen things."

I step onto the porch, let the screen door bang to announce my presence. "What's up?" I say.

Adrian's voice is flat. "What are you doing up?"

"Can't sleep."

A short distance out in the water, something big makes a splash, and we turn, but see nothing but an expanding ring on the surface of the water. I look at Taina. "I want you to paint me. And you—" I look at Adrian. "How 'bout you compose a song for my funeral?"

"Jesus, David. Stop being so morbid."

"C'mon, you so-called artists. Where's the guitar? The sketchbook? The tackle box full of fancy art gear? Come on inside. I don't have forever, you know."

Stirring my siblings' creative juices is easy—just lounge on the couch, listen to Adrian play around with his guitar and watch Taina sketch. To lighten the mood, I open a trunk in the hall and exchange my baseball hat for a tall black leather grenadier hat with a brass eagle on the front.

"Que guapo," says Adrian. "Don't you think, Tai?"

I run a finger across the brim of the hat and begin to dance around, singing, *"I'm too sexy for my hat . . ."*

Taina's face melts into the first smile I've seen from her in days.

"It's a great hat," Adrian says, and tries to play "Too Sexy" while I dance around.

"Don't move," Taina orders, holding out her hands. She tapes a fresh sheet of paper to her easel. She begins to sketch me. I sit. I don't move.

After a half-hour, I get up and look at the picture. It looks exactly like one of her Caribbean Lagoon designs that have become a cash cow for her former employer. She even sketched a palm tree behind my head. Gone is the hat that I'm so obviously wearing. Instead, I have a full head of thick, dark hair. It's ridiculous. She smiles at me hopefully, expecting praise.

I pull at the edges of the paper and rip it off. I ball it up and throw it across the room so it lands in the empty fireplace.

"You can do better," I say. "You're blocked."

Her mouth hangs open for a moment, and then she says, "Go to hell." Her eyes actually fill with tears.

Sure, I feel bad. But I press on, emboldened by the soldier who once wore this hat: Lieutenant August Bradley the Fourth, a Griswold by marriage. If he could stand up to the Confederates, then surely I can stand up to my sister. So I say, "You gave up on yourself and your talent. I want to help you get it back."

I can tell she's really pissed, because her lower lip is trembling. "I'm not painting you, asshole. Forget it."

"Stay in the present moment," I say, doing my best Buddhist monk imitation. "Just draw like you did before fear moved in." I tap at the hat. "Honor your gift." I grab her hand and point to the starfish tattoo that Adrian said looks like a frozen crab. "Let's defrost that little bugger."

Adrian throws his head and laughs. "Can't say no one listens to you, Tai."

So Taina marches over to where Adrian's sitting and starts tearing out the pages of his notebook, crumpling them up and throwing them across the room. "See how *you* like it," she mumbles, frowning. She looks like a little girl, suddenly, a sister being teased by two older brothers who might be throwing her favorite doll back and forth between them. Adrian lunges at her and tries to get his papers back. "Hey! Hey!"

"Lame." She holds up a sheet. "This one sounds like a . . ." she screws up her face, "like a hemorrhoid commercial."

I hold my Zenlike calm. "Taina," I say, taking the paper away from her and putting my hands on her shoulders. "You just said it yourself—you weren't made for commercial work, at least, not forever. You told me that, and I'm never going to let you forget it."

She shakes her head. "Are you saying my work is mediocre? Speak for yourself. You're the most mediocre person I ever met, David."

"Exactly!" I say. "That's my point. You're extraordinary, and I'm not. My job therefore, is to repeat to you what you told me ten years ago—that you would consider your life a failure if you never saw your work hanging in a gallery. I'm here telling you it's time to start that journey. Now."

I guess I hit a bee's nest because not even my monkish charm can calm her. "You don't get to be a dick just because you have a brain tumor," she yells. "And the whole 'what I've learned from the Griswolds thing' is getting old. Screw the Griswolds."

I trace an imaginary rainbow between us. "This is great. Let it out."

"Great job, man," Adrian pipes in. "Creativity's just *oozing* out her ears."

I take a deep breath. I try a more direct approach. "Look. I know that was harsh, Tai. But you didn't waste your time.

Once you know what isn't working, you're free to discover what does."

Adrian looked up from his guitar. "He's got a point. That's how I work."

Then I did something I rarely do. I hugged her. I held her head to my neck and said, "I *am* mediocre, always have been. And that's why I'm trying so hard *not* to be. I have so little time left to make my mark, to be extraordinary at something." I pull her back and look into her eyes. "Even if it's only at being a brother."

Chapter

28

In the late morning, on the fourth day, Julia came running out of the house and breathlessly announced that David was missing. They were all out on the lawn, waiting for him to get up and join them. Adrian and Ray, already in their swim trunks, were in the process of setting up a volleyball net. Holly was kickboxing a tire swing underneath the old cedar. Taina was sunning herself in a macramé bikini out on the seawall and had recently caused a passing sailboat to run aground. The guys had helped an embarrassed pair of brothers push their boat back out, and the incident had served as after-breakfast entertainment.

"Missing? Not too many places to hide on a one-acre island," Ray told Julia. "Did you check the bathrooms?"

"He must have left before we got up. The blue kayak is gone," Julia said. "He does this." She shook her head. "He craves solitude."

"But he shouldn't be alone," Ray said, squinting and shading his face in the sun. "What if he has a seizure or something?"

Julia said, "Exactly."

"A thousand bucks says he's in one of the nature preserves, being bitten by ticks as we speak. Let's go check it out," Adrian said, looking out to the water. "When we spot him, we leave him alone."

"I have a first-aid kit, a Swiss Army knife, a cell phone, some snacks, water bottles . . ." said Ray, patting at his chest and pants pockets, as if he were looking for his car keys.

"Hang on there, Eagle Scout," Adrian said. "Two is enough."

"Cool. You and me, man."

Adrian shook his head. "Julia knows the islands better than anyone. I'll go with her."

Ray saw the guilty look pass over Julia's face, but she didn't say anything, she just folded her arms and looked away. They wanted to be alone with each other, Ray understood suddenly, so he nodded and backed away. He got back to work untangling the volleyball net. When Julia and Adrian disappeared from sight in the motorboat, he followed the stone path to the back of the house. He walked around Uncle Jim's grave, calling out "Morning, sir!" A gentle breeze animated the beach towels and ladies' cover-ups hanging on the clothesline, and they parted for him as he passed through. He stood before the rock tub full of beverages, the captain's punch bowl. He put his hand into the icy water in search of something to drink. He sucked in air at the sight of the vodka bottle, a tall, Scandinavian beauty with its seal still unbroken. He ran his fingers along the bottle's neck, then picked it up out of the water. By the time he reached for the plastic bottle of Canadian spring water, his fingers were blue and completely numb. It took everything he had to put the vodka back.

The sky was dull with a thin cover of clouds, but the breeze sweeping over the Thimble Islands was fragrant with the scent of charcoal and grilled meat of early lunches. As Julia and Adrian wove their way through the channel, each Thimble showed activity of some kind, whether it was children diving off rocks into the water or someone lounging with a newspaper on a porch. Only the nature preserves and bird sanctuaries were quiet.

"Wow. This is a great spot for a hotel and casino," Adrian joked. "Why waste it on birds?"

Julia gasped. "Watch it. You're in Connecticut, boy. We executed eleven people for practicing witchcraft. These days it's for proposing land development. To us, it's the same thing."

Even though she had given her guests a tour of the islands already, she hit some of the points she may have failed to mention, such as the names of the aboriginal inhabitants, the Mattabesek, also known as the Quinnipiac. "Only twenty-five or so of the islands are inhabited," Julia explained. "There are just under a hundred 'homes' of varying sizes." She pointed to Roger's Island, upon which stood a twenty-room English Tudor mansion, and then pointed behind them, at Cedar Island, which was nothing but a pile of rocks with a gazebo on top. Adrian asked how many islands there were in total. "It's hard to say, because some of the islands are just rock piles that disappear at high tide. At some point, everyone just agreed on three-hundred-and-sixty-five islands, one for each day of the year." As she spoke, she swept the landscape for signs of a blue kayak, and seeing none, continued weaving between the islands. Julia explained the history behind quirky names like Cut-in-Two Island, Mother-in-Law Island, and Dogfish Island. The infamous pirate Captain Kidd supposedly buried treasure on Money Island, she told him. She pointed to her favorite, Pot Rock Island, the site of the Thimble's first hotel, built in 1846. "They had clambakes there every weekend. At the turn of the century, yachts from New York stopped there to picnic," she said. "And locals from the city of Branford came too. You could take a midnight sail to the islands that had bands and dancing. This area became the Newport of Connecticut. The golden era was from 1890 to the early 1930s. The Great Depression put the kibosh on all the fun. The cottages emptied and the big yachts stopped coming. And then came the Great New England Hurricane, which crushed most of the houses and killed seven people here." Suddenly, Julia stood and pointed to a Crayola-blue kayak on the shore of Outer Island. There was also a speedboat off shore. Julia raised the binoculars and saw that David was talking to a woman wearing a pink baseball hat while standing on a huge boulder. "She must be someone from the university," Julia said. "Or from the forestry social circuit."

"Forestry social circuit? There is such a thing?"

"It's an oxymoron, I know." She stood up and began waving, then shouted, "*David*!" It was too far for him to hear, he was just a small figure. They saw him and the woman turn and walk deeper into the heart of the island.

"Let's leave him alone," Adrian said. "He's fine."

Julia turned to look at Adrian. "He shouldn't be standing on that rock. His balance is off."

"He's not alone," Adrian said.

Julia took her cell phone out of the pocket of her shorts. She hit one key and listened. Adrian could hear the slap of water underneath the boat as he waited. "Dammit," Julia said, "this is still part of the dead zone. How are we supposed to keep him safe?"

Adrian drew his eyebrows together. "Are you . . . jealous?"

Julia chuckled dryly. "First of all, I'd bet a million dollars he's annoyed that she's intruding upon his solitude. And second, if there's any monkey business going on up there, I'm happy for him."

"Then why are we spying on him?"

She pulled the bill of her Gap canvas bucket hat a bit lower, half-shielding her eyes. "I'm not spying," she said, putting her hand on her chest. "I feel responsible—" She stopped. "The whole point of this gathering was for me to begin to detach."

"And how's that working out?"

She sighed. "So take over, dammit. Give me some proof that that tattoo means something."

They sat on the boat in silence, letting the water rock them up and down, just listening to the distant sound of children splashing and laughing.

"What do you want me to do that I'm not already doing?" He leaned forward, elbows resting on his knees.

"You can start by giving up your DNA," she said. "Please, Adrian. It's the right thing to do at this point."

He looked up at her. "You want my DNA?"

"Yeah, I want your DNA," she echoed, realizing too late, how it sounded. He half-closed his eyes and rocked his head back and forth. "Well, well." Then he threw his head back and laughed.

"You're not going to rattle me into forgetting about it," she said. She yanked the cord of the boat's engine. "I'm asking you to return to *me* the trust that I have placed in *you*." The motor trembled and roared to life. Not waiting for him to respond, she shouted, "Hey, how'd you like to go sailing?"

After cleaning up the porch and washing the morning dishes, Holly found Taina in the second-floor sitting room, looking through the footed telescope.

"Let it go, Tai," Holly said. "They didn't mean to exclude you."

"Like hell."

Holly sat down, stretching her legs across a cushioned bench.

The deck outside overlooked stunning rooftop views of blue sky and colorful sailboats. "Did I ever tell you about the time I was hypnotized?" Holly said.

Taina sighed, just to let Holly know that she knew full well that she was trying to distract her. "It was a long time ago, right?" Taina kept up her vigilance, her back to her sister, telescope pointed outward.

Holly nodded even though her sister wasn't looking at her. "The last time I pursued our biological roots was before I had kids. I'm not the type to bother looking up records and such, so I thought I'd cheat. I figured the truth about what happened to us is somewhere in my brain." She put an index finger on each temple. "This was before David's brain tumor proved that I was right." She looked back out to the water. "While I was being hypnotized, I remember feeling like my mind was like a heavy metal ball that was sinking into deep, deep water. The hypnotist made a tape of our session. It was hard to hear."

"Hard to hear?"

"In both senses of the word. During the entire interview I stuttered."

Taina blinked and turned back for a quick glance at her sister. "What did you say in the tape, in the stuttering voice?"

Holly shrugged. "I spoke Spanish, so I didn't understand a word. I just remember that strange voice coming out of me. It was creepy."

Taina's voice rose. "Do you still have the tape?"

"Nah, I threw it out. Too freaky." She twisted a lock of her hair.

"That was dumb. You should've kept it."

"Turn around. Look at me."

Taina twisted around slowly.

"Adrian is our brother."

"He's not."

"To hell with DNA, Taina. It doesn't mean anything. I agree with David. We came into this life—*this life*, not that *other* life, not the one back when we were babies, but the life we've known for thirty years—*together*."

Taina turned back to scouring the horizon. She saw a couple that looked a lot like Julia and Adrian depart on a sailboat from the neighboring island. The woman—yes, it was Julia—unfurled the sail. The sail trembled, opened up, and the vessel glided off into the shimmering sea. She felt her stomach clench. "Oh come on, Holly, haven't you ever wanted something you couldn't have?"

Holly stood up. "I want a baby daughter. And I want this house, Taina. I want this life."

Taina made a face. "Your house has five bedrooms and a pool. You have a husband you love and three beautiful boys. Are you out of your mind? What's wrong with your life?"

Holly sighed again then held up a catalog of preppy clothes that was resting on her lap. It had a picture of a man bending over a lobster pot, the sea, and a lighthouse in the background. "It's not *this* life. I want to be anchored in permanence and surrounded by beauty. These people aren't transient."

"We were unwanted, abandoned orphans, lucky to have what we have. What makes you think it's okay to want more?"

"Being American, Taina."

Taina shook her head. "Even Julia doesn't have 'this life.' Her parents worked their asses off to keep up their stake, and they have to share it with like, fifty other people. Personally, I'd be happy with a little condo on South Beach."

Holly wrinkled her nose. "To be near Adrian."

Taina took the magazine out of Holly's hands. "If we have sons, we want daughters. If we live in Florida, we want to live in New England. If we have a detective husband, we want a singer instead. C'mon, admit it—don't you find your pilot to be a little dull? After all, we always want the opposite of what we have," Taina said. "Don't we?"

Holly's face turned red. "Fine," she said, getting up. "I'll leave you alone with your incestuous jealousy and your voyeurism." She stomped off, and Taina heard her footsteps descending the creaky stairs. Taina fiddled with the telescope, because she couldn't seem to hold the view. She found a switch that made all the difference, and the image came in steadily and as sharply as if they were standing ten feet away. She witnessed the moment that Adrian leaned over to reach a rope that was on the floor of the boat, and with his other hand, gripped Julia's bare thigh for support for just a few seconds. She saw how Julia stopped what she was doing and stared at that hand before Adrian quickly withdrew it. Taina noticed the main sail's tentative flapping, saw how it leaned, cupped, and filled with wind. The vessel turned just a few degrees and suddenly picked up speed and glided away.

Taina hated this feeling of agonized rapture. Like a moth, attracted by a bare light bulb; mesmerized, drunk with admiration, bashing herself again and again against the barriers that surrounded Adrian's life.

The Griswolds' sailboat was being repaired, so Julia borrowed the *Lil' Pearl*, a sloop that belonged to the Rigbys, longtime family friends on Governor's Island. Julia docked the motorboat at the Rigbys' cottage and they headed out before a brisk wind.

The sunshine and wind speed was exhilarating to Julia, so it took her by surprise to see that Adrian's face was tight with fear. Julia eased off the wind a bit and the boat slowed down. But Adrian couldn't relax while they were out in the Sound, so they headed back in toward the islands. He relaxed when the islands came back into view. Julia got the boat as close as she could to a sand bar, anchored, and they paddled around in the water.

"You've got to start trusting me," Julia told him, just as a passing wave deposited her into his arms. In the water she was weightless, and he held her up like a child so she wouldn't be pulled away. She looked down at him, put a hand on his cheek and felt the prickliness of his razor stubble. There was that moment of consideration, the weighing of consequences, the probing, testing of their capacity to give in to instinct. Adrian took one last close-up look at the curve of her jaw line, her eyes, her hair. He drank in the image of water droplets rolling down along the length of her skin. They pooled and grew heavy, then split into rivulets that fled into the shadowed crevice where her breasts met. He put her down, and took a step back. "Sorry," she said, and they both laughed, but nervously.

Adrian knew then, without a doubt, that they would become lovers. But he knew that it had to be a long time off, because he could not, would not, take her away from David. His longing for her began at that moment. Like the mechanism on an old clock, it held itself back, ticking and marking the seconds, minutes, hours, and days.

It was four in the morning and Adrian couldn't sleep. The Griswold house was his first experience inhabiting an old home, and he marveled at how different it was from the concrete structures he had known all his life. The family had decently kept up the repairs, but the house was so old that it was sagging in places. He imagined that the whole thing could collapse and fall into the sea at any time.

It was hot and damp in his room. The one window had swollen shut and was impossible to open, so he lay with a fan pointed directly at him. There was always the option of sleeping in the hammocks that were hung out on the veranda, and that was okay for a night, two at the most. The dilemma reminded him too much of nights in Puerto Rico, in the two-bedroom cinderblock house he and his dad had lived in for so many years, without air-conditioning, without much privacy, the neighbors carrying on day and night, never quiet. Here, it was the incessant cawing of the seagulls that kept him from napping by day and the sound of waves breaking against the seawall that kept him up at night. He lay in bed, hot, wide awake, and achingly horny.

Holly told him again and again to relax, to not be so jittery. Never in his life would he carve out idle time like this again, he knew, so he was glad that he had come to Griswold Island. And who knew, he could die in a plane crash on the way to a concert, and he would take inventory of his life and he would be glad he had taken advantage of this time with the girls, with David, and with Ray. The meals were a group effort that he greatly enjoyed. And who would have known that adults could have so much fun with a Slip 'n Slide and a piñata? And in the late afternoon, Julia brewed sun tea and they sat on the rocking chairs lined up on the veranda overlooking the water, with ice cubes clinking in tall glasses of cold tea, drifting in and out of sleep while Holly and Ray chatted away. It vaguely reminded him of village life. He sat up in bed. He had been trying to figure out what it was that was drawing him so dangerously close to his pseudo-sister-in-law. He had never known that someone like her could exist. While he hurled himself into the world, Julia seemed still, anchored, rocklike, uncomplicated.

The bed groaned below him. He stood up and put his shorts on. He turned the brass knob and opened the door. He stepped into the hall. Below his foot, the wood made a low creaking noise. He began to walk down the hall, past Raymond's snoring, past Holly's door, past Taina's room. In the pale moonlight he saw the eyes of Julia's relatives watching him from behind their gilded frames, some of the expressions stern and disapproving, some blank and distant.

David's door was half-open. It was the last door at the end of the hall, the room just before the stairwell that went up to the master bedroom. Adrian listened to hear snoring or deep breathing, but he heard nothing. He went up the stairs, lured by the cool air that was escaping from under Julia's door. At the top of the stairs, cut glass doorknobs glowed in the moonlight like huge diamonds. A bead of sweat rolled down his temple and down the length of his cheek. He heard the hypnotic hum of the AC unit inside Julia's room.

Chapter
29

David

I'm sleeping in Julia's room tonight—special circumstances. The night is extra hot and sticky, so she set up a daybed in her air-conditioned room for me. I've just returned from the bathroom for the third time tonight; the meds always keep me from locking in a straight sleep. So I'm lying in the coolness of the master suite, trying to fall back asleep, when I hear footsteps in the hall. I might not have heard them over the hum of the AC, except for the creaking wood. I see feet underneath the crack of the door; two dark circles that move in the soft light from the hall. As they move closer, I can actually hear the weight on the wood floor, too heavy to be one of the girls, to light to be Raymond's. At first, I thought that someone was disoriented, lost in the labyrinth of partitioned rooms. Then I remembered that the guests were all on the floor below us. The person had to come up a set of stairs. We don't have any sleepwalkers among us, and no one got drunk.

The dark shapes under the door come together, then stop. This is the point where someone who is lost might think, *hey, this isn't my room,* and turn back. But they stand there for twenty seconds or more. Then they step closer, the toes touching the wood of the door for a few seconds before turning away. Inside my rib cage, my heart flops over itself like a cold, meaty fish.

He won't dare. I know him. He won't. And now he's lying alone in his hot, muggy room. He's staring at the ceiling, wondering what the hell to do with his dick. I get out of my bed and crawl into Julia's. When she wakes I tell her that I had a nightmare, and can I please lie next to her? She kisses my forehead and says, "Sure. Go back to sleep." She rolls over. I lie next to her, eyes wide open. I suddenly remember the time, back when we lived together, that she told me she was having a sexy dream. She confessed that it hadn't been about me, and I didn't even care. Now, I wonder. Now I very much want to know who she thinks about when she closes her eyes.

30

On the fifth day, David had a medical appointment, a test that could be handled locally, at Yale–New Haven Hospital. The plan was for Raymond to take David across the water to meet a friend at Stony Creek dock, later that morning. The friend would drive David and Ray from there to his appointment and bring him back to the dock.

Everyone was amazed when Taina walked into the kitchen at eight. "I haven't actually been to bed yet," she said. "I'm really screwed up." Julia, Holly, and Ray were having coffee at the kitchen table. David was upstairs getting dressed. Julia slipped some films out of a large square blue sleeve and held them up to the light. "Have any of you ever seen what a brain tumor looks like?"

"What a question," Holly said. "It's like asking if I've ever seen an elephant's ovaries. Of course not."

"I found this photo of David in the office," Julia explained, and held the X-ray film up against an eight-by-ten photo of David. They looked back and forth between them. One captured David in what appeared to be health, the other in illness.

"But they're the same, really," Julia said. "He already had it, in this picture, he just didn't know."

In both images, David is looking in the same direction, and they could see the similarities in the shape of the skull, the arch of the nose, the tilt of the cheekbones. Julia pointed. "See this wispy thing? It looks like a raw egg dropped into boiling water. That was the tumor they took out."

Julia picked up the envelope and began to look at some of the other views, looking over her shoulder occasionally to see if David was coming down. "That stupid tumor," Holly whispered, unable to take her eyes off it. "It doesn't even know what it's doing."

"Or who it's doing it to," Taina echoed. "It just lives. A useless nothing."

Julia said, "Cancer's purpose is to destroy life." Then, in a trancelike voice, "Cancer is, therefore, the purest definition of evil."

"A *gee-oh-blastoma*," Holly attempted. "I heard it's like a Xerox machine with the copy button jammed. It can't stop copying itself."

"*Glee-oh, blast.* With an 'L.'"

They looked up.

"Glee, as in fun," said David. He was dressed in a fresh blue shirt, ready to go. "Blast, as in, having a fun time."

Taina had found his comment unnerving, and the image of the tumor in the MRI was utterly terrifying. After they left, Taina stared at the photograph of David for a long, long time. She hadn't been able to touch her sketchbook or the canvases since the day David had ripped up her work. The thought of drawing and painting again sickened her, like the remorse after a drunken one-night stand. She had once thought of visual art as transcendental, but now she just saw it as impotent, because you could only deal with what was seen—and that neglected so much. Like cancer. She had once believed that she had the power and the talent to create something really perceptive. But how superficial it was, this image of a healthy David, how incomplete.

Chapter
31

David

The friend who's taking me to my appointment is running late. Ray and I are sitting together on a park bench in the Stony Creek parking lot. I'm brooding over last night's incident, trying, in vain, to convince myself that I dreamed the whole thing. Ray is prattling on about things that don't interest either of us, and I wish he would shut up and leave me to my thoughts. It's all nervous chatter. He's building up to something, I can tell. The wind is lifting his crazy hair, and then he looks out to the water and asks, totally out of the blue, something no one else has ever dared to ask me. "So what's it like?"—he looks me in the eye— "Knowing that you're going to die?"

"You tell *me*," I retort. "You tried to kill yourself."

"Not the same," he says. "I just wanted to stop feeling bad. I wasn't thinking about dying. I just wanted peace." His tone is so matter-of-fact, as if we weren't discussing death but rather our favorite kind of music, and his teenager-like openness is refreshing. I've never been one to pontificate, and now that I have aphasia, I take even greater care to be succinct. So I take a deep breath, to let him know that I'm working on an answer. I tap my knuckles on the envelope that contains my MRIs. "I'm not afraid of being dead, Ray. I'm afraid of losing my mind, and still being alive. I'm afraid of it being a long, hard road."

He nods, as if this was exactly the answer he expected. Then he clasps his hands together, and touches them to his forehead for a moment, like he's praying. "If you need help, when the time comes, I'll do whatever needs to be done." He nods once, and turns to looks at me. For a moment or two I assume that he's talking about being of service in a general way, like paying my bills or rotating my tires. But then he looks up at me and his eyes are so heavy. The rims of his eyes fill, ever so slightly, and suddenly I understand that he means *anything*.

I don't know what to say, so I get busy throwing pebbles into the water. I feel the sun's warmth being sucked up by my navy baseball hat. I put my arm around his wide back. "Thanks, brother," I say, bumping his tattoo with the other hand. "I'm not leaving anytime soon. Besides, I don't think I'd need anything beyond the stage of morphine. It's not like Huntington's Disease where you live for years all messed up. But it's good to know you got my back."

He raises his hand above his head like some kind of Spanish dancer, then snaps his fingers once, twice, three times. "That's the hand signal, okay? If you can't talk anymore, and you want out, then snap your fingers like that."

"Oh yeah," I say. "Like in the Mayagüez police report, when I supposedly snapped my fingers for the policeman who found us on the boat. I wonder what it meant. We may never know."

He shrugs. "Now it means put a friggin' pillow over my head already."

"Ray," I say. "If it comes to that, just see to it that I have a ton of morphine if I start to get . . ." I make a circling motion next to my temple. He laughs nervously, and that's how we end the conversation.

I don't think I ever loved Ray until right now. I slap him on the back and tell him to tell me more about the restaurant business; I let him talk endlessly about his video game tournaments and I realize how lonely he is. I notice that he has chewed his cuticles raw. I feel guilty the whole time that I'm having my follow-up tests with Ray by my side, guilty because I know that I will leave them all *someday*.

32

It took Holly all of about twenty minutes to regret her decision to invite her family to Griswold Island. Erick looked about the property suspiciously, mumbling about the stone cliffs and the depth of the water below. He embarrassed Holly before he even got up the steps, complaining in Julia's presence about the gaps in the wooden stairway that led from the dock down to the water. "Dangerous," he said, to Holly's count, seven times before he even got inside the house. She was ready to kill him.

Patrick, Daniel, and Bobby were indeed a force of nature. With their backward clothes ("we let them dress themselves") jack-o'-lantern smiles, red buzz cuts, and freckles, *here comes trouble* was the first thing that came to mind. They made their rounds inside the house like a pack of dogs, exploring and touching everything. Daniel found a spinning wheel in the corner which he immediately whipped into motion, only to have Julia stop him, mumbling something about it being one hundred and seventy years old.

When David and Ray arrived, the boys pawed at them and shouted their names. Holly came upon Patrick, the eldest, staring up at the enormous wood figurehead that hovered over the dining table. She could see by his expression that his nine-year-old imagination had converted the dining room to a more proper setting for such a treasure. He was far away, on the high seas, with crashing waves all around, in a galleon fighting pirates with booming cannons, amid thick fog and smoke. When he finally looked away, he smiled at her, and said, "The real Captain Kidd hid from the British Navy in the Thimble Islands. Did you know that, Mom?"

From the moment they set foot on the island, "British and pirates" was the continuous theme of their play. They found sticks in the yard and waved them dangerously close to each other's eyes, and the seawall became a perfect plank for prisoners. They howled at passing vessels from the veranda, shouting "Bad guys!" and scrambled to equip themselves with their makeshift weapons. A tour boat of passengers ogled, holding up cameras and taking off sunglasses to get a better look at the family that, they presumed, owned the island. The captain waved politely, even as the boys brandished clubs and shouted threats from the seawall. Holly waved back, turning to smile at a scowling Erick.

At lunch, none of the boys would eat what Julia had prepared, and a separate meal of hot dogs and Kool-Aid replaced the lovely egg salad sandwiches and thimbleberry tea that the adults ate. In the afternoon, after their lunch had settled, Holly sent them out to go swimming, complete with an inflated raft and pool noodles, buckets and balls, flippers, masks, and tools for digging in the sand. They loved every minute. They hooted and howled and screamed and fought and laughed. Wonderful stuff, except Holly knew, by having been at the house for five days already, that the sound of their voices would carry into the open windows of the house, and that the noise was keeping David from his nap, and that a tired David was a cranky David, and that tiredness increases his aphasia and therefore his frustration. Taina, who was sleep-deprived herself, held a finger to her lips and said, "Boys! Keep it down!" The boys stopped to look at her for a moment, and went right back to shouting and fighting. But to her credit, Taina started art lessons the very first night after dinner, setting up the easels in the kitchen, after Holly battled with them to come inside to take showers, eat dinner, and put on their pajamas. Adrian was the uncle the boys knew best and loved the most, but he was unusually distracted and disinterested in them. And as the hours passed, the boys soon found their Uncle David to be cranky and bizarre. Ray happily claimed the role of uncle-hero, with his Slip 'n Slide, his magic tricks, and his snow-cone maker. He showed them how to make some cash by charging everyone a buck for the snow cones they made in the afternoon. Julia was constantly correcting them, but gently and with the ease of a pro. She was the only one they listened to, really.

The next afternoon, on the sixth day of the reunion, Taina appeared with boxes wrapped in shiny parrot-green wrapping paper with huge red bows on top. "Early Christmas gifts," she said. For Erick, there was a "Caribbean Lagoon" silk tie. For Holly, a pair of Crocs.

Holly sat the boys down to unwrap their gifts. They tore through the boxes and did nothing to mask their disappointment at the clothing inside. Not toys, but some delicate linen garments, including a sailor suit for the little one. "I modeled them after the original outfits that Adrian, Raymond, and David were found in all those years ago. Three boys," she said pointing at the garments. "And you have three boys." Holly did her best to cover for them, a useless gesture in light of the fact that the little one tossed the garment into the air and yelled, "Stupid!" and scrambled away before it even hit the floor.

If Taina was secretly disappointed, she didn't let it show. "Oh, I knew the gift was really for you, Hol."

Holly touched the soft folds of the fabric. Her eyes filled with tears. She picked up all three of them and held them to her chest. She extended a hand and looked at Taina. "Thank you," she said. "I can't imagine a more special gift than this."

From the other room came the sound of something like glass smashing. They both jumped up and went to see what it was. Daniel had tried to reach a toy car on a shelf, and had knocked down a crystal candlestick in the process. The candlestick lay in pieces on the floor. David was standing over the boys. He had been napping in a hammock on the porch, and heard the commotion through an open window.

"Brat!" He shouted, and little Daniel started to cry. Then Bobby's face scrunched up and he joined his older brother. The big one, Patrick, let it rip too. The room filled with a chorus of howls. Erick had been nearby, and was about to apologize until he heard David snarling at the kids. His ears turned red as he shouted back at David, "I don't care if you're sick! You don't treat little kids like that just because you're pissed off!"

Holly put her face in her hands. Erick said, "Bringing three little boys here while David is sick? Are you insane? And this place is one big child-hazard."

With fists clenched, Holly screamed, "I thought it would be a once in a lifetime experience!"

"It is, it is," Taina reassured her. "Your heart is in the right place, Hol."

"I'm calling the airline," Erick said. "We're not staying four more days; this was a mistake."

"What's going on?" Julia said from the hallway. "I was gathering some seaweed for tonight's clambake and I heard all the shouting. Holly, why are you crying?" She looked down and her face fell. "Oh. Those candlesticks are antiques. Early Tiffany."

"*Were*," Taina said, picking up the shards and putting them in a paper towel.

Julia gathered herself up. "Look, Holly, we all know that people are more important than things. Don't worry."

Holly rubbed tears out of her eyes with the back of her hand. "Did you hear that Erick?"

"Tell that to David," he said. "Hell, I don't blame him for getting mad, even if he wasn't sick, these kids will drive anyone crazy. The place isn't for children. That's all."

Holly sat on the floor and dropped her head onto her folded arms, mumbling something about pilots being arrogant jerks.

"So—need help finding seaweed?" Taina said, a not-so subtle prompt to get out.

"Sure," Julia said, and grabbed her by the elbow. She led her down a hall and through the kitchen, then out to the back area of the veranda. Taina put her hand on her forehead. "Oh God, they give me a headache."

Julia wiped the sweat off her brow with the back of her hand. She took a deep breath. "It's gonna be fine."

They looked at each other, and it dawned on Julia, for the first time, that Taina had been giving her the cold shoulder lately. But suddenly the incident with Holly and the kids loosened the tension between them a bit.

"I have a little som'n som'n up here," a voice said out of nowhere. Ray was sitting alone on the veranda above them. All of a sudden, they smelled pot smoke. They stepped off the porch back onto the lawn so they could see him.

Taina said, "Ray! You can't!"

"Sure I can. I do it all the time. How do you think I was able to give up booze?"

"Help!" said Taina, touching the tips of her fingers to her forehead. "I'm in the cuckoo's nest."

"Is that a yes?"

"I'm not sure," called Julia. "I'll be right up." Taina followed her up the outdoor spiral that led to the veranda off Ray's room.

Thirty seconds later, Julia had declared that it was okay to smoke because technically, they were outside. Holly joined them, and they waved at the water taxi and the tour boats, the canoes and the Coast Guard boats. This act of rebellion relaxed Holly and dried her tears. She inhaled heartily, with all the force of the tension inside her. She sucked in smoke until her lungs burned and the ash at the tip of the joint glowed bright orange and the smoke made her eyes burn. Then she exhaled for the last time before disassembling the minuscule roach from its wet wrapper and ate the burnt buds with the meticulous intensity of a starving monkey. "They should go home," Holly said. "The boys had a wonderful two days. They got to see their uncles and aunts and they enjoyed this incredible house, but we should quit while we're ahead. Mission accomplished. I don't want them to remember David and Erick arguing or David being frustrated with them. They should go."

"They can jump-seat right?" Ray asked.

"Yeah, so it's not like we made this huge investment." She shrugged, then her face brightened. "I really loved the outfits, Taina," she said softly, touching a hand to Taina's knee. "And I love the idea of putting them on the boys so we can take a group photo, everyone gathered around the seawall, smiling and looking happy, like we had the best time and got along. Just like in J. Crew world."

Julia leaned forward. "You did get along. You did have a wonderful time, and it's not over. It's just that you crammed in years of family tension into just six days. That's how siblings are. Not some fantasy you see in a catalog that arrives at your house every month. It's this." She pushed a thumb back in the direction of the house. "This is what you've been missing out on. The beautiful messiness."

Holly's fantasy had been jerked away by the irony that it had, at last, come true, and she burst out laughing at the realization. Taina got the bug too, and they giggled like two teenagers. "This is what we've been missing!" Holly repeated, and howled again, shaking her head and scissoring her feet in the air. "Yelling at kids! DNA tests! Alcoholism!" Finally, Holly stopped. Her expression grew serious and she looked up at Ray. "Seriously, though, is it a bad thing that you're smoking pot?"

Raymond shrugged. "Is it a bad thing that *you're* smoking it?"

"I'm not a recovering alcoholic."

"This isn't alcohol." He shrugged again. "I'm cool with it. How about you?" He tilted his head toward the house.

Holly let her breath out and her head fell back against the chair. "We love you is all. Where did you get the pot anyway?"

He pointed toward Stony Creek. "A kid I met in the park the other day. He sells it out the town gazebo over there."

Julia shook her head. "Right under our noses. The nerve," she said, as she sucked in another lungful of smoke.

Ray held up two fingers. "Peace," he said, and took one last hit before turning his head, closing his eyes, and falling asleep. Taina and Holly dozed off too. From somewhere below, Erick was calling, frustration in his voice. Eventually, Holly shook her head and got up. "I must confess something to you, and you'll never hear me admit this ever again. There's nothing like kids to kill the fun in a marriage." She wrinkled her nose and whispered, "It's just work, work, work, argue, argue, and argue." She opened the wooden porch door, took a step up, then turned and stopped. She leaned forward and whispered, more to herself than Taina, "But"—she sighed—"this is what I wanted." She stepped into the house and disappeared.

Later that night, David and Erick mended fences. It was Tuesday, the seventh day, and David convinced Erick to stay until Sunday, the final day of the reunion. But it took him another day to summon the energy to wander back into their circle. He had some bait sent over from Stony Creek and he taught the boys to fish, thus greatly improving his uncle ranking. Erick and Holly were delighted to see their picky sons so determined to eat their catch, although they actually only ate a few flakes before going back to the safety of macaroni and cheese.

Adrian, Raymond, Taina, and Julia were on the porch having afternoon coffee and pie. Technically, they were babysitting. Erick had gone for a nice long run in Stony Creek and left the kids with Holly, who in turn decided that she needed some "alone time" too, and snuck off in a kayak, leaving the boys to the whole group of uncles and aunts.

David said that he wanted to bond with his nephews, and he set them up with fishing rods on the deep end of the island, on the backside of the house. On the lawn in the front of the house, Julia was in the middle of telling a story about her great-great-uncle's unsuccessful attempts to market an amphibious unicycle when they all heard a soft, hollow popping noise, followed by peals of laughter. After ten years of teaching, she knew mischievous laughter when she heard it. She jumped to her feet. "I'll check on the kids," she told Ray and Adrian.

"Allow *me*," Adrian said with a nod and a quick smile that implied that he was trying to take more responsibility. Ray went back inside the house and Julia followed Adrian. They rounded the house and came to a jungly space where the seagrass was as tall as a person, and peeked from behind the plants. David, Patrick, Daniel, and Bobby were all wearing black felt pirate hats and clutching their plastic swords. They were crouching behind the interior side of the seawall. The beach below was littered with what looked like a half-dozen giant balls of popcorn. The boys moved like ants, and one of them shouted "Pirates!"

Out on the water, the *Summer Salt* tour boat was passing by and people were waving. There was the hollow pop sound again—some kind of small explosion. An object whizzed across the water and landed a few feet from the boat. One of the white puffy things was lying on the grass close to the house, and Adrian scrambled to retrieve it and bring it back without being detected. It appeared to be made out of cotton that was partially burned. Adrian held it up to his nose. "It smells like gasoline," he said, just as they spotted a jar filled with a yellow liquid and a small blue cardboard box that was instantly recognizable to Julia. She gripped Adrian's wrist when she saw David crack the paper wrapper off a tampon, pull the cotton center out of the applicator tube, and dip both the string and the center into the jar of gasoline. They watched, in stunned silence, as David re-inserted the tampon into its cardboard applicator by tugging it back in with the string. He pinched it into a makeshift slingshot and lit it with a match. Then he pulled back the sling, and shot it into the air. The kids ducked. The tampon shot across the water, then *poof!* It detonated and rained white puffy bits over the water. The remains of the cardboard applicator landed on top of one of the loudspeakers of the tour boat. From behind the seawall came triumphant shouts, hooting, and a commando-style crawl for cover behind the seawall, as if the tour boat might return fire.

Julia's first impulse was to grab David by the collar, and march everyone up to their rooms. But this was, after all, traditional Griswold mischief. Her older cousins had invented this game when they were children. They must have told David about it. Behind her, Adrian was laughing so hard he had tears rolling down his face. She whispered to him that this was dangerous play, that they'd soon have to answer to the captain of the boat. The young captain's father's boat had also been attacked with tampons over the last forty years, and he probably wouldn't find it amusing in the least. And then there was Erick. But Adrian pulled Julia back by the waist, and said, "Julia, listen to me. This is probably the only glimpse of fatherhood that David is ever going to get."

"But playing with gas and matches? That's not fatherhood. He's acting like he's twelve. Which is how old my cousins were when they invented that game."

Then suddenly she remembered how her friend had run a finger across the glaze of the chocolate cake and said, "His time is running out." For a moment Julia wondered if David was regressing into childhood as a part of his illness, but then she saw how protective he was, making the boys stand back five feet before firing. "Keep going, keep going," she heard David say, and the boys would move back a hair, if at all, until he moved them himself. The longer Julia and Adrian watched, the less they dared to intrude. David had always been a man of logic, order, and calm. It had been so long since he had been so happy and free. Julia folded her arms and leaned into the tree, and she and Adrian secretly supervised the game. They snuck in closer, hiding behind the old cedars. "I feel like we're Joe Hardy and Nancy Drew," Julia whispered, to which Adrian replied, "Yeah, in *The Mystery of the Exploding Tampons*."

When they had catapulted the last tampon into the water, David put his flippers on and waded out to retrieve the floating pieces while the boys located them from the dock. They gathered them up and dropped them one by one into a garbage bag. They high-fived each other, and declared victory. Behind the cedars, Adrian turned to Julia and did the same thing.

The next day, Julia was feeling antisocial and preferred to just sit with the kids out on the dock. Her feelings for Adrian were multiplying exponentially, and she felt a kind of emotional vertigo. She wanted to keep her distance as best she could. She tossed quarters, one by one, into the shallow water around the dock, and handed each boy a set of snorkel gear. She didn't even have to explain that the goal was to find the most coins possible. "I'm gonna win!" Patrick shouted, his eyes already sparkling with the fever of competition. There was a splash, followed by another, followed by a "Wait for me!" and a third splash.

Erick appeared, arms folded in front of him, while Raymond served watermelon margaritas on the porch. Adrian and Julia had shared the tampon story with Taina and Ray, but they all agreed it was not a good idea to tell Holly, much less Erick. Erick kept looking over his shoulder. Julia said, "Erick. Go relax. Your kids aren't drowning on my watch."

"C'mon, honey," Holly called from the porch steps. "We can watch them from up here."

When Erick turned to look at Julia, it was like he was peering into the pit of her soul. "Will you dive in and rescue them if something happens? Will you risk your life if need be?" He demanded.

"Absolutely. In fact, I was a lifeguard in high school. But they'll be okay; it's shallow near the dock."

He lowered his eyes. "You know why I'm like this, right? It's because of my brother."

"Holly told me, Erick. I'm so sorry."

Erick's eyes softened and he nodded.

"Uh, Erick?" Julia said, grabbing hold of his arm. "Daniel is throwing rocks at a huge swan."

Erick turned around and sure enough, a swan the size of a small ostrich was circling and fluffing up its feathers, ready to go on the attack, while the three boys whipped coins at it. Erick turned and sprinted toward the water, yelling at the swan first, then at the boys. Holly bolted toward her family, giving Julia a grateful squeeze as she passed.

Later that day, Bobby was crying, and his parents couldn't console him. Holly and Erick were arguing again. The boy was hot, tired, and grouchy. His brothers were excluding him. Dinner was still an hour away. Julia ran out to the beach and came back with a periwinkle, a tiny mud snail. Julia sat the boy down on her lap and told him that if he said "Rum," slowly, over and over, that the snail would come out of its shell and crawl around on his hand. They began chanting, "*Ruuuuum. Ruuuuum,*" singing it lower on the second note. The boy was silent for the first few repetitions, but then he began to sing it with her, feeling the vibration of the "m" in his mouth and throat, elongating it so they harmonized the "mmmmm" until their breath ran out. When they got really good at it, they both laughed and had to concentrate not to crack up and break their perfect harmony. The snail extended one eye stalk, then the other, and slowly came out of its shell and crawled around the boy's hand. After that, the little boy declined invitations and taunts from his brothers, choosing rather, to gather more snails with Julia. At dinner that night, Bobby declared that Julia was his "favorite aunt", which didn't go over well with Taina or Holly. But on her right, David gave Julia a little kick under the table. On her left, Adrian did the same thing.

In the Northeast, in mid- to late August, there comes a day when it's unexpectedly cool, quite suddenly. This day happened on Friday, the third-to-last day of the reunion. David was upstairs napping, while Julia entertained the others, describing the often sharp transition to autumn: "You think that it's just a hint, a quick, premature leap toward fall; you expect the heat and mugginess to return, but no, it's over. A curtain comes down." She made a dramatic downward cutting motion. Then, "driving through town, you notice a single red leaf high up in a maple tree. You're on your way to the beach when a neighbor hands you a tiny pumpkin over the fence instead of the usual bagful of tomatoes. And that's it. What follows is a quick slide into autumn."

Sure enough, that afternoon, the hooded sweatshirts came out. They all laughed when Holly came down wearing a woolly Armenian sweater she found in an armoire. "It's sixty-two degrees, Florida girl," Julia said, shaking her head. "And you claim that you want to live here all year?" She tipped her head back. "Ha!"

The reason Julia mentioned the seasons was because she had begun to worry that the changing landscape might negatively affect David's state of mind. She looked at Taina and said, "You're a visual kind of person, so you know that winter landscapes can be so depressing." Taina agreed and Holly and Erick decided to invite him to Fort Lauderdale in late winter, even though they all knew that David wasn't a fan of flat, over-developed South Florida. "No hills, no real forests and way too much cement," he once told Julia. "What's the point?" But they all believed in the curative powers of rumrunners and sunshine, and Holly was home all day so he wouldn't be alone. It wouldn't be easy with David's medical needs, the longest he could be away was three weeks if everything went well, and you couldn't count on that. His treatments had side effects and complications that needed almost constant monitoring. Still, they understood the need for a plan to keep his spirits up all year. Suddenly Julia sighed and pointed behind her. "I'm going to go up and see what's taking David so long to come down. Then I'm going to make sure he takes his afternoon pills and make sure that he brings down his stress ball." She stood up, then sat back down. "Wait a minute," she said, as she looked at Adrian, then Taina, then Holly, and finally Raymond. "Guys, it's time for you to start doing these things automatically," she snapped her fingers, "and consistently. I can't be the default all the time."

Adrian nodded once and stood up. "I'll go check on him."

Taina had winced when Julia snapped her fingers, but she got up, reluctantly. She muttered, "You keep them in the fridge, right?"

Ray got up too. "He needs to take them with milk, or it'll mess up his stomach. I'll go get it."

"Thank you," said Julia. "Ray I know you're cooking Thai food tonight, so I'll go start the chopping."

Holly and Erick stayed put because they were watching over their boys, who were playing nearby in the yard. "Julia, I think you should get a starfish tattoo," Holly said. She passed her hand gently over the blank surface of Julia's hand. "You're the third sister. You know that, right?"

Julia looked at the empty chair where Taina had been sitting, and a cloud passed over Holly's face. It confirmed what

Julia had begun to suspect—that Taina wasn't feeling so sisterly these days.

David showed up at cocktail hour wearing a white panama hat with a black band around the crown. "I found it in the attic," he said. It used to belong to Julia's dad. He flicked a finger at the brim of the hat, raising it a bit over his eyes. At that moment, Adrian plucked Julia's empty martini glass from her and handed it to Raymond. "Bartending rule number one. Always give them a fresh glass." Raymond took it from him and disappeared into the kitchen.

"Why is Ray bartending for you?" Erick asked. "That's just wrong."

"I can wash my own glass," Julia called out, giving Erick a look of agreement. She followed Ray into the kitchen. Inside the house, the jazz was so loud that Ray didn't hear Julia following behind. He stopped at the sink and grabbed a sponge to wash the martini glass, then he held the glass up to the light to see if there was still vodka at the bottom. He swirled it around. He looked at it for a long time, and Julia got the impression that he had found something out of place, like a shard of glass or a dead bug.

Ray brought the glass up to his lips and tipped it back. Julia couldn't see his face, but she could almost taste it with him, that sting of warmed vodka, the salty taste of olive juice, prickling the front of the mouth. Recognizing the potential gravity of what he had done, Julia instinctively turned and stepped into the butler's pantry. She waited a few seconds and then went back into the kitchen, pretending that she had not been in there all along. Raymond gave her back her glass, clean and dry, with fresh vodka that had ice crystals on top. She thanked him, avoiding his eyes, and went outside, but she was no longer interested in drinking it. She filled a glass with cranberry juice and seltzer, Ray's signature drink. David was laughing and joking and she noticed, suddenly, how happy he seemed. Soon, she forgot all about the incident in the kitchen.

Ray's seafood and noodles had a spicy, lemony, coconut sauce that deserved nothing less than the moans of delight it got. They soothed their burning mouths with ice-cold beer. During the evening toast, David took off his white panama hat, held his drink up, and said, "There is nowhere I'd rather be than right here with all of you. There are people who live their whole lives without ever experiencing the feeling of being at the right place at the right time, of just standing at the center of your own life. I feel that way right now; and I want to thank you all for showing up here, in this moment." He said it flawlessly, with no aphasia.

Even the three boys stared at him, blinking and crunching their baby carrots. Julia remembered their talk at the Christmas tree farm back in the spring, how David had defined his idea of holiness as an encounter with a beast in the woods. Only Julia could have predicted that they would find communion in a house filled with family, bickering kids, competition, noise, and chaos. It was as if their affection for each other appeared amid rustling leaves, long enough for everyone to see it, then spooked and disappeared from wherever it came. David took Julia's hand and thanked the Griswold family, "who are all here with us right now." His eyes roamed the porch, stopping at intervals, smiling sometimes, as if to make eye contact with invisible people sitting in the gallery of wicker chairs. So convincing was his acknowledgement of the unseen that the boys' eyes grew huge, and they scooted closer to their parents.

Chapter

33

David

As I toast my siblings, I see the uncles across the lawn. They tip the brims of their ubiquitous panama hats, but I also spot safari hats, felt bowlers, fishing hats, fedoras, and a few hunting boonies. The Griswold personalities are coming through more clearly every day. Today, I notice that the adventurer who invented the water unicycle is wearing a leather race cap with goggles fastened to the top of his visor. Julia's third cousin, a hulking teenager, is wearing wrestling headgear. The Vietnam-era "conscientious objector" in the family is wearing John Lennon glasses and has a bandana tied around his head. The old guys look happy as usual, and they join in on the toast by raising their odd-sized bottles of beer, brands that no longer exist. The more contemporary men raise gleaming cans of Coors in the sunshine, and I can tell, by the way they hold them—uncomfortably, with two fingers—that the cans have been sitting in ice too long and are half-frozen. The aunts are scattered across the lawn, their faces concealed behind colorful straw hats. All around me, the trees serve as a sundial; I notice that the shadows falling across the lawn have lengthened by at least three inches since we got here. I'm in "the hilltop hour" as Helen Keller called these moments of pure happiness. It's that perfect moment, as my grandmother used to say, "before everything goes to hell."

Chapter

34

Julia lowered a handful of dirty dinner dishes into the sink. When she turned, there was Adrian, holding a bowl in one hand and a spoon in the other. "Try this," he said, advancing with a spoonful of sticky coconut-rice pudding, topped with a thin slice of ripe mango. Adrian's lips were red and swollen from the spicy heat of the last course. Julia opened her mouth and he slid the spoon inside and deposited a mouthful of contrasts: warm, sticky rice and cool, slippery mango. As it melted in her mouth, she closed her eyes and moaned. She felt him step closer, and closer still, so that one of his arms was touching hers.

Holly walked in with an armful of dishes. Julia opened her eyes just in time to see Holly's expression change. Holly blinked quickly, locked eyes with Adrian, then swung her gaze over to Julia. "Wow, you're flushed," she said. Julia pivoted around and hastened to wipe scraps of food off plates with a wad of soiled napkins.

Holly grabbed Adrian's arm. "Would you mind playing some music? It doesn't have to be anything fancy. Just so we're together, having fun."

Adrian smiled and put a finger under Holly's chin and kissed her on one cheek. "You're a good egg, you know that?"

Holly shook her head. "I didn't have to cancel eleven gigs to be here. You did, sweetie." After David's cocktail hour toast, everyone was affable like that, calling each other pet names, hugging and backslapping, thanking each other for every little thing.

Adrian put a hand on Julia's shoulder. "If you accompany me with the piano, I can play guitar."

"Okay, but I suck," Julia said. "Just so we're clear on that."

Holly waved a dishrag at them and pushed them both out the door. "Taina and Erick will do the dishes while I put the boys to bed. Be ready in an hour or you'll find us all passed out."

Adrian and Julia found five songs that they both knew well, among them "Piano Man" and "Tiny Dancer." The last one they would sing was "This Guy's in Love with You," as Adrian had promised to do back in the spring. When he put the sheet music of that song in front of her, Julia remembered the strong attraction she had felt that day that they had come to the house alone, and how confusing that feeling had been. How shockingly natural it felt to be around him now. She felt like she'd known him for years. Adrian kept his eyes on his fingers, plucking the strings of his guitar:

> *I've heard some talk*
> *They say you think I'm fine*

Yes, Julia thought as she pressed down on the keys of the piano, *you absolutely are*. They played under the veiled gaze of a bridal grandmother and her groom. Julia played well that night, beyond her normal range, due in part to the euphoria that kept her from feeling self-conscious. But she also felt connected to Adrian's talent, and therefore for a brief moment, it felt like her own. She was inside his magic, not just standing outside, admiring it like everyone else. She was exhilarated by this heightened state of awareness, this glow-in-the-dark, heart-on-fire undercurrent. Perhaps it shouldn't be so surprising that David's illness was bringing them closer together, uniting them all in a grander way. Sadness, lust, melancholy, and happiness all mixed together into an unlikely cocktail that had Julia utterly intoxicated.

When the song was over, David stood and called for an encore, but a few notes into it, David asked Julia to dance. She stepped away from the piano and Adrian sang and played guitar unaccompanied. This time it was David's voice that rose over Adrian's, *"Say you're in love, in love, with this guy."*

Julia held David closer, as if to protect him from . . . what? Herself? She felt a knot form in her throat, at the familiar warmth of his body, and she kept her focus on the steps of the dance to keep from thinking too much. Suddenly, he pushed her away, but gently. He put a hand up, signaling Adrian to stop. The room grew quiet.

David got down on one knee, still holding on to her hand. The soft light in the room made his gray eyes shift to a sparkling, mineral blue. He pulled out a ring from the front pocket of his camp shirt and took his hat off to reveal his bald head and six-inch brain-surgery scar. "Julia Griswold," he said. "I love you and want to spend every day of my life with you. Will you marry me?"

Chapter

35

David

Even as I'm dropping down on one knee, I know this proposal is doomed. I know that I'm being fueled by a spirit called gin and by a demon called jealousy. I may have brain damage, but I'm not stupid. I can see that Julia's all goo-goo eyed over Adrian's singing, and I'm utterly terrified by the prospect that the feeling might be mutual. I don't know what I thought her answer would be, but I was confident that she'd at least consider it. But cool as can be, she cups my head with her hands and says, "Oh hon, you're just beer-goggling." She wrinkles up that cute little freckled nose and says, "You won't like me this much when the Beefeater wears off."

"I'm not beer-goggling! I love you!" I bark, looking over my shoulder at Adrian, just to make sure he's listening.

"Say yes!" Taina calls out in a low, smoky voice. Ray jabs her with an elbow and mumbles, "*Shh*. Friends don't let friends drink and propose."

Holly is just staring at the floor in horror, and so is Erick.

Julia butts her forehead softy against mine and looks into my eyes. "You know perfectly well that the answer is a big, fat, hairy 'no.'"

"So did you," I point out. "On that morning at Long Wharf. But you asked me anyway."

She smiles, flicks her head a little to the side, points to me, and says, "Touché."

I shake my head, this is going down the wrong track. "This isn't a fencing match, Julia, I'm beg—" A grandfather clock gongs somewhere downstairs; a warning from the masculine spirits of the house. So I stop, before I totally humiliate myself. I gather up my pride. I'll never resort to begging anyone to marry me. Not even Julia.

She looks relieved. She gives me her hand, and pulls me up. With her arms and with the swaying of her hips she induces me to dance with her again, as Adrian plays "Just the Way You Are."

"I took the good times," she sings along, still looking straight at me. "I'll take the bad times."

I don't know how she does it, but she calms that tempest inside me and I just sort of melt. I just hold her and we sing along, while Ray and Taina and Holly and Erick dance beside us. Adrian has shifted over to the piano, he keeps his head down, concentrating on the keys, and I can pretend that the whole thing never happened, especially since I'm drunk. When the show is over, we all go back for one last cocktail. I pour myself another gin martini, but I'm starting to feel pretty sorry for myself.

36

David's limbs seemed to drift onto Julia's body; his arms draped themselves around her shoulders, his fingers brushed her thighs. Now and then Adrian shot Julia an apologetic look, the way guys do when they have a drunk and unruly friend.

Ray brought out the karaoke machine, and David put his hat back on and they had great fun singing until David couldn't remember the lyrics to "Just a Gigolo," and since he couldn't read, his mood spiraled down fast. At one point, he whipped the stress ball at Adrian, but his aim was so bad that it got stuck on top of one of the kitchen cabinets and everyone laughed. That did it. He sat down at the kitchen table, held his chin up with his hand, and said, to no one in particular, "I'm *sick* of being a dying man. How can it be my time? It's so stupid. And pointless. Why did I go to college? Why did I get a job? Save money? Why did I exercise . . . for what? The future was a lie!" He pounded a fist on the table. "I was wasting my time!"

"Time to put the gin away," Julia said to Adrian.

"Pour me another one, will ya, sweetheart?" David said to

Julia, and so Julia went to the refrigerator and brought him a tall glass full of ice and seltzer, which David pushed away.

"Tell us, *Flaco*," Adrian said, sitting down across from him, "What would you have done differently? Do you really regret spending four years studying botany? Meeting new and interesting people in college? Securing a good job?"

"Oh, c'mon, you've had many a day in the sun," Taina chimed in.

David raised a fist like an activist as he spoke. "I should have climbed freakin' Everest! I was afraid of getting myself killed! HA! I shoulda gone bungee jumping, I shoulda parachuted from airplanes! I shoulda had seven wives and twenty kids! I shoulda taken my parents to Hawaii!"

"You didn't even want *one* wife," Julia said coolly.

"You can still take your parents to Hawaii," Holly soothed, stroking David's shoulders. "Let's go."

"I can't afford it *now*," he wined. "I need to hold on to my cash for experimental drugs not covered by insurgents."

"Insurance."

"See? I can't even talk right. I'm David-who's-dying-of-cancer-David!" He was slurring his words, but his rant was the most he'd spoken the entire time they'd been on the island. He turned to Erick, as if to fill him in. "See. There's this dude that follows me around everywhere I go, his name's cancer. He talks for me, you know? Before I even open my mouth cancer shakes people's hands and takes over. It's like that movie, *Twins*, the one with Arnold Schwarzenegger as the good twin and Danny DeVito as the evil twin? The cancer is Danny DeVito—mean, bossy, big-mouthed, impossible to live with. Only not funny like Danny DeVito. Not funny at all."

Erick shrugged. "Then don't compare him to Danny DeVito. I love Danny DeVito."

Julia rolled her eyes and pointed at David with her thumb. "Never in six years has he ever mentioned going to Hawaii."

"Did too," David said, holding up a finger. "Once." He burped loudly.

"Do you want to go somewhere David?" Holly said. "Because if you do, tell us. Maybe we can make it happen."

"Yeah, you know, like Make-a-Wish Foundation," Ray said. "Wanna go to Disney, David? I'd definitely do that with you."

Adrian groaned. David had his head down on the table, over his folded arms. "I hate Disney," he mumbled.

"Is there any 'naturey' thing you'd like to see?" Holly persisted. "Or have you seen it all?"

"I'm not going camping in Alaska," Julia said. "Just letting you all know."

"He hasn't seen anything," Adrian said. They all turned to look. David lifted his head. "He's never seen full-wattage bioluminescence."

David's eyes sparkled for just a second or two. "I've been to La Parguera. It's pretty cool."

Adrian shook his head. "La Parguera? Dead as a doornail."

"Huh?"

"Another victim of tourism. The motor fuel from the boats polluted the water and the ecosystem no longer works." He pointed to the lamp on the side of the house. "And there's tons of light pollution, so what little bioluminescence there is you can't even see." Adrian took a sip of wine and spoke in a slow, low voice. He looked at the women first. "Vieques is an island off the coast of Puerto Rico. It's the most undeveloped, pristine place in the entire Caribbean because access was restricted by the U.S. Navy. The Navy left in 2003 and now it's a nature preserve and home to the best bio-bay in the world. But Vieques learned a lesson from La Parguera. They guard

Mosquito Bay like it's full of holy water. No motorboats are allowed, and they don't even let you use insect repellent when you go in the water. The water has these microscopic organisms in it that suck up sunlight like solar batteries. They release the light when provoked by motion. You go out at night, in kayaks, and everything that moves glows and sparkles, the waves, the fish below, and if you swim in it, you literally glow. Dip your hand in the water, and it sparkles like tiny fireworks as it rolls down your body. It's almost a religious experience. It's insane."

David's mouth was hanging open as he listened. Then he blinked and said, "Dude. You never told me about this."

Adrian shrugged. "I thought you were only into hiking."

David sat upright, slammed his hand on the table, which sent the salt shaker flying. "I have to see that. Right now."

"What about Hawaii?" Julia said. "Can *I* go with your parents to Hawaii?"

"We'll do that too, babe," David said, pointing at her. "And then we'll have twenty kids." Julia balled up her napkin and threw it at him. He blocked it and it bounced back at her.

Holly yawned, stood up, and stretched. "Sounds like a plan," she said as her joints cracked loudly and they all got up and called it a night. For the first time in eight days, Julia didn't put David to bed. She asked Ray to do it. She passed his room on her way up, after she went through the house turning off all the lights. From the hallway, she could hear the two of them laughing and she guessed, by Ray's sudden shrieks, that David was modeling her Uncle Charles's secret collection of mustaches and toupees.

In her bedroom, Julia lit a candle, a no-no, but even she broke the house rules now and then. Humming softly, she bathed in the claw-foot tub, in warm saltwater. She was a little drunk, but not necessarily on alcohol. She couldn't stop thinking about Adrian. She had left her bedroom door unlocked. She could barely admit it to herself, but she very much wanted Adrian to sneak in. He never would do such a thing of course, but the fantasy occupied her mind from the moment she went upstairs. As she scrubbed her skin with a washcloth, she imagined a vinyl disc falling. A crackly recording of "Only You" playing softly. Adrian stepping into in the claw-foot tub with her. Outside the window, she could hear the sound of waves bashing into rocks and being shredded into ribbons of silver that tumbled back to sea.

As if the fantasy had shifted from her imagination to reality, she heard footsteps outside her door. She watched the jewel-shaped glass door handle of the bathroom turn in the dim light. Her heart quickened. She sank lower into her bath, until she tasted the saltiness of the seawater.

It wasn't Adrian, it was David. He stopped at the door, then took a step forward and stood over her. Julia's arms flew over her bare chest.

"I should've married you while I had the chance," he whispered. She was about to protest, but he put his hands up. "Don't. I just wanted to see you like this one last time, because I couldn't remember, Julia." He pointed at his temple. "What you look like naked. It's like someone stole it from me." But he was looking at her eyes, not her body. He seemed clear-headed and lucid, and his eyes were shiny with emotion. So Julia let her arms fall back for a moment. Then she stood up and let him see. Slowly, she grabbed a towel and wrapped it around herself.

"I wasn't beer-goggling," he whispered, "when I said that you're beautiful." Then he turned around and left, closing the door behind him. Julia stared at the glass door handle for what seemed like an eternity, until she felt cold.

Julia had trouble sleeping that night. In the early morning hours, a door slammed. She closed her eyes and hoped that it would all dissolve back into sweet oblivion. Her stomach was acidic and generally offended after so many days of continuous consumption of rich foods and alcohol. Truth be told, entertaining on the island was exhausting and the logistics were a nightmare. As much as guests pitched in, it was the hostess who had to stay on top of the meal planning and making sure everyone was comfortable. She was so ready for the gathering to be over. It had been a success, overall. The DNA test results were in, and her mother had agreed to pass them on to the water taxi operator after she got home from work, that way they could know the results before they left. Then Julia would have to clean the place, wash all the bedding and towels. The whole job would take more than two days to complete and she couldn't rely on David. She sunk deeper into the pillow, tired at the very thought of it, but it was useless. She was awake. She got up and wandered the house, making a mental checklist of everything that had to be done. In the boiler room, the laundry baskets were overstuffed, and she could smell the gasoline-soaked tampon trash from the bin just outside the door. The tide was low and the whole house stunk of seaweed. She remembered that David had drunk too much the night before. In the hall she ran into Ray, who assured her that he would take care of David, so she went back up to her room to read.

Chapter

37

David

It's Saturday, the second-to-the-last day. I've decided that I'm never gonna drink alcohol ever, ever again. I'm resting my head on the edge of the toilet. As if being sick isn't bad enough, I now have this indelible emotional connection between nausea and chemotherapy, so what follows is a profound kind of sorrow over the fact that I chose to do this to myself. There's a special kind of shame waiting for me inside the toilet bowl, in the water that reflects back this image of myself, miserable and barfing. A lot of last night is fuzzy, but how can I forget the moment I asked Julia to marry me? Or that it turned into a sloppy, pathetic joke? I behaved like a jealous drunk. Now I'm hungover, exhausted, and I've never felt more ashamed of myself. I go back to bed, partly to rest, partly to forget.

Not long after, I am forcibly ejected from the bliss of sleep. Ray is at my bedside, insisting that I sit up. There is a dusty thudding in my head. Even the pale rectangle of light that surrounds the shaded window does me harm. My mouth tastes like a small animal crawled inside and died. Ray makes me chew a chalky antacid tablet, which makes my stomach rise up and push against my throat. I lay back down, as the whole scene beats like a pulse before me, and Ray puts a cold, damp cloth on my forehead. "Been there, done that, got the t-shirt," he intones, as he pulls a light blanket over my shoulders. I thank him and go back to sleep. When I wake up, hours later, the glass of water is full and there's a plate of saltines at my bedside. I'm still hungover, but much improved. A tiny thread of optimism bubbles up, and then burst when I look at the clock. Two o'clock in the afternoon, and I haven't seen or heard from Julia. I eat the saltines, drink the water, and go back to sleep.

When I finally make it downstairs, it's four o'clock and I'm famished. I look around for my family. Holly and Ray are out on the dock with the boys. Erick and Taina have kitchen duty today; Erick is peeling potatoes and Taina is peeling peaches. Even in my self-absorbed misery, I can't help but notice the copper bags under Taina's eyes. I'm too trashed to do anything but utter the basics: "Where's Julia?" Erick points behind him and tells me that Julia is in the parlor with Adrian. "They have this game where she teaches him something about American history through Griswold memorabilia," Erick says. "Turns out Adrian is interested in history. Sounds like they're having a ball in there." He turns to look at Taina. "I hated history class. You?" Taina sticks out her tongue, points a finger into her mouth, and makes a gagging noise. Which reminds me that I need to get some food into my stomach, so I toast some bread and think, would it have killed Julia to bring me some tea and ask how I'm feeling?

I peek my head into the parlor, where Adrian and Julia are sitting on the floor, books open on their laps. Elvis's "Are You Lonesome Tonight?" is playing on the Victrola. They don't see me standing here in the doorway, watching them. Instead, my eyes meet those of the human skull on the bookshelf, which reminds me suddenly of my MRI films. It's depressing to think that that was a real person, and that his head ended up as a book-end at a beach house. Suddenly, everything about the Griswold house repulses me. The presence of the dead is no longer subtle; it is overpowering. I feel a wave of nausea at the thought that maybe the dead had been preparing me all along.

"What the hell!" Julia shouts all of a sudden. She stands up, but with a great deal of effort, still holding the heavy copy of *The Griswolds of New Haven County*. She points. Adrian leans over to take a look. She looks up with a stunned expression on her face.

"What?" I step into the room and they see me.

"Someone ripped out a page," says Adrian.

I go to Julia's side to inspect the book, and sure enough, a page has been ripped clean. I peek at the cover. "This is the newest one," I say.

"It's the page that has my birth," says Julia. "Someone ripped it out . . . like in the last few days."

I feel terrible that the book has been damaged, but at the same time, I'm secretly glad for this distraction, because I'm still dragging around the heavy, stinking awkwardness of the previous night like the pelt of a freshly killed moose. It takes the focus off of my shame.

Erick and Taina appear in the doorway. Erick is giving Taina a strange look, and Taina looks kind of panicked. She points out the window. "I think I saw a kid running around with it." Adrian and I turn and look out the window, at the partial view of the boys fishing off the dock outside with their mother.

"Are you kidding me?" Erick jerks his head back. "I watch them like a hawk. That's impossible."

"Maybe it happened while you were jogging in Stony Creek," Taina says with a shrug. She is wearing her sunglasses pulled up over her head, and she reaches up and pulls them down to cover her eyes.

"Holly was watching them the one time I went into town," Erick replies. "And she wouldn't let them wander the house unsupervised."

Taina smiles and folds her hands in front of her. "Uh . . . Holly left them with David," she says, flashing a tight, sassy smile. "She went kayaking."

"We were outside the whole time," I assure Erick, putting my hands up. "Don't get pissed at Holly, okay? It was just for a little while." Adrian, Julia, and I share a conspiratorial look, but Taina can't help herself: "Yeah, teaching them to make little gasoline bombs."

"Come again?" Erick looks hard to the side. I know that look; it's all too familiar.

"She's just kidding," Adrian says, making a cutting motion across his throat. "And of course the boys didn't rip the book. Why would the kids pick *the* page that documents Julia's birth? How would they even know?" He puts a hand on Erick's shoulder. "Relax." He looks back and mumbles, "Tai, why the hell would you throw the kids under the bus?"

Erick points at Taina. "You did it, didn't you?"

"Ha ha." Taina feigns laughter. "Very funny."

"You're jealous of Julia. So you ripped her out of the history books."

"Jealous?" Adrian says.

Taina puts her hands on her hips and warns Erick to stay out of it, to which Erick replies, "I would've kept my mouth shut if you hadn't chosen to accuse my children," he says. "I won't have it."

"Alright," Adrian says wearily. "We're all tired, but Tai hasn't slept much in the last three days. She's extremely sleep-deprived. Let's just calm down."

"Hold on," Julia says, stepping forward. "Let me just get this straight. Erick thinks that Taina did it." She turns to Taina. "Did you?"

Taina squints, turns her head to the side, and snaps, "That's insulting."

Julia gets a strange look on her face. "Why are you wearing sunglasses inside the house?"

"Taina, put your hand on David's starfish tattoo and say you didn't do it," says Erick.

Taina scoffs, "It's not like it's the Bible."

"Enough," Adrian says. "We'll find the missing page, and I'll tape it back. I'm sure it was an accident."

"You're right, Erick. The tattoo *is* our Bible," I say, suddenly understanding the power in the symbol, given the timing.

"The DNA test results will be here," Julia says and looks at her watch, "in about twenty minutes, so if you want to make a statement of faith, do it right now."

I hold my hand out. Taina doesn't move. She sighs, lowers her eyes, and says, "Okay, I did it."

I swallow hard. "But *why*? By accident?"

She raises her sunglasses and looks into my eyes. "Because of Adrian and Julia." She nods in their direction without looking at them. "I had a feeling that they were falling in love with each other, and it enraged me because I knew that you . . ." With her right hand, she tugs at the ring finger of her other hand. "You were gonna ask her to marry you. Which you did, and well . . . look what a disaster that was."

Adrian withdraws his arm from around Taina and throws me a glance. "Jesus, Taina, why would you bring *that* up?"

"Now wait a minute," Erick interjects. "That's only half the story. Don't you get it, Adrian? Taina's been in love with you for years." He takes a step back with downcast eyes. "There. I said it. Cat's out of the bag." He holds his hands out in a surrendering gesture and turns to Taina. "Maybe I'm throwing Holly under the bus here, but you should know that she tells me *everything*." He turns and walks out, but in his haste to leave the room, Erick's shoulder bumps the edge of a picture frame. The picture falls off the wall and the glass smashes on the ground. The thumping in my head picks up an extra beat. I make my hands into fists. I close my eyes and suddenly I remember going into Julia's bathroom last night. I recall what I said. How she let me see her naked, out of pity. I remembered the look on her face when I asked her to marry me. How she laughed and said, "The answer is a big, fat, hairy 'no.'" I remember how she glowed, how bewitched she looked when Adrian was singing like he was singing to her, which, I suddenly realize—he was. I want to kill him.

I rush at Adrian. I slap my hands onto the tops of his shoulders and shove him back. He falls and I go down with him. I hear a loud *thunk* as Adrian hits his head against the ledge of a table so hard that it bounces forward. I look down, where Adrian is sitting, his head tilted to the side. He touches the back of his head, then looks at his hand. His fingers are wet with blood, a bright cherry-colored splotch that lingers, and then trickles slowly down the length of his wrist. "Son of a bitch," he says, pushing me off of him. He leaves a bright, bloody fingerprint on the breast of my white t-shirt.

Something makes me look up, toward the parlor, toward the gilded mirror over the fireplace. I glimpse the reflection of the skull sitting on a bookshelf on the opposite wall. Its ghoulish sockets are dark, its teeth yellow and slightly parted, as if the person died in the middle a good laugh.

38

As Ray walked through the door with the DNA results, he noticed, as he passed through the dining room, that the expression on the figurehead's face was all wrong. Serena looked chaste, more like a church statue, worried eyes downcast as if to say, "Oh no."

From the kitchen, Ray heard Julia and David arguing. There was some kind of commotion going on, and Julia came bounding in, sobbing. She threw open the door of the icebox and reached inside. Taina was behind her, and Ray caught the tail end of some kind of argument between them. "It would kill him," Taina was saying.

"What would kill who?" Ray asked. Taina didn't answer and Julia kept her lips pressed together and didn't say anything as she filled a Ziploc bag with ice. She sealed the ice pack and wrapped it in a towel. Taina spotted her cigarettes on the windowsill and opened the package, hands trembling. Her eyes were bloodshot and she had bruised circles under her eyes. She had told Ray that she had slept no more than twelve hours in the past four days.

"Don't," Julia said, pointing to the cigarette in Taina's hand.

Taina struck a match and held it to the tip of her Marlboro. She inhaled, without taking her eyes off Julia. The tip of the cigarette ignited.

Julia put the bag of ice down, stunned. "Are you out of your mind?"

"Don't come closer," Taina said in a low voice. She squinted at the smoke rising in front of her eyes.

"Put it out, Tai," Ray said. "C'mon."

"I've never seen this side of you," Julia said, staring hard at Taina. "Your behavior is appalling. You have three seconds to get the hell out of my house with that cigarette."

Something inside Ray was stirred by that imperative. Those words were familiar to him; his girlfriend had said she didn't know him anymore just before she left. It had been almost eight years now, and he had been consistently sober since then. But the words still stung, or rather, awakened memories of feeling out of control. He recognized that Taina was on the same bad ride, saw the pain in her eyes as she took a long, slow drag of her cigarette. She slid one shoulder forward, in the slow, bone-by-bone retreat of a cowboy making an exit from a saloon while trying to hold on to pride. She went outside and smoked half the cigarette, then she tossed it, still lit, on Uncle James's grave. Ray followed her, and when she disappeared back into the house, he looked down at the lit cigarette, with the smoke curling up from its tip just below the line that spelled out the name "Griswold." "Sorry about that, sir," he said, and he picked up the cigarette. His fingers were trembling as he put it to his lips and inhaled. He finished it off and looked at the tattoo on his left hand. He was thinking about the envelope sitting on the kitchen table. Like a mother hen, Ray made his way through the house checking up on everyone. He could hear that Erick and Holly were arguing, even through the closed bedroom door. The children were in an adjacent room, playing a board game. Taina was on the veranda, apparently trying to sketch, but when he came up behind her, she was staring at a blank sheet of paper, and there were at least four wads of crumpled paper at her feet. David was up in his room, fuming. His aphasia was worse than ever, probably due to the hangover, and he had gotten even more frustrated trying to express himself, although he did manage to fill Ray in on what had happened.

Julia had attended to Adrian's head wound, and she told Ray that she wanted to make sure that Adrian didn't have a concussion. Adrian refused to go to the emergency room, but he admitted that he was a little nauseated and wanted to lie down. Julia took him up to her room and turned on the air-conditioning. The only thing left for Ray to do was cook. He thought he might be able to restore peace with a final meal, and he headed downstairs, his great heart heavy with worry.

Ray opened the envelope, alone. He thought it was a bad omen that he got a paper cut as he ripped open the envelope from DNA Concepts. He held up his finger and watched a tiny line of blood rise up along the surface of his skin. He wondered how something as abstract as DNA could contain the power to bond people—legally, physically, morally, and emotionally.

The individual reports were full of jargon, numbers, charts, but he immediately saw that David and Adrian had common mitochondrial DNA, and therefore it was likely that they had the same mother. There were no other genetic matches between any of them. So Adrian had finally caved in, Ray thought. He had given David what he wanted. And where did that leave them? The only two that shared blood had gotten into a fistfight. What hope was there for the rest of them to stick together?

Ray had not been able to gather them, so there had been no final dinner. Holly and her family had eaten on the porch, while Taina, David, and Adrian had taken plates up to their rooms. Julia ate standing up, and then retreated upstairs to watch over Adrian. She told Ray that even though she understood that David has lost some impulse control after his brain surgery, she was still upset with him and preferred not to deal with him that night. Ray asked her point blank if she and Adrian were an item. He half-expected her to say that it was none of his business, but instead she turned and said, "Adrian is all about family loyalty. You know that." Yeah, he thought. But Adrian had been right. Genetics could and would change everything. As loyal as Adrian was, he would see that their family was just an illusion. And Ray felt all alone again.

Nighttime came and everyone went to bed. Julia kept a vigil over Adrian, who would sleep in the cot next to her bed on the third floor, so she could wake him up every hour to make sure his head injury wasn't worse than he thought. David holed up in his room. "I'm mashing," he mumbled, which Ray assumed was "crashing" spoken through aphasia.

"I'm mashing too, buddy," Ray answered, and retreated from David's room and walked downstairs, through a house that seemed completely empty of life. In the pantry, Ray found the last of the gin, which, he guessed, wasn't going to be nearly enough. He drank it straight out of a tall milk glass. When it was gone, he went to the parlor and found a half-empty bottle of premium Scotch, displayed like a dead fairy-tale princess in a pearly, satin-lined coffin, inside an otherwise barren liquor cabinet. Oh, that lovely bottle, with its blue-and-gold sash across its square breast. He dug his fingers into the creamy satin of the casket and lifted it out by the neck. He uncapped it, inhaled deeply, and tipped it back. He drank in long, thirsty gulps. Inside his heart, the devil put his head down. *God, that's smooth*, he thought. He looked closer at the label, squinting. No wonder. It was forty years old. Inexplicably, he had smelled tobacco and Old Spice aftershave when he opened the liquor cabinet, and those scents had kept him company the whole time he was drinking the Scotch. In the kitchen, he found Taina's cigarettes and her lighter. He lit up and drank alone until the whisky was gone. Then he was about to drop the cigarette into a large trash bin outside the boiler room when he saw pieces of broken glass and some paper towels stained with blood, evidence of the war that had taken place earlier. He got the DNA test results and put them in the trash. Then he tossed the cigarette in the trash bin, and went to bed.

The cigarette smoldered through several days' worth of trash until it reached the bag of gasoline-soaked tampons, well past midnight. There was an energetic *poof*, as an exuberant breath of fire blew off the lid of the trashcan. It ignited a dry vine, and the fire spread to a trellis attached to the house. The wood shingles caught fire, as did the curtains of the boiler room, via an open window. The piles of laundry ignited and the fire progressed into the kitchen, where it easily devoured the cabinets. Once it entered the kitchen, it set off the smoke alarms. By the time Erick's feet hit the stairs, the hall was already filling with smoke. He ran to get Holly and the kids, shouting to anyone who might hear him. There were loud popping noises, and a hiss. Within minutes, there was an exponential growth of flames and heat. They heard the mesmerizing crackle of a fire's consumption of wood, not just any wood, but century-old wood.

"Fire!" Erick shouted and realized with growing horror, that Julia and Adrian were upstairs, on the third floor. Erick got his family out first. He left Holly in charge of the children and ran to find a cell phone, and to do his very best to rouse her siblings, but was only able to wake up Taina, who told him to go back outside to protect his family. Then she went back inside to help Raymond and David. Erick reminded her, with rising panic, that Adrian might have a concussion.

On land, a boy who had been selling marijuana from inside the Stony Creek gazebo called the fire department. He described what he saw to the dispatcher—that the fire was thicker at the base, shaped like a tulip, and that the flames rose from the bottom like petals drawn together, opening up, "like a bloomin' onion."

The fire trucks howled their way through the winding roads down to shore. Fire rescue boats and marine police boats circled the island, blasting the sides of the Griswold house with water, hoping for the best. A strong breeze lifted and blew hard across Long Island Sound, a huge breath that only gave the fire more life. The Griswold house was consumed from its core to its chipping gray shingles. A few moments later, the cupola imploded and there was a terrible roar as the floors inside collapsed. Every shred of paper, every photo, every relic, all of it, burned.

Chapter

39

At the hospital, Julia faced a roomful of Griswold family members. She had a bandage on her arm and shoulder, and her hair was chopped off because it had been singed right up to the neck. David had no burns but he had twisted an ankle after he jumped out of a second-story balcony, into the hydrangeas. Taina's burns were mild but diffuse; Ray had suffered smoke inhalation. Adrian had a second-degree burn on his leg. Only Ray and Adrian stayed in the hospital overnight. It appeared, however, that no one suffered irreparable harm. No one, that was, but the Griswolds.

Julia was trembling as she explained what little she knew at that point. David felt bitter frustration that his aphasia prevented him from stepping in and taking the heat. He tried a few times, interrupting and slowing down the conversation, until Julia stopped him, and with a quick pat to the knee, reassured him that she could handle it. She turned back to the crowd and insisted that she didn't blame any one person for the accident. A profound change had come over the siblings over the course of the ten days together, and that tensions had been running high.

The fire had been the physical realization of that energy, albeit accidental. David expressed his regret and asked the family for forgiveness. He wanted so badly to be like them, he explained, that he had driven his siblings to the edge by forcing genetic self-knowledge upon them, something that, he could see now, they weren't ready to handle.

But the family wasn't quite ready to forgive. While the house itself was insured, there was the loss of the irreplaceable contents.

"Memory is like water, if you don't contain it, it drains away," said an aunt, dabbing at her eyes. "We loved that house so much."

The ninety-three-year-old patriarch, Uncle Mick, had been the one to make the decision to loan David the house for the ten days. He said, "It's a great shock to all of us to lose the old house. But we're grateful that everyone got out alive."

Chapter
40

David

Once it's determined that everyone is going to be okay, and once everyone goes home, I feel absolutely stricken. Julia's mother, who is not a Griswold by blood, has the emotional distance to remind me, over and over, that no Griswolds were harmed in the fire, and that in the end, a house is just a material thing. "A very old thing that had served the family well," she assures me, but I still feel awful. Every time I put on a hat I try to conjure the ghosts of the men that I have been remembering but they don't come to me anymore. Hats, I realize, contain our essence when we put them on, because everything that we are is stored in the brain. It's no surprise then that after we got out of the burning house, I thought I saw the lawn strewn with hats. But there were no Griswolds. It was as if they had all evaporated. The lawn looked empty, the way a field does after a graduation, when everyone has tossed their caps up in the air and moved on.

Quite suddenly, Labor Day is upon us. That means that the school year starts up again. Julia has her nose to the grindstone this term. I see her for only a handful of hours in the month of September, and she seems tense, always in a rush. She says that she's forgiven us, and holds no ill will toward Ray, who she feels should never have been talked into taking the DNA test. Taina and Julia had it out, although she didn't tell me the details and I don't want to know anything more about that whole messiness. It makes my stomach turn. In the end, Taina was the one who saved Julia's and Adrian's lives, so that earned her a few points with Julia and the Griswolds. They've made peace, but Taina has withdrawn. Maybe she's behind at work, or maybe she's just had enough of all of us, especially me, because she won't answer the phone when I call. Ray is back in rehab, but struggling. His sobriety is, of course, a work in progress. He seems distant the few times we've talked.

In early October, Julia tells me that there are those in the Griswold family who are eager to make a fresh start, to rebuild a house that is safer, stronger, and more modern. Now that everyone put their vision for the new home on the table, the older folks are excited to have luxuries like central air and walk-in showers and bedrooms on the first floor.

I haven't heard from Adrian in a month, and Julia and I don't talk about him. We talk around the subject, but I can't get myself to say his name. I am mute with shame over hurting him, especially knowing that he would never, ever, hit me back. But I'm too proud to pick up the phone. In the end it is he that reaches out to me. Not with a phone call, not with a letter or a message delivered through a second party. No, Adrian isn't mediocre at anything, especially at being a brother. When he decides to do something it's 100 percent. So he blows the lid off Pandora's Box, blows it open with a dozen sticks of dynamite, and says go on, kid, take a look inside. Are you happy now?

Chapter

41

Kathy Cooper saw the article online, right there on the home-page of her computer, about the budding Latino heartthrob who was hospitalized with second-degree burns after a fire in Con-necticut. Otherwise, she might have heard it from Rashid, who also saw it, or from her secretary, who knew she'd been in the Do-minican Republic, or from her teenage daughters, who saw it in *Teen People*. Kathy didn't reply to the staff reporter, as the article requested, but rather, she sent a message directly to the website of Adrian Vega. As proof of her identity, she named the children she remembered one by one: there was Javier, Miguel, Rafael, Rosita, and Emely ("Emily" spelled phonetically in Spanish, she explained). Adrian, Taina, and Kathy met at a Boston café. That little Miguel was now a successful musician took Kathy's breath away because Sister Juana had recognized his talent and passion for music at such a young age. "And to think that I was the first person to put a pick in your hand," Kathy said, shaking her head, blue eyes sparkling.

Miguel and Rosita eyed her with curiosity. Now in her early fifties, with blonde hair graying at the temples, Kathy was very different from the troubled but idealistic hippie-chick she'd been in 1979. Her life in the Boston suburbs was a world away, but she clung to her youthful, globe-trotting persona by dressing the part. She was wrapped in a saffron-and-garnet-colored sari and had a red dot painted on her forehead. "I was supposed to have become a Supreme Court Justice by now," she explained. "That was my parents' career track and that's what they expected of me. And then something happened that changed everything. Rather than tell my parents that I had no intention to go to law school, I convinced them that 'a detour' on the road to law school would round me out. That detour was joining the Peace Corps."

Kathy had been sent to the Dominican Republic, where she was assigned to create a resource network for orphanages, schools, and nursing homes. She paused at that part of the story, because it was where their lives intersected. Her hand instinctively went to her throat, and she fingered an amber pendant. In the Dominican Republic, she told them, she had met her husband, Rashid, who had been serving in a nearby village at the time. After two years of service in the DR, they had gone together to serve in India for a second term, and they married shortly after. "By this time, my parents had figured out that I wasn't going to law school," Kathy told them. "I was inspired by the work of a nun in the DR, who had a special way of using singing to help speech-delayed children, and it changed the direction of my life. I'm a speech pathologist now and I use a similar method, called melodic intonation therapy, to treat autistic children." She watched Miguel's face, how his strong jaw sagged and his lips parted when she mentioned the part about music. She finished up her introduction by adding that she and Rashid still lived in Boston, with their two teenage daughters, who had downloaded his songs and had not stopped playing them and dancing around their bedrooms ever since. Adrian encouraged her to tell them more about her daughters, but Kathy intuited that he was just delaying the moment of truth. Rosita alternately hid and revealed her dark eyes behind a pair of fashionable sunglasses even though it was a dim afternoon, just before Thanksgiving. Kathy gently turned the conversation back to them, and their past. "You're here in the U.S., because both Sister Juana and I—" She paused, as if to gather up courage. "We were each trying to atone for something we'd done in our private lives—pain we had caused that was eating at us." She held her hand over her stomach.

Kathy began with a simple fact: they were all from the Dominican Republic, and they had each been orphaned. The wondrous part, she told them, was that despite what they may think, they were very much loved. Sister Juana de Arce, and two other nuns, had cared for them at *La Casa Azul*, a small, Catholic Church–sponsored orphanage. Then Kathy looked down and sighed. "I hope it's not too shocking for you to know that you were all born to prostitutes." She gritted her teeth and her forehead wrinkled up with worry. Adrian's hand had lingered on his rib cage, as if he was protecting an injury, but he nodded for her to continue.

"*La Casa Azul* is in the southern part of the island, and about half of the children came from the northern coast, from the Aguas Negras slums outside of Puerto Plata. Puerto Plata, as you may know, is known for its beautiful resorts. But tourists from around the world wander to the outskirts of the town to find prostitutes. These girls are often underage and uneducated about birth control. Your fathers were probably tourists; guys just passing by. One of the things that struck me the very first time I went to *La Casa Azul* was that many of kids had foreign features," she pointed at her own blue eyes and smiled.

"Caucasian, black, Asian, mixed with Dominican blood, which is already a mix of ethnicities. The combinations are so striking. You have this international community stuck in the middle of nowhere." She smiled at both of them. "Tiny citizens of the world."

"Tsk. Citizens of the world of prostitution," Adrian said, turning to Taina. "That's what I was afraid of."

"Ah, but there's a lot more to it," Kathy continued. The nun who cared for them, she said, had raised hundreds of children before them and since, but she had chosen the five for a unique journey because she had considered them each to be special in some way. "She made enormous personal sacrifices for you because of your musical inclinations," she told Adrian. "Because of your beauty and fierce will to survive," She turned to Taina. It was then that Kathy noticed the green starfish tattoos on their hands, making a mental note to ask about their significance. She was well into her second glass of wine when she learned the enduring significance of the markings that she herself had drawn on their hands almost thirty years earlier.

Just before she began to tell the story, Kathy asked if it could remain confidential. Taina said she could speak for the others, and confirmed that no one was interested in publicizing the story. "*I* certainly don't want the publicity," Adrian said, putting a hand on his chest. "It wasn't my idea to blow this open in the first place. David has been pushing for it."

"And ironically," Taina pointed out, "those two aren't speaking to one another. Since the fire."

Adrian looked at Kathy out of the corner of his eyes. "I haven't done anything wrong, Kathy, but I upset him, and he's struggling with a health challenge that I can't even fathom. So you're my olive branch."

"That fire," Kathy said. "Thank God you guys are all okay."

"It was bad," Taina said, pulling back her sleeve to reveal a large scab on her arm. "Adrian still has a bandage on one leg."

Kathy pressed her hands together. "It sounds like the whole incident was just a lot of old energy expending itself. Listen to me carefully, Adrian and Taina, because I'm going to tell you something about yourselves that will explain a lot of what's happened in your adult lives. As traumatized children, you became master survivors at a very young age. Once you hear the whole story, you'll understand that it's no coincidence that you escaped through a window, across a rooftop, and down a tree," she told Adrian. "Or that you, Rosita—I mean, Taina—risked your life by going up to the third story to alert Adrian and Julia about the blaze." Adrian and Taina each looked down and to the side, shifting away from each other in their chairs, and Kathy got the impression that it was a sore subject. She leaned forward and said in a very serious voice, "This wasn't the first time that you've been in grave danger. We're here right now," she tapped the table with her index finger, "because of something that happened almost thirty years ago. It all started when Hurricane David ripped its way through Santo Domingo. But it wasn't the hurricane . . . " Her eyes grew distant, and a shiver ran through her at the memory. "The entire southwest and western parts of the country were badly battered. Our orphanage was on the outskirts of a small village, an agricultural area about thirty miles west of the capital city; close enough so that it broke windows and put holes in the roof. But when it was over, it looked like we were going to be just fine." Their lunches arrived and Kathy took a good long swig of her chardonnay before she sat back, crossed her arms, and said, "It wasn't until the hurricane had passed, after the rivers had swollen and flooded the villages to our north, that the real trouble started."

Part III

Chapter

42

Dominican Republic
September 1979

When the eye wall of Hurricane David passed over the village, it dawned on Kathy Copper that there was a good chance that they were all going to die. She considered the silver lining of this kind of end— huddled with three nuns and twenty-five orphaned children. If there was such a thing as heaven, she just might be able to sneak past the pearly gates by saying, "I'm with them."

As the storm raged outside, Sister Juana, who was defiant of every kind of authority, even nature, stubbornly played Brahms on the upright piano as she did every night. One could barely hear anything through the whistling of the wind and the drumming of the rain outside, but the nun knew that children are comforted by routines, and so she played by candlelight. Her fingers hovered delicately over the keys while she waited for the cold blue lightning to spend itself and the thunder to dull before continuing on to Mozart's "Lullaby" and then to *"Los Pollitos Dicen."* The children sang along with her, but soon the thunder became so loud and came so frequently that they could only see the nun's fingers dancing across the keys. At eight o'clock, Sister Juana's small brown hands glided over the last note of *"Arroz con Leche."* When she was done, everyone clapped, but nervously, and Sister Juana nodded and joined the children and the other nuns clustered in the center of the room. The circle parted for her, and then closed again. A tiny girl reached for her, one-armed as she sucked the thumb on her other hand, eyes clamped shut. The older children looked at Sister Juana with wide, frightened eyes, as if to ask, what now? Without singing, there was only the sound of the storm and its freakish peculiarities: the rattling of the front door in its frame, the whistling noise coming up from inside the sink, and a persistent and malevolent pounding on the wall behind the framed photo of the pope. A rumor spread among the older children that it was the devil knocking on their door. Sisters Juana, Antonia, and Teresa were busy holding, stroking, and comforting frightened children.

While the nuns moved the group of children under a tent of mattresses that they had set up in the windowless corner of the hallway, Kathy was too restless to stay put. She paced the orphanage, policing the situation. She found an unobstructed window and tried to see out, but the window was just below a rain gutter, and the glass was opaqued and marbled with cascading water. *Good God*, she thought, was the wind actually bending the glass? She scurried away, in case it blew. Almost immediately, from down the hall came the sound of glass shattering, startling her so badly that she bit her tongue. A small, round object tumbled down the hall and landed halfway into the room. Sister Teresa illuminated it with a candle and it turned out to be a green coconut. Kathy half-walked, half-crouched down the hall to inspect the damage to the house. In the boys' room, the glass jalousies were in shards across the children's beds and cribs. The double set of curtains had been sucked out the window. The roar of the wind was so loud that she couldn't hear the clanging of metal as the curtain rod bashed itself against the widely spaced iron bars on the window. She tried to grab the curtain rod, but the wind turned it first, and it slipped cleanly between the bars and disappeared into the gloaming. The mosquito nets suspended from the ceiling over the children's beds were wet and had gathered themselves into thick lassos that whipped around in frenzied circles. The air was wet and thick with the smell of sulfur and gasoline, most likely from some kind of spill in town. Outside, power lines were swinging and crackling across the rooftops and spitting sparks into the flooded streets. As Kathy stepped into the safety of the hall, closing the bedroom door behind her, her frayed nerves snapped and she began to sob.

Javier had followed her. He was holding the coconut like a grenade, and Kathy led him back to the main room. Kathy realized with a start that the little man was trying to protect her. A laugh burst out of her and she wiped her tears with her sleeve. Suddenly, the nauseating fear that had been bashing itself against the inside of her rib cage stopped. The boy's valiant gesture calmed her panic and brought her back to center. They weren't going to die, she told herself. The building was made of reinforced concrete block, and the sea was a mile away—a decent margin anyway. Once she calmed down, Kathy was able to process the curious wonders of hurricane phenomena, like horizontal rain. She had seen several chickens, cats, and even a small goat tumble by in a scene straight out of *The Wizard of Oz*.

An hour later, the howling outside downgraded from murderous to mournful. It slowed, petered out, then nothing. *"¡Se fué!"* the children cheered.

A few moments later, Sister Juana called Kathy into the

bathroom, and Kathy found the nun standing over the toilet bowl, which was gurgling. Do you know what that means?" she said, massaging the area behind her eardrums.

Noticing the dull ache in her own ears, Kathy said, "Low atmospheric pressure." When she realized what that meant, she exclaimed to herself, in English, "Shit!"

Sister Juana raised an eyebrow and said, "Exactly. We're in the eye."

They could hear the voices of their neighbors outside. Sister Teresa opened the front door and shouted, as she ran out, that she was going to see if anyone needed help. Sister Juana stood at the gate shouting, "It's not over! If anything happens to you, I'm not rescuing you, Teresa! I'm not!" But it wasn't long before people started calling for everyone to go back inside. Despite her threats, Sister Juana ran out and grabbed a fistful of the younger nun's habit and practically dragged her along the front path and slammed the door behind her.

"*Tranquilo,*" Sister Teresa said in a trance-like voice, pointing up. "You can see the stars up in the sky. It's beautiful." With this break in the tension, Sisters Antonia and Teresa began to praise the power of God.

"You mean His *fury,*" Sister Juana corrected them. "His destructive, maniacal moods." The other two nuns exchanged a look, but there was no time for one of their epic religious debates. The mist outside quickly thickened into rain. They could hear the sound of the wind rising in pitch. Not one to candy coat anything, Sister Juana informed the children that it would be worse this time. Some of the children began to cry as she gathered them back under the mattresses. Kathy suddenly remembered that she had several large packs of Juicy Fruit gum in her day bag, which she gave to the kids and the nuns to relieve the pressure on their eardrums. In the minutes that followed, the tears and wails ceased entirely. Chewing gum was a rare, delicious, and comforting treat, even for nuns. Next, Kathy told the story of "The Three Little Pigs," pointing out that they too lived in a house made of concrete block, and no matter how much the wolf blew and blew, he could never blow down the walls (indeed she had confidence in the walls, it was the roof she was worried about). The kids grew more confident each time they chanted "and he huffed and he puffed." The nuns always howled with delight at Kathy's occasional mispronunciations, so she threw in a few extra mistakes for their entertainment.

After the all-too-brief respite, the roar of the wind started up again. During another round of guard duty, Kathy and Sister Juana discovered that water had begun to seep under the kitchen door. They gathered towels and rags and were piling them against the door when there was a loud crash against the opposite wall. They stood paralyzed, expecting the wall in front of them to split open and crush them. But the wall held. From a window in the hall, they saw that their neighbor's whole sun porch—roof, jalousie windows, and wood siding—had been ripped off by the wind. It remained suspended against the wall of the orphanage for a few minutes, then, suddenly, the wind lifted it up and it tumbled down the street. It jumped over the six-foot iron fence of a nearby farm and rolled end-to-end until it disappeared into the darkness.

Once the storm died down a bit, Kathy was able to entertain the kids with her guitar. She took Miguel onto her lap and let him play with the strings. She sang, "How many years must a man . . ." she nodded, prompting them. Javier used his hands to sign, "I am afraid."

She put an arm around him. "When you can't talk," she said, "you can always sing. What's the matter with you guys? You want to sing *en Español*?" She made a funny face. "Aren't you sick of '*de colores*'?"

When the storm was over, nobody at the orphanage suffered a scratch, and save for a few broken windows, two holes in the roof, and a big mess outside, the orphanage was relatively unharmed. In the early morning hours, Sister Juana told Kathy that she had inspected the building herself before the archdiocese purchased it. "Miracles are 99 percent planning, and one percent luck," she said.

"Luck? Not prayer?"

Sister Juana swatted at a mosquito. "Same thing."

Outside the sky was still cloudy. The whole town looked trashed. There were dangling power lines, broken windows, shredded foliage, and decapitated palm trees that looked like giant eels sticking out of the ground. Just about everything was coated in mud and sand. Kathy couldn't believe what she found lying in the middle of the yard—a starfish, alive and still writhing. The creature was something that you would expect to see depicted in a storybook, an exaggeration of nature, big as a bear's paw. Either the wind had lifted and carried it, or a wave must have come dangerously close during the storm. The thought sent a shiver down her spine. She tossed the creature into a puddle.

The news from the outside was not good. Down the street, a man had been killed just after the eye passed over, while trying to secure the propane gas tank his family used for cooking. Two houses down, a twenty-foot tree trunk had gone through someone's roof. By transistor radio they heard about the floods and landslides in the mountainous interior of the island. In the village of Padre las Casas, an entire church and a school were washed away during the storm, killing several hundred people who were inside. There was no power, and yet there were dozens of electrocutions. There was no running water. A chemical spill had contaminated a reservoir in the capital. For Kathy, there was no way to call home. She would have to rely on the Peace Corps to send word to her parents. She headed to the boardinghouse where she rented a room, wondering if it was still standing.

The walk that should have taken five minutes took almost an hour because of downed trees, storm debris, and potentially deadly pools of water. But the boardinghouse was in working order. In her room on the second floor, a rat had made himself at home during her absence. He was so full that he barely moved when she opened the door. He had knocked over, opened, and gorged himself on a box of Lucky Charms cereal she had left on the nightstand. This was her comfort food, a treat sent from home by a thoughtful friend. Kathy opened the glass jalousies and the rat sauntered out reluctantly, looking back a few times at the box. She pulled the blanket off her bed, took it to the balcony, and shook out the cereal and rat droppings. She desperately wanted to wash it, but she couldn't afford to use up her meager water supply to wash a whole blanket.

Kathy had had the foresight to fill a large plastic tub with water the day before, which would have to last the duration of the crisis. She washed her body and some panties, careful not to use up more than two quarts of water. Despite the rodents, she relished the privacy and silence of her room. She sprayed her armpits with deodorant, holding down the trigger a full six seconds. It was going to be a long, hot, miserable day. She replaced the cap and, on second thought, misted her entire body with deodorant and spread some aloe on her arms. She dabbed anti-itch cream on a dozen swollen mosquito bites and changed into a fresh sundress. She ate two cereal bars and drank from her supply of bottled water.

The small mirror that hung above Kathy's dresser was lined with photographs of her life in Boston. Among her favorites was the one of her father teaching her to clean the engine of their motorboat, and the one of them sailing with the whole family off the coast of Nantucket. The moment that she had recognized that doing these things was not in the least bit ordinary, that most people in this world couldn't even imagine such a lifestyle, was the day that Kathy knew that she wouldn't live the life her parents had prepared her for. In the months since she had arrived in the DR, she had become exasperated at her inability to communicate to her parents the level of poverty that she had witnessed. After one such earnest attempt, her mother wrote back bemoaning the tragic state of the family dog, who was "so sick that he won't even touch a pile of freshly carved roast beef."

Not all her photographs were on display. She kept the photos of Jared in a suitcase. She had to sit down on the bed to be able to look at them. The first one in the stack was taken on a family outing to Niagara Falls when she was a kid. Kathy and her childhood friend were both wearing moccasins and yellow rubber raincoats. Jared was grinning, his two front teeth far too big for his head, Kathy awkward in her prairie braids and too-big feet. The second photo was of Jared in high school, picking at the strings of a guitar. The third showed Jared in cap and gown at Princeton, heading off to medical school. The fourth was a photo taken a year later, the night they got engaged; the stress and exhaustion of medical school showed in his face. He had his arms around Kathy's shoulders and they were standing in front of the fireplace at his parents' house. His eyes were on Kathy, or rather, fixed on her profile. Kathy was looking at the man behind the camera, Dr. Joe Patterson, Jared's dad, who by then had begun making secret visits to Kathy's college dorm room on weekends.

Fast-forward six months: Jared in a wheelchair, living in a nursing home. Bony, blank-faced Jared would never speak again. Everyone assumed that the pressures of medical school had overwhelmed him. That was true, but it wasn't the whole story. To this day, only Kathy and Jared's father knew what had triggered his act of self-destruction. Jared's father, Joe, had told Kathy that he would deny anything she said in regard to their affair; he had his medical career, his wife, and his reputation to think of. He reminded her that their affair had been consensual, and that Kathy was the one who had "given Jared such a shock," after all, not him. Jared's mother, Lilly, never knew, but Joe's history of infidelity wasn't new to Jared. Kathy's confession, along with his access to prescription drugs and lack of sleep, put Jared in a such a state of despair that he went to his aunt's house, asked to see her tiny, mother-of-pearl-inlayed pistol, went back to his car and shot himself through the temple. The bullet's trajectory had been a little too far left to kill him, and too far to the right for him to ever be normal again.

Kathy's mother and Lilly Patterson were close friends, and so the Coopers were a fixture at the hospital. But Kathy had gone to see Jared only once at the nursing home, despite her mother's badgering. By then Jared was alert enough to recognize her. How much he remembered or understood was unclear, but he never took his one good eye off Kathy (over the other was a black eye-patch). He tried to say something to her, but it came out in moans. His eyes roamed over her hands. Kathy presumed that he was searching for her engagement ring. Kathy stepped back from the bed, ashamed. She had given the ring back to Lilly. She had not had the courage to see Jared again for many years. His mother kept sending cards and photos of Jared. On the other side of that most recent photo, Lilly had written: "Kathy, in my heart you'll always be my daughter-in-law."

A fascinating course in Latin American political history followed by a conversation with a Peace Corps recruiter at a career fair had gotten Kathy to thinking about making an escape. And unlike any other post-graduation pursuits, the Peace Corps also offered the possibility of redemption. She hoped that forgiveness could be achieved by doing hard work in a third world country. She also wanted to escape being seen as a victim, to keep her hands busy, to do the kind of challenging labor that anchored the mind to the present and allowed her to forget the past. She needed to be needed and she needed to be able to sleep at night. When the acceptance letter arrived from the Peace Corps, she was elated. She would work on a unique project and would help create a resource-sharing network that involved orphanages, schools, churches, and health-care organizations in the Dominican Republic. *Hogar Infantil Casa Azul* was the first orphanage in the sequence, a training ground where she could assess the needs of residential units for children.

Kathy tucked Jared's photos back inside the liner and shoved the suitcase back under the twin-sized bed, although not too far back. She might need to look at Jared's photo if the water ran out, if she got robbed again, or got another spider bite, or if she came down with the dreaded dengue, or malaria, which she was sure was headed her way. It was the penance, after all, that she had come for.

When she got back to the orphanage, the two nuns asked her to watch the kids while they combed the streets for government workers, supplies, and information. By early afternoon, the children were worried that another hurricane was on its way. Kathy was shocked to learn that it was true. And more bad news: the big bridge that connected their cluster of villages to the capital was not passable. They were cut off.

The children were extra unruly that day. Kathy suddenly remembered the giant starfish, and she fetched it from the place she had left it in the yard. It was lethargic but still alive. She made up a story. Back home, she told them, if you find a starfish it's considered very good luck. Kathy had found rural Dominicans to be highly superstitious, and she thought that given the circumstances, it was okay to capitalize on this cultural trait. Many of the children believed that they were parentless because someone had cursed them with the "evil eye," the dreaded *mal de ojo*. The children passed the dishpan around with the stinky, half-dead creature around like it was something holy. They believed her. Kathy fetched a Sharpie from her bag and proceeded to make drawings of the starfish on the backs of the kids' hands as "proof" of their good fortune. All at once they stuck their hands out, pushing each other to be the next. The little ones did the same, not knowing what it was for, but wanting to do everything the older ones did. A half-hour later, they all had matching green starfish drawings on their hands. The last one she drew was on herself. They put their fists together. They were safe.

"God help us," Sister Teresa lamented. "It wasn't easy taking care of these *mocosos* before the hurricane. How are we going to manage now?"

"Don't worry, we're prepared," Sister Juana assured them. "We'll be self-sufficient for two weeks." She leaned in and frowned. "That is, if you two don't go giving our supplies away." No sooner had she said this when someone hit the buzzer at the front gate. The visitor was the first of dozens to follow. Red Cross volunteers, police, firemen, neighbors, utility workers, priests, and neighbors came knocking on the door. They didn't bring food or supplies, only children—injured, traumatized, hungry, dazed, mud-caked children found wandering the streets, alone. The number increased steadily as the long hours passed. In twenty-four hours, every room of the small orphanage was packed. *Casa Azul* became a triage and emergency shelter. The Red Cross delivered five mentally and physically disabled adolescents, forced them on the nuns, really, despite the fact that the age-cap of the orphanage was ten. One of them easily weighed two hundred pounds. One of the older girls remembered Kathy's story of "The Three Little Pigs," and suggested, with hands on hips, that the newcomers "should have been smart enough to make their houses out of cement."

In spite of the orphanage's humble resources and the fastidious routines of communal life, the children normally had one great luxury: a long and elaborate bedtime routine. A few years before, a local widow, who had attended grade school with Sister Juana, had donated an upright piano to the orphanage, and even had the instrument tuned every few years. Every night, Sister Juana played, and the children developed a Pavlovian response. The little ones nodded off and the older ones grew calm and sleepy. Kathy's arrival at the orphanage had added yet another rich layer to their routine, because she read to them a half-hour *before* the music. So bedtime was drawn out to a solid hour, plus ten minutes of prayer, a snack (three sips of water and half a dinner roll), teeth brushing, hand-and-face washing, medicines and ointments, and dressing for bed. The nuns did all this even as they complained that the children were being spoiled. The nuns went to bed exhausted but deeply satisfied. But after the newcomers flooded in, bedtime came and the original children went without the usual coddling. Sister Juana just shooed everyone off to bed, out of exhaustion and because the orphanage was woefully understaffed. The new children were noisy *malcriados* who wouldn't let anyone else hear the story or listen to the music. Moreover, she couldn't take her eyes off of them for a second anyway. Sister Juana feared that the years of progress they had made in restoring her children's trust in adults was eroding, as demonstrated by their bed-wetting, biting, tantrums, nightmares, their acts of defiance, and the attempts to escape their cribs. But the plight of the newcomers pulled at the nuns' heartstrings too. One day, Sister Juana asked Kathy to take some of the older girls to use the bathroom. The orphanage's restrooms were out of service, so the adults and older kids had to use a crudely built outhouse in the neighbor's field. A nine-year-old girl refused to go into the latrine without Kathy by her side. Her eyes were huge as she gripped Kathy's hand. "You're going to leave me here, aren't you?" Kathy assured the girl that she would wait for her right outside the door, but the girl would not go, even as she squirmed, squatted, and crossed her legs. At last Kathy found a way to reassure her. She tucked the tips of her Keds under the gap at the bottom of the door, so the girl could keep her eyes on them from behind the closed door. Kathy chitchatted away to distract the girl from whatever had happened to her. Only then was the girl able to trust Kathy enough to relax and go to the bathroom.

While the original children felt neglected, the new children took notice, within hours of arriving, that the original children got fed first. They had pillows and blankets and slept in beds, never on the floor. They got their teeth brushed and their hair combed and they got utensils to eat their rice and beans. They had adults who cared about them, even a lovely, blue-eyed *madrina* who tickled and cuddled them and whispered secrets in their ears. In the meantime, the original children watched the orphanage's stash of food, water, and supplies dwindle. They were forced to share their blankets with the muddy, foul-smelling foreigners who used bad language and had snot oozing from their noses; creatures with boils and shingles and bloody scabs that wouldn't heal. They were monsters who mocked them when they prayed, and flashed their private parts to the nuns. The toilets were overflowing and their rags were piling up in the wash basin. They saw Sister Antonia fly into a rage when a boy tossed a lizard into the cauldron of beans she had just cooked for supper. They saw Sister Juana cry after she found three children jumping up and down on top of the piano while another banged at the ivory keys with a rock. They heard Kathy arguing with someone through the gate, refusing to unlock the iron portal to accept more children. At night, they looked out at the lonely moon though a broken window that no one had the time to fix. A bat took up residence in the girls' room. Fights broke out. A fever started to go around.

The women had to concern themselves with bigger things, so the squabbles among the children took a backseat to worries about food, space, and medicine. Four of the children were diabetic, and the newcomers had come with rashes and stomach parasites. But had Kathy and the nuns known the meaning that the green starfish drawings on the kids' hands would take on, they would have scrubbed them off with what little rubbing alcohol they had left (the ink was "permanent" and would continue to be visible on the skin a very long time, especially without regular washing). Perhaps they might have drawn similar stars upon the hands of the outsiders. But since they weren't a part of the children's inner world they didn't know. It wasn't until much later that they learned that the drawings had become a visual marker of who "belonged" at the orphanage and who didn't. Only the permanent residents had the starfish;

Kathy had drawn them the morning after the storm. During the next twenty-four hours, a fierce pack instinct sprung up among them, and they instinctively polarized into two distinct clans: the citizens and foreigners.

On the fifth day, when the last of the rice and beans were gone, Sister Teresa confiscated a nine-inch shard of broken glass from three of the outsiders who had been plotting to slice up ten-year-old Mauricio, the oldest of the original twenty-five. That same night, the nuns had awoken to terrified screams from the nursery. Two boys, around seven and nine, had climbed into a crib shared by Javier and his brother Miguel. A nine year-old boy had stripped Miguel and was lying on top of him. The other had his hand over Javier's mouth until Javier bit him. The nuns had brought Javier and Miguel to their own beds that night, but it was Sister Antonia who had said, "Sisters, we can't go on like this."

Kathy refused the Peace Corps's offer to send her home once the airport reopened. Her ability to speak English and her connection to the Peace Corps were two critical resources for the orphanage. They needed her now more than ever, and when she fell into bed the night after the hurricane, she slept peacefully for the first time in over a year. Still, the job was exhausting and the tension at the orphanage was overwhelming. What kept Kathy sane was that she didn't *have* to be there. She chose it, and at the end of the day, there was sanctuary in a rented room two blocks away. She had her stash of comforts: a stack of novels (before the storm she had been deep into Robert Ludlum's *The Holcroft Covenant*), a bottle of Dominican rum, an oversized bar of Toblerone chocolate nougat from the duty-free shop at the airport, a radio-cassette player, and a dozen mixtapes. UNESCO had declared 1979 to be the "International

Year of the Child," and Kathy loved the album they released after the televised UNICEF benefit concert, featuring the Bee Gees, Donna Summer, Elton John, Olivia Newton-John, and Earth, Wind & Fire. She also had a generous supply of Valium and prescription sleeping pills that Joe Patterson had given her just before she left for the Peace Corps. "Something to take the edge off," he had said. They did come in handy, but she was careful not to overdo it. Now she wondered if Dr. Patterson was hoping that she'd OD so that their terrible secret would die with her.

On the day that the orphan wars began, Kathy thought Sister Juana was going to have a nervous breakdown. Sisters Teresa and Antonia had taken leave to go take care of some of their own relatives. But Sister Juana had no family beyond her brother Alejandro. Besides, she was the director, so she was stuck. In the meantime, the archdiocese in Santo Domingo stubbornly continued to send provisions in proportion to the needs of the original population of residents, despite Sister Juana's pleas that they send volunteers and at least double the amount of rice, beans, and bottled water. Flooding from of the Ocoa River had knocked out the bridge that connected *Casa Azul* to the main road, and so the church's deliveryman had to drive more than triple the normal distance to get around the flooding and deliver their ration of goods from the west, rather than the usual direct approach from the east. And as if things weren't bad enough, Alejandro dropped a bomb on Sister Juana. He was going to try to enter Puerto Rico illegally, by boat.

Kathy was touched that Sister Juana chose to confide in her. The nun described how the odyssey across the famously treacherous stretch of sea would be led by smugglers in rickety, overloaded, wooden boats. The track record for this sort of thing wasn't good. Even if they didn't capsize and get eaten by sharks or drift and die of exposure, they ran the risk of being caught by either the Dominican or U.S. Coast Guard. But Alejandro had given up hope on immigrating legally and he couldn't afford a plane ticket even if someone did grant him permission to emigrate. He said that Hurricane David had wiped out his last chance of making a living in the DR, and he was desperate for work. After the hurricane, word on the street was that authorities in both the DR and Puerto Rico were completely absorbed with post-hurricane activities and that for once they weren't bothering with illegal immigrants. It was a rare window of opportunity and the weather was perfect to make a go of it. "Don't go!" she begged. "There's another storm coming!"

They would leave right after the new storm, Frederic, passed. He was determined to start a new life in Puerto Rico.

In the meantime, Sister Juana estimated that the number of orphans in her unit would double by the end of the week. Once or twice, a bandaged relative showed up at the orphanage to claim a child, but reductions to the population of the orphanage were rare, and when they did, they came for the wrong children. Most of the original children at *Casa Azul* were children of prostitutes who either couldn't afford to take care of them, didn't want to, or had tried but been grossly neglectful. It was normal for mothers to show up now and then trying to claim or see their children. Rosita's mother had scampered out of the alley like a cockroach, drunk and filthy and crusted with blood, claiming she would take her girl to a "special school."

"You want to sell her to buy drugs and *trago*, don't you?" Sister Juana said, taking the woman's arm to get a better look at her needle marks. "You'll have to kill me first," she said, and slammed the door in the woman's face. Later that same day, a well-dressed man in dark glasses came by claiming that he was the uncle of a missing boy, and could he take a look around? He pointed to a sweet, fat-cheeked boy, Rafael, but couldn't provide any papers to prove his relation, so Sister Juana wouldn't release the child. The mysterious man never returned. "Of course not, he was a pervert," she said. "I've had three women try to pull the same thing, just looking to find a child-slave." It soon became obvious that overcrowding at the orphanage could potentially open the door for predators and unfit parents to take advantage. Still, the decision to close the door to more children weighed heavily on her. The next day, tropical storm Frederic passed over them, and with it, more flooding. "More flooding means more children," Kathy said wearily. Even she was starting to break down. But once Frederic passed, one week after David, their situation actually improved. First, a farmer brought sacks upon sacks of fallen oranges that they feasted on all day. You could tell that some of the kids needed a little sugar in their blood, because their overall behavior improved. A neighbor tapped at the front door with news that there were plantains and avocados washing up on the beach. But Teresa and Antonia had not come back yet, and neither Kathy nor Sister Juana dared leave the other loaded with so much responsibility. Their lucky break came when a German couple, both Red Cross volunteers, showed up at the door. This meant that the direct route from the capital was now passable, and the Germans came with a drum of powdered milk and bottled water. They told Kathy (in German, but she understood and was able to translate) that they couldn't tolerate the heat and stink of dead bodies trapped under the rubble of the shantytowns where they had been working. They had begged for an easier assignment and had thus been delivered to the front steps of *Casa Azul*, a cushy job by comparison. The Germans wanted to know how they could help entertain the children. Kathy translated Sister Juana's swift reply: "Teach them how to make German cars." Then she took Kathy's hand and pulled her out the door. "We'll be back in an hour!" Kathy called out as they hurried to the shore.

Kathy pushed a wheelbarrow filled with empty potato sacks a mile down to the sea. Her back was killing her by the time she got there, and she wondered how she would manage when they loaded it up. Indeed the shore was strewn with robust avocados, what appeared to be a whole shipment or harvest of them, as if they'd been dumped by a cargo ship. Kathy and Sister Juana got to work. They slowly drifted east as they combed the beach for more fruit. Neither of them noticed anything out of the ordinary until Kathy's sharp hearing caught a familiar *slap, slap, slap* sound. She looked up.

It was a boat, about a hundred yards out. It appeared to have gotten stuck, and was motionless, slightly tilted to the side. The local fishermen had told Kathy that there were sandbars and sharp rocks just off that beach, which was why boats always fished at a safe distance. It shouldn't be so close to the shore, Kathy thought. Certainly not a boat that size—it was a cabined fishing boat with twin engines, roughly the same size as one her father had once owned. "It must be stuck or wrecked," said Sister Juana. "But I don't see anyone, do you?"

"I wish I had better eyes," Kathy said, making barrels with her fingers and raising them to her face. The nun dropped the avocados and kicked off her shoes. *"Ve a ver,"* she told Kathy. "It must have drifted over from one of those fancy marinas in Santo Domingo."

The boat, named *For Tuna*, was a Hatteras, close to forty feet. Homeport was San Juan, Puerto Rico. By the time Kathy got to the boat, the water was up to her shoulders. She grabbed onto the narrow ladder that led up to the deck. When she got to the top, she peered into the boat. It was filled with debris and had flooded with several inches of water on deck; a bouillabaisse of dead fish and shrimp, palm fronds, seaweed, a ripped plastic tarp, a gutted grapefruit, and a phone book. The hatch appeared to have a tight seal and was padlocked from the outside, so she climbed over the side rail and knocked on the hatch door. She didn't get, or expect, any response. She swam back to Sister Juana and reported that the boat was abandoned.

"*Fortuna*," Sister Juana echoed when Kathy told her the boat's name.

"In English it doesn't mean 'fortune' like it does in Spanish. It just means that someone is looking for that kind of fish. *Atún*."

"You need luck to catch tuna," Sister Juana said. "Alejandro has tried, but all he catches are crabs, grunt, and barracuda. Fortune from Puerto Rico." Sister Juana narrowed her eyes. "What a name. The Spaniards should have considered the implications before they named it 'port of riches.' Why *wouldn't* it attract pirates and rivals—with that name?" She inspected the boat from another angle, trying to figure out what to do about it. "How in the name of God do we alert an owner in Puerto Rico that their boat has drifted all the way over here? There isn't any Coast Guard around."

"Smugglers will steal it," Kathy said. "That boat's not going back to home port on its own. But that's not our problem." Kathy looked down at her wet sundress. She was already feeling embarrassed at how the cloth clung to her, and now she had to walk through town in it.

Who thought of it first, they would never know for sure. Kathy's whole body stiffened. "My God," she said.

"My God," echoed the nun in the same stunned voice. Juana would come to believe that God (whom she alternately believed in and didn't believe in, but whom she argued with constantly) was mocking her. *You don't believe in miracles, old girl? Ha! I'll show you a miracle.* She looked up at the sky. Squinting, she spread her gaze across the heavens, waiting, listening. She saw and heard nothing. God's blue eye was blank and indifferent.

As soon as they got home, they sent the oldest of the original children into the neighboring village to go find Alejandro, to bring him back with a single word: *"urgente."* In the time it took them to cook up a feast of fried plantains with salted avocado slices on the side, Sister Juana had hatched the plan that had already been quietly unfolding in the secret recesses of her heart.

In the Dominican Republic, Kathy Cooper stood out. She was tall, wide, milky-skinned, blue-eyed. She had a mouthful of perfect white teeth and a narrow bite, which she clamped tightly whenever she smiled, like a Texan beauty queen. She was so beautiful, everyone said. Some people called her *muñeca*, "doll," although Kathy insisted she was not considered beautiful back home. But in the DR, she was a magnet for attention. In the village, men (single or otherwise) saw her as either a sexual trophy or as a potential green card. Kathy regularly got marriage proposals from strangers. Children sat very close to her, stroking the blonde hairs on her arms and squealing with amazement at their blondness. "In the DR, even bugs, rats, and stray dogs adore me," she would joke, as she slapped off mosquitoes. She had a solid command of the Spanish language, but her accent was heavy and her textbook Spanish was highly entertaining to the locals. She often missed jokes and other cultural nuances, but never missed the meaning of anything important.

During Kathy's first month at the orphanage, the youngest

nun, Sister Antonia, had declared that Kathy had the "soul of a nun." Kathy had flinched, then smiled graciously and thanked her for the compliment. When Antonia was out of hearing range, Sister Juana had patted her thigh and said, "Don't worry, you don't remind anyone of a nun. She didn't consider how unflattering that must sound to a modern young woman." But Sister Juana somehow knew that the cause of Kathy's inadvertent flinch probably had nothing to do with vanity. "You have a hurt inside," she ventured one day, and Kathy only nodded, but wouldn't say more. And on the one occasion that Sister Juana probed, Kathy evaded the subject. "Since I came here, Sister Juana, I've realized that nuns are stereotyped in my country. You're not cloistered or cut off. You're more like social workers." She pointed to the nun's calloused hands. "You're up to your elbows in the muck and grit of life, not dreaming about angels playing harps in the clouds."

Sister Juana nodded. "We raise the unwanted children of prostitutes, criminals, and drug users. We know the smell of marijuana; we know what moonshine smells like when you sweat it out, what sniffing glue does to the pupils. We know how to recognize the signs of rape and mental illness. Before coming here, I ministered over at the women's prison. After that, nothing could shock me. And after seeing what I've seen, no sacrifice is too great to try to save my children from that kind of destiny."

It wasn't long before Kathy began to open up a bit, if only about the lighter aspects of her life. Juana especially enjoyed the gossip about the other Peace Corp volunteers, and whenever Kathy had a meeting in the capital, she'd bring back updates that the nun heard with the rapture of a soap opera addict.

Several months prior to the hurricane, after they had put

the children to bed, the two women had been sitting in the backyard together. Juana had shared something that she could never confess to any other member of the clergy. "I don't love God," she said, looking up at the sky, as if to include Him in the conversation, for she had been raised to never say anything about anyone that you wouldn't say to their face. "I don't even like Him."

Kathy had shaken her head. "What?" She laughed. "That's absurd. You serve God every day."

Sister Juana had her hands pressed together as if in prayer. She bit the tips of her index fingers softly, and said, *"Le sirvo sin quererlo. Somos como un matrimonio, sin ilusiones ni juegos seguimos adelante.* I am his resentful servant. I watch as He creates life, then He goes on to other things, never looking back. He doesn't *steward* his creation." The words rushed out. "It's irresponsible and cruel. And every day the orphans keep piling up, those little souls." She stopped, swallowed, blinked, and then wiped the edge of her eye. *"Yo le grito desde la cocina que no sea tan haragán.* He's a very lazy God. I remind Him every day." She lifted a finger, wagged it in the air. Then she sat back and looked at Kathy. "Blasphemy, right? But look." She waited. She looked up, then said, "See? He won't do me the favor of striking me dead. He knows that I deserve some rest. But no. He's a brutal and demanding *patrón*."

Kathy was shocked, amused, and a bit in awe. "I have never heard of anyone having such an intimate relationship with their God," Kathy said. "You talk like He's a living, breathing being."

Sister Juana shook her head. "It torments me to know that the cycle will continue. Our children will reach the age of ten and go to the house for adolescents, where they are pooled with other children who will contaminate them with . . ." She made a face and looked away. "When they hit puberty they'll make more unwanted children, who will commit crimes and prostitute themselves only to procreate more orphans."

"But there are those who make it, right?" Kathy said. "And some get adopted."

"A few," she conceded. "But it's rare. Even the smartest, kindest children hit adolescence and then they teeter on the edge," she said. "And no one's going to adopt the ones that aren't babies. Foreign couples want infants."

"I'd love to take them all back to the States, just drop them off somewhere safe and let my countrymen figure it out." She sighed. "But how would we get them off the island?" It was a rhetorical question.

Sister Juana said, "Your country has opened its arms to so many people from all over the world. I am a great admirer of the United States, and especially its little outpost here in the Caribbean, Puerto Rico."

And then an abandoned boat from Puerto Rico appeared with the words *"For Tuna"* written across the back. Coincidence? Juana was suspicious, thrilled, challenged. But more than anything, she was convinced that her brother would have safe passage into Puerto Rico.

Kathy would never forget the moment when they snuck back out with Alejandro and his friend to show him the stranded boat (thanks to the Germans again). Juana took Kathy's hand. "You said that you know how to navigate a boat, right? Then transport my brother to Puerto Rico. And take some children with you too. Deliver them somewhere safe."

The nun had figured out almost every detail of the plan, but Kathy had to consult with an outsider, someone to play devil's advocate. She ran across town to find a phone to call Rashid, her friend, confidant, and fellow Peace Corps volunteer from a nearby village. She wanted him to cover for her absence during the two days she would be gone. It was prudent for someone to know where she was, just in case the Peace Corps came looking for her. She needed access to nautical weather forecasts. There were so many things that could go wrong. He had ticked them off: "The engines could malfunction. You could run out of fuel or get lost and die of exposure. You could encounter drug runners who will rape you, kill you, and throw you to the sharks." He sat down and said, "Kathy, it's like driving a camper full of kids through the badlands of Mexico, only with ocean currents trying to sweep you out to the open Atlantic. Then there's the fact that the Dominican or U.S. Coast Guard or marine police aren't going to appreciate you smuggling immigrants into the United States. If the Feds catch you, they're gonna charge you with a felony or two. Let's see. Kidnapping, aiding or trafficking of illegal aliens while aboard 'stolen' property. Or how about abandonment and willful neglect of minors? How about you get kicked out of the Peace Corps, and get a criminal record? Good-bye law school. And how well do you know these two characters, Alejandro and Raúl?"

All true. And the more Rashid talked, the deeper Kathy felt her decision take hold, because she kept thinking of reasons it was right. And she had imagined those grown children, in their graduation gowns or in business suits, or maybe just standing in front of a simple house, alive and healthy but not prostituting, not sniffing glue or cutting sugar cane until their hands are bloody. This is what she was thinking when Rashid ran a hand through his shiny black hair and said, "With that said, if you pull it off, Cooper, it'll be the greatest accomplishment of your life. Hell, it might be the biggest accomplishment of *my* life just to support you in this."

After Sister Juana had spelled out the plan, Kathy had looked out at the ocean of children in the yard and realized that nobody would even notice if a handful of them were gone. And yet it was such a huge risk. She remembered reading something in a religious pamphlet about the futility of tossing starfish back to sea when thousands of them were beached. The moral of the story was that the opportunity for a second chance mattered immensely to the one starfish that got a second chance. Whether it registered at that time or later, the appearance of the starfish on the lawn emerged as a powerful trigger, some kind of divine push or big hint from the cosmos. The starfish had died in the dishpan, but the spirit of the metaphor persisted. *Insisted. Yes. Yes. Yes*, her heart said. *Do it.*

In the end, Rashid gave her his blessing, support, and vow of secrecy. Kathy could see that Rashid saw her with new eyes. "You've got some balls, Cooper," he had said, and she thanked him for his counsel because it helped her make a few "worst-case scenario" adjustments to the plans with the men, as well as a "let's get our story straight" session with Sister Juana.

The nun had made the sign of the cross over Kathy's forehead and asked her if she was sure. What might the nun herself be risking, Kathy could only imagine. But of one thing Kathy was sure: Sister Juana suffered from the same ailment of the spirit that she did.

Kathy, Alejandro, his friend Rául, and Sister Juana sat at the kitchen table at the orphanage, surrounded by screaming children. No need for Rashid to send maps and nautical charts, they had found everything they needed inside the boat after they broke the lock and went below. The boat's navigational instruments were in perfect working order. Kathy and the men had taken it for a test drive (it still had fuel in the tank) and it had turned out to be perfectly seaworthy. They were to leave early the next morning. They had moved the boat to a safe and remote anchorage a few miles down the coast. Alejandro had spent the day gathering supplies and preparing the boat. Raúl, who Kathy suspected was a small-time thief, quickly showed himself to be indispensable. He somehow found more fuel, no questions asked. The two men were jubilant, almost giddy. They had found a white captain's hat with a shiny black bill in the *For Tuna*. "Tell me, Sister, what kind of illegal immigrant wears a captain's hat?" Alejandro said. "I have a suit jacket that belonged to my father that I'm going to wear, in case anyone spots us, and a cigar, so I look like a gentleman." The men would be met by a friend in town, and they would start their new lives by washing dishes at a small neighborhood restaurant. Alejandro's eyes sparkled in the light of the gas lamp. "I'll send you money, Juana, I promise. I'll send you money. And when I become a citizen, I'll figure out a way to come back and get you."

Sister Juana had waved him off. "I'm not going anywhere. I just want you to be safe, get a job, get married, be happy." She paused, changed her mind. "A little money now and then would be nice." Alejandro threw his head back and laughed.

Sister Juana demanded that the boat be returned to a legitimate port, dock, or marina in Puerto Rico. Also, she made them promise to help any *yolas* that were in trouble out in the open waters. "Remember that you two might have been on a *yola* too if it hadn't been for the miracle of the motorboat. If you see anyone in trouble, help them. Come back if you have to. And don't forget to check the beach at *Isla Mona*. People get stranded there."

Once in Mayagüez, they would tie up and vacate the boat, at a dock identified as safe by their friend in Puerto Rico, at the site of an abandoned condominium where he had worked as foreman before the owner went bankrupt. Then they would place a phone call and let the police return the boat to its rightful owners. As an American citizen, Kathy could easily get back to the DR by ferry from Puerto Rico.

The children would be strategically abandoned. It was very important to stage it right, Sister Juana insisted. The U.S. authorities would have to operate on the assumption that they were Puerto Rican children. No one would report them missing. As it was, the Dominican government hadn't sent a social worker to check in on the orphanage in months. As abandoned, unaccompanied minors, the U.S. government would be obligated to assume custody. They'd have a chance at something better.

The children, they agreed, had to be young enough to not give away any real information about their origin. "Señorita Kathy, grab a few babies and let's get going," said Raúl.

"You can fit twelve or more in there," Juana said.

He balked. "And if we get stopped by the Coast Guard they're not going to believe that they're our children, Juana. It'll look like we just emptied out an orphanage, which, by the way, we did."

"But six is so few," Sister Juana said.

"Five," Kathy said. "We don't want to have so many kids that they crawl overboard, or cause an accident."

Raúl said, "The children represent an unnecessary risk. I don't think we should take them at all. It's crazy, Sister."

"You're taking them," Sister Juana said, hands raised. "Or you're not going."

"You don't know where the boat is," Raúl dared.

Sister Juana turned her head two degrees to the left, and narrowed her eyes.

Alejandro patted his friend's shoulder nervously. "C'mon,

Rául, we can handle five kids." He put the captain's hat on Kathy. "Nothing bad can happen—we're transporting orphans, after all. God will be with us."

"Five. Five kids but that's it," Rául said, turning back to Sister Juana. "So pick out the ones who won't give us away."

Juana took a deep breath. "Ay-ay-ay-ay. I'll have to consult with Charles Darwin," she muttered.

"Darwin?" Kathy echoed.

Alejandro raised an eyebrow. "She wanted to be a scientist when we were kids. Read every book in school about science."

"But of all the scientists . . . Darwin?" Kathy asked. She was interrupted when a fight broke out in the kitchen. She rushed off to break it up.

When she returned, Rául was asking Sister Juana, "How many are there under the age of three?"

"Nine," Sister Juana replied. If you include four-year-olds the number jumps to thirteen."

"We're not taking thirteen, we're taking five. And no four-year-olds. They talk too much, especially girls." He pointed to a group of little girls jabbering in a corner of the kitchen.

"Let's go pick them out, Sister," Kathy said. "And you're right about Darwin. We have to identify our strongest children, the ones that have demonstrated excellent health, endurance, brains, *something*."

"If we're taking them to Puerto Rico, then they should *look* Puerto Rican," Rául said. "Even better if they're white, like the boy with the gray eyes." He shrugged. "I'm just saying. They should look like they're part of a family or a community. Not a hodge-podge of Dominican orphans."

"What's wrong with Dominican orphans?" Sister Juana shot back.

"Out there? In the world of *jankees* and *blancos*? Are you kidding me? You haven't been out there, *hermana*. You don't know."

"Neither have you," Sister Juana snapped. "I bet you've never even been off the island."

Rául said, "I've been to *Nuevayol*," he declared. "I know."

"You were three," Alejandro said.

"Everyone knows that the police on the mainland don't like Latinos or *prietos*," he said. "And we're both. So pick the ones who can blend in."

Sister Juana narrowed her eyes, deep in thought. She turned without saying anything, and they followed her into the nursery.

That night, Sister Juana became judge, talent scout, behavioral scientist, God. She tapped the headboard of a crib where a tiny boy was asleep. "Miguel has the soul of a musician," she said. "When I play the piano he listens, enraptured. He consistently becomes excited anytime he hears music." She lifted his shirt, revealing a half-dozen round, knotted scars on his chest and belly. Juana said, "His mother's boyfriend did that to him. The boy is lucky to be alive." She kissed him on the forehead.

Rául narrowed his eyes. "But what qualifies him, Sister?"

"Passion," Juana said. "He loves something already and that's a rare gift. Besides, there is a certain natural intelligence needed to appreciate music." Next, she signaled the crib of a sleeping baby girl. The crib was covered with a crude frame topped with chicken wire. "Rosita is a master escape artist. A genius at self-preservation. There was a mentally ill girl, a cousin, I believe, living in her house. The girl was twelve, and she doused herself with gasoline and set herself on fire. Rosita saw it." Sister Juana shook her head and turned to Rául. "She goes. She's also beautiful, and that will serve her well."

During this part of the story, Taina gasped audibly and pressed a hand to her chest. Kathy and Adrian thought she might be choking, but she said that she was fine, and so they ordered a glass of water for her, but she looked shaken for a good while. Adrian asked how Holly and Ray had been chosen for the voyage.

Alejandro followed Sister Juana to the crib of a scrawny brown girl. "Emely is smart, loving, obedient, and motivated to learn. She watches over younger children like a little hen and she potty-trained when she was two. She goes." Next, Sister Juana pointed to a chubby boy with a headful of curls. "Rafael has a good soul. He laughs at everything and always offers what he has to the others. Plus he's fat and healthy; just look at those pink cheeks. That's four."

Lastly, she lifted a small boy, who was still awake in his crib, "This *hombrecito* is Javier, Miguel's half-brother. He has two strengths. First, he's curious about everything, and that's a sign of intelligence. He loves to explore things. He looks, he touches, he smells, he tastes. I found him tipping back a bottle of *colonia Mennen* just because he wanted to know what cologne tastes like. This gets him into trouble too. Before he came to us, he was living with his grandmother. At least he wasn't being abused like Miguel, but she was old and couldn't keep up with him and so he got into a bag of rat poison. He ate some of it and almost died. He was in the hospital for months. That's how he ended up here. Since he's recovered, he's never so much as had a sniffle. We've had break-outs of dengue, malaria, meningitis, whooping cough, but Javier is the strongest and healthiest one."

"But Juana, he's almost four and he can't talk. Are you sure he's a contender for adoption?" Alejandro asked.

"He's mute because of his trauma, but he can hear perfectly.

See?" She clicked her nails on the side of the bed, and the boy's eyes drifted over to the source of the noise. "He's intelligent and his will to survive is phenomenal. His grandmother said that he was vocalizing before the poisoning, so there's nothing wrong with him. He'll speak when he's ready. If he has survived his life so far, he can survive anything. He will do well." Sister Juana held the boy close. She pushed the little boy's head down onto her shoulder and closed her eyes. She swayed left and right. Kathy had never seen this kind of open tenderness from the nun. She began to sing, *"Arrurú mi niño . . ."* Keeping her hand on the back of the boy's head she swept around, turning her back to the adults.

"Oh, Sister, I think you fell a little in love with that one," Kathy said.

Sister Juana had looked at Kathy over the boy's shoulder. "This is the one who will find us. He's the one who will lead them all back to me someday. He's the explorer. *El curioso.*"

Alejandro turned to Kathy and said, "Javier and Miguel's mother tried to make it over to Puerto Rico in a *yola* six months ago. Neither she nor the thirty people on that boat were ever heard from again."

A single sob escaped out of Sister Juana's throat, and Kathy didn't know if it was because of what Alejandro had said or because she was just sad about the kids, or both. Suddenly the nun straightened her shoulders, took a deep breath, and gave the boy to Alejandro.

With his hand around her waist, Alejandro swept his sister away, speaking close to her ear, in a hushed voice. They were saying their good-byes, and Kathy lowered her eyes and walked out of the room. Rául came in. "Everything is ready."

"Did I give you sedatives for the children?" Sister Juana asked.

"I have them," Kathy said, patting the canvas bag slung on her shoulder. "Along with the powdered milk, the bottles, the cereal, and the bread."

"Wait," Juana said. "You have to take one more thing with you. Come with me, Kathy."

Kathy followed Juana to the closet where she kept the children's clothes. "The clothes you brought the children from the United States," she said, handing Kathy outfits hanging on padded satin hangers. "We've never used them because they're so fancy. But they're perfect for the trip. Except for the fact that they didn't come with shoes. Their worn-looking rubber sandals will give them away, so we'll leave them barefoot. No one will notice."

Kathy shook her head. She didn't understand. "Dress them up, why?"

"So they look like they belong on that fancy boat. It's important that they not look like poor children."

Kathy nodded. These were clothes that Jared's mother, Lilly, had sent upon Kathy's arrival as a gift for the orphanage. There were ten girl and ten boy outfits, ranging from size two to size seven. They were hand stitched and designed by Lilly's company, Lilly Pad Designs. They even came with little matching accessories and headbands, but not shoes.

"This is a wonderful use of Lilly's outfits. I can't believe I didn't think of it myself," Kathy said.

"Nice, well-to-do *Cristianitos*," Sister Juana said. "Here's a balloon. Blow it up and tie it to the boat, so the police can spot it after you make the call."

Kathy exhaled and closed her eyes for a second. "I feel like I'm breaking up a family," she said. "This is awful."

When she picked up Javier, Sister Juana spoke to him in the firm voice one would use to address another adult. "Remember this, my boy: Don't be afraid. Everything that has happened to you will help you. You will succeed." She held him for a long, long time. Kathy had to pry him out of her arms.

Twenty minutes later, Juana handed the last child to Kathy, who was waiting in the backseat of a borrowed car. Rául's other contribution was his brother, who drove the "getaway" truck to the anchorage down the coast.

Sister Juana went back inside. She collapsed in her bed. Sleep took possession of her body like an illness. When she woke up, she had no idea how much time had passed. The sun was already high in the sky. She could hear the high pitch of the children's voices, the sound of their small hands banging on the door. She fell back asleep, and saw, in her mind's eye, the vastness of the sea, the choppy waters of the passage, and the shining, walled city of San Juan, port of riches. She didn't pray for the journey of Alejandro, Kathy, Rául, and the children. Her confession to Kathy that she didn't admire God was incomplete and mildly put. The status of her soul was even more precarious than that. She had lost her grip on faith in a single moment, years before.

Sister Juana hoped that she had begun a silent chain of benevolent guardianship, a network that would carry the five children across the sea, and over every obstacle, until they arrived at the place where they had everything they deserved: parents, homes, siblings, toys, pets, friends, educations, professions, spouses, and eventually, children of their own. Perhaps their paths might lead them back to their island, but, she hoped, not for a long, long time. She knew that she had sentenced herself to a certain kind of unresolved grief. She would wonder, every day, perhaps for her whole life—if she had made the right decision.

After Kathy and Alejandro left with the children, a strange thing happened. A thin and distant rip appeared in the thick cloud cover that had hovered over the region for ten days straight. Maybe, just maybe, she thought, God was showing Himself.

Maybe He was doing what little He could. She comforted herself with the knowledge that her orphans were on a sturdy vessel in the care of three responsible adults, and that each child was equipped with special gifts that would give them a foothold on happiness. It seemed impossible, after everything they'd been through, but there it was: someone banging at the gate, a stranger holding five new children to fill the five empty beds.

When they reached Puerto Rico, Kathy had placed the call directly to the desk of a Mayagüez police officer, who, according to Rául's contact, was reputedly sympathetic to the plight of Dominicans. She waited on the roof of the construction site until the two officers arrived. She watched them through the boat's binoculars, which she regretted having to steal, but she needed to make sure the children made it into police custody. She saw Officer Castillo toss the can of dry milk in the water, chastising herself for being so careless. But she knew by that small but deliberate act, that the children were in good hands.

When she was nineteen, shortly after she had taken her vows, Sister Juana was visiting her parents and her brother in Santo Domingo. Her father owned an off-road vehicle, a real luxury back then. They loved to take it up to her uncle's farm high up in the hills. Sister Juana was a tomboy at heart, and she loved to drive fast. It had rained a great deal that month, and the ground was soft. She was at the wheel, and she took a sharp turn too widely. Her vehicle almost collided with a rickety, short bus. The bus swerved, perilously close to the shoulder of the road. Then the soft ground under the shoulder of the road crumbled and the bus rolled down the mountain, front to rear, with fifteen tobacco pickers inside. "It rolled, and it rolled, and Sister Juana won't say more." Kathy's voice cracked and her eyes welled up as she looked into Taina's and Adrian's eyes. "We recognized in each other a drive to undo a colossal mistake. She has spent her whole life trying to make up for what happened that day. And you being here, in the United States, happy, healthy, thriving—is the flowering of that grief."

Adrian's shoulders had been rising slowly, throughout the whole telling of the story, as if someone was lifting a burden off him. But his eyes seemed to contain the shadow of skepticism. Taina had lifted her sunglasses and appeared serene, her eyes wide and moist. Kathy said, "Now that I'm a mother, I think that I was crazy to do what we did. It was too risky." She shook her head, and she looked down to one side, her face clouded with images of what could have gone wrong.

"What happened to the men?" Adrian asked.

"Both Alejandro and Rául became legal citizens and still live in Puerto Rico, Alejandro owns his own restaurant in San Juan, and is able to help Sister Juana financially. He has a wife and five children, who all work in the restaurant. Alejandro is fond of saying that he is blessed because he has the favor of Saint Jerome Emiliani, the patron saint of orphans. Anyway, Alejandro did some recon for us over the years, and when we learned that you had all been adopted into families, Sister Juana was so relieved. She's in her seventies now, retired and living in a convent in Santo Domingo."

The waiter brought the bill and Kathy reached into her bag, suddenly remembering that she had some old photographs of *Casa Azul* to show them. But first, she leaned forward and made an impassioned plea for them to embrace the orphanage, told them what it could mean to the orphanage to have ambassadors such as them. She took each of their hands in hers. "Always remember that with privilege comes responsibility. You must go to *Casa Azul* and see the place you came from. Only then will you be able to understand how far you've come."

Chapter
43

David

It's barely necessary to discuss it. We have to go. Even Julia, who is making a deliberate effort to withdraw from me now that I've had nine months of clean scans, knew she had to figure out a way to see the orphanage. So we all agree on the February school break. I'm paying for Ray's airfare, although the poor guy will have to do without the week's income. We've been talking about him making a career change into rehab nursing after I pointed out to him how great he was when I was hungover. But he knows he has to get his own house in order before he can help anyone else. Going to see the orphanage is part of that process for all of us, and so it will be the five of us plus Julia. Making the trip isn't a small deal for me either—staying cancer-free without being over-medicated is a very complex, finely calibrated process. So with my oncologist's approval, and pending a round of tests, we confirmed plans to fly to the Dominican Republic, with a detour to Puerto Rico tacked on at the end.

I'm sure Taina is freaking out about being with Adrian and Julia again but we all know that this trip holds too much significance to let our personal conflicts stop us. I give her credit though; she didn't try to exclude Julia. Adrian and I have spoken five times since he called with the news about Kathy. It was very hard, but I apologized, and told him that I love him. We've never spoken about the Julia thing, but I know that they are in contact. So now I'm nervous about them being together again, but I want her at my side thoughout this journey. I haven't given up on us. The day I willingly let her go is the day I stop fighting for life itself. I know that I've arrived at the heart of my own selfishness, but I just can't let go of Julia, who I still think of as my future wife.

We agree to spend a day in Santo Domingo taking in the capital city before heading to *Casa Azul*. Adrian is our translator and we hire a driver with a minivan to give us the grand tour of Santo Domingo, its suburbs, and the outskirts. I had no idea that so much affluence could exist so close to poverty. We see new construction and a tree-lined neighborhood of stately, walled-in homes. As we drive by, a maid dressed in a traditional black-and-white uniform rings the front gate, her arms full of groceries.

"Why couldn't we be from *this* part of town?" Taina whines, as she tugs at the ties of a long silk scarf she has wrapped around her head. In the DR, everyone assumes she's a *Dominicana*. There's always this shocked look when they find out she doesn't even speak Spanish. All three girls have been attracting a lot of attention, but the only one who *enjoys* the catcalls is Holly. I swear, I'm ready to throw burqas on all three of them, it's so annoying. Next, we pass a slick financial district. We get off at the *Zona Colonial*, to do a little shopping and have some lunch. Just as we get situated at an outdoor restaurant, a movie house empties. They must have been playing a chick-flick because out spills a crowd of young women. They are the most jaw-droppingly beautiful women I have ever seen in my life. I kick Ray under the table.

"Smokin' . . ." he says.

We both turn to Adrian, our leader in the fine sport of girl watching. But Adrian doesn't seem to care. He pans the faces for a second or two and just keeps talking, maintaining eye contact with Julia, who's sitting across from him, her back to the crowd. He asks her if she would like to switch seats, because her chair is in the partial sun and the skin on one of her arms is turning red. Since the fire, we're are all sensitive to heat and light now, like a bunch of vampires. She says yes, and they switch seats, and he sits with his good arm in the sun, his back to the eye-candy, like nothing. Like he didn't just give up the equivalent of first-row seats at the Super Bowl. Ray gives me a worried look but doesn't say anything, he just picks at his plantains.

Taina is sitting across from me, and I admire the necklace I bought for her this morning as a gift. It's a thick gold chain with twenty tears of the ubiquitous Dominican amber. Amber is fossilized tree resin. The color of the stones vary a great deal, from a near-clear, light honey, to chunks of burnt orange, glowing with bright yellow sparks inside. Taina doesn't see me admiring my purchase; she's lost in thought, twisted around to watch the women in the exact, unabashed way I had expected Adrian to do. "Those women are goddesses," I say. "You fit right in there, Tai. As long as you don't open your mouth." She turns and looks at me like it's the single most fascinating thing she's ever heard me say. "Go stand over there," I say, and she rises and steps into the crowd, lingering among the flock of tawny, hourglass-shaped women. I take my camera out and follow her. I snap a bunch of pictures of her posing, draping a hand across a rail, or sitting next to a coral stone fountain. I get a shot of her looking up at me, arms open, with a secret Mona Lisa smile pulling at her lips. I'm not sure if I've witnessed something significant here or not, but I get the feeling that Taina is enjoying this new side to her identity. If this doesn't make her creative juices flow, I don't know what will.

Back on the road, I'm surprised at the generally festive vibe I get, even in poor towns. Maybe because of the reggaeton blasting from cars, or the merenge coming from the houses, or maybe it's that someone's always trying to sell you something— pirated DVDs, designer knock-offs, lottery tickets. Every time we come to a stoplight, dudes with baseball hats on backward try to wash our van. We scramble to pay them, while our driver waves a fist at them and says *"joder"* about five times. We pass the city limits and travel through a series of small towns with crowded plazas bursting with brightly colored plastic junk for sale. These towns are not easy on the van. There are potholes where it is paved, but plenty of streets that are just dirt. There are naked kids roaming alone. All the buildings have iron bars over the windows and some of the dwellings are made of cardboard with tin plate. Prostitutes blow kisses and tap the windows of our van in broad daylight. "Hey, Adrian. That's your mom," Ray says, pointing.

"Ray. That's sick," Holly says, and folds her arms in disapproval.

Adrian is normally sensitive about that stuff, but he loves that it offended Holly, so he high-fives Ray, and Ray giggles like the Pillsbury Doughboy.

When we get out of the car and look around, Holly says, "This is where we might have grown up."

"But we didn't," Taina says.

"We've never had to endure any of this, even thought it was our lot in life to live here," she says, looking skyward.

There are plumes of Saharan dust floating across the atmosphere. It gives the illusion that the sky is dirty. Thin, horizontal bands of darkness are blemishes against the fluffy while clouds, as if someone has dragged a sharp stick of charcoal across a clean piece of paper. By afternoon, the rain comes down in sheets; it pounds on the tin roofs in the shanty towns and the streets grow flooded and quiet. We pull over to the side of the road to wait it out. Our driver sticks a hand out the narrow crack in his window. He lets the raindrops run down his hand, as if he were playing with a living thing. "See this? This is the rain that our ancestral deserts of Africa thirst for, but can never have." Adrian got his pen out and wrote it down.

Four young nuns run *Casa Azul* now, and there is time for a tour before Sister Juana arrives from the capital. There are thirty kids. Kathy was right, this little crowd belongs on a UNICEF poster. There are sixteen black kids, nine brown, and at least three of them have gringo genes like me. One little girl, who everyone agrees looks like Vanessa Williams, is a stunning combination of dark skin and muted green eyes that look like beach glass. Another has a halo of flaming red hair encircling a bronze, freckled face with big, dark-chocolate eyes. I can't help but wonder what the carrot-top who sired her would think if he knew he left this daughter in a Dominican orphanage. Like her, my father would have no knowledge of me; I was brought into the world through a transaction between strangers. I wonder, is he a CEO, a machinist, an actor, a dentist, a stay-at-home dad? Do I have other siblings out there? Our fathers don't even know we exist. It strikes me that my arrival in the world contained a kind of randomness that is echoed in the appearance of cancer at such a young age. At last my life has become purposeful and defiant of such disorder.

How can I begin to describe what it feels like to meet someone who has saved your life? Sister Juana has known me longer than I've known myself. She holds my hand constantly and commands the other nuns to put their hands on my scarred head. They pile them up, warm against my scalp. They shut their eyes tight and pray like crazy. I'm not disappointed that Sister Juana isn't a healer or a saint. In fact, Kathy told us that Sister Juana has struggled with faith all her life. We're taken aback when she looks us all in the eye and asks for our forgiveness. No, no, we assure her, we are *grateful*. We beg Adrian to be very clear: she did the right thing. We love our adoptive families. We know Kathy has told her all this but she's only at peace when she hears it from us that we weren't harmed, and that we harbor no resentment toward her. Taina says, "The greatest threat to our happiness and well-being has been fear and uncertainty about our origins. Coming here has shut down the source of its power over us. We are healed by our return to you."

Still, we've come a long way and this is our big chance to get some specifics, of course, and so Raymond is the first to inquire about his mother. Sister Juana doesn't mince words: "You will find her, if you want, by going to the *old* red light district in Santo Domingo. If she's still alive, and I believe she is, she will have boils on her arms; she will be filthy with disease and vices of every kind, because that's how she was thirty years ago. You also have to be prepared for the likelihood that she won't remember you." She floats an upturned palm across the scene of children playing in the sunny yard of *Casa Azul*. "*This* was your real home. You were loved here." She cups his broad cheek with her hand. "And you still are, *mijo*."

Our stories are all similar, but only Raymond has had two other siblings pass through the orphanage over the years. He's utterly stunned by this news, and one of the nuns is assigned to arrange a reunion with his half-sisters before we leave. Sister Juana remembers nothing of Taina's mother, but if we ever want names, there are records, of course, back at the archdiocese. But knowing that she's a prostitute's daughter is more than enough information for Taina. She decides to leave it at that. Holly asks for just one detail about her mother. Sister Juana taps at her temple, as if to dislodge something. Julia leans over and whispers that she doubts that the nun could possibly distinguish one particular prostitute over the dozens of others, especially after so many years. *"Sí, sí,"* Sister Juana says, and Adrian translates. "She came from moneyed people who lost everything in the era of Trujillo. She stuttered. Yes, I remember that clearly."

"Stuttered," Holly echoes, looking stricken. Her hands slide over her abdomen. I suppose that it is there that she bears the mark of having become a mother; and before that, a daughter. Taina puts a hand on Holly's back and says, "Can I tell them, Hol?" Holly nods, and Taina tells us about Holly's experience with hypnosis; that when she played back a recording of the session, she heard herself speaking with a stutter. "You must have been imitating your mom, Hol," says Taina.

Taina also learns something about her childhood. While we tour the sleep hall, we pass rows and rows of railed bunk beds. Taina gasps and cries out, "My doll!" She picks up a small, faceless rag doll. "There are dozens of them!" she says, pointing to other beds.

Sister Juana explains that the ladies' auxiliary from the local church makes them, and that they are modeled after the famous faceless Dominican ceramic dolls. "If you go to the craft market you will see them everywhere. They represent the mix of cultures and races here in the Dominican Republic, that are the result of centuries of international commerce, colonization, conquest, and the slave trade. The facelessness means that there is no 'typical' Dominican woman."

Taina collapses on one of the children's beds and clutches the doll to her heart. "There's so much history," she whispers, putting a hand over her heart, "in my blood."

And finally, we meet some of the ones who were part of our original group but who weren't chosen for the voyage. The nuns are able to summon a half-dozen former "starfish" children from town. One brings an armful of dazzling, colorful *helconia*—lobster claws and false birds of paradise. He is a flower vendor. He is my age but looks fifty. Next comes a woman with clothes in tatters, who supports herself by peddling fly-covered candied fruit from a falling-apart wicker basket in the local market. There is a civil servant, a hairdresser, a bookkeeper, and an out-of-work handyman. We're told that the eldest, Mauricio, has died in prison. We learn that not all the girls escaped the grasp of prostitution. Curiously, none of them remember anything about the starfish drawings. They forgot its significance long ago, lost that memory somewhere in their daily struggle for survival. I overhear Taina mumble to Julia, "They haven't had the luxury of fixating on their traumas, like me."

We get to hear a bit about Kathy, and how much Sister Juana appreciated her. "Kathy managed you children with stories and clever, imaginative little psychological tricks," Sister Juana said. "I remember when she first came. She told all of you that she could control the air temperature by snapping her fingers. The older children didn't believe it, so she snapped her fingers and said, 'Do you feel the cool air?' and again, 'Feel it get warm again?' One of the children, Mauricio, I think, said, 'Yes, yes,

I felt it!' and then everyone was convinced they had felt the change in the air too." The nun laughed at the memory of the gullible kids. "They believed she was magic, and Javier, you followed her like a shadow. Ever since then, the snapping of the fingers was sign language for the name 'Kathy.'"

"So that's what it means!" Ray gives me a little slap on the shoulder.

Sister Juana says, "We worried that the emotional damage of that abandonment would be irreparable. Both of us were in pure agony for weeks on end until my brother began to telegram updates of what he heard on the news in Puerto Rico." She puts a hand to her heart and kind of swoons and sits down.

Chapter
44

Julia moved apart from the five, and observed them as they sat on the tile floor surrounded by thirty orphans. While Sister Juana played songs on her old piano, Julia alone saw the expression on Adrian's, David's, Ray's, Taina's, and Holly's faces as they realized that they remembered every word of one of the songs. She saw Holly embrace a little girl who sucked her thumb and clutched a tiny, faceless rag doll. The girl looked up at Holly with enormous, bright, wet eyes. Julia saw the look of admiration on the faces of those kids with dirty feet and torn clothes who sat in their laps—how they imitated their every gesture, and talked gibberish, mimicking the English language, which they were hearing for the first time. To the children, the visitors were rock stars—celestial beings who owned cars and houses and traveled by airplane to distant places.

Adrian had a little girl on his lap, and was making her laugh by telling her a story in Spanish. David was teaching a little boy how to play "Rock Paper Scissors." Ray came back from the van with a bag of cookies and a nun almost got run down in the stampede. Taina and Holly were led by tiny hands to the corner of the room, where they were put to work rocking, feeding, and burping faceless dolls that slept in cardboard boxes.

That night, long after everyone had gone to bed, Taina decided to go down to the hotel bar for a glass of wine. At 3 a.m. there were still a few couples drinking and dancing to merenge music. The backside of the bar was encircled with rails that led to a garden. The previous morning, they had all noticed a very large cactus plant just beyond the bar. It was studded with ugly, asparaguslike stems. Sitting at the bar, Taina realized that the plant had literally bloomed overnight. As she got closer, she saw that the flowers had a fierce, desert quality to them. They had a base of spiked leaves, but inside each flower was a nest of delicate petals that were luminous and moist. She dipped her nose in and smelled its lovely, strange perfume.

"That cactus is called 'lady of the night,' " said the barman, in English.

"I've never seen anything like it," Taina replied, as she signed for the wine.

"They close up all day to conserve moisture and only blossom at night. I've been watching that plant for a year now." He looked up toward the sparkling sky. "I think they open up to see the stars."

Taina smiled. "Ah, a poet." She winked and slid a five-dollar bill across the bar. As she walked across the stone path back to her room, she looked up at the diffusion of light across the heavens. She wondered about the woman who had brought her into this world. Long ago, Taina had made up the story about the trauma of foster care, about the girl with the burning eyes so people wouldn't think she was crazy. She had been stunned to learn that the girl who haunted her dreams was real—a troubled older cousin who had set herself on fire. Neither Kathy nor Sister

Juana had any knowledge of what had become of the girl, or why she had done such a thing, but the scene had obviously branded itself into the deepest folds of her memory. Taina crawled into bed and prepared herself for hours of insomnia. Lying in bed, she suddenly made a connection between her life-long insomnia and the ugly, rugged cactus plant that only revealed its lovely, vulnerable places to the gentle darkness of night. Outside, it began to rain. She heard the frogs rejoice and the rainwater dripping down the length of palm fronds, scattering across emerald leaves and slipping quietly into the opened hearts of the cacti flowers. She remembered that she had fallen in love with Doug at night, out on Block Island, surrounded by inky, star-lit darkness. Now she understood that their marriage had been damaged by their nightly separation. Doug had been right, it was the insomnia, and their inability to be together at night, that created the distance and distrust between them. Taina recognized herself to be very much like the mysterious plant that could only unclothe its heart after dusk.

That night, a dark-skinned woman dressed in a nightgown stamped with her "Caribbean Lagoon" theme came into her dream. The woman went to the closet and opened the doors, where Taina's cousin was screaming that her eyes were burning. But the girl's trunk was just a cactus plant, with its arms reaching up toward the light of the morning sun. Only when the woman carried the cactus-girl out of the room and quietly closed the door behind her did Taina realize that the woman was her birth mother. When Taina woke up, she felt as if she had slept for weeks on end, when in fact, it had been only four hours.

Holly banged on the door at eight. It was time to check out of the hotel and move on to the final leg of their trip. The weather was beautiful. The transcontinental Saharan dust had been washed clean away by the rain, and the sky was a flawless blue. As she made her way along the breakfast buffet, Taina observed that the flowers were gone, and the ugly green fists of the plant were tightly clenched again. She asked the waitress for a pencil, and in a half-hour she had sketched Holly and the plant on the back of the resort's breakfast menu. From that day on, she sketched frequently and compulsively.

Chapter 45

David

In Mayagüez, Puerto Rico, we watch Coast Guard officials fingerprint a group of men whose boat had been interdicted just off the coast. Homeland Security has this new biometrics program to track wanted criminals and immigration violators. "Otherwise," the Coast Guard officer explains, "we're just a taxi service for people to get back home after they fail to sneak in."

We didn't have time to make the arrangements to go to Mona Island like I had hoped. Mona is an ecological preserve, considered to be the Galapagos of the Caribbean, with dazzling coral reefs, unspoiled lime caves, a one-of-a-kind species of giant iguana, and a rusted lighthouse that was built by the architects of the Eiffel Tower. But it turns out you need permits from the municipal government to disembark and we didn't have enough time to apply. So we charter a boat with a captain to take us and we'll just have to be satisfied with seeing it from the water. The truth is that our curiosity about the island is secondary; we are most interested in the sea all around it. Adrian and I have come hoping to connect with our biological mother.

Kathy and Sister Juana told us about her fate after she took to the sea, and that the day before she left, she had begged Sister Juana to release us to her. We are haunted by this: this idea that we might have died here.

We follow our mother's trail, and it leads us across a glimmering field of silver and blue. It isn't long before we spot the fin of a nurse shark, following alongside our boat.

We imagine the nauseating roller-coaster ride of the high seas, people throwing up, the cold spray of seawater, the boat beginning to fill with water, possessions thrown overboard to stay afloat. After all the screaming and arm flailing and cries for God's mercy, none comes. The stern slowly sinks below the surface as the sharks begin to circle. Then hope dies in an explosion of pink bubbles. Maybe she watched it all go down around her; the water is so clear out here. And right before they came for her, before the water rushed into her lungs and she felt herself being pulled apart, I'd like to believe that her last thoughts were for us—for Adrian and me. Maybe she became a real mother in the moment the creature sunk its teeth into her flesh. Maybe the last emotion she felt wasn't panic, or fear, but rather, a sense of relief. *Thank God I didn't bring them. My boys are safe, up there.*

After visiting the Passage, we head to the opposite side of Puerto Rico, to the eastern coast. Our melancholy burns off like fog with every mile. We're all impressed and amused by Adrian's celebrity status everywhere we go. Even a pair of sunburned tourists from Ohio sniff out his star quality. At the bar of a place where we stop for lunch, a woman calls out, "Hey, aren't you that singer? The one who dated what's her name? She was on the TV the other day. Oh God, my son loves her."

He's not in the mood to entertain drunk, lobster-skinned, middle-aged women, so he just makes a face. "Me? Nah. I'm just a local salt," he says, and takes a swig from his beer. And then the woman's eyes drop to his muscled arms, his thin waist, his lean hard legs. "Yeah," she says, licking her lips. "Like the salt on my margarita." Her friend howls with laughter. We pay for the beers and move on.

We take a ferry from Fajardo to Vieques, to the decommissioned U.S. Navy bomb test site that is home to the world's best bio-bay. The lower level of the ferry smells like fried food from the snack bar. None of us can take the smell, so we gather our things and head to the upper deck, where guys in *guayaberas* and panama hats are playing dominoes.

The waters on the eastern side of the island have an entirely different character than the white-capped, choppy waters of the west. This feels like a real tropical escape, as in piña coladas and long naps in hammocks. We pass tiny, storybook islands with nothing on them but palm trees. I half-expect to see a laughing skeleton propped up against a dome-top treasure chest; or maybe a bandaged Wile E. Coyote waving for rescue. Suddenly, I'm in the mood for fun and adventure. I'm reminded, once again, that nothing is more life-affirming than the simple, child-like joy of exploring the world.

In Vieques, our tour guide explains that Mosquito Bay has an opening to the sea that is so narrow that it's practically a lagoon. Mangrove leaves fall into this contained aquatic environment and create a unique, protein-rich, brackish soup. This special ecosystem contains a kind of bioluminescent marine plankton called dinoflagellates. We set off into the water as part of a caravan of kayaks, just after sunset, in dimming light. At first we don't see anything unusual. Then, we notice an eerie blue glow each time we dip an oar into the water. Adrian was right, there is zero light pollution, and the stars sparkle with a clean, bright fiery light from the heavens. As the darkness deepens, anything that moves provokes a release of light in the water, including the waves themselves, which glow eerily as they pass by. By the time we bungee our kayaks to each other in the middle of the bay, we are floating in an otherworldly field of curling, sparkling light. Never before have I heard adults giggle and squeal and carry on the way we do tonight. We don't know what to do with ourselves; we can't believe what we're seeing. Adrian and Ray are hee-hawing like a pair donkeys, so I swim over to find out what's going on. Ray has discovered that you can fart in the water and that the bubbles glow and rise like champagne in a glass. We have ourselves a hearty juvenile moment, while Holly, Taina, and Julia protest and paddle away from us. Then Ray shouts, "Hey, Holly, is that a shark fin behind you?"

Holly starts thrashing and screaming and hurls herself into the kayak, which immediately tips over. The annoyed tour guide assures everyone that there are no sharks in Mosquito Bay because the entrance is too shallow, even at high tide. We get back into our kayaks and our guide leads us along the edge of a mangrove. He shows us how we can disturb shrimp by banging our oars against the side of our boats to see a hundred squiggle marks of light moving though the water. I drift away on my own for a bit. Suddenly, I see a pair of winged creatures speeding through the darkness, below my kayak. "Rays!" I shout. They pass underneath me in a radiant formation of blue, and then they're gone. The glow lingers for a few seconds, then fades to dark, and disappears.

Back at Blue Caribe Kayaks in Esperanza, the tour guide gives us vinegar to pour over our jellyfish stings, a small hazard they failed to mention before the tour. Only two people in the kayak party of twelve escaped the jellyfish stings (one of them being Holly, who never got out of her kayak again after the shark scare). They hurt a lot less than you would think, no more than a paper cut. Then, while we're rinsing off the sand and salt at the outdoor showers behind the tour shack, Adrian and Ray, still excited by what they had experienced, talk of future trips together. I don't know if they're even aware that "we" might not include me. I feel the weight of my spirit swing hard toward sadness. But I force myself to stay in the moment, and to remember that I'm on vacation, after all, about to go out for drinks and dinner with people I love. I stay focused on the fact that I've seen something today that most people will never see in their whole life, something strange and wonderful.

As we gather our things, we're discussing the mechanical aspects of bioluminescence when Adrian absently poses the question that would reverberate in my soul for the rest of the night: "What good does it do for light to follow prey as they move away from their predators? To be of use, light should lead, rather than follow." The tour guide knows the science well, and he explains that bioluminescence is simply a defense mechanism for the plankton. The flash of light is a kind of alarm, meant to make its predator jump and worry, and also to attract a secondary predator that will be more likely to attack the initial predator. Pretty darn clever.

In my bed that night, I sit up. I look at the clock: 4 a.m. Adrian and I refused to bunk up with Ray during the trip because he snores like an elephant with a chest full of phlegm. In fact, I can hear him now, two doors down. I sit on the edge of Adrian's bed. I feel bad waking him but I can't help it, I need to talk. He stirs and so I go right ahead and tell him that I have just figured out the parable of the bio-bay. "The what of the who?" he says, and flips over, turning his back to me.

"It's only in absolute darkness that dinoflagellates fully release their light. They charge up in the daylight. Until darkness falls, it's like they don't exist."

"So?"

"Think of it. Finding Kathy. Finding Sister Juana. Seeing the Passage. Going back to *Casa Azul*. It released a kind of light into our lives. The bioluminescence we saw last night represents a physical or literal release of light. I think our brain and our immune system conspire to do what the plankton do. We release every bit of love, energy, and intelligence we have in the hopes of scaring away the predator. Look at me. The last year has been this huge burst of life and energy."

He rolls over again, facing me this time. He rubs his eyes and sits up but doesn't say anything. What the heck, I think, and I hop into bed next to him. "Move over," I say.

"Okay, but just don't try to spoon me," he says, and I lie down next to him. He asks me to repeat what I just said, and I do, for both of us, and we sit with it for a moment. "Jesus. You ought to write that down," he says. "I think you're on to something."

"Maybe I can outsmart cancer," I continue. "I guess that that's what I've been trying to do." I tap a finger to my lips. "Back at the kayak shack, you asked something like, 'what good does it do for the light to *follow* rather than lead?' As in, why must experience follow rather than precede?"

He clutches a pillow to his bare chest. "Exactly. That makes no sense. What's the point of being wiser *after* the experience, after the risk, after the mistake," he says. "Take Erick, for example. He's wise about child safety because his little brother drowned in a lake when he was a kid. Why couldn't that knowledge have come before the event, so that they might have saved the child? That's why Erick is so protective of his kids. The other plankton in the bio-bay see the light as a kind of warning to change their course. Are we that smart? I don't know."

An hour passes and we're still talking. He tells me that he had predicted, last summer, that I would find comfort and meaning in experiencing the luminescence of Mosquito Bay.

"A slam dunk," I say. I hold up a hand and he high-fives me.

"Oye Flaco," he says, placing a hand over his heart. "Going to *Casa Azul* has given me peace. You're not the only one who's 'releasing light' and all that shit." He looks away.

"So what are you gonna to do with all that Zen, bro?"

He sighs. "I have to figure out a way for those thirty kids at *Casa* to get some kind of formal education or training beyond elementary school. That's my mission in life."

"Anything else?" I fold my arms in front of me.

His eyes roll up. "Uh . . ." his expression reminds me of a little kid trying to make something up to satisfy an adult. ". . . keep my eyes on the plankton."

"Spend your life being worthy of the sacrifices those women made for us. We could've been shark meat, Adrian. But Sister Juana didn't let that happen. We might have lived in poverty, but we didn't, because she saw an opportunity to help us and she took it. Do something with that, okay? Do something with that, Adrian, now that you know the whole story."

"What about you?"

"I'm already living my life differently. I appreciate everything I used to take for granted." I tap him on the shoulder and point to my eyes with two fingers. "Eyes on the plankton, man. Don't make the same mistakes I've made." Then I hold up a hand to let him know the discussion is over. "That's all."

Chapter
46

Julia and David were in the Muñoz Airport, waiting at the gate for a flight to Hartford. They had already said goodbye to Raymond, who was flying home to Phoenix. Adrian and Holly were together on a flight to Miami, and Taina was headed to LaGuardia. Suddenly, David turned to Julia and said, "Who's that girl?" He pointed to the empty runway. Julia looked up and saw only the flawless blue sky and the green hills beyond. He cocked his head to the side. "She kind of looks like me."

Julia stared at him. Coldness spread across the pit of her stomach. David waved at the invisible girl. Julia remembered that he had skipped his last MRI because he had a cold, and wanted to save up his energy for the trip. She calmed herself by ticking off all of the crazy things that happened as a result of the interaction of his medicines. It didn't necessarily mean that the cancer was back. Regardless, she was terrified of being the only one responsible for him during the flight. This was *supposed* to have been the very last time that she would be in charge. But the siblings each had their jobs and their lives elsewhere.

No one, not even Adrian—who was eager to take the reins—knew exactly how they could complete the transition.

During the flight, David paced the center isle until everyone was unnerved and the flight staff asked him to sit down and he refused. Julia told them that David was in treatment for brain cancer. The bewildered staff handed Julia three free nippers of vodka and some soda, which she mixed and gave to him immediately. He finally settled down and fell asleep. Julia thought she would have a heart attack from the stress and worry that was rising inside her. By the time they began the descent, David couldn't be roused. At the insistence of the airline, there was a stretcher brought to the gate. They took him directly to Sloan-Kettering, and they called Dr. Levine at home. The doctor on duty began to run tests.

The MRI showed that David had two small but fast-growing tumors. One of them was in his parietal lobe, so this time, he *was* hallucinating. One was embedded deep at the center of his brain, nested right on top of his hypothalamus. That one was inoperable.

A month later, having exhausted the boundaries of conventional medicine, David began experimental drug treatments as a last resort. They ceased chemotherapy. His hair grew back, curly this time.

Julia phoned Adrian, who was in a hotel in Chicago. She informed him that she would be spending her nights in the O'Farrells' guest room from then on. Her gift to David would be to stay by his side for the rest of his life.

"Thank you," Adrian said, relief in his voice. In the background, someone called his name. "I'm on in five minutes," he said. "I have to go." They said their good-byes and just as Julia was about to hang up Adrian said, "Wait." Silence. "Julia? I *love* you," he said simply. "I miss you, and I want to get on a plane right now and be with you and my brother." He paused, took a deep breath. "Oh God, Julia, I'm so scared."

•   •   •

By day, Marcia was the caretaker. At night, Julia watched over David. That was the worst time. The situation became asphyxiating in the dark, as if it were being gassed into the room as daylight disappeared. In his bed, David looked like a mound of dirt beneath the blankets, and every night that mound looked smaller. He snored softly, while the evil twins grew safe and warm inside his head. Julia lay with him sometimes, so that each night's routine was the same as it had always been. She eventually came to understand that siblings could only come in so close. That Julia and David were no longer lovers didn't matter anymore. What mattered was that they had been. Having someone in your room at night is profoundly intimate, and David relished his privacy. Even his parents could only come in so close. He had even used the old "What if I'm having sex?" threat on them again, after his dad came into his room without knocking first.

She glided her hand along the runway of his arm, which rested at his side. She wished that she could strap him down and anchor him to this world. Other times, she was like a child in thinking that she could just plain refuse to let it happen. *No, you're not taking him, and that's it. And that's it, and that's it.* After he fell asleep, she got up, closed the door softly behind her, gulping huge gasps of air in the hallway. She went downstairs, grabbed a blanket, and lied down on the couch. She immediately felt guilty that he was alone in his room. What if he woke up? She got up, fell back, sat up, fell back. She stared up at the ceiling and wondered why and how this came to be. When had those glial cells staged their vicious coup?

Spring was on its way again, and Julia made it a priority to make sure David got outside. Some days he walked, some days he had to sit in a wheelchair, covered in rain gear. He had begun to lose mobility on his left side. On a particularly good day, when David was feeling "well" (he was able to walk down the driveway and back, holding on to her arm), he asked Julia what she planned to wear to his service. He knew her well enough to assume that she was ready, and he was right. Julia asked if he was sure he wanted to know, and when he said yes, she brought the dress to show him. She put it on and modeled it for him. When she put on the diamond earring studs he had bought her for her birthday, he started to cry. She apologized, but he stopped her. "No, no, no. It's just that you look so beautiful," he said, wiping his eyes.

Then she asked David something she had been curious about for more than a year. "What did you wish for that night at Tre Scalini, David, when you blew out the candles of my chocolate lava cake? It wasn't to marry me, because you turned me down the next day. So what did you wish for?" He looked off in the distance for a moment, and then his eyes turned down to the left. She would never know if he truly remembered the moment, or was making something up. His lips pulled up on one side and he said, "I wished that you would always feel loved."

Within a week of their conversation, David's Spanish almost eclipsed his English. Julia wrote his words in her pink notepad: *Pelota, mesa, vaso, calsetines, arroz, leche, perro, pájaro, camiseta,* and *tengo hambre . . . sed . . . sueño.* She translated them for Dr. Levine, who pointed out that it was the vocabulary of a child, and that each referred to household items, toys, animals, or a physical need. He explained that language is stored in layers that deepen as we grow older, so that as more recent data was lost, the more primitive vocabulary remains intact. Where he lost an English word, his brain dug deeper, and so retrieved a Spanish version instead. "This is how aphasia can manifest itself in the bilingual brain," he said. "It's very curious, I know."

Chapter
47

April 2009

When there was no more they could do at the hospital, they moved David to the Connecticut Hospice in Branford, just a short distance down the shore from the Thimble Islands. He had begun to have seizures and had become aggressive. To control him, they gave him anticonvulsants and tied his wrists to the rails of the bed. Julia couldn't stand to see him like that so when the nurse on duty wasn't looking, she untied him. The tumor on the hypothalamus had thrown his internal thermostat out of whack, and he sweated profusely despite the cool temperature. When his wrists were free, he immediately stripped naked and tried to get out of the bed. Julia ended up with a fractured wrist, so they tied him down again. She thought, *this is it, he's strapped in for the ride.* He was already somewhere they couldn't reach him, in a delirious, agitated state of mumblings. But she was sure that something or someone was helping him through the churning waters of this passage, because he often said things that implied the hustle of moving with a crowd: "Better hurry!" and "You've got to be kidding!" and "Come on!"

Everyone came, even Kathy, who stayed for a whole day at David's bedside, speaking quietly and singing to him. "So what ever happened to Jared?" Adrian asked Kathy one day.

"I have him in the same nursing home as my dad," Kathy said. "Now that his parents are both dead, I'm it. One of my daughters visits him twice a week, and I'm there every Saturday afternoon." She looked down at her hands. "I had to run away from him in order to find my way back. It took years."

Adrian began to carry a notebook, monitoring and recording every detail of David's care from doses to times of catheter changes. Everything Julia used to do, but no longer did, because she finally understood that it wasn't going to be of any use. Adrian's state of denial lasted a bit longer, and so he persisted in recording David's mumblings, because, "You never know, this could be useful." It wasn't, Julia knew, but she didn't discourage him because Sue Lorens, the wife of the ten-year survivor, had been right. One has to find ways to pass the time and feel useful. The second thing Adrian did to try to keep himself busy was to volunteer as an entertainer at the hospice. He brought his guitar and wandered around the halls, asking patients and their relatives if they were in the mood for a song. Julia was with him when an old man in a wheelchair pulled on the hem of his shirt.

"Excuse me." The old man put his hand out like he was begging. "Can you please tell me who I am?" Adrian and Julia looked around. They couldn't find a nurse.

"Hmm. Well, let's figure it out," Adrian answered, sitting on a nearby chair and setting his guitar on his knee. "What kind of music do you like?"

Five minutes later they were all singing "When Johnnie Comes Marching Home" at the top of their lungs. At last the old man raised his chin, high and proud, and cried out,

"Edward! First Sergeant Edward McGuiness. A Company, 187th Infantry Regiment, 101st Airborne Division!" His watery blue eyes sparkled with pride. The janitor, who had been emptying the garbage in the hall, saluted him, and Julia and Adrian did the same. First Sergeant McGuiness put his face in his arthritic hands and wept with relief and gratitude at having remembered himself.

That same day, a woman requested "Clementine" for her comatose father. She said he had sung this to her as a girl, and she smiled a little as she told them that her father had taken guitar lessons, but that he never progressed beyond a few songs. "But he had 'Clementine' down cold," she said, with a soft chuckle. Julia thought that Adrian would be stumped for sure. How could someone growing up in Puerto Rico know that old American folk song? But he knew it. "I don't believe it, Adrian. You're like a human jukebox," Julia told him.

When Adrian got to the line, "You are lost and gone forever, dreadful sorry, Clementine," the woman's face had crumpled up and she reached over to hold her father's hand. Adrian had helped move her along the long and difficult road of saying good-bye not only to her father, but to her childhood. And it was through this intense and focused attention on the grief of total strangers, that Adrian Vega became a little more like his father. He stepped into a new maturity; an expansion of the spirit that, by necessity, hurt.

"Keep it up and you'll be famous, kid!" shouted an old lady in a wheelchair who had been listening to him sing from the hallway.

Adrian kept a constant river of warm Spanish sounds flowing over his brother. Sometimes David surprised them by stopping his thrashing and mumbling long enough to listen, or even mouth a few of the lines. One morning, a week after he'd been admitted into hospice, Julia had buds in her ears and was singing along with her playlist of favorite songs. She was lost in thought as she shaved David's face. "Some people want to fill the world with silly love songs," she sang out loud. She was rinsing the razor when David turned his head and sang, "What's wrong with that?"

After that, she prompted him all the time, trying to get him to communicate his needs by introducing songs that could help him express thirst, hunger, or pain. When Marcia cracked open a Diet Coke, David started humming the jingle to the latest Coca-Cola commercial. Julia asked Marcia for the can and gave it to David, who happily sucked up the entire drink. The doctor on duty explained that the human central nervous system doesn't process musical sounds the same way it does the auditory patterns of speech. Musical ability isn't necessarily affected by damage localized in areas that control language. This is what Kathy and Sister Juana had discovered all on their own in working with speech-delayed children at the orphanage. "If one avenue to or from the brain is blocked, you try another. The brain isn't a road, it's a labyrinth," Kathy added when Julia explained it on the phone. Soon, they could only communicate with David through sign language and music, first popular music and then through nursery songs in both Spanish and English. It was as if, through the songs, Adrian was able to take his brother to a safer place, and still keep him close.

Adrian and Julia's first kiss was in the elevator of the Connecticut Hospice. There had been ample opportunity, up in the master bedroom of the Griswold house, the night that Julia had nursed Adrian's wounded head. But they had agreed that it would be disrespectful to start something right under David's nose. Their resolve was emboldened by the fact that Adrian had a colossal headache, and a few hours later, they were jumping out a window to escape a fire. They had fallen in love again during the trip to *Casa Azul*—and once that happened, the rest of the trip had been an exercise in torturous self-restraint. They would have dropped everything to be together after the trip, but then David started seeing imaginary little girls and they all knew that it was the beginning of the end.

David had been at the hospice for two weeks when they all gathered out on the lawn. Adrian and Julia were alone in the elevator, standing face to face as it descended to the ground floor. When the doors shut, Adrian took her face in his hands, closed his eyes, and kissed her on the lips. His kiss was so tentative, so restrained, their lips barely touched. "I love you," he said, and he marveled at the sound of those strange words coming out of his mouth.

"Am I crazy? David doesn't even understand what's going on," Julia said, clutching a pearl on her necklace. "Why am I doing this again?"

"You're doing it for David," Adrian replied. "Choosing to honor his parents' faith, even though faith eluded him, is in itself a kind of faith." The doors opened and Adrian led Julia out to the lawn. Taina, Doug, Holly, Ray, Julia's mother, and her three brothers and their spouses were all waiting. David's bed had wheels, and the staff had rolled him out to the patio, as they often did when patients wanted to get fresh air. The O'Farrells' parish priest presided over the ceremony. Adrian, handsome in a gray suit, walked Julia down the path to where David was waiting. Adrian gave Julia away and spoke David's wedding vows for him. Julia wore a white dress and the stud earrings that David had given her for her birthday.

"My daughter-in-law," Marcia said as she placed her mother's diamond ring on Julia's finger. "You were right. Symbols of belonging *are* powerful." The priest pronounced David and Julia husband and wife. Julia leaned over David's bed and kissed him on the lips.

Julia watched over David that day and the next and the next until his pulse slowed by half a beat beneath her touch. Soon, he was no longer able to sing, eat, or drink. Even the flecks of Italian ice that the hospice supplied just sat on his tongue and melted, making him cough. There was a rattle inside his lungs and a bad smell emanated from his mouth. Adrian made the decision to withhold life support. Ray lobbied for, and won, an increase in David's dose of morphine, and David didn't recover any awareness after that. He wasted away in a matter of a few days. His jaw became razor-sharp. He got that waxy, candlelit look. But the varying expressions on his face convinced Julia and Adrian that he was on a great adventure. "Not *too* much fun," Adrian teased, fussing with his brother's blanket and combing David's hair with his fingers. "Remember you're a married man now, *Flaco.*" Outside, the still-cold May wind picked up and rattled the glass of the windows. When Adrian looked out and down to the ground level, he saw a blue lady's hat tumbling across the lawn of the hospice. It danced and floated and spun like a Frisbee before it finally got hooked by the wiry branch of a high tree. When the wind moved the limbs of the tree just so, it looked as if there was someone in it, an old lady perhaps, with her legs dangling off the branches. Adrian noticed that the limbs kicked to a quicker beat than the melancholy gusts of wind would have them move. It was as if they were dancing to the sound of a distant music that no one else could hear.

Chapter
48

David

I'm thinking about the women in my life: grateful, ardent thoughts of mothers and nuns and sisters and friends and lovers; even about the daughters and granddaughters I might have had. There's this bony, pony-tailed girl who won't leave my side. She's wearing shorts and t-shirt but her head is covered with a first communion veil and a pair of white gloves, fastened at the wrist with pearls. Through the veil I can see that she has my eyes, but with Julia's blonde hair and small, fine nose, so I know she's the daughter we would have had. She offers her hand to me, and says, "Papa, I have to show you something." I take it and suddenly we're at Griswold Island, standing before that terrible fire, and I have to close my eyes as the wind stirs up the smoke and ashes of Julia's destroyed history. I pull the girl back from the heat, down to the beach, because I don't want the smoke to hurt her eyes.

What happened during my brain surgery is happening again. I must have encoded the last moments of the fire and stored the scene away somewhere inaccessible to the conscious mind. I know perfectly well that I'm dying, and that I'm getting access to the *classified* stuff. Only now am I able to process, interpret, and remember the secret things that happened during the fire. Or maybe it's just that the closer death is, the stronger life can be felt, seen, and heard. In this rush of energy, in this process by which we release our spiritual light, time simply has no place. What I can see now is this: as the house went up in flames, every dead Griswold rose in a great funnel, like a waterspout. There was literally a Griswold explosion, an exuberant stampede of souls that bounded across the lawn like a herd of buffalo across a plain.

I'm seeing it, as I linger in this porous in between place. The Griswolds scatter across the lawn, some stand, some sit, some lie flat on their backs. They crush hydrangea bushes and knock over the geraniums in their terra-cotta pots. They're unharmed and strangely unconcerned by the fact their homestead is being consumed in flames. They are all barefoot. Several of them have binoculars, telescopes, spyglasses, opera glasses, and I suspected that they have been watching us all along. At first, they wait patiently for a man to mount what has to be the infamous "water unicycle." It looks like a combination between a unicycle and a hay-cutter; a wide contraption that allows the cyclist to pedal his way on top of the water. Then he rises up into the air and glides across the Sound like he's one of the Wright brothers. Once he reaches a comfortable cruising altitude, the crowd cheers and they rush across the lawn toward the beach, shouting and shoving each other to get ahead.

"What took you so long?" barks a stooped man who has to squint in order to keep a monocle in place. I think it's Uncle Jim, the one buried in the garden. We're shaking hands when a tall, bald man in a yellow satin baseball jacket holds a black mop of hair in the open palm of his hand. "Thanks for finding my hairpiece," he whispers in my ear. He flops it over his dome. He parts the bangs so he can see.

"It looks good, man," I lie. I know it's his "Italian Stallion" wig, because I remember seeing the packaging it came in. "Eye of the tiger," I say, and hold my fists up to my face. He does the same, like were going to spar, but then he rushes off into the crowd. The girl at my side covers her mouth and giggles.

"They're nuts," I tell her, shaking my head. "But you gotta love 'em."

I turn to see John Crew Griswold, Julia's father. He slaps me on the back and peers at me from behind his mustache. "You kids have been a breath of fresh air. We enjoyed every minute with you. Only *you* could have done this," he said, pointing at the house on fire. "You set us free!"

"But we burned down your house!" I say. "Aren't you angry?"

"Our need to have every one of our quirks remembered has reached a point of saturation. There is a time to let go. It's been way too long for some." He holds up a wrist, and I see that he has reclaimed his wristwatch from the bowl in the parlor. The metal band gleams in the sun as he gives me a quick salute, then he runs off toward the beach.

A group of Victorian ladies circle us. A pretty lady in her forties, who was probably *the* original Mother Griswold, leans down to kiss my daughter, whom, I suppose, is one of her descendants. *"Javier es el mas fuerte,"* the lady says, and she puts her index finger to her lips.

I'm amazed to see that all the women have green starfish tattoos on their hands. I take one lady's hand and examine it. "I'll be damned," I say, and the woman says, "Bite your tongue, young man, we hope not."

They put their hands on my back. It's so comforting, so nice.

I have a thousand mothers now. And I have a wife. Julia and I are bound in a way that is deeper, stronger, *stranger*, and more meaningful than any definition of love that I could have invented on my own. We were married last week on the lawn of the hospice; I knew what was going on the whole time. It's so great to be able to say that one of the last moments of my life was also one of the best moments of my life.

The Griswold women crowd into my hospice room. They pull my hand, urging me to get up and follow. "No, I'm not ready. I like it here. Just look at that view," I say, pointing at the window, at the wide yard, rocky shoreline, and blue water. But the matriarch steps forward. She has this really serious look on her face, and suddenly I'm scared shitless.

She puts one hand on the top of my head, like a queen, and says, *"No tengas miedo. Todo lo que te ha pasado te ayudará.* You're ready. Don't be afraid."

"¿Ustedes hablan español?" I ask. They didn't bother to answer, because obviously they can speak whatever language they want, they're dead. I take one small, hesitant step forward, but I'm so, so scared. I close my eyes and gradually I feel myself leaving the indoor space of the hospice. The chorus of "shhhhhh" blends into the hiss of the wind all around me, and the branches, heavy with leaves, tremble and dance in the sky. The Griswold ladies give me one last shove and I tumble forward. I fall though space until I am in a beautiful forest. I hear the crunch of sticks and leaves beneath my feet. I smell moss and rotting wood in the cool air. The path is lined with all the trees I have saved in the course of my short life, my good deeds standing in formation, like an honor guard. I recognize them, the hickory, the elm, a whole lot of white birches that escaped that terrible fungal rot of a few years ago. Bright sunlight flashes through the canopy of leaves now and then as

I walk. I catch pine needles in bunches of five, "Great Eastern Pine," I inform no one in particular. The trees shade me from the sun, and I walk until the landscape becomes tropical and the air grows moist and warm. Mangroves are clustered like an arthritic tribe, with tangled limbs intertwining in a nearby swamp. Bird of paradise flowers dot the landscape with orange, yellow, and red, like small fires ablaze in the forest of green. I stand waiting for the leaves to part; for the magnificent beast of death's forest to show himself. I hear something stirring nearby. My heart muscle pumps inside my chest, an insistent fist banging on a door. I scan the landscape and wait, motionless.

I sense that I'm being watched. So I turn around and I see Julia, my parents, my siblings, my friends and relatives, all crouching up in the branches of the trees, waving. They're just a flickering presence now, as the dead Griswolds once were to me. I want to say some final words, something to comfort them, but I know they can't hear me. My girl takes her place next to the grandest tree, and I suddenly understand her role in all this. She's my final guide, my last love. She pulls back a branch, and the leaves part. A world opens up. I hear water. I see the eerie blue glow of souls zipping through a dark lagoon and I realize that I've come to the place where all things begin. I hear voices, and laughter. I see that my birth mother is waiting for me. I wave to let her know that I see her, that I'm coming at last. The girl rips off her veil, plucks the gloves off tip by tip, and tosses them into the bushes. She runs inside ahead of me.

I turn to the ones I'm leaving behind. I wish I could tell them this: in the end, we return to our most elemental state, which for me is simply playfulness and curiosity.

"See you on the other side!" shouts Julia. "I love you!" I feel wind on my face. I turn, and step inside.

Julia kissed him slowly, on the lips. "See you on the other side. I love you!" is all she could think to say. David's skin was cooling, so she dug her face deep into the cavity between his neck and his shoulder blade, inhaling his smell so as not to waste a single bit of it, even as it began to evaporate. His scent took off on wings and flew up in bursts, like butterflies, and then he was gone. David's days released the last of their light, and went dark.

David was cremated, as per his wishes. Once again Julia went through a kind of post-traumatic shock when she asked the funeral services director to detail the process. They had placed him in a wood box, she was told, and a conveyor belt rolled him into a flaming oven. He was reduced to ashes. They put them in an urn and later spread the ashes in the forest near his parents' home. David had agreed to every last Catholic sacrament, including a mass in his honor. His three nephews looked miserable in their tiny black suits and slick hair, and they stumbled around, alternately proud and uncomfortable in their fancy clothes. At the celebration of life, Julia was the one who remembered to pass the boys the microphone when everyone was talking about the impact that David had had in their lives. The boys said that they would never forget their Uncle David, because he had been their captain, and together they had fought and won a war against a pirate ship called the *Summer Salt*.

Epilogue

Late 2009

David had a life insurance policy through his employer, and the payout, after funeral expenses, was close to two hundred thousand dollars. The marriage to Julia had been symbolic, not legal, because of David's compromised mental state. Julia wanted none of the money, not even as retribution for the damages to the house. They had worked out the formula together. Half of it went to his parents in a trust for elder care, a portion was put into a college fund for Holly's boys, and the rest went to the orphanage. Ray got David's Jeep and his books. Adrian got his hiking and camping equipment. Julia wanted only his collection of hats.

Inside the "Pandora's Box" that David had managed to pry open, Holly found the one thing that was missing in her life. She and Erick began the process of adopting the "brown-eyed girl" that she had bonded with so quickly at the orphanage. The Dominican Republic has a ninety-day residency requirement for adoption, so Raymond, who was between jobs, volunteered to stay with Holly and her boys near the orphanage for the required time period. Holly was concerned about Ray being away from his rehab for so long, but they worked out a plan that included ways to make Ray feel productive. He helped out at the orphanage, took Spanish lessons, and began what for him was a highly spiritual endeavor—mastering Dominican cooking. He found some ladies in the village who let him look on as they prepared a traditional *sancocho*, a stew made with pork and a variety of starch vegetables like *yuca*, *ñame*, *yautia*, potato, and plantain. Since he had so much time on his hands, he began to read the books that David had left him. He struggled with *Walden* and the essays and the poetry of Ralph Waldo Emerson, but it made him feel closer to David, so he read just a few paragraphs a day. In the second month of their stay, he met a buxom young lady who cooked him a meal of stewed goat and mashed green banana *mangú*. In a day she had him smitten. In a week he was wondering how he could ever stand to go back home to Arizona. In three weeks, she agreed to marry him someday.

Erick adjusted his flight schedule so he could see Holly and the boys in the Dominican Republic several times during their stay. The three boys learned to converse in Spanish with the nuns and the other children in a matter of weeks, and to recite the Lord's Prayer before bed in a single, mumbled streak of Spanish. They spent most of their energy playing *beisbol* every day with the local kids in an empty lot. They played to the sound of reggaeton blasting from a falling-apart boombox, with a ninety-year-old neighbor serving as umpire. This made Holly recognize all the isolating cultural and economic barriers that kept them from enjoying the same kind of rich, meaningful exchanges with people outside of their socioeconomic circles back home. Of course, the boys also picked up more dubious behaviors, such as referring to each other as *pendejo*, and keeping a stash of rubber bands around their wrists to shoot rocks at lizards and baby birds.

Holly's boys were exited about their new little sister, a two-year-old whom they would call Emely, Holly's original baby name. One rainy afternoon, when little Emely was cranky, Holly found Bobby soothing his new little sister by rocking her in a hammock and chanting *"rum, rum,"* until the little girl grew quiet and fell asleep in his arms.

Adrian kept his promise to David, and immediately became devoted to raising funds for *Casa Azul.* He and Kathy formed a strong bond, and she remained in contact with the five ever since her first meeting with Adrian and Taina in Boston. The siblings made a new pact. Every time they got together, they would leave a fifth chair empty, in "Missing Man" formation. One of David's favorite hats would be left on the chair, as if he might arrive at any moment, put on the hat, and sit down. It was a way to give their loss a shape; an invitation for David's spirit to be as alive as he wishes to be, or as real as they needed him to be, or both.

Paul O'Farrell was having a hard time with Marcia's belief that the human spirit can visit loved ones. He believed in a distant heaven and completely rejected Marcia's suggestion that David was behind the unusual number of wildlife appearances in their lives in the months after his death. Deer and wild turkeys routinely wandered into their yard, and given David's love of nature, she couldn't help but draw a connection. Julia reported that she had found a barn owl nesting in her mother's garage. Holly and the boys had seen a manatee in a Florida canal. Ray had seen a coyote in the desert. "Not only do I not believe it," Paul confided to Adrian's father, Reinaldo, in a phone conversation, "but I can't understand why anyone would take comfort in it. As much as I appreciate animals, I would hate to think of our David, with his stubborn independence and fierce intelligence, reduced to sending mute signals by way of tick-infested animals."

Unintentionally, and by way of their terrible loss, the O'Farrells began to draw the other parents into their lives. Julia's mother, Diane, began to have breakfast with Marcia once a month. Taina's parents invited Paul and Marcia to join them for a weekend in New York City. Ray's mother flew in from Arizona, to meet the O'Farrells for the first time.

Taina became the keeper of David's now-sacred bonsai forest. Terrified that it would die under her watch, she read three books and consulted with experts on how to keep it alive and well. By spending hours obsessively staring at the minuscule trees, Taina began to experience stillness for the first time in her life. She had left her insomnia in the Dominican Republic. Immediately after David's death, she did almost nothing but work and sleep, and she refused to see or talk to Doug for four months. Finally he agreed to sign the divorce papers. They met at a coffee shop, started talking, and by the time they stopped, three hours later, Taina said that she wasn't sure about wanting a divorce anymore. Doug slipped the papers back into his satchel and asked if she'd like to go see an art exhibit with him. She agreed and the papers ended up getting tossed into the fireplace a week later. She enrolled in art classes by night.

David had sensed that Griswold Island, with its placid gray waters, was a parallel universe to *Casa Azul*, that there was a passage between those unlikely places. Because of him, *Casa Azul* underwent many improvements. New rooms were added, a school house, and a playground, a new cistern, and private bathrooms for the nuns. The Griswold house, on the other hand, was razed, and the island lay empty for many months. Once the insurance money was collected, a new house was designed and scheduled to be completed by the spring of 2011. The family decided to make it a simpler structure, but it would be safer, stronger, more cleverly designed, a blank canvas for future generations to paint their days in the sun.

When Adrian and Julia passed the three-month mark, Adrian asked her to move to Miami. When she finished the school year, Julia packed up and moved in with him. She soon got the idea to write an innovative textbook about Connecticut inventions, both the successes and the failures, along with colorful stories of fortunes and blunders. The project got a jump-start by a grant from a private foundation that promotes entrepreneurship, and a magnet business program in public schools. The book included stories about the invention of the Wiffle Ball, the topsider shoe, the Sunfish, the Pez dispenser, the first combat submarine, the gun silencer, and of course, the amphibious water unicycle. "I had to leave my home to truly see it," she told Adrian the day she began to tap away at the computer. "Living in Miami, with its pink newness and transient character, is like a blank canvas to my mind. I had no idea how stimulating gaining distance can be."

At cocktail parties, Adrian joked that he "couldn't wait to get off the sex roller coaster of bachelorhood and settle down." At first, Julia thought the joke was hilarious, but after he told the joke a half-dozen times, she didn't think it was so funny anymore. So he stopped telling it. In truth, they thrilled each other in every way and he was as ardent about their life together as he had been passionate about bachelorhood. Adrian asked Julia to marry him one evening, over a bowl of the charred *sancocho* that he had attempted to prepare with Ray coaching him on the phone.

Julia and Adrian planned a small wedding at *Casa Azul* with a honeymoon at one of the luxury resorts on the Dominican coast. They agreed to adopt at least one child from *Casa Azul*, probably more. But sharing genes with a child was important to both of them, and replenishing the Griswold bloodline never stopped being a sacred mission for Julia. Their family, they decided, would be bound by love, history, *and* biology, an homage to the tragic but serendipitous way that they came to become a family in the first place.

David's hiking watch was the first to be put in the family's new bowl of watches. Both David and Adrian would be listed in the next volume of *The Griswolds of New Haven County* as spouses of Julia Abigail Griswold. In the meantime, the story of the fire at the Griswold house appeared in five major magazines. The media's interest in the Griswold family, by extension, was stimulated by footage of the dramatic fire rescue, and of course, the connection to Adrian Vega. Julia began to write the Vega family history in her own hand, with a fountain pen, the way the first *Griswolds of New Haven County* volume was written in 1789. Shortly thereafter, the historian who was working on volume nine informed the Griswolds that instead of receiving the usual leather-bound tome for their library, they should expect to get an "eco-friendly" paperless version—an e-mailed link to the central archive. The Griswold story would exist, henceforth, only in cyberspace. Surprisingly, this was universally appealing to all members of the clan. The younger generation was comfortable with technology, but the elders loved it because the electronic world is a place that's far more permanent than the paper world; an infinite space that's invulnerable to fire, water, or light. In the end, the exotic tale of the starfish children merged into the Griswold family's long and convoluted history, like fiery birds of paradise thriving amid New England's oldest forests of pine. Memory, after all, is a place both the living and the dead can inhabit. Days overlap, laughter commingles, a bottle of scotch is passed around for a century. Memory is a trick whereby a sip of tea can be tasted by seven generations of women sitting in the same chair and drinking from the same cup at the same moment. And when each person's light is released, it is witnessed, registered, learned from, honored. Individuals become families and families become clans who welcome more souls with whom they will share their lives.

On Griswold Island, the barren windows and freshly painted walls are bathed in an orange juice–colored light that no one had ever seen before. A few of the family members have a new way of thinking. If they keep the island, it's because they choose to do so, not because they are obligated by tradition. If they are bound to one another, it's not because they share common blood; but rather, because life has given them the chance to be essential to one another, and they have each chosen to accept that invitation. They are kindred by the power of the mind, rather than by the mindlessness of chance: a family because they choose to be.

Acknowledgments

I wish to thank Jeanette Perez for her patience and guidance and Julie Castiglia, for her enthusiasm and support of my work. For enabling and celebrating my debut novel, I would like to thank Rene Alegria, Melinda Moore, Cecilia Molinari, Isabel Allende, Pernod Ricard, the Miami Book Fair International, the Bread Loaf Writers' Conference, the International Latino Book Awards, *Las Comadres Para Las Americas*, and Marcela Landres.

Love and gratitude to my husband, Robert O. Barron, whose support has brought forth two novels. As always, thank you to my mother, Yolanda Rodriguez, and to my family and friends for years of inspiration and encouragement. Special thanks to Suzanne Donahue and Judith Cooper Haden.

I couldn't have written about the beauty and magic of bioluminescence without financial support from the Ford Foundation, JPMorgan Chase, the Andy Warhol Foundation for the Visual Arts and Southwest Airlines, through a grant from the NALAC Fund for the Arts. *Muchísimas gracias.*

ALSO BY
SANDRA RODRIGUEZ BARRON

THE HEIRESS OF WATER
A Novel

ISBN 978-0-06-114281-9 (paperback)

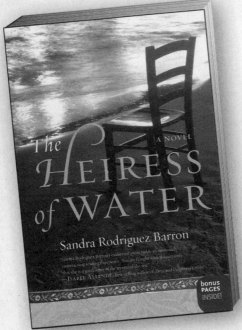

The beautiful and lyrical first novel from Sandra Rodriguez Barron is an odyssey centered on the story of Monica Winters, a woman haunted by her mother's sudden disappearance in 1985, at the height of El Salvador's violent civil war.

Monica's journey back to the land of her childhood to unravel the mystery of her mother's death finds heartbreaking answers to questions she has had her whole life. But there she will also discover a new and extraordinary love that contains the power to heal a family torn apart by greed and betrayal.

"Secrets and lies drive the intricate plot of this first novel, which is both a gripping mystery and an intimate drama of love and betrayal."

—*Booklist*